The LEAVING KIND

A Hearts & Crafts Story

KELLY JENSEN

RIPTIDE
PUBLISHING

Riptide Publishing
PO Box 1537
Burnsville, NC 28714
www.riptidepublishing.com

The Leaving Kind

Cover art: L.C. Chase, lcchase.com
Editor: Carole-ann Galloway
Layout: L.C. Chase, lcchase.com

ISBN: 978-1-62649-984-3

First edition
September, 2023

Also available in ebook:
ISBN: 978-1-62649-985-0

The LEAVING KIND

 A Hearts & Crafts Story

KELLY JENSEN

 RIPTIDE PUBLISHING

For Susan. I wish you could have met Victor. I think you would have loved him.

Stop leaving and you will arrive.
Stop searching and you will see.
Stop running away and you will be found.
—Lao Tzu

TABLE of CONTENTS

Chapter One

Spent firecrackers littered the gravel lot outside Shepard's Tree Farm. Brightly colored plastic cones and cardboard rings. Scorched and ragged boxes. Dozens of slender lengths of wire, one end blackened. Cameron steered his niece's car around the largest clumps of debris and parked near the gate. He hopped out, key in hand for the padlock, and jumped about a mile in the air as a lost popper detonated beneath his shoe sole.

"Jesus. Fuck!"

Seven in the a.m. was way too early for that kind of startlement.

Cam stood still a moment, as he waited for his breath to slow. Then he made for the gate, eyes glued to the ground. The next popper, hidden under a curl of paper, jacked his pulse back up, but he didn't jump.

"Damn kids." That it could have been him thirty years ago—no, make that thirty-five—wasn't lost on him. He'd done his share of sneaking out on a holiday weekend. Setting off firecrackers in empty lots. Tossing the odd cherry bomb in a dumpster and running like a rabid dog was biting at his heels to make the corner of the Dollar General where Gerry and Nate had been crouched low, waiting for him.

God, that boom. Always sounded like a bomb going off. To them, it might have been a real bomb.

Cam winced at the memory. If only they'd known. The sound a real bomb made? It varied. But the feeling of it . . . The nanosecond of surprise, the punch of air. The way the earth kicked and bucked. The screams.

He squeezed his eyes shut. *Breathe. In and out.*

July Fourth was not his favorite holiday. The detritus strewn across the parking lot put him on edge. Back on edge. Shading his eyes against the rising sun, Cam gazed across the highway toward the housing development on the other side. Rows of houses nestled beneath low trees. Siding mostly the same color, the pitches of the roofs almost soothingly even. Beneath those eaves rested the punk-ass kids who'd left him all this extra work.

They weren't the same folks who'd terrorized his own neighborhood last night and the night before, but Cam scowled at them anyway. Then he dropped his hand, dropped his shoulders, unlocked the gate, and got back in the car.

The drive to the farm wound down a long slope, through a quarter mile of fledgling trees. Spruce and pine on one side, sweet gum, honey locust, and dogwoods on the other. Apples and pears too. Small parking bays lay off to each side, spaces for customers who liked to wander the rows and pick their trees right out of the ground. A popular pastime late in November and early December.

Cam drove past the collection of small buildings at the bottom of the slope—the store and indoor plant nursery—and pulled around to the rear of the premises to park beside a pair of green pickup trucks, both printed with *Shepard's Tree Farm* and the unimaginative Christmas tree logo. It was what it was.

His boss's car was already there. Sometimes he thought Luisa Narvaez slept on the couch in her office. But she did have a shorter commute than him, living only five minutes away on the other side of Dingmans Ferry. Cam had to drive down from Milford. Took him about seventeen minutes on a quiet morning.

Well, sixteen minutes and forty-three seconds, on average. If he wanted to be precise, which he did not. That was his brother Nick's thing. Cam preferred a life with rounder edges.

Pocketing his keys, he ducked into the rear of the shop and stopped at the coffee station. He helped himself to a cup from the pot Luisa had already started. Judging by the volume, she hadn't gotten herself any yet. He grabbed an extra mug, poured it half full, topped it up with cream, and added three sugars.

After giving it a stir, he carried both mugs into the back office and set one on Luisa's desk.

She looked up with a smile that quickly faded. "*Caray*! Did you pull an all-nighter?"

Cam snorted. "No, the kids in my neighborhood did." He slumped onto the couch, setting his mug on the armrest. "Plenty of adults out there too. All yelling and screaming, as if setting off fireworks until one in the morning wasn't enough noise."

Luisa studied him closely for a moment, and Cam met her gaze with a lift of his chin, meaning, *I'm cool. Don't worry about me.* If he weren't so tired, he'd add a wink and a playful smile. She'd see through the ruse, though.

Luisa would know what the Fourth must feel like to him. She'd lost a husband to war. She knew all about the scars war could leave on a person's body and soul. Her eyes were slightly glassy as she turned toward the computer monitor. The ache of loss never ceased.

She hit a few keys.

"Only two deliveries this morning." Business had slowed a little after the large chain hardware store opened in Dingmans Ferry earlier that spring. Lately, though, it seemed to have ground to a halt.

She lifted her gaze, briefly. Cam kept his features as far from wince territory as possible.

Attention back on the computer, she tapped another key. The printer on the credenza chuffed to life. "More might come in. I'll text you."

"It's always quiet the week after a holiday," he noted.

Luisa met his gaze again. "Not this quiet. At this rate, I'm not sure whether I should be reordering mulch and soil. We might have sold all we're going to sell for the season."

Cam reached for the smile Luisa would definitely need now, and a yawn cracked his jaw open. Man, he was tired. Still, his deficit of sleep over the weekend had one thread of silver on the underside: tonight, he'd crash out as though a train had hit him.

He could not wait. Deep, dreamless slumber was addictive. The more he got, the more he craved. Mother Nature seemed disinterested in letting him have his fair share, though. Like she thought it wasn't good for him.

Outside, gravel crunched under tires as another car pulled into the lot. That'd be Jorge, the large, quiet man who did a lot of the heavy lifting around the farm. A car door squeaked open and squawked closed. Jorge drove a Mercury Cougar that had probably graduated from high school the same year as Cam. Jorge's somber step paused by the coffee maker a moment later, then his shadow darkened the doorway to Luisa's office.

Cam lifted his mug in a morning salute.

"Good morning," Luisa said.

Jorge returned the salute and slurped at his coffee. Cam took another mouthful of his and Luisa sipped hers. The three of them shared a long, silent moment where presumably their thoughts wandered in different directions. But Cam guessed they were all thinking pretty much the same. It was just the three of them now. There was a weekend manager, and a couple of college students on summer break who worked weekend shifts, but on a Tuesday at the beginning of July? Just them. Should have been more. Last year, there had been more.

Cam drained his mug and stood. He grabbed the printouts from the tray and glanced at the orders. Gravel and sand to an address down in Bushkill and trees and mulch to a house halfway between here and Milford. So, the opposite direction. He couldn't fit both orders in one truck, anyway.

Bushkill first. He handed the slip to Jorge. "Want to load the sand and gravel? I'll start cleaning up the mess around the gate."

Silently, Jorge took the delivery slips. With another slight lift of his mug, he left. Cam took no offense from the wordless exchange. That was Jorge. Cam hadn't been sure he could speak until they'd been working together for four months. He got it, though. Jorge was another vet. Like him.

Or maybe not like him. Jorge was . . .

Cam shook the thought away. Degrees of damage didn't really matter. It was how they were now. How they related to the real world. Sensing the weight of Luisa's gaze again, Cam glanced over his shoulder. He shot her his most confident smile and raised his now-empty mug.

She smiled back and then busied herself at the computer.

His brother called while he was on the road to the second delivery. Cam tapped the dash-mounted phone and answered, "Nick." For a long time, Nick had been Nicky, his little bro. But that had been decades ago, and Nicky was now Nick. A man. A somewhat odd but very talented craftsman. "What's up?"

"I only have two minutes to talk."

"All right."

"I'm on a break."

"Breaks are good."

Nick's partner, Oliver, had insisted Nick break his day into more than two halves. The rationale, as Cam remembered it, was to give Nick additional opportunities to engage outside of his work. To make phone calls and entertain visitors to his small gallery.

"Are you free on Saturday?" Nick asked.

"Probably. I didn't think Oliver was doing a market this week?" Two weekends a month, Oliver paid Cam to run a second farmers' market stall up in Milford for him. Used to be every weekend, but logistics and the growth of Oliver's catering business had reduced the number of markets he attended. Cam didn't mind that it meant less cash for him. Running the stall had never been about the money. It was about staying busy.

"I'm delivering a dollhouse to a client in Doylestown and would like help getting it into and out of the truck," Nick said.

"Oh, sure. Text me a time and a place and I'll be there."

"Thank you."

"You're—"

Nick had disconnected the call. Cam chuckled. His little bro wasn't big on small talk. The drive down to Doylestown would give them the opportunity to catch up, though.

With the empty hours of his Saturday potentially filled, Cam smiled his way along Milford Road as he looked for the turn off. There, Raymondskill Road.

He'd made a delivery somewhere along here before. As he navigated the dips and turns, Cameron studied the houses, mostly hidden behind the trees. Was it that place? No—that one. He slowed the truck as he passed a place set closer to the road. Yeah, that one. He recognized the house but not the garden. It seemed kinda sad, as if the owner had stopped caring for it. That was a shame. As he remembered, the garden, while small, used to show years of labor and love. It had resembled the garden back at his place—the house he was babysitting while his niece finished college—established so long ago that even the weeds knew where they were supposed to grow. Here, the weeds had gotten out of hand and the grass was way too long. The barberry bushes lining the driveway had merged into an unruly mess, and there were broken tree branches gathered into messy clumps and not cleared away.

Huh.

Wasn't his business. This wasn't the address for the delivery he had in the back of the truck: three cubic yards of hardwood mulch and four trees, two firebirds and two cloud nines. The firebirds were pretty, with a dark pink edge to the leaves that would darken to a fiery red in the fall. Cam had planted one at the corner of the drive last year and enjoyed watching the foliage change throughout the seasons.

He drove on.

Half a mile later, he caught sight of a mailbox printed with the house number and name from his docket. 693, Ness. The name rang a distant bell, which happened sometimes. Cam had grown up here.

He turned into an almost hidden driveway that rose in a long curve around a gentle slope. Midsummer had the trees on either side almost meeting overhead, creating a tunnel of green. Low beds flanked the drive, thick with the spiky fronds of lilies, a few orange heads still bobbing in the afternoon heat. The drive flattened and widened at the top, opening out into a broad circle of gravel with a water-stained fountain at the center. The lilies continued around the outside, breaking for paths that led off into trees on the right, rolling lawn and flower beds on the left.

As pretty as the garden was, though, the drama taking place on the small front lawn quickly drew all of Cameron's attention. The grass was littered with objects: Boxes, garbage bags, and stacks of what might be clothing. In the middle of it all, two men screaming at each other. Actually, only one was screaming. The other held a defensive posture with an arm held up across his forehead as though to fend off an attack.

The reason why became apparent as the other man stooped to pick something up, cocked his arm back, and made an attempt to toss it. Whatever it was resisted his efforts, however, being perhaps too light for any sort of dramatic momentum. He overextended his arm, yelled—shrilled, really—and spun three-quarters of the way through a circle, the robe he wore fluttering open in an arc around him.

Cam blinked at the sudden exposure of skin. A lot of skin. Pale, as though the owner hid from the sun. With his cap of almost colorless hair, hiding was a good idea. He'd burn in no seconds flat. Was *he* Mr. Victor Ness?

Thankfully, *he* wasn't completely naked. Tight black briefs covered his junk, worn under an insubstantial robe of purple with swirls of teal, blue, and green, as though peacock feathers had been woven together to form a material. The way the sun sparked through the fabric, it might be silk.

Okay, then.

The other man stepped forward, as though to offer a hand.

Mr. Ness screamed again and made a very definite gesture, using a single sweep of the hand. Even over the grumble of the engine, Cam heard his words.

"Get out! Go. And never come back."

Chapter Two

This was not how it was supposed to happen. But when had his fantasy life ever lined up with reality?

Victor drew in a breath and tried to hold it this time. To not let it go like the last one, the echo of which still battered his ears. Or maybe his ears were ringing. His head felt a bit like a gong, and the universe—or reality, the snarky bitch—had one of those little hammers. Blood pounded across his temples and over the back of his skull, down his neck, and into his chest. When he placed a hand there, his fingers curled across bare skin.

Victor looked down. Oh, dear Lord. This was not what he was supposed to be wearing.

He recalled one imagined scenario in which he'd open the door to Tholo the Betrayer while wearing an outfit that said either *I don't care* or *I've moved on*. He did not recall that outfit being a pair of briefs.

The breath he'd been holding leaked out, and the sound emerging from his lips was suspiciously thin. Employing the hand at his chest like a bellows, Victor pushed the rest of the air out of his lungs. Drew in a new breath and, what the heck, he'd throw in another screech. He'd already lost his dignity. Had perhaps left most of it at the bottom of a wine bottle last night.

"And another thing!" He stooped to pick up one of Tholo's award statues.

"Victor, no!" Tholo held his hands out in a placating gesture. "Please don't."

Victor cocked his arm back. "Why not?" He sucked in more air. His head throbbed; his lungs convulsed. "You broke my heart.

It seems only fitting I should break yours." These cheesy statues were what turned the cogs in Tholo's chest. Victor knew that. Had known that ever since the first one landed on the trophy shelf Tholo had screwed into the wall the day he moved in. A beveled length of faux hardwood. Into the beautiful, quite authentic hardwood paneling to the side of the fireplace.

Tholo stepped closer, hands still outstretched. "Victor. Vic. Let me take it. I'll take all of them."

Victor let the statue drop into Tholo's hands. He then swooped to pick up a second and tossed it underhand toward his very much ex-lover. Tholo caught that one but had a hard time catching the next. And in between the *clink* of each award landing in Tholo's full hands, Victor got shrill again, because why not? It would be a lot harder to remain silent at this point, and he was done with hard.

Done with pretending to be the adult in this relationship. The cool, calm, and collected one. The man who lived a perfectly arranged life, with everything he had ever wanted. The soft-spoken and gentle artist who saved his temper for the studio.

He was done with being gentle. With politeness. With pretending he liked sex the way Tholo liked sex. When had their dynamic become stuck in so deep a groove, and why had he let it slip down there in the first place?

Why couldn't Tholo worship him for once?

Because you're not a little statue engraved with his name, Victor.

Humph.

Victor picked up the shelf, the one he'd ripped out of the wall—oh, his poor hardwood paneling—and braced it over one upraised knee, prepared to snap it in half.

"Victor! Oh my God!"

Tholo nearly dropped the awards in his rush to stop the destruction.

Victor whacked the board down and cried out as it smashed into his knee. "Goddamn it!" He raised the shelf again and brought it down only to have it thud into the other side of his knee. A shockwave of pain rolled through his leg. His toes tingled. His head continued to throb.

And his mouth—so dry. Spit clung to the corner of his lips.

Hauling his arm back, Victor searched for somewhere to throw the shelf, a surface that would guarantee its destruction, and noticed a pickup truck idling in the drive. The driver's side window was rolled down, with one tanned arm folded over the sill. Above, an equally tanned face framed by windblown brown hair.

The contrast between the mysterious stranger in his driveway and the beautiful man now easing the shelf out of his numb fingers was startling.

"Thank you," Tholo breathed as Victor let go of the shelf.

The wash of air against Victor's cheek made him shiver. He glanced at his former lover, at the man who hadn't so much broken his heart as let him carry on believing they could last.

His thoughts flashed toward the magazine resting on his kitchen table, the one where Tholo was framed by inset pictures of two different partners—one young and stupidly attractive, the other quite obviously older, with every wrinkle rendered in high contrast, his pale cap of hair more silver than blond. *Out With the Old, in With the New* the headline read.

Victor's throat constricted. He'd known it was over, but did the rest of America have to share his pain? And see him at his most unattractive? Whereas Tholo, with glossy black hair falling across his eyes—his large, dark eyes fringed with absurdly long lashes—was gorgeous. Almost unreal in his loveliness. An image of harmonious beauty with the squareness of his jaw, the perfect curve of his full lips, the smoothness of his skin—the color a blend of yellow ochre and burnt sienna. His straight nose with delicate nostrils. Even his stubble, the way it framed his mouth and curved below his cheekbones, his ridiculously high and sharp cheekbones.

How was he real? He wasn't, was he? Tholo Smit hadn't been born looking like this, surely.

Suddenly weary beyond belief, Victor put a hand to the center of Tholo's chest and pushed him back. The warmth beneath his palm almost surprised him, as though he hadn't expected Tholo to have any substance. "You need to go."

Tholo briefly resisted the push. He met Victor's gaze. "I'm truly sorry, Victor. For the way—"

"Save your breath. We both know this should have happened eight months go." Victor's heart contracted. "Or was it a year and a half ago?" His vision narrowed. "When did you shoot that film with Amir?"

"That's—"

"Forget it. I don't want to know. I already know."

The pain in his knee throbbed upward, and that leg wobbled beneath him. Victor staggered back a step and reached for the doorframe. He missed. Even as Tholo leaned forward, as though to steady him, Victor batted at his hands.

"Just go. Leave me alone."

And then he fell backward, half-in and half-out of his doorway, the jamb catching his tailbone. His head smacked the Spanish tile and something bit his elbow.

Jesus Christ.

Victor blinked against blackness and starlight. Bile rose up the back of his throat, and he swallowed, wincing at the taste of sour wine and regret. Tears stung the corners of his eyes.

Hands pulled at his, the touch familiar. Then a stranger's voice. "Don't move him. Don't pull him up. Check his head and neck first." A different hand, large and warm, cupped the back of Victor's shoulder. "Hey."

Victor forced his vision into focus. Two faces swam in front of him, one too beautiful to be genuine, the other all too real. He blinked and tried again. Still two faces. Tholo and the stranger from the pickup. Closer, Victor could see the lines etched across the stranger's face. Crinkled around the eyes and mouth, as though he spent a good portion of the time in laughter. Serious across the brow.

His eyes were the color of coffee, or perhaps Hershey's chocolate. His nose crooked slightly leftward, a telltale bump at the bridge. A wide mouth, not quite even, and two days of stubble. Perhaps more. Whoever this stranger was, he hadn't slept well the night before. Victor could tell that with a glance from the red roadmaps in his eyes and the familiarity of bone-deep weariness.

And he wasn't exactly happy to be here, crouched in Victor's front hallway. And yet there was a kindness to his voice and beneath the scrunch of his brow.

Victor blinked and his vision blurred. Was he crying?

So not what he had planned.

But as the sobs heaved out of his chest—shrilly, because of course he couldn't even cry with dignity—Victor let his last fuck go. Why ever not? He no longer cared what Tholo thought of him, and the man prodding his neck and shoulders was a stranger. They'd never see each other again.

"Does this hurt?" the stranger asked.

"Everything hurts," Victor wailed.

"Should I call for an ambulance?" Tholo asked, his accent suddenly pronounced.

Dear lord, was he flirting? Now? Victor could be lying here with a broken back and Tholo was flirting with the . . . the . . . truck driver.

Who was this unmasked man?

A giggle welled up from beneath the bubble of confusion now filling Victor's chest. It came out on a burp—a burp that burned. Victor tasted wine.

Drinking last night, until he passed out on the couch, had also not been a part of the plan.

Fuck the plan.

Victor giggled again.

"I think he might have a concussion," the stranger said.

"I will call—"

"No." Victor forced his neurons into neutral. Swallowed another burp. "I'll be fine." Debatable, but ending up in the emergency room was most definitely *not* how today was supposed to go.

He pushed his palms into the nice cool tile beneath his ass and began to lever himself upward.

"Are you sure you should move?" the stranger asked.

"Nothing is broken. I can feel my extremities." He hurt all over, though. Even before this, he'd woken with the vicious edge of a hangover poking at his temples and a relentless pounding that sounded as if it was coming from outside his head. That'd been the front door.

Now he had more bruises than he'd collected in a week at the playground in elementary school, but he'd heal. In fact, that's all he wanted to do. Everyone needed to leave so he could shower, toss the outfit he'd laid out for today off of his bed, peel back the covers, and crawl into oblivion.

Sitting up, Victor turned to the stranger crouched beside him. "Really. I just need to pull myself together."

Tholo forced his way into the conversation. "How about we—"

"How about you fuck off, Tholo? As in pick up your crap and leave the premises."

Nothing like a good, sharp whack to the head to reorganize his priorities. The urge to toss Tholo's belongings across the lawn had faded, along with the need to make a fool of himself. Cool reality had been reestablished, and Victor couldn't even find it within himself to call her a bitch. She was only doing her job.

He turned back to the stranger. "Thank you for your assistance, but I'm fine."

Dark brown eyebrows dipping, the man studied him with the same mild concern before nodding and pushing to his feet. He then extended a hand toward Victor. "How about if you try standing up?"

"Sure." Victor grasped the broad, callused palm and hauled himself upward, noting that the stranger hadn't done much more than provide a steady handhold. Interesting. Victor had half expected to be pulled to his feet. His slight stature usually inferred weakness in the eyes of others. People assumed he lacked any sort of strength, whether physical or mental. Apparently, Mr. Pickup Driver had read him differently.

"Victor." Tholo's voice was quiet and flat. His accent once again almost absent.

"I thought I asked you to leave."

"I am. I will. I . . ." Tholo glanced toward the stranger, and for once, he appeared uncomfortable, as though he'd stepped into an audition he hadn't read the script for. When he returned his gaze to Victor, his expression was appropriately sad. And almost . . . Was that a real, live tear in the corner of his eye?

Tholo reached inside the lapel of his light sport coat and withdrew a lavender envelope. He held it out. "This is for you."

Victor couldn't make himself take it.

Mr. Pickup Driver eventually plucked it from Tholo's fingers. Then he lifted his chin toward the drive. Tholo's car—the oddly understated BMW that spent more time in long-term parking than on the road—waited there like an unwilling spectator.

As Victor watched, Tholo and the stranger picked up the rest of Tholo's belongings, the boxes Victor had packed yesterday afternoon before he'd started drinking. They carried them to the car, stowed them in the trunk and the back seat, and then Tholo was gone. Their life together, four years and change—three wonderful, the last a badly stitched article that should have been two separate pieces of material—reduced to a slowly retreating crunch of gravel.

Tears threatened again. Victor blinked them back. His throat hurt. The center of his torso ached, as though his heart had coerced all of his internal organs into revolt. Or perhaps that was also the wine.

The back of his head felt tender, and Victor was almost afraid to touch it. Instead, he turned his gaze toward the floor. No blood on the tile. Despite feeling less than together, he'd not done a Humpty-Dumpty.

He could already feel the bruise forming on his tailbone, though, and for some reason, his left knee hurt. Twitching the cloth of his robe aside, he inspected the joint and gasped at the rising welt there. *The shelf. Damn it.*

When he looked up, the stranger stood in front of him, his gaze also fixed on Victor's knee. His lips twitched.

"Don't even think about it," Victor warned.

The man's lips narrowed and flattened. Then he extended a hand. "I'm Cam. I'm here with your mulch and trees. From Shepard's?"

Victor stared at him a second. Then he shook the offered hand. "Victor. I'm here with . . ." A bruised heart and butt.

Cam's lips twitched again.

Victor bit the inside of his cheek.

"I don't mean to—" A smile overtook Cam's mouth.

"You certainly shouldn't." Victor would bite harder, but he'd injured himself enough for one day, thank you very much.

Cam's brown eyes were sparkling. He still wasn't what Victor would call handsome, but there was something there. Years of life. Of living. Pain, but happiness too. The gentleness Victor kept noticing amidst the chaos of the afternoon. Empathy as well. Hard-earned and genuine. Or perhaps that had always been there.

A kernel of interest popped inside Victor's chest.

Oh, no. Nope. No way. Not happening. This was, most definitely, not a part of the plan.

Victor cleared this throat. "Ah . . ." He leaned out sideways, past the bulk of Cam's shoulder, and eyed the pickup truck still idling in his driveway. "You can dump the mulch there, in front of the garage. On the right side, please. Try not to block the left door. And the trees can go behind the mulch, I guess." He returned his attention to the man in front of him. The not-at-all interesting delivery driver. "Thank you." He patted his hip and winced as his hands slid over the silken fabric of his robe. He was standing there in his underwear.

Well, then.

Spinning with enough drama to flare the robe around his calves—why wear a garment designed for such a display and not use it?—Victor stalked along the hall to his kitchen and plucked a twenty from the cookie jar on the counter. When he got back to the front door, Cam stood where he'd been left, his not-in-any-way-lovely face now creased with bemusement.

Victor handed him the tip. "Thank you."

Then he shut the door in Cam's face. Because he needed it to be gone from his sight. He needed this day to be over. The weariness from earlier was seeping back into the corners of the recently reinstated reality. Beneath it lurked a deepening fatigue.

A wave was building in the troughs of his mood, and soon it would crash over him. Victor needed to prepare. He didn't have time to moon over strange delivery men in his driveway, handsome or not. He didn't have the wherewithal to follow such whims, anyway.

He was done with men.

For the time being.

And beyond done with love. So very done.

Chapter Three

The following afternoon, for reasons he couldn't articulate—that would mean giving them space in his head—Cam found himself driving along Raymondskill Road. It was a hot day, and heat shimmered up from the blacktop as he navigated the long curves, his niece's car whining when he hit another slope.

He should get his own ride. Had thought about it on and off, and had some cash put aside. But until Emma's car died on him—full-on stopped working in a way he couldn't fix—he lacked the impetus. Besides, when they talked, Emma always asked how the car was, as though it was a pet Cam was taking care of while she spent the summer in the city. So, he kept driving it.

He slowed down as he passed the house with the unkempt lawn, and then stopped altogether. A figure with a long ponytail the same color as Emma's stood in the middle of a chewed-up strip of grass with what appeared to be a dead mower in front of them. Two determined kicks to the body of the mower didn't start it. Didn't even budge it. A grin pulled at Cam's mouth as the kid wound up for another round. Had to be a young person with all that energy. Also, who else would dress in shorts so wide their legs resembled sticks and a shirt loose enough it might be draped on a hanger? In Cam's experience, the older a person got, the better their clothes fit, if not only because a person filled out a bit.

Briefly, he glanced at his own belly. He should stop eating bacon sandwiches and drinking beer. A chicken and whiskey diet for the win. Easing his foot onto the accelerator, Cam moved on along the street.

He'd check in with the kid on his way back, because apparently that was his job now: Raymondskill Road Rescue. Not that Victor Ness would need rescuing today—unless he kept more than one lover in residence and was scheduled to throw another out on the lawn.

Another grin tugged at Cam's mouth. Making deliveries to people's homes, he saw some things. One day last fall, he'd dropped off a truckload of trees to a place out toward Honesdale that *had* to belong to a cult. Six-foot chain-link fencing followed the road for a full two miles before breaking at a gate. He hadn't really clocked the gatekeeper's outfit until he reached the end of the long drive. Then he'd had to take a second to wonder if she'd run behind the truck for the past half mile, because hadn't she been wearing denim overalls and a bright yellow blouse? But, wait, she'd had sandy-blonde hair, and the woman who'd met his truck had dark curls.

Then he'd seen everyone else—denim overalls and yellow blouses for all of them.

He hadn't asked and, thankfully, they hadn't tried to recruit him. He'd temporarily suspended the dating apps on his phone the week before, thinking he should stop tooling around so much, and a house full of women—cultish women—would have been tempting. But yellow wasn't his color. And besides, he hadn't known if they were that kind of cult. They might have been celibate. Or not into dick.

At the bottom of Victor's driveway, Cam again slowed to a stop. He'd forgotten that the house wouldn't be visible from the road. Since not making space in his head for thought was the theme of the day, Cam turned into the driveway and began the long and winding ascent to the house. He could always say he thought he'd messed up the order. Delivered the wrong trees.

Or he could tell the truth.

Not the whole of it. Victor didn't need to know Cam had spent some time thinking about him last night. And whacking off. He was taking another break from the dating apps, so masturbating and watching TV were about all he did at night now, and he hadn't needed much imagination when it came to how a passion strong enough to drive a man like Victor to make a scene on his front lawn might translate to *other* activities.

Victor wasn't Cam's type, insomuch as Cam had a type, which he didn't, fantasies about sex cults aside. His libido carried no physical restrictions. He sure had some mental ones, though. Cam wasn't looking for a relationship, and Victor had *commitment* written all over him. He'd be a serial monogamist who thought each and every lover was The One. Victor believed in love and was—obviously—surprised when it didn't work out.

Or so Cam suspected.

At the top of the driveway, he parked and shut off the engine. The large red house lay quiet, and Cam took a moment to appraise the rambling structure. Like the tree farm offices, it was more a collection of buildings than a single one, except these were all joined in some way. The roofline at the center had the pitch of a typical Pennsylvania barn, steeper at the sides, a gentler bend toward the peak. The brick-red paint reinforced the image, as did the hayloft shutters framing the highest window. From there, roofs jutted out at different points, on different sides, as though rooms had been added here and there, as needed. Then rooms added to those rooms.

The front door was closed, any drama having already unfurled or perhaps still waiting in the wings. He didn't think so, though. The place had too restful a feel. No science would ever back him up, but Cam reckoned tension gathered in spots where something might happen, as though the universe knew in advance that shit was going to go down. Right there.

A soldier always knew.

Nothing was happening here today. Not even garden work. The mulch remained piled in front of the second garage door, undisturbed. The trees lined up like sentries behind. Where was the mulch supposed to go?

His car door opened, and then he was standing in the driveway, scanning the adjacent beds. Despite the anxious tick of his heart—why was he out of the car?—his fingers itched to give the beds the attention they needed: weeds were struggling up beneath a too-thin layer of mulch. The path between the detached garage and the closest rambling edge of the house could also use some TLC. The flat stones surrounded by gravel were uneven, as though the ground beneath had settled. Bound to trip someone who wasn't watching their feet.

He followed the path around to the back of the house.

Forgetting, momentarily, that he was somewhere he didn't belong, Cam stopped at another small lawn, this one not as trim as the front, abutting a patio put together with larger stones than the path. Proper pavers, set again between gravel. Weeds sprouted between the stones here and there, and moss crawled out from the shade of two gnarled trees at the rear. Furniture had been piled to one side as though someone had intended to tidy up the space but had then found something else to do.

Like tossing packed boxes out onto the front lawn?

"Can I help you?"

Cam landed back on his feet before he was aware he'd jumped. Catching his breath, he turned toward the house. Victor stood in an open doorway, wearing the same robe as the day before. This time, it was pulled closed and tied with a belt. His legs remained bare except for the black cat winding around his ankles. The visible V of his chest, however, indicated he was still only wearing briefs.

Had he not changed since yesterday?

"Hello?" Victor said.

"Shit, sorry. I . . ."

"You appear to be trespassing."

After trying and failing to find an amusing quip to explain his presence, Cam fell back on the excuse he'd invented on the way over. "The trees," he mumbled.

"What?"

"I thought I might have delivered the wrong trees."

Victor narrowed his eyes.

Cam let the rest of his breath trickle from his lungs and hauled in some fresh oxygen. "Sorry. I was checking in on you."

"You were *what?*"

"You fell yesterday, and you seemed kind of upset."

Victor's expression fluttered between surprise, horror, embarrassment, and a recognizable what-the-fuck. Then he said, "I'm fine."

"So I see." Though Cam didn't. They were six feet apart, and he could still smell wine and a hint of sweet smoke. Weed, maybe?

Hey, he wouldn't judge. Cam liked a toke. Also, if he'd suffered as dramatic a breakup as Victor had, he might want to drift around in his robe and drink for a couple of days as well.

"Okay, um . . ." Cam glanced up at the sky and nodded in that direction. "Rain forecast tomorrow. Most of the rest of the week, actually. If you don't want to lose your mulch to that gully off the side of your drive, you should drag a tarp over it." Or spread the mulch into some beds so it could take that rain and lock it down into the soil for the hot months ahead.

Victor made no answer.

Nodding again, toward Victor this time, Cam produced a confident smile—*I was meant to be here, this meeting prearranged, but now I'm leaving, as agreed*—and raised one hand in a half wave. Then he retraced his steps along the path to the driveway, got into his car, circled the fountain, and drove back toward the road.

Leaving was definitely the best course. He *had* been trespassing, after all. But a part of him wished he hadn't left quite so quickly. The part that had noticed the forlorn set of Victor's shoulders and the downward curve of his mouth. The fact he was still wearing yesterday's clothes, and that yesterday, he hadn't appeared to have gotten dressed at all. The pallor of an already pale face. The dark thumbprints beneath Victor's eyes.

Cam couldn't put his finger on what it was that called to him. It wasn't simple attraction, despite Victor's otherwise fit state. It was something else.

Back around the longest curve of Raymondskill Road, Cam noted the kid had taken a seat in the long grass next to the mower. She—? He couldn't see a face beneath the bill of a ball cap. *They* appeared to be studying their hands. Probably a cell phone. Emma was rarely without hers.

The itch to help still unscratched, Cam pulled into the bottom of the drive and parked. He got out and climbed the small slope to the lawn and pushed through grass up to his knees. Pausing a good distance away from the kid, he called out, "Everything all right over there?"

The kid looked up and waved a single hand in a nonchalant gesture, as if they were used to strangers appearing in their driveway. "Hold on."

A soft voice. Feminine features. She shook her head at the phone, then stood in a quick but graceful gesture, rising as though pulled from the ground by invisible wires. If Cam had been sitting with his legs crossed, he'd have had to lean sideways and get his hands under him. Then his knees would have snapped, crackled, and popped and his left would have threatened to buckle before he stood.

Ah, the wonders of middle age.

She strode across the lawn to meet him. "You know anything about mowers?"

"A bit."

She held out the phone. "I found this video, but—"

Cam touched the phone, glanced at her for permission, then eased it out of her hand. He tapped the screen, closing her video, and brought up the one she should be studying. *Why Your Mower Stalls When Cutting Long Grass*. He handed it back.

"Oh." Her brow scrunched.

"But you don't need to watch that. I can take a look and help you fix what's up."

Whatever preservation instincts she possessed chose that moment to kick in. "Are you a neighbor? Like, do you live next door?"

"I work at Shepard's Tree Farm. I delivered mulch and some shrubs to this house last year. Just made a delivery along here yesterday. I had to check in on it and saw you were having problems with your mower."

"Oh." More brow scrunching.

Cam held up his hands. "I can head off if you want. I get it. Can't be too careful."

A half smile dimpled one of her cheeks. "I really could use some help."

"The old guy . . ." Cam poked at the gray matter in his head. "Mr. Gregory? No, Gregory Burke. He still here?"

Her smile died. "That was my grandfather. No, he passed a while back. Three months ago."

Which would account for the state of the lawn. "I'm so sorry. He was nice. Friendly. Came out to chat while I unloaded the mulch." Cam frowned at the lawn again. "He was keeping up the lawn all by himself? Or were you . . .?"

"No, he had a service, but that stopped when he died." She glanced back at the house. "He left it to me. The house. I'm his only grandchild. I was finishing my last year of college, though, so I couldn't come out until now and . . ." Her shoulders dropped. "It's so much. I thought if I could get the lawn clear, then at least I could see what else needed to be done, you know? But I couldn't even manage that."

Raymondskill Road Rescue to the rescue it was. "I could give you a hand. If you want. I've got time this afternoon." Too few deliveries again this morning meant he was pretty much done for the day. "How about we get this mower running and the lawn cleared and see what else needs doing? Then I can help you make a list and give you some advice on where to source materials and such."

"Oh my God, that would be amazing."

"Your parents . . ." Cam let the question trail off, unsure whether he should have asked.

"Texas. We moved down there when I was young. I was at college up here, though, so I used to come stay for the weekend with Gramps. We were pretty close."

"Again, I'm sorry for your loss."

She shrugged one shoulder. "Like he would have said, he had a good run. He was ninety-two."

"No kidding. I'd have said eighty-two."

"Right?" She stuck out her hand. "I'm Melanie, by the way. Melanie Burke"

"Cam. Cameron Zimmermann." They shook. "Let's see what's up with your mower."

As he'd suspected, the grass had choked the blade, causing the mower to overload. He showed her how to free the tangle, and they both marveled at the length of the grass wound around the rotor. When it was clear, he reset the safety and started the engine. Smoke belched out over a rough idle. Cam winced and shut the mower off.

"Do you know the last time this thing was used?"

"The lawn service probably didn't use it, did they?"

"This old beast? No." He wheeled it toward the driveway. "Let's get it serviced and then we'll take another swing at the lawn." He turned to ponder the long grass. Serviced or not, the mower wasn't going to cut it. "Don't suppose you've got a weed whacker?"

Three hours later, as the sun finally dropped behind the trees, casting long evening shadows across the road, Cam pulled into his own driveway and parked in the now-empty garage. With Nick living in Stroudsburg, the first space was free. Nick had left his workout equipment in the second bay and all the tools at the back—he'd hardly need them living over the shop with Oliver and working out at the nearby gym with their friends. Still, the garage felt curiously empty.

So did the house, most nights, when Cam couldn't summon the energy to find company. Which he hadn't for a while. His need for intimacy scrolled through cycles. Incessant and infrequent. He was enjoying a low ebb at the moment but might want to think about reactivating an app or two soon. Especially with how long the days were in summer. He'd watched every DVD in the house four times and all that appealed on the streaming apps.

He looped his fingers through the couple of shopping bags on the passenger seat and crawled out of the car. Man, he was tired. A good, achy tired. He wouldn't need to stream a movie tonight. Should have no trouble sleeping at all.

Dinner was a rotisserie chicken from the supermarket and a tumbler of whiskey. In concession to health and because eating vegetables made him think of his little brother, Cam plucked some lettuce, a tomato, two radishes, and a cucumber from the garden and put together a salad.

Then he poured himself another whiskey and carried it into the living room, where he flopped onto the couch and picked up the remote. After surfing through the front-page offerings of three different services, he decided to continue watching *Star Trek: Voyager*. He'd finished *Next Gen* about a month ago and had debated the merits of *DS9* and *Voyager* for all of sixty seconds before going for the latter. B'Elanna Torres was easily his favorite Star Trek character of all time; not only could she fix anything, she wasn't afraid to express herself.

He toasted the screen. "Here's to you, B'Elanna."

But his focus wasn't up to the challenge of whatever the Hirogen had planned for this intrepid band of explorers. Instead, Cam's thoughts kept drifting back to Raymondskill Road. First to Melanie. He'd enjoyed helping her. Turned out her degree was in social work, and she reckoned she could read people pretty well. She'd determined he was mostly harmless.

She wouldn't define the *mostly* for him.

Cam smiled at the TV. Sipped his whiskey.

Melanie had the summer to herself and planned to fix up the house. If she could get a job within a reasonable distance, she might keep it. Social work didn't pay a lot. Owning her own home would allow her to take positions she might not otherwise consider while she continued to study part-time.

Cam couldn't imagine getting two degrees. He didn't know anyone who had one. Well, he supposed Oliver had a degree. And Victor . . . What did Mr. Victor Ness have a degree in? What did he do, aside from float around his home, getting lost in all those odd and extra rooms? Did his robe get caught on furniture or in doorways? Snag on the stairs, perhaps?

Maybe he was . . . What was the term? Independently wealthy? If Cam had wealth, he could stand to wander around in his underwear and a robe. He'd get bored pretty quick, though. And a day of wandering, tugging his robe free of tight corners, wouldn't wear him out half enough to sleep at night.

Cam drained his glass and reached for the bottle. Poured himself another round.

The real question was: Would he be visiting Victor again tomorrow?

Or maybe the question was: What would be his excuse for stopping by?

He could say he had another customer in the area. Melanie was expecting him to drop off some organic weed killer for the tangled mess choking the garden. He could drop some off for Victor too. As an apology for trespassing. And because Victor could use some in those front beds. Could use a little Preen, too, under the mulch. Or maybe he'd prefer weed cloth. Friendlier for the environment, even if it did encourage mold.

Maybe not around the house, but on the other side of the patio?

His glass was empty again.

On the TV, people were screaming. He'd missed half the episode.

Cam grabbed the bottle and portioned out another mouthful. Then he tipped himself sideways on the couch and closed his eyes. A sweet face, too young, too innocent, too familiar, fluttered behind his lids, jacking his pulse rate up. As always, the concussive boom of an explosion followed. Waves of heat and noise. The stench of human wreckage. The young face wavered and became covered in blood.

Gasping, Cam pushed the images aside. *Trees. Think of trees.*

Trees and flowers and the smell of the forest after rain. A big red house. A man in a flowing robe. The cloth sparkled, light straining through, and Cam saw blue and teal and green. Heard the call of a peacock, the shrill caw and an answering warble.

Then he was drifting, falling, wrapped in someone. Warm. Safe.

Then he was asleep.

Chapter Four

Victor jabbed his brush at the blank canvas in front of him and smirked at the resulting daub of paint. "Acrylics one-oh-one, folks. We put the paint on the brush and the brush to the canvas. It's that simple."

Except it wasn't. Not today. Even the gray light pushing through the heavy cloud cover outside was enough to sting his eyes and spark painfully off of the crushed glass inside his head. Every time he turned, his neck crackled. His back hurt. The swelling in his knee had subsided, but the bruise was ugly, as though a giant hand had wrapped around the joint and squeezed. His tailbone throbbed.

He felt as though he'd lost a fight. The worst of it, however, was that the damage was self-inflicted; every single flare of pain, including whatever was up with his head.

"It's the wine, Victor, dear," he grumbled.

Vodka would have been kinder. He'd have passed out sooner. Woken up less hungover.

Victor squinted at the canvas in front of him. His brush hand had drooped to his side. Holding it up had become painful because his arms also ached for no discernible reason whatsoever.

God, he was a mess.

It had only been two days since he'd tossed his heart out onto the front lawn, though. Not that Tholo had entirely owned it at that point. Still, the incident had to leave a mark, and it certainly had.

With an overly dramatic sigh (one that sent a twinge down the spine to his coccyx and back up), Victor swirled the brush through the jar of water beside his palette and laid it out on the paper-covered table to dry. Then he sighed again.

He had a single spot of paint on a canvas. Best landscape ever. Perhaps if he invited the audience to squint? He could encourage them to look for the world inside that one brush stroke. Infer this was his new style. It was about time he tried a new direction, no?

His head throbbed and Victor nodded gently. "I know. We're not painting today." Thunder rumbled outside. "We'll use the dreary weather as an excuse."

From deep inside the house, Dexter let out a mournful wail. Victor rolled his eyes and turned away from the windows, calling out, "It's all right, Dexie. The thunder can't hurt you." He offered the same reassurance every storm, as if the cat might one day become fluent in human, and then take him at his word.

Sinister, Dexter's smaller, sneakier brother, arrived in the studio doorway and stood there with his slender black tail wrapped around the doorframe.

"Where have you been?" Victor asked. "I've been out here talking to myself for about half an hour. You're supposed to be my muse."

Sinister answered with a petulant squawk. From wherever he'd chosen to hide, Dexter howled. Victor flicked his fingers toward Sinister. "Go help your brother. He thinks the sky is falling again."

Outside, the wind picked up with a sudden gust and roared through the trees like a freight train. Summer always brought storms, but the weather had been wild and wooly lately. End-of-times wooly. Victor frowned at the windows surrounding his studio. If this trend toward apocalyptic storms continued, he might have to consider shutters for this room. Thankfully, his studio was on the south side of the house, facing away from the wind.

Lightning arced over the trees across the lawn. Thunder boomed close by, making the house vibrate. Drafts sprang up from everywhere. His house was gorgeous in a mysteriously rambling way but leaky as a junkyard sieve. Victor tugged his robe closed over his chest and got a whiff of two-day-old body odor. He looked down at himself and sighed.

Dear God, had he changed his underwear since Tuesday?

Dexter wailed again.

No. No, he had not. And Dexter wasn't the only one who should be upset by this. Was it safe to shower during a thunderstorm? Victor could never remember. He seemed to recall his mother had always warned him against it, with stories about people being zapped through walls. Dutifully, he'd passed the stories along to his own progeny. He also seemed to recall his son, Sage, reporting the rumors as false, however.

Had he ever fact-checked? He should set Cori on to it. She loved proving her brother wrong.

He was reaching inside a robe pocket for his phone when the lights went out.

Dexter hissed and growled from his hiding spot. Victor squatted to run a hand along Sinister's furry back before nudging the cat toward the interior of the house. "Go. We don't want to be here if this room tears away and takes off for parts unknown."

Sinister disappeared into the deepening shadows, and Victor woke the screen on his phone. Despite the darkness outside, it was still midafternoon. And, surprise, surprise, he had no signal. He often didn't in the midst of a storm. Pocketing the phone, Victor shut the door to the studio behind him in an effort to begin compartmentalizing the house. He had no central air to worry about, but preferred to keep the ghosts to a minimum.

A wry smile cornered his mouth as he recalled Sage's year-long campaign regarding the Ghosts of Ness Manor. He could feel their fingers around his ankles and legs, he'd said. And on the back of his neck and sometimes in his hair. Tereza, the children's mother and the more sensible parent, had not approved of Victor and Cori's plan to stage an exorcism. Thankfully, such shenanigans had proven unnecessary when the ghosts had invaded the family room one night, teasing the back of every neck and wrapping around all exposed ankles and wrists, the mystery resolving into the Drafts of Ness Manor.

In the kitchen, Victor contemplated the weather whipping across the patio and wondered whether he could be bothered heading to the garage to hook up the generator. Depended on how long the power would be out, and how much water he wanted to use. He could leave it for now. The smell wafting up from his pits wasn't going to kill anyone but him. Hell, if it rained, he could stand outside.

The phone in his pocket rang. Eyebrows crawling upward, Victor retrieved it and blinked at the screen. Then, smiling, he answered. "Tereza! Your ears must be burning. I was thinking about you. Also, I don't know how you're getting me. The weather is ferocious up here and a minute ago, I had no signal."

"I'm surprised I had one," she said. "It's crazy down here." She lived about forty minutes south of him in Stroudsburg. "I know it's always hairier up your way, though. Do you have power?"

"Just lost it. How about you?" The infrastructure in Stroudsburg usually proved more robust, which was part of the reason Tez had relocated there. She'd rather have a steady supply of electricity to run her kiln than a steady supply of unbaked clay. She did not love drama as much as Victor—her words, not his.

"Still humming along," she said now.

Dexter added a loud howl to the conversation. He was probably in the dining room, crouched under the buffet.

"Was that Dexie?" Tereza asked.

"It was."

"Poor thing. So, listen. I planned to call you today, anyway. Are you all set for the weekend?"

The weekend? Victor consulted his phone screen. How in the heck was it Thursday already and what was happening this weekend? He put the phone back to his ear. "Yes?"

"Victor!"

"What? I drank a little too much last night." The subtle pressure in his chest suggested he'd smoked a little too much as well. "We're artists. It's what we do."

"It's what we did when we were twenty. These days, you only— Oh." Her voice lowered, and Victor could barely hear her over the rain now battering the kitchen windows. "Did Tholo come home?"

"Came and went. I tossed him out on his beautiful ass."

"About time."

"Tez!"

"What? He's been on-again, off-again with that other beautiful ass, Amir, for how long now?"

"Eight months, according to *Us Weekly*." Victor cast a glance toward the magazine resting on the kitchen table.

He didn't need to see the picture on the cover to remember every detail. The slightly grainy photo of Tholo and Amir strolling hand in hand through some remote Italian village—the set of their latest film together.

Victor had assumed Amir was someone Tholo kept company with on occasion. He'd minded but not terribly much. So long as Tholo came home, Victor had never minded. He hadn't dwelled. But this . . .

Eh, he'd known Amir and Tholo were more than keeping company. Had known for some time.

As though sensing his thoughts, Tereza said, "You weren't in love with him anymore."

"I wasn't."

"But you're still a mess." For decades, Tez had had front-row tickets to the play of his moods. She'd know exactly how badly he was handling the breakup.

Victor dragged a chair out from beneath the kitchen table and slumped into it. His robe billowed up around him and the funk of a two-day bender rose up in a cloud. Ugh. He did need to wash. And to stop drinking wine. And to change his goddamned underwear. Call an end to this pity party and rejoin the world.

"I'm a mess," he admitted to Tereza.

"Are you going to be all right for Sunday?"

Sunday, Sunday, Sunday. Wait, it was his grandson's first birthday. And he was hosting. He'd had mulch delivered. And trees, though only the horses of Jupiter knew why he'd decided he needed new trees, which was to say *no one*. Instead of drinking himself into a stupor, he should have been tidying up the patio.

A voice whispered in the back of his mind, dry, slightly amused. *"Rain forecast tomorrow. If you don't want to lose your mulch to that gully off the side of your drive, you should drag a tarp over it."*

"Vic?"

"I'm here. I'll be fine." Did he sound confident?

"Are you sure?" Tez sounded tired, as though she wished she didn't have to ask. And she shouldn't have to. She really shouldn't.

"I'm sure. Though, if you want to come out early and help with the food . . ."

"Sounds like a plan. I'll see you bright and early Sunday morning, okay?"

Another gust of wind leaned against the house. Rain drummed against the roof and not-so-distant thunder rumbled. "If I still have a house by then."

Chuckling, Tereza wished him farewell and ended the call.

Victor sat staring at the blank screen of his phone for a few seconds, then slid it across the kitchen table, turning it face down over the magazine cover. A corner of purple poked out from beneath. The envelope Tholo had left behind. Scowling at it, Victor wrapped his robe around his torso and tied it off as tightly as he could. No point in getting dressed. The rain would drench him in seconds.

By the kitchen door stood a row of boots and shoes. Leftovers from when everyone had lived here: Tereza, Coriander, and Sage. Victor smiled as he contemplated the family of footwear. He left the shoes there as a reminder and because the kids always liked seeing them when they visited. They'd tease him but smile fondly at the row nonetheless.

He shoved his feet into bright red rain boots festooned with yellow chickens. Tereza had given them to him for Christmas two years ago, knowing he'd adore them and he did. Then he opened the kitchen door and stepped out into the storm.

The wind tugged his robe free of the belt within thirty seconds. Leaves leftover from last fall hit him in the face. Victor clawed the leaves away, clutched at his robe, and leaned into the weather. God, this wind. Perhaps he wouldn't need to plant the new trees. They could all be snapped off at the base. And the mulch might already be gone.

The wind dropped off sharply as he entered the narrow space between the house and the garage, and Victor used the interlude to catch his breath.

Then he was around the corner and back into the storm, the wind doing its best to undress him entirely. And, there, in his driveway, was the Kelly-green pickup truck emblazoned with the Christmas tree logo. *Of course he's here.* Exhaust puffed out behind the tailgate, but Victor couldn't hear the engine over the storm. Neither could he see the driver until he noted a tarp flapping near the mulch pile that appeared to be wrapped around a man.

Gritting his teeth, Victor went to help flatten the tarp over the mulch. "You didn't have to do this," he yelled into the wind. "I was on my way outside to do it."

Cam poked his head over the edge of the blue plastic. "I was in the area."

"Where did this tarp come from?"

"My truck."

Victor wrestled the edge closest to him toward the ground. "Grab one of those rocks? The pile, there . . ."

Cam glanced in the direction Victor was pointing and nodded before selecting one of the flat stones by the corner of the garage. Victor had piled them up as he cleared new beds and then used them to build low walls and pave walkways. One day, he'd carve a path through the trees to the mailbox and pave it with reclaimed stones. One day.

The wind fought them every inch of the way, but finally, they got the tarp secured on all four corners, without losing a lot of mulch to the side of the drive. Dusting his hands, Victor straightened, only to have the wind nearly knock him backward.

Cam caught his shoulder. Victor's robe fluttered out behind him, exposing him to the weather. They both looked down. Rather than try to fight nature, Victor shrugged and held his hands out as if to say, *What can you do?*

A lot, according to the set of Cam's eyebrows when he finished inspecting Victor's underpants. Despite the wind and rain, he'd seemed rather focused there, as though he'd never seen a man's crotch before. Perhaps he hadn't, outside his own, but Victor suspected he had. Cam's expression wasn't confounded or distressed, as though he'd rather not see another man's skin. No. Cam liked what he saw. He might not like the fact Victor had been wearing this robe and these underpants for coming up on three days now, but . . .

The wind tugged Victor away from Cameron's grasp, breaking the brief spell, and Victor took a careful step back. "If you've finished meddling in my business, I need to . . ." He gestured toward the house. "Shower. Change."

"You have power?"

"Not at the moment, no. But I have a generator."

"I can help—"

"Who *are* you?"

Cam rocked back. Thunder cracked overhead and he flinched. Then the wind pushed between them, and the rain turned heavy again, coming down in sheets now. The sort of rain that drenched.

Victor waved Cam toward his truck. "You're getting soaked."

When Cam's mouth opened—probably in protest, or to outline all he could do for Victor on his odd mission to save him from himself—Victor waved. "Please. Go."

Cam got into his truck, backed it away from the garage, turned slowly around the circle, and left. Victor could feel his gaze through the mirror the entire time. Knew Cam was wondering how long he'd stand here in his robe and underwear, soaking in the rain.

Hell, he was starting to wonder the same thing himself.

Lightning shattered the sky above the road and thunder boomed.

He should get inside.

Victor retraced his steps along the path to the back patio, his feet squelching inside the boots. By the time he reached the kitchen, he was so wet, his robe seemed to weigh a hundred pounds and his briefs were sagging around his ass. Wonderful. He should snap a picture of himself and send it to *Us Weekly*. They could use it next time they wanted to show who was losing the love war.

With the door closed behind him and his robe dripping onto the floor, Victor eyed the collection of empty wine bottles next to the sink. The ashtray and joint butts beside it. The remains of a sandwich he might have made yesterday.

Quickly, he checked the bowls on the floor beside the fridge. Still stocked with kibble. No matter how low he dipped, he always remembered to feed the cats.

Dex let out a mournful howl.

He should clean up. Make a fresh sandwich.

His gaze cut to the purple envelope. Victor snatched it off the table, flipped it over, and slid his finger beneath the flap. Inside, were two slender lengths of heavy cardstock emblazoned with the title of Tholo's latest film. Tickets to the premiere in Manhattan.

Of all the . . .

Victor dropped the tickets on the table and then turned the envelope upside down, looking for the accompanying note, the card, the anything that would hold a word of . . . What? Apology? Caught between a snort and something like a sob, he crumpled the envelope and tossed it toward the row of empty wine bottles. His throw fell short, the purple ball dropping out of sight between the table and the counter.

Victor drew in a ragged breath. Where was he? Shower or sandwich.

Or he could open a fresh bottle of wine. The day's events, thus far, certainly warranted it.

Decisions, decisions.

Chapter Five

C am parked to the side of his brother's truck and got out of the car before digging his phone from a pocket. He'd have checked the dash clock, but the displays hadn't lit up this morning. He'd had to estimate his speed on the drive, and now he had no idea what time it was.

As he glanced at his phone, two more points occurred: he couldn't remember how much fuel he'd had, and no dash meant an electrical short somewhere and those were generally a bitch to find. That was his Sunday taken care of.

One of the double doors at the rear of the shop banged open, and Nick poked his head out. A crooked smile quickly lit his face, and Cam strode forward with his arms extended. As he always did, Nick waited to be hugged rather than moving into the gesture. That he didn't shrink away meant he was into it, though. Nick wasn't shy about letting people know when he didn't want to be touched.

When his little brother's arms folded around his back, Cam breathed out a deeply held sigh. A release he'd probably needed for a week. Before letting Nicky—*Nick* go, he pressed a kiss to the side of his head. Nick endured. In fact, he might have leaned in. After they separated, he still wore his wonky smile.

Then, "You're twelve minutes early."

Cam shrugged. "Not a lot of traffic at eight on a Saturday. Got some coffee on?"

"Sure. Come on up."

Nick led the way into the shop and toward the stairs that connected to the apartments above. He and Oliver lived on the second floor. Nick's custom dollhouse business occupied most of the ground floor, which had been divided into three sections. A shopfront and small gallery for houses that more resembled models and replicas than children's toys. He also stocked handmade miniature furniture and fixtures for other enthusiasts. Behind the gallery sat Nick's workshop. The final, rear slice of the ground floor was taken up by Oliver's kitchen and the huge walk-in refrigerator he used to store the meatless, cheese-less pastries and pies that had proven so popular, he'd been able to start his own business.

The world truly was a strange place.

The scent of coffee caught Cam halfway up the stairs and he quickened his stride. Oliver had the carafe and a mug in hand when they reached the open apartment door.

"Cam." Smiling, Oliver filled the mug and handed it over. "Milk's on the counter."

Deciding it was another black coffee morning, Cam lifted his mug in salute and drained about half of the near-scalding liquid in one gulp. Immediately, the world seemed brighter, and not only because his tongue and throat had banded together in a chorus of what-the-fuck. Caffeine, oh blessed drug, was seeping into his bloodstream and working minor miracles. Right in that moment, Cam didn't feel as though he'd barely slept the night before—that it'd been a light sleep week. His brain cells were in concert, making anything possible.

Cam smiled.

Oliver did not smile this time. Nick appeared beside his lover, leaning against Oliver's side in the unconscious way he had, and he wasn't smiling either.

"What?" Cam asked.

"Late night?" Oliver asked.

"Yeah. Caught up with a few friends," Cam blithely lied. "You know how it is."

Nick would remember the rotating schedule of company Cam had kept when he'd first moved back to Milford. He liked to let his brother believe he still played around. There'd been a stage—about a year ago—when Nick had decided that because he was coupled up, Cam should be too. Cam's only defense had been to point out his need for variety. That and the fact he was too old to settle down, which, according to Nick, made no sense.

Whatever. As long as Nick was worried about Cam's romantic future, he wasn't thinking about why Cam didn't sleep well at night.

"So, we going to load up this house? Get on the road?" Cam gestured in the vague direction of the shop.

Nick picked up a mug. "In a minute."

Turning to Oliver, Cam asked, "What's on your schedule for the day?"

"I'm catering a wedding if you can believe it. In fact"—Oliver put his mug down—"I need to start baking. The reception doesn't start until three, but I want to make sure I have enough time to make up for any mistakes."

"I hear you." Cam clapped Oliver on the shoulder. "Good luck with it. If you need a hand when I get back, I've got nothing on this afternoon."

Oliver frowned. "Sorry I'm not doing a market this weekend. I find they're not as well attended in July. It's too hot or people are away."

"It's all good," Cam assured him. "I can use the time to catch up on my sleep."

In fact, an afternoon nap could work out for him. He wasn't fond of sleeping in the middle of the day; there was something wrong or decadent about catching zees when the sun was up, though he'd learned to sleep whenever and wherever. He seemed to have lost that ability after leaving the military, though. Along with several other essential life skills.

But right now? The idea of a nap was all kinds of inviting. Cam finished his coffee and followed Nick and Oliver back downstairs.

The house Nick had to deliver to Doylestown was beautiful. Three stories, the upper one housed in the attic, the white-painted dormers framed by dark blue tile. Cream-colored siding wrapped the lower two stories with the same wide-framed windows. Columns and a low triangular portico staked out the front door.

The shutters matched the roof tile. Cam could see a bit of the inside through the windows: miniature hardwood lined the floors and curtains hung from brass rods. Fireplaces, kitchen cabinets, built-in bookshelves.

Next to the house, two taped cardboard boxes held the furniture.

Cam placed the second one into Nick's pickup and glanced over at his brother, who was nudging the first toward the side of the bed so that it lined up with the grooves running along the floor.

Before Cam could suggest the first turn would knock it all out of place, Nick gestured for him to pass the second box over. "I want to strap them down. I've packed them pretty well, but the furniture is still delicate."

Cam grinned. *Packed well* in Nick-speak meant the boxes could be dropped from orbit and the furniture would be fine. But he knew Nick would have spent hours on every piece, making sure it replicated the original perfectly. His brother had the sort of talent that stunned. Granted, the cost of a Nicholas Zimmermann custom dollhouse also left more than a few people without air, but for his customers, every penny was well spent.

Cam looked forward to seeing how the owners of this treasure reacted. He also wished he had the patience and dexterity to do what Nick did. He enjoyed working with Luisa, Jorge, and the others at Shepard's. It was the best job he'd had in years. He pretty much set his own hours, working as often as Luisa needed him, and as hard as he wanted.

But loading and delivering soil and trees didn't take a lot of brainpower. Sometimes Cam needed a break from thinking. He'd enjoyed that aspect of being a mechanic in the army; being able to lose himself in maintenance and repairs often helped him forget where he was and where he'd been. Never for long, though.

Here, he could drift through a day, his thoughts touching off anything and everything. Enjoy conversation with customers, one-sided banter with Jorge, and yelling at whatever talk radio program he could find. Other days, he'd plug into an audiobook and while away the hours feeling almost productive. He'd listen to lectures on the history of the Roman Empire or artificial intelligence and finish a delivery with his thoughts whirling faster than the blades of a Black Hawk helicopter.

It was a rare day that truly challenged him, though.

"What are you thinking about?"

They were somewhere along Route 33. Cam refocused his gaze on the passing scenery outside and determined they were just past the Nazareth exit. Not quite halfway there. He turned to Nick. "Daydreaming. Sorry. A bit drifty. Late night and all that. What's up with you?"

"I want to talk about marriage."

There you had it. Nick could probably have managed to get the dollhouse into and out of the truck by himself. He'd asked his big brother along for the ride because he wanted to talk. About—

"Wait, marriage? Did you . . ." No, Nick wouldn't have asked Oliver. Not without preparing an elaborate plan. "Did Oliver—"

"Oliver and I are not getting married."

Cam leaned toward the center of the vehicle. "I'm listening for the 'yet.' Tell me there's a 'yet.'"

The corner of Nick's mouth twitched. "Yet." He glanced at Cam. "I don't know if he's thought of it. Or if he wants that. He's been married twice already."

"To women."

"Maybe he doesn't believe in marriage between men."

"I doubt that. Oliver's all about family. Being a unit. I think marriage suits him regardless of his partner's gender. I absolutely guarantee he's thought about marrying you. He probably doesn't know how to ask, but I'll bet he has a half-formed plan."

Nick full-on smiled. "You think?"

"For sure."

Nick's smile narrowed. He glanced over again. "Have you ever been married?"

A mule kick to the center of his forehead might have surprised him less. By the time Cam had gathered enough air to speak, Nick seemed to be paying more attention to him than the road. Cam waved at the sign for the upcoming merge with Highway 78. "Want to take the river down, or head along to 309?"

"Let's take the river. It's scenic."

"I figured you'd be all about efficient use of time."

"Then why ask which way I wanted to go?"

"Just making conversation."

Nick guided the truck into a merge lane. "You were changing the subject and much less subtly than I would."

"Pretty much."

Nick looked at him, concern etched into the fine lines of his face, and Cam got one of those rare glimpses of all of history. His brother as an uncoordinated and spirited young boy who used to practice awkward cartwheels on the back lawn for hours at a stretch.

His silly side had vanished the night their parents had died.

He also saw Nick as a young man—snapshots from when Cam chose to spend his leave at home in Pennsylvania. And Nick as an adult: a familiar but sad stranger.

Their sister's death five years ago had changed him further. After they'd lost their parents, Rebecca had practically raised Nick while Cam had run off to find a war. Her passing had devastated Nick. When Cam had arrived home again, nearly two years ago, he'd found a ghost living in a house full of them.

Cam had seen himself in all of those faces too. Seen his shitty history as a brother. As the boy and then the man who always ran away.

A dull pain spread out from the center of his chest, and he resisted the urge to press his fist there. He'd had a conversation with Nick last year about this very pain. Cam had called it *grief* and had told his little bro that everyone felt it.

Truth. But Cam's pain wasn't only a sense of loss. Or maybe it was—just deeper and more profound than the absence of family. Of having only Nick and Rebecca's daughter, Emma, who Nick had raised in turn after Rebecca passed away.

Cam had been quiet for so long, the signs for 611, the route along the river, were already counting down. He glanced over at his brother again, then back through the window.

"There was someone. Once. A few years ago," he said to the trees along the highway.

The truck slowed, then sped up again. "Who?"

"A woman up in Connecticut. She . . ." He didn't want to talk about this. Cam forced a smile. "Tell me your plan for asking Oliver."

"I'm at the part where I ask other people why they decided to get married."

A surprised laugh shot out of Cam's lungs. "That's a part of your plan?"

"I'm in the research phase."

"Oh my God, Nick. You slay me."

Lips pursed, Nick guided the truck onto the exit. "I don't understand why you find my planning so funny."

"I don't. It's just *this* plan. Marriage is . . ." Cam let out another breath, this one a lesser held sigh. "I guess it does require some forethought. I mean, it's not something you're supposed to take lightly. But what you and Ollie have works on a number of levels. You're friends and you're lovers. You have the sort of adult relationship I envy. You admire and support each other's talents and respect the differences. You've made a home together and a place where both of you can work. You get along with each other's families. Heck, the most important part? You genuinely like each other and that's a lot. Love—love can be overwhelming. It can blind you to reality. Like is so much better."

"I love Oliver."

"I know you do, but it's the kind of love that comes from intense like and admiration. Respect."

Nick's brow crunched. He glanced at Cam. "You don't think I'm capable of a passionate love?"

"I didn't say that. I meant to infer you weren't the type to lose your head to it."

"But I did. When I thought Oliver might move to Texas, I very much lost my head."

Nick had also destroyed several of the new trees Cam had planted in their backyard. "Sorry, little bro. I didn't mean to sound like . . . Fuck. I wasn't trying to . . . I'm not the one to ask, okay? About love and marriage. But what I was trying to say is that you've got whatever it takes. You and Oliver have it. That spark.

The deep kind of love that's a shared deal." Cam smacked the dash in front of him. "It's not mindless infatuation. That's what I was trying to say."

Nick nodded. "I understand." He glanced over, his expression sad. "You haven't had a deep love? Not even with the woman you wanted to marry?"

"I didn't say I wanted to marry her."

"Your face did."

"Damn your observant ass." Cam waved toward the windshield. "Pay attention to the road."

Nick snorted.

"She wasn't into it," Cam continued, relating only the relevant part of the story.

"I'm sorry."

"Don't be. I'd make a shitty husband. I lost the best part of myself in Afghanistan, Nick. There's not enough left to partner up with someone now."

A sharp inhale. "I don't believe that."

"You can believe what you like. I know who I am."

Nick pulled into a gas station. He did not sidle up to a pump, but parked by the air-filling station. He killed the engine and turned to face Cam.

"I love you, Cameron. I don't say it often enough. I used to carry a checklist of the people I loved, so I could remember to tell them how I feel. But I don't use it anymore because I think—I choose to believe that you all know." He pressed his fist to his heart.

Cam found himself echoing the gesture. He also found himself hoping Oliver didn't have to rely on Nick's newfound discovery that people simply knew he loved them. Then again, how could Oliver not know? Nick's adoration of his partner shone brightly whenever he and Oliver were in the same room.

They should totally get married.

Nick evidently wasn't finished talking, though. He took a breath and lowered his fist. "Last year, you suggested I talk to someone. Well, I did. I mean, I am. I . . ." High color bloomed across his cheeks. He ducked his head, but the sweep of his long hair failed to hide the blush. "I started seeing a therapist. I don't like it—the talking. But she's helping me deal with my losses in a way I wasn't able to on my own. And I think it's because I've been seeing her that I can talk to you now."

For sure.

Nick lifted his chin. "You were right. Now it's my turn to say it back to you. You know how when you first came back I'd ask when you were leaving?"

Cam nodded.

"At the same time, I was terrified you'd actually go. You didn't. Not then." Nick grimaced and winced and growled softly.

Used to the time it sometimes took his brother to express himself or work out what he was feeling and then find the accurate words for it, Cam waited. And the waiting was kind of nice, as though he'd needed Nick to need *him* in this way. When had his brother grown so far past him?

Nick touched Cam's forearm before closing his fingers in a slow, firm grip. "Anyway, if you want to start with me, I'll try to help. I can listen. I might not be able to tell you the right things afterward, but I can listen."

This was so typically Nick. First, because he had a partner, he wanted Cam to have one. Now, he'd found solace in therapy and thought Cam might too. But although slightly annoyed, Cam knew the suggestion came directly from the heart. Nick was saying *I love you*, again, in his own, awkward way.

Cam put his hand over Nick's. "You do just fine. And . . . thanks. I'll, ah, keep that in mind."

Nick smiled. Nodded. Squeezed Cam's arm again.

"And Nick?"

"Yes?"

"I'm here for you. Always. Even if you want to talk about marriage. Mom and Dad made a pretty good go of it."

"They did."

"I'll see what I can remember for you."

"Good. Because I have more questions."

Cam grinned, and as his face cracked upward, he felt lighter than he had in quite some time. "Bring them on."

Chapter Six

Victor followed the sound of banging along a hallway that didn't bend where it was supposed to. Where the hell had the front door gotten to? And whose house was this anyway? He ended up in an odd cul-de-sac of paneled walls and turned a full circle, the familiarity of the scene prickling his senses. His house used to be this confusing, before they'd joined a few of the smaller rooms together.

Was this his house?

The banging—knocking?—sounded again, and Victor chose a new direction. The front door was this way. Always had been. When he found himself in a new corner, this one lit by windows, he turned another circle.

The knocking continued, louder now, and the tone had changed from a rap against wood to a sharper, rhythmic *tock*.

"Victor!"

Eyes peeling open suddenly and somewhat painfully, Victor struggled to focus on the face in front of him. Looming over him. Tight dark curls framing a sun-browned face. Large, expressive eyes— Oh, he knew those eyes and recognized that expression: anger, disappointment, and exasperation. Tereza had mastered each one individually over the course of their friendship and all three in the years they'd lived together.

Victor licked his lips, and that was a mistake. "Ugh."

"Jesus Christo, you are a mess. Thank fuck I decided to come extra early." Tereza wrinkled her nose. "When was the last time you showered? And where on Earth did you find that robe? I thought we gave it to Goodwill six years ago."

He was on the couch in the living room, sprawled indelicately, with his beautiful peacock robe spread out like a picnic blanket, which it might as well have been if he hadn't been wearing it. As he reached for handfuls of the silken fabric—in defense of it and himself—he encountered crumbs. And a sticky patch. And— Oh dear lord, when had he torn it?

Squawking in distress, Victor sat up and immediately regretted it. His stomach gurgled, and bitter fluid stalked the back of his throat. Only the fierce pain across his temples stopped him from opening his mouth in a liquid yawn. Vomiting would only exacerbate his headache. Also, Tereza was already mad.

Why was she mad?

Perhaps not trusting his sense of self-preservation or control, Tereza stepped back, her chunky heels *tock*ing against the hardwood.

"Where's the rug?" Victor asked, blinking stupidly at the floor. A vague memory prodded. He mentally batted it away. His head hurt too much.

"Oh, Vic. What have you been doing to yourself?"

He glanced up at her but didn't answer.

Tez shook her head and sighed. "Come on, we need to get you through the shower, and then you can clean while I cook."

"You're a terrible cook," Victor mumbled as he hoisted himself to his feet. "I'll clean and you can cook. No, I'll cook and you can clean."

"Fine, fine. As long as we get started soon. Sage will be here at one. Cori said she'd try to come early. She's bringing the balloons."

Balloons. For his grandson's birthday.

A weight dropped through the center of Victor's torso. "Why did our son have to clone himself so soon? I'm only fifty-two. That's much too young to be a grandfather."

Tez rolled her eyes. "Could you keep it in your pants at his age? It's a wonder he doesn't already have six kids."

"I wasn't sticking my dick into people who could grow babies." Victor shuddered.

Tez's chuckle had a reluctant sound, as though she'd rather not be amused. Sobering, she gripped his shoulder. "Are you going to be all right today? Seriously, Vic. You—" She cut herself off with a sigh. Then, "Why don't we move it all to my place or reschedule?"

"No, no, I'm good." If not for Tez's hand, he might tip forward and face-plant where the living room rug used to be, but . . . "What did I do with the goddamn rug?"

Fur wrapped around his ankles. Victor glanced down and smiled. Curving his lips upward hurt his head a whole lot less than curving them downward. He stooped—ill-advised—to stroke Dexter's long, white fur. "Where did the rug go, Dexie?"

Shaking her head, Tez helped him stand again. "I'll look for it while you shower." She held out a hand. "Give me that robe. I'm going to burn it."

"No. It's . . ." Victor stroked the filthy silk again, then shrugged it off. "Put it into a bag. I'll take it to the cleaners." His eyes widened. "Oh my God. It's Sunday? I didn't shop. Tez, I didn't shop. I haven't—"

"It's just hitting you now that I had to let myself in because you were passed out on the living room couch in your underwear when you promised me two days ago that you'd be ready for this party?"

Don't cry.

Victor sniffed. "I am a mess. Why am I such a mess? I didn't love him anymore, Tez."

The weary annoyance in Tez's expression softened. She went to curl an arm around his shoulders and then hesitated. "I'll hug you after you shower."

Another vague memory resolved out of the mist of the past few days. A thunderstorm with heavy rain. Lightning. A blue tarp. The guy from the tree farm.

"I dripped on the rug," he said.

"What?"

"The day it rained. Thursday?" That had been Thursday? Vic glanced down at himself, at his pale, sticky skin, his underwear—he'd changed into bright red briefs. Okay, that was good. He'd at least done that. Three days ago. "I got wet and came in here and dripped all over the rug and then worried about the wet rug on the floor. I have no idea what I did with it, though."

"We'll find it. Now go shower."

He shook himself like a wet dog. "Right. Yes. Shower."

As he reached the doorway, Tez said, "It was the idea of him you were in love with, and ideas are hard to let go of."

A half smile tugged at a corner of his mouth, one of sad and strained humor. Bracing a hand against the door jamb, he swung his head in her direction. "You ever wonder whether we should have gotten married? Bought the whole farm?"

She shrugged. "Sometimes. But then we wouldn't have had the fun of all these disastrous other relationships." She met his tired smile with a wry one. "We got to have our cake and eat it too, my darling Victory. Just like we wanted." Gay best friends deciding to have kids together. Because why not.

"You know, the years we lived in this house, doing the parent thing, were the best of my life."

"*So far*," Tez said. "And, yeah, me too. But we're still young and hip."

"No one says that anymore."

"Whatever. I'm fifty-three. I can say it however I want to say it."

He blew her a kiss. "Go find my rug."

"Go shower away that funk."

"Thanks, Tez."

She answered with a flick of the fingers. *Get out of here.*

After a long, hot shower that relieved his headache better than the pain killers he'd swallowed while the water heated up, Victor felt almost human. He wouldn't be operating at peak efficiency today, but he wouldn't embarrass his children, either. Lingering in the doorway to his closet, he surveyed the row of hanging shirts, hoping for one that said *first birthday party*.

Lord, a first birthday. He was going to cry, wasn't he? Happy tears, of course, but also nostalgic and sentimental ones. Sage would blush with embarrassment, and Cori would pat his shoulder fondly and whisper in his ear, "It's okay, Dad."

Tez would snug an arm around his waist and squeeze tight.

Did he need more than that? Why did he want someone else so much that he'd endure the sort of behavior Tholo displayed?

Had they ever been this happy?

After brushing white cat hairs away from the quilt, Victor laid three shirts out on the bed and went in search of pants to go with them. Should he dress up or down? Tereza was wearing an orange and gold sundress, which looked fabulous with her complexion. She'd have already lost the heels, though. She loved the idea of them but could never wear them for long.

Vic chose a pair of jeans in a pale lavender denim and a loose button-down with a mosaic print. Red, orange, gold, pink, purple, blue, and green. The pattern was small enough that all the colors were only visible up close. From a distance, the shirt almost resembled static.

Posing in the mirror, he asked Sinister, who'd appeared on the bed as though by magic, what he thought. "Too casual or just right?"

Yawning, the black cat put his head between his paws and closed his eyes.

Victor left him to his nap. Halfway through the family room, he remembered the pain in his tailbone only because it had faded. His knee still caused him to wince, though. He'd inspected it in the shower, and the bruise matched his shirt for range of colors.

Tez had the front door wedged open, and a warm breeze had flooded the house, airing out corners and the funk of his five-day bender. Victor drifted into the kitchen and silently thanked her for starting the cleaning in there. He'd been afraid to count how many empty bottles might be gathered around the sink. She had the door to the patio propped open too, and the scent of old leaves and sunbaked stone drifted inside.

Glancing through the windows, Victor admired the greenery gathered around the edge of the large patio. The hibiscus had started to bud, and the lilies were already aflame. Behind the bright orange, star-shaped flowers spread a veritable hedge of lavender. Purple echinacea swayed over the top, and black-eyed Susans poked through at irregular intervals. Buddleia flowered behind it all, their drooping, ethereal blooms almost alien in shape. The rhododendrons were done with their display, but their strong, green leaves served as a thick screen, protecting the patio from the weather.

It was a beautiful space, and gazing at it, Victor wondered why he'd never painted the patio garden. Probably because painting had been all too hard, lately. Riotous color hadn't answered his call. If he were alone, he could pick up a pencil and start sketching. Studies of the different flowers, the shape of their petals, and the way the light hit each one. He could prepare compositions. One ordered and one chaotic.

But he wasn't alone. Not today. Today, his children were coming home to visit him, and with a sudden sense of longing, he realized he'd missed them. He always missed his kids. It'd been hard to watch them leave the nest—five years ago for Cori, four for Sage. Thankfully, neither of them had decided to move to the other side of the country, though Cori might at some point. She loved the ocean—specifically the Pacific. She was the more laid-back and potentially Californian of the family.

Thoughts of his family pushing the residue of Tholo aside—for the time being—Victor turned his attention back to the kitchen and plucked the shopping list pad from the side of the fridge. He needed a to-do list.

Tez popped out of the basement door. "Your rug is downstairs. Somehow, you got it to the basement without breaking your neck and hung it in front of the furnace."

"The furnace that is not currently lit."

She smirked at him.

"I'm lucky to be alive."

"Aren't we all?" She leaned against the kitchen counter.

"Leave it down there. I'll hang it outside this evening. After the party." He tapped a pencil to the pad. "Okay, what are we feeding everyone?"

Two hours later, Victor was stuffing his fridge with salads, side dishes, and snacks. Tez had finished tidying the house—it hadn't been that bad—had unstacked and arranged the patio furniture, and had charcoal going in the grill. The smell of smoke and old barbecues had Victor's stomach rumbling. He had little idea what he'd fed himself over the past few days. Hopefully not cat food.

"Hello, the house!"

Victor shut the fridge door, wiped his hands, and went to greet his son.

Both of their children more resembled Tereza than Victor, with their tall stature, golden skin, and dark curls. But they had Victor's eyes, Sage's a grayer blue, and always startling by contrast. Victor pulled him into a hug, surprised, even ten years after the fact, at how small he felt in Sage's embrace.

"Hello, my boy."

"Hey, Dad." Sage clapped his back, the signal their hug should probably end soon.

Chuckling, Victor let him go and turned to hug Sage's girlfriend, Ashni. She was, thankfully, shorter than he was, beautifully curvy, and had the glossiest black hair Victor had ever seen outside of a magazine. She was also an absolute dear. She had a smile that encouraged everyone else to be happy, even if they didn't know why. Perched on her hip, his chubby little legs kicking back and forth, was his grandson, Billy. He was a perfect combination of Sage and Ashni, all smooth, dusky skin, dark curls, and a huge smile.

"Hello, number one grandson!" Victor said, ducking a little to stroke the boy's cheek. Then he leaned in to kiss Ashni's cheek. "And number two daughter."

Chuckling, she kissed him back.

"Come in, come in." He hustled them into the hall. "Cori isn't here yet, but Tez has the grill going, and I've made enough food to keep us through the apocalypse."

Tires crunched on gravel, and Victor glanced over Ashni's shoulder. "Speak of the devil, here she is." He turned a smile to Billy. "And she has balloons for you!"

He was vaguely aware he sounded mildly ridiculous, but fathers and grandfathers were supposed to. One of the aspects of being a parent he'd always loved was the license to let go and be embarrassing. To give in to the hugeness of his emotions during worthy moments.

A moment later, Cori and her phalanx of balloons joined the huddle in the hallway and another round of hugs and kisses ensued. She'd brought along her best friend, Raya. Cori and Raya had been friends since high school, and Victor sometimes wondered whether they were the generational equivalent of him and Tereza. Cori always offered oblique responses to his equally slanted questions about the relationship, though, so he left it alone.

He hugged her as hard as he had Sage, and she clapped him on the back when it was time for him to let go.

Another pair of gray-blue eyes, these a bluer gray, met his. Tez had never understood how both of her children had won such an unlikely genetic lottery, though with Cori's slightly fairer complexion, the color was less of a surprise.

"You smell like you've spent the week inside a wine bottle, Dad," she murmured. "Everything okay?"

"I'm fine."

She had a hand on his arm and didn't seem inclined to let go. "It's been a while since you last took a deep dive."

Oh, his oldest child. Not always sensible, but oh so wise. Cori took after her mother there.

Victor made his mouth smile. "I finally tossed Tholo out on his behind."

Her smile echoed his for a second before spreading wide. "Good." She squeezed his arm and let go. "Call me if you need to talk about it."

"Of course." He never would. It was a parent's duty to be there for their children, not the other way around. But he loved Cori for the offer. How had he ever produced such kind people? Must be Tez's genes. He'd given his kids eyes in various shades of blue, and she had given them everything worthwhile.

Curling an arm around his daughter's waist, Victor guided her into the house. "So, tell me about your latest project." After college, she'd taken a job with a landscape architecture firm in

New Jersey that dealt with city parks and infrastructure. He loved hearing her enthusiasm for the work and only hoped Sage would eventually enjoy publishing as much. Perhaps when he graduated from the slush pile to actual editing, he'd have a better time.

The afternoon continued to pass pleasantly, and it was only as the evening cooled and Victor trod the path to the garage in search of wood for the firepit that he remembered fully his encounter with the landscaping guy. Cam? Cameron? Victor couldn't recall exactly how he'd introduced himself, but his memory of the man's face was clear. The way his features refused to be plain, even while unremarkable. The concern in his eyes and the care he'd taken with Victor every time he'd been here.

The blue tarp, flapping gently at the corners in the early evening breeze.

For no reason whatsoever, he wondered how Cam would fit into his family, into the close-knit group of loved ones currently gathered on the patio. As he stacked cut wood into his arms, he reasoned his thoughts likely hinged on the fact that Cam had obviously had as little to do with his life this week as Victor had. That time weighed heavily on him—and that Cam had not sought solace at the bottom of a wine bottle. Instead, he'd turned his attention toward helping a stranger.

Victor studied the tarp, still held down by six flat rocks despite the ferocity of Thursday's storm, and wondered if he'd ever see him again. His guardian angel. He also wondered whether he'd like that.

He was wondering why he was doing all this wondering when Sage called from the side of the garage. "Need a hand?"

Victor held out his armful of wood for Sage to take. "Here."

Sage took the wood but didn't move. "You all right, Dad?"

"Hmm? I'm fine. Why?"

"You're quiet. And you're not drinking."

"Just thinking about a new series of paintings." If only that wasn't such a lie. "You know how I get when I'm lost in my head."

Sage frowned and hefted his wood. "Okay." Then, "I'm glad you got rid of Tholo."

Victor found perhaps his first genuinely effortless smile of the day. "Me too, Sage. Me too."

Chapter Seven

A combined sense of accomplishment and letdown assailed Cam every time he passed Raymondskill Road without making the turn. By Tuesday, however, a week after having reacquainted himself with the neighborhood, the feeling was more an itch than anything else. An itch that caught him miles away.

After making a delivery of soil and stone to a place in Bushkill, he passed a house painted a similar shade of red and had to force his hands to remain at the wheel. No, he would not turn into a complete stranger's house and stand there doing only God and the devil knew what.

An order of dogwoods—not for immediate delivery, but to be put on reserve for the fall, when one *should* plant trees—caused an itch at the back of his skull. With each plastic tag he wrapped around a slender trunk, the scratch deepened. Had Victor planted *his* trees yet? Or were they still suffering in pots? Had he spread the mulch?

Was he still dressed in a robe and underwear and subsisting on a diet of white wine?

Hands on his hips, head tipped back so that the late-afternoon sun fell full on his face, Cam breathed in and out. The scent of soil grounded him. The quiet rush of leaves from the gentle breeze soothed his thoughts. But the itch persisted.

He checked his phone, saw it was past five, and decided enough was enough. He'd be making no further deliveries today. It was time to see if he could drive past Raymondskill Road without turning.

Luisa wasn't in the office when Cam ducked inside to hang up the keys to the truck. He found her in the nursery seeding a plug tray. The work looked meditative. Soil, seed, soil. Soil, seed, soil. After completing a row, she glanced up.

"Heading out?"

"Yeah. I marked the trees for that order."

With a wry smile and soft shrug, Luisa said, "Not that it matters. I doubt we'll sell so many between now and then that we'll be left scrambling."

"You never know."

She rubbed her forehead, her gloved fingers leaving a smudge of soil below the graying hair that had escaped her bun. "I should be advertising. Doing a sale. Didn't we do a sale last summer?"

"We did."

"Does it make sense that I . . ." She shook her head. "*Olvidate.* You should go enjoy the rest of your day."

Cam folded his arms and leaned a hip against a nearby table. "I'm in no hurry. Just a chicken potpie, a six-pack, and two or three episodes of boldly going where none have gone before waiting for me."

Chuckling, Luisa shook her head again. "A young man like you. You should be out having a good time."

"I'm forty-nine, Luisa. And I've had my share of good times." He lifted his chin. "I get it, you know? Sometimes enough is enough. If you want to take some time, Jorge and I can handle business. Maybe head out west to visit your kids. If something comes up that we can't figure out, we can always call you. And you can log into the shop's inventory systems and whatnot from about anywhere, right?"

"I . . ." Surprise widened Luisa's eyes. "I could. But there is the ordering for fall."

"You did that already. I know how to check stock off the invoice as it arrives." Seasonal stuff such as hay bales, pumpkins, and apple cider. Corn stalks and scarecrows. Then there were the mainstays—fertilizer, mums, bulbs—and the monthly deliveries of products they always kept on hand. Natural pesticides and herbicides. Tree food. Stock for the small shop in front of the nursery, the seedlings Luisa raised herself. The colorful pots from local artisans and other assorted crafts. Plant stands, hangars, wall plaques.

As Cam finished compiling his mental list, he realized Luisa had been watching him. He met her gaze, and she smiled. "Maybe I will move to Oregon. Leave the business to you. Hmm?"

It was Cam's turn to express surprise. "I, ah, um, I'm not . . . That's not what I meant."

She touched his arm. "I know. But it's worth considering. I'm old, Cameron. Much older than your forty-nine. I'm tired. I miss my children. My grandchildren. I think it is time for me to consider these things. To either find someone who has the energy to keep this business running, or sell it, maybe."

"If you sell it, some developer will pull up all the trees and build a bunch of houses."

"Probably."

Luisa could make a lot of money on a deal like that. Enough to retire on, easily. More than enough to move out west to be with her kids.

She patted his arm and gestured toward the door. "Off you go to your Star Trek. I'll see you tomorrow, yes?"

"Tomorrow."

Ten minutes later, heading north on Milford Road, Cam sucked in a breath as he approached an all-too-familiar turn. Would he or wouldn't he? Luisa had given him enough to think about that he could go straight home, crack open that sixer, and contemplate all the ways in which he could a) fuck up a tree farm or b) make something of it. Luisa had done an admirable job of maintaining a business that had been around for decades. It was a part of the landscape and the community. What had started as a Christmas tree farm had become much, much more.

Where would he find the money to compete with any offers she might get from a property developer, though? And did he even want to? His one and only previous attempt to invest in a business had gone the way of the woman he'd thought about marrying—quite literally—and he only had himself to blame. Naivete and absolutely no business sense whatsoever, apparently.

He should have known how to tell whether a deal was too good to be true. Or if someone wasn't actually into him.

Blinking back to awareness, Cam frowned at the scenery outside the car and realized he'd made the turn. He was on Raymondskill Road.

Damn.

He slowed down for the curve by Melanie's place. The lawn already needed another trim. Also, now that the long grass had been cut away from the beds lining the front and the hedges running up either side of the lawn, further signs of neglect were evident. Weeds and woody shrubs, perennials that needed thinning out or replacing. The brickwork beneath the front windows of the house could use some mortar. He'd bet the windows leaked as well.

He'd put together another list, he decided as he cruised past and into the long curve that would bring him to his next decision. Unfortunately, thought did not sweep him away, letting his hands guide the car to where his subconscious wanted to go. Cam was fully cognizant of his surroundings when he slowed to a pause before Victor Ness's driveway. Then, because other people might like to use the road, he indicated and turned. What the heck. He didn't have to go all the way up. He could sit there a minute and then back out. Turn around and go home.

Or he could go all the way up to the circle at the top, check whether Victor had spread his mulch. He'd need to remove the tarp soon if he hadn't. Let some air in.

He was at the top of the driveway. *Thank you, subconscious.* Now what?

The house sat quiet and still in the late-afternoon light. Not that houses generally made noise or danced, but the silence felt off somehow. Vacant. Maybe Victor wasn't home? That would be fortuitous, seeing as Cam had arrived uninvited. Again.

The tarp still covered the mulch, but the trees had been moved. Cam nodded in approval before discovering he'd opened the car door and put a foot out onto the gravel. He'd check the mulch. Make sure rot hadn't already set in.

He crunched over to the tarp and peeled back a corner. Given the position, off to the side of the drive and beneath the shade of some grand old oaks, it wasn't doing too badly. After replacing the tarp and stone, Cam peered through the windows running across the upper quadrant of the garage doors. The lack of light inside meant he could see practically nothing. He could make out the hulking shadow of a car on the left side, though.

Unless someone else had picked him up, Victor was home.

So why did the house feel so still?

Cam ducked into the path between the garage and the house, the one that led to the patio behind the kitchen. He stepped quietly, anxiety prickling his scalp. He'd check on the trees and go before Victor caught him trespassing again.

The arrangement of furniture across the patio had changed. Chairs moved into groups around the fire pit, the table dragged near to the grill. Small cuts of ribbon fluttered from the backs of two of the chairs. A red Solo cup had caught in between the low wall of flat rocks lining one of the beds and the red-painted siding of the house.

The first of the trees had been placed, pot and all, on the far side of the patio in a spot that would suit it. The colorful leaves would brighten the view from that side of the kitchen and offer shade.

Cam crossed to the tree and crouched to dig his fingers into the pot. Well-watered, but it should be in the ground.

The second of the trees faced a set of narrow, uneven windows. Cam hadn't seen this part of the house—being the back. The windows almost resembled arrow slits, and the towering shape of the wall made him think of castle staircases. With its odd and sprawling layout, the house might have more than one way to the second floor. He'd love to see the inside. It must be a veritable rabbit warren of rooms in all different sizes and with ceilings of different heights.

How had such a house come to be?

The third tree sat in the middle of a south-facing lawn. The placement seemed odd. Perhaps Victor had left it there until he decided exactly where it should go. Hopefully not into the line of trees behind it. A dogwood like this one should have a home all its own. A small circle of friends to bask in its glory but not a lot of shade.

He glanced toward the windows gazing out over the lawn and realized he'd nearly circumnavigated the house. Still treading carefully, quietly, Cam approached the windows. The sense of trespassing grew heavier with each step, pinching his shoulders and elevating his pulse. He could hear the blood swishing through his veins.

I should go back to the car.

He should stop being so goddamn curious. Or nosy. Or—

"Oh my God." Was that a body?

Raising his hands to shade the window, Cam peered through the glass. A vast studio space lay beyond. Several easels were set at different angles, some facing the window, some away. Canvases of different dimensions sat on a couple, but most were empty. He registered an ordered sort of clutter surrounding the walls: tables, a couple of chairs, narrow shelves and cubbies. His most immediate concern, however, was the figure supine on the floor.

Arms slack at his sides, feet turned out, and with a goddamned cat curled up on his chest, lay Victor. His lips were parted, his eyes closed. And not a muscle twitched. Not a hair stirred.

No longer caring whether his presence was appropriate or legal, Cam tapped on the window. Victor did not move.

Shit, shit, shit.

Cam scanned the length of the studio for a door and located one back the way he'd already come, set into the side of the tower. He trotted over to it and tugged at the handle. Locked.

He ran back to the window and smacked a palm to the glass. The cat looked up, but Victor didn't move. Was he sleeping? This late in the day, the sun had traveled to the other side of the house. Cam squinted through the afternoon gloom and watched Victor's chest. The cat made any movement impossible to detect. Christ. Was the cat absorbing the last of his body heat?

What would it do when Victor's body cooled?

Stop thinking and move.

Trained instinct took over as Cam quickly assessed his options. He could call for an ambulance, but he should see if he could gain access first. Check for a pulse before he diverted emergency services from someone who actually needed them.

Victor might—

Cam jogged toward the kitchen and tried the door that led out to the patio. The handle turned, and he let himself into the house. The quiet, slightly guilty swish of blood had become a roar. His heart hammered in his chest. But already the image of Victor flat-out on his back had become overlaid with scenes of horror. Cam wouldn't be able to dispel either until the situation reached its conclusion.

Despite the confusion of rooms, he quickly found his way to the studio. The French doors separating it from a large, comfortable living room were open. Cam slipped through and rushed to kneel beside Victor's body. Beside Victor.

Before his knees hit the ground, the cat leaped away with a surprised yowl, its white fur fluffed, its tail the width of a corn cob. With a gasp, Victor opened his eyes, took one look at Cam, and yelled.

Cam fell backward, his arms raised as though to ward off an attack of the undead.

It was only after Victor sat up, rising from the floor like a freshly animated corpse, that Cam registered the low note of his yell. Not at all similar to the screeching sounds he'd made a week ago. Also, how in the hell had he sat up like that? Man must have sick ab muscles.

Victor turned on him and blinked. Then he plucked a dark blue cylinder of plastic from each ear. "What the fuck."

"I thought you were dead!" Cam whisper-shouted. The atmosphere of the house continued to feel off, though that was probably due to his uninvited presence.

Victor scrubbed a hand over his face. "What the ever loving— What are you doing here?"

Having landed on his ass, Cam scrambled to his hands and knees. "I was checking on the mulch and . . ." An explanation for his subsequent exploration failed him. "I really thought you were dead, man. You weren't moving. Your cat was waiting for you to cool down."

"Jesus, fuck."

Hearing his own oft-repeated phrase drop from another set of lips almost made Cam smile. Sensibly, he overrode the impulse.

Victor glared at him. "What are you? The Mulch Whisperer or something?"

"No. Yes? I—" Kneeling now, Cam spread his hands and exhaled. "I know it's none of my business. But you hit your head pretty hard on Tuesday. Or it seemed like you did. And you were upset. I've been worried about you. I explained that the other day? Anyway, concussions can be more than a headache. And I am— Okay, I wanted to check on the mulch. I know that's not my business either, except it sort of is? You don't want it to rot. And those trees need planting. Moving a tree in summer is pretty dicey already."

Surprisingly, or perhaps not, Victor hadn't interrupted him. In fact, he seemed almost broken. He still sat facing Cam. Continued to stare at him in wonder. But whatever he might have wanted to say seemed stuck in this throat.

After about thirty seconds, he shook his head. "Well."

Cam leaned forward a little. Not brave enough to ask *Well, what?* but keen to know regardless.

"I guess if you were going to rob me, or murder me, you'd have done it by now."

Before he could stop himself, Cam said, "Had to check if you had a pulse first. Couldn't have you waking up while I was taking inventory."

Victor blinked.

Cam coughed. "Sorry." More quietly, he continued, "I seriously thought you were dead, man. I was going to check for a pulse before calling 911."

"I see." Sighing, Victor scrubbed his face again. "I was meditating." He shot Cam a rueful look. "You're right. Last week was difficult. But my pride took the biggest beating, and after spending four—no, five days at the bottom of a bottle, I am a reformed man." He swept a hand up and down, drawing Cam's attention to the sweatpants and T-shirt he wore, both more colorful than should be allowed. The sweatpants were splattered with paint and the T-shirt had a rainbow band across the front with the words *Hearts & Crafts* wrapped around a design at the center.

"I just finished doing yoga," Victor explained. He touched his ear and then held out his hand to display a wireless earbud. "And was somewhere on the road to Nirvana when a weight seemed to launch itself off my chest, and then you were here and I was yelling."

"That was a cat." Cam sat on his heels.

"I beg your pardon?"

"On your chest. A cat."

Victor smiled. "So you mentioned. White?" Cam nodded. "Dexter. He'll take advantage when he can. Sleeps on my head every night. One of these mornings, I'll wake up with a mouthful of fur. Or not wake up at all."

Cam didn't have to feign his shudder.

Victor laughed. "I take it you're not fond of cats."

"I'm not really an animal person."

"I find that odd."

What was odd was the fact they appeared to be having a perfectly reasonable conversation after Cam had broken into this man's house and roused him from death.

Clearing his throat, Cam pushed to his feet and dusted his hands off on his knees. Victor stood in a single, fluid motion, rising from the ground without support. Cam swept his lithe form with an appraising glance. When he met Victor's gaze, he found amusement there. He thought about returning a certain sort of smile before deciding now was so not the time.

"Are you looking for extra work?" Victor asked.

"Huh?"

"You seem to have a lot of time on your hands. Would you like to fill it?"

An odd energy passed between them. Was he being propositioned? Cam had just started to wonder whether he'd accept, when Victor broke the spell.

"You're absolutely right about the trees. I had planned to spend last week weeding, spreading the mulch, and planting.

Unfortunately, I found other, less constructive uses for my time, and I really must get back to work. Do you have a rate for landscaping? At the tree farm?"

Cam found words. "Ah, no. I mean, no. We don't do that."

"Oh."

"But I could. It's not busy at the moment. I'd, ah, I could do that for you."

Victor's smile had a weary edge to it. "Excellent. To be honest, I'm not sure giving you an excuse to check up on me is entirely sensible, but that mulch isn't going to spread itself."

"Be great if it could. Maybe with nanobots or something."

Now, Victor laughed. "Yes." He gestured toward the door. "Well, I have cats to feed. Wouldn't want to wake up in the middle of the night and find they'd taken a chunk out of my cooling corpse now, would I?"

Cam swallowed a horrified chuckle.

Victor smirked. "Can you start tomorrow?"

"Ah, sure. I mean, probably. I'll confirm when I get back to the office." He didn't like to use his cellphone for Shepard's business.

They had reached the front door. Victor opened it. Cam stepped through. He was halfway across the front lawn when Victor called after him.

"Thank you, by the way. For checking up on me. It's weird, but had I actually been dead, I'm glad someone would have found me before I started to smell."

Cam forced himself to smile and wave. But as he sat in the car, the remembered odor of dead and decaying bodies seemed to fill the air. For a minute, his lungs seized. Closing his eyes, he whispered, "In and out. In and out."

He didn't know why his head kept going back to places he'd rather it didn't go. He'd been home for over a decade. Fourteen years. But some days, he only had to look and he'd see the desperate faces. Smell blood and ash. Hear the sound of war.

That was why he preferred to stay busy, so he'd forget to look.

Some days, though, he saw without trying.

Chapter Eight

"**Mr.** Ness?"

Victor paused in the doorway of the community center and turned to smile at Cassidy. He wasn't supposed to have favorite students or insist that one was more artistic than another. But Cassidy could easily be the most talented kid he'd taught over the past fifteen years. Victor considered himself lucky that she continued to sign up for his summer courses—even though he'd encouraged her to apply for several programs in New York.

"What's up?" he asked as she stopped beside him, hoping she wasn't going to critique that day's lesson. He had promised himself he'd come up with new projects for his summer class, but between work, Tholo, and deep dives to the cellar, he'd been feeling less inspired than usual.

Cassidy bit her lip and frowned. "So, um, you know how Beck wasn't in class today?"

"Mm-hmm."

"Their, um, parents kicked them out over the July Fourth break."

Victor felt his eyebrows shoot upward, though the news, sadly, didn't surprise him. But it had to have been at least a year since an area family had rejected their child's identity—that he'd heard about, anyway. He'd been running the Hearts & Crafts program at the LGBTQ community center in Milford for nearly twelve years, though. He'd heard all the stories, and it always hurt. It always felt personal.

"Does Beck have somewhere to stay?" he asked.

"They're staying with Morgan right now, but Morgan is going away to college in the fall and his parents said Beck has to find somewhere else then."

Oh–kay.

Cassidy bit her lip again. "We, um, tried calling you. I know you sometimes have kids stay with you."

"From our program and only temporarily." Victor would love to house all the homeless LGBTQ youth in the world, but he wasn't officially licensed as a foster parent. Regardless, he'd housed up to four kids before and would have taken in another if Tez hadn't sat him down and forced him to make a choice. Either complete the training, certify, and become more active with that aspect of the community, or continue as he was—as an advocate who occasionally housed at-risk youth until a better situation came along.

He'd have liked to continue doing both, but he couldn't teach, remain active in the arts community, participate in as many outreach programs, maintain his career as a working artist, and care for children, temporarily, at his home.

"I'm sorry I wasn't there to answer your call," he told Cassidy now. He'd missed a few important calls last week, but this would probably be the one he regretted the most. "Let me talk to Georgia"—the program director—"and see if we can't find a permanent placement for Beck. They graduated high school in May, didn't they? Are they eighteen yet? Do they have plans for the fall? Are they working at the moment?"

Cassidy shook her head. "No. Beck's a year younger. They have one year of school to go. And no job. They don't have a car."

A serious handicap in an area where infrequent busses were the only form of public transportation.

"We'll see what we can do. Thanks for letting me know."

"I figured you'd want to."

Normally, he would, and when he had a moment to himself, he'd kick his own ass for being too self-absorbed to question a student's absence. Moving out of the doorway, Victor gestured for Cassidy to precede him. "I might pop back in and chat with Georgia now. Thanks again, Cassidy. Enjoy the rest of your day."

"You too, Mr. Ness!"

He watched as she joined a circle of friends in the center's parking lot. Kids who, at a glance, didn't belong in Northeast Pennsylvania. And, yet, here they were. Brown skin and white skin. Brown hair, black hair, bright pink hair, and a mohawk with green tips. Earrings dangling from lobe to shoulder, sparkling eyeshadow, and a swipe of glittering gloss across the cheeks. Short skirts for every gender identity. Leggings, shorts, and T-shirts. Ripped jeans and shitkickers too. Rainbows and quieter pins for each tribe.

In one sense, these kids—these young adults—were no different to the art-club kids of his generation. But they *were* different. These kids, whether their parents approved or not, lived mostly out and mostly proud. Thanks to programs like his, and the community center that hosted them. And, thankfully, most of their parents continued to love and support them. It had been a while since he'd had to chat with Georgia about how they could help.

Victor had just turned away when Georgia appeared at the end of the hall. She caught Victor's eye and smiled. "Hey." Her gaze shifted to the window and the view of the parking lot. "Cassidy told you what's up?"

"Yeah, I was coming to talk with you. See what we could do for Beck."

"Getting them a job is first priority. They're safe where they are at the moment. Once they're earning money, we can talk about next steps."

Victor nodded. "Sounds good. I'll keep my ear to the ground and let you know if I hear of any opportunities. And I've got room if they need somewhere else to stay while they save up for a place of their own."

"Got you on the list." Georgia cocked her head to one side. "Everything all right with you?"

"Yeah, why do you ask?"

"I tried calling you last week. Frank and Tom were hosting a game night at the inn. None of us have seen you in ages."

"It was my grandson's first birthday."

"All week?"

"First I had to kick Tholo out on his ass and then feel sad about it."

Georgia smiled.

"Why are you smiling? I was very sad."

"I'm sure you were. But now that you've shed your excess baggage, you can only be happy."

What mockery was this? Victor put on an affronted expression. "Did no one like Tholo?"

"Nope."

"Why didn't anyone say so?"

"We did, Vic. At least once a year. Your standard response was to start describing parts of his anatomy. Artistically, of course, but I still didn't want to hear about his dick."

"He did have a rather spectacular—"

Georgia had clapped her hands to her ears and started singing.

"Fine. Fine. I'll let it go. I have let it go." His affrontery melted into a pout. "I shall never touch it again."

"That's the spirit. Now go home and recycle all those wine bottles in your kitchen."

"What makes you think there are multiple bottles? Or that they're not already in the recycle bin?"

At Georgia's *I've known you since we were in high school* look, Victor held up his hands. "Fine, fine. This is why I had babies with Tez instead of you. In case you were wondering."

"I was not."

Flipping one of his hands upward in a dismissive wave, Victor spun on his heel and pushed out of the door, managing all of it with flair—none of it overly dramatic. "Keep telling yourself that," he said as he crossed the lot to his car.

Georgia might have been snickering behind him. But the traffic and the birds and the sounds of a small town swallowed it all.

Two hours later, Victor stood in front of the canvas he'd daubed with a simple blot of paint some uncounted number of days before. Had that been Thursday? Friday? Lord, how on Earth had he managed to lose so much time? And why hadn't he painted while he was drunk? His drunk paintings were often inspired.

Or they used to be.

Now they tended to show twenty minutes of brilliance and four hours of *should I or shouldn't I have another drink*, followed by a day and a half of *I really shouldn't drink anymore*.

Truth was, he painted better sober and always had.

He stared at the dot of paint on the canvas. What was it supposed to be? What had he had in mind when he'd started this piece? He'd planned his current series around the idea of movement, but the dot appeared rather static. Also, why was the canvas standing up rather than across the easel? He didn't often paint tall.

Had he been trying for a waterfall?

A distant bell clanked somewhere far back in his skull. He had notes for this piece. Heck, he had notes for all of his pieces, commissioned and otherwise. Where was his sketchbook?

Victor flipped through the piles of sketchbooks balanced around the edges of the two tables at the back of the studio, knowing the one he wanted wouldn't be there. His workspace might present as chaos to the casual bystander, but he knew where each brush, tube, jar, and rag was. Possessed an archeological knowledge of the layers of paper piled at each corner of these tables, including the splotches of paint beneath. Every scuff, every scratch.

Kitchen. He'd been sketching the flowers on the patio last night, hadn't he? The muted palette of sunset and then the starker highlights and deepened shadows brought out by the outdoor lights.

Victor left the studio.

Yes! There it is.

He scooped up the sketch pad and flipped back past six pages of flower sketches to the notes regarding his latest series. He had a show in September, two pieces to complete, and this second-to-last painting was supposed to show a wave formation through foliage rather than water. He found a tiny sketch of trees.

Trees?

"God, where do I come up with this shit?"

Movement outside the kitchen windows caught his attention. Victor glanced up from his sketch pad and nearly swallowed his tongue. A shirtless man stood at the edge of the patio, wiping his forehead with a rag. No, with his shirt.

Who had invited this Adonis to pose in the sunniest spot of the backyard? And when?

The shirt slid down to reveal brown hair, dark brows, and eyes Victor knew were brown. It was Cam. On his patio. Again. Without a shirt.

Cam tucked the shirt into the back of his belt and leaned to collect a shovel from the— Oh! The wheelbarrow of mulch. He was spreading the mulch. Right. Victor had hired him to do that. And apparently, he was doing it shirtless.

Oh my. Victor fully acknowledged his shallow nature when it came to men. He had a penchant for certain features and characteristics. He was willingly swayed and manipulated by his idea of beauty. But Cam was more interesting than beautiful. The clothed version, anyway. This shirtless wonder with muscles shifting beneath his shoulder blades and flexing across his back with every swing of the shovel?

Breathtaking.

Cam had broad shoulders and narrow hips. If he were to turn again, Victor planned to check whether one of those remarkable V shapes dove beneath the waistband of his jeans. The afternoon sunlight played off the hollows of his ribs as he lifted the shovel. Lean musculature contracted and released.

His skin wasn't uniformly sun-kissed. A scattering of moles, likely from sun exposure, dotted his spine, and a tattoo completely covered the back of his left shoulder. Victor couldn't quite make it out but guessed the regular lines at the top and the bottom were letters and numbers.

When Cam turned to dig the shovel back into the wheelbarrow, Victor lost his breath in a very real sense. Where the shirt had covered him before were scars. A large, painful-looking ridge twisted up over Cam's ribs, and there were two marks in front of his left shoulder. At a distance, they resembled small splotches of wet paint. One almost star-shaped and shiny. The other spoke of a deeper, angrier wound. Both of them obviously—

Victor's stomach pinched. He swallowed.

What did it mean that the man in his backyard had been shot at some point in his life? Shot twice. And what had caused the larger scar, that awful line over his ribs? Victor squinted. Were those other marks scars?

He thought back to the few times he'd been face-to-face with Cam, and the brief stories he'd read in the other man's eyes. The kindness and empathy but also the hint of brittleness. Victor had been working with at-risk youth for over a decade, and while Cam was years beyond the usual age of his charges, his attachment to the periphery of Victor's life started to make a little sense.

The stuff about making sure Victor hadn't had a concussion? True. Absolutely. And Victor had believed the excuse the moment Cam had given it. But that wasn't all, was it? Cam had suffered some tremendous loss. His scars might not be a part of it, but Victor wouldn't be surprised if they were.

And now he was looking for ways to fill the empty spaces inside of himself.

Oh, yes. I know all about that one. Victor loved his children, but in his quieter and more introspective moments—all right, in his broodier moments—he did sometimes wonder if having them had been his version of filling space. The awful gaping hole left behind by the death of his father.

A sunny face intruded on his thoughts for a moment before Victor gently brushed him aside. He had other thinking to do. And sketching.

But as Victor picked up the closest pen and flipped to a fresh page of his sketchbook, a knock of certainty sounded somewhere inside his soul. There'd been a familiarity about Cam the first time they'd met. Victor had put that down to the highly emotional circumstances. Now, however, he suspected yet another abandoned child might be seeking a home.

Not that Cam was a child, or abandoned, or in need of a place to stay.

It was all just a feeling, but Victor lived by his emotions. His art—his best art—came directly from what he felt.

And right now? He was not feeling the movement of the wind through trees.

But as he sketched the first outline of the man in his garden, a new sort of movement rippled through his torso, from the base of his skull, down his spine, and around his ribs, where it tightened into a squeeze. Gasping softly, Victor put the sketch pad down.

There was a reason he stuck to landscapes. To abstract concepts. He didn't love his trees in quite the same way he loved the humans surrounding him. But when he painted them, he could pretend he did. That they were the be-all and end-all of his existence. His family, his precious children, the best friend a man could have, his parents.

Victor closed his eyes against the bright yellow of a name that always left an ache across his heart. He could paint the sun, but never Sunshine—the one who'd left him behind.

Swallowing old pain, Victor turned away from the kitchen and the invitation to try, one more time, to paint past that particular block.

Chapter Nine

The following Monday, Cam sauntered through the office door shortly after 8 a.m. and stopped at the coffee maker. Noting the level in the pot, he filled a second cup for Luisa, doctored it with cream and sugar, and carried it over to her desk. She didn't look up, and cold fingers of dread pinched a path down Cam's spine.

He set the cup in front of her and sat on the couch along the wall. "What don't you want to tell me?"

Luisa continued to stare fixedly at the monitor in front of her, though Cam knew for a fact there wouldn't be more than two or three orders listed there. Well, he didn't know for a fact, but he could guess with a reasonable certainty. He'd been trained to read patterns, after all, and he was good at it.

Or he had been.

He'd also learned to read faces, and Luisa wasn't trying to hide what she felt. Remorse, fatigue, and perhaps relief.

Sucking her lips so that they nearly disappeared, she finally looked away from the screen. Glanced at Cam, then down at her coffee. She didn't pick up the mug. A sudden urge to spill his mug washed through him. He could delay this moment by making a mess. He could—

"I've talked it over with my kids, and I've decided to sell the tree farm."

Though the news wasn't unexpected, it still hurt. But if asked, Cam wouldn't be able to express why. Luisa's decision didn't amount to a rejection of his ideas or a lack of faith in his ability to keep the ball rolling. He knew that. His place in the grand scheme was not her primary concern. Yet, he felt as though he'd let her down.

How could he not? His mission, since he'd started working for the tree farm some twenty months ago, had been to be the best he could be. To be an asset. To be valuable. No matter the job, Cam always gave it his all. He didn't know how to do otherwise. This job, though? He'd liked it. Loved it.

Luisa reached across the desk as though to touch the hand he had wrapped around his coffee mug. "This isn't on you or your lack of effort. You're one of the best employees I've ever had. You and Jorge both. But I don't have the energy to do it anymore. I'm tired, Cameron. I want to retire. And if I sell before I start to lose money, I can retire well."

"Will you head out west, live near your kids?"

"I spoke to Nadia last night." Now her smile held warmth.

A reciprocal glow kindled in Cam's chest. Despite the fact he'd soon be out of a job, he was happy for her. Luisa was a good person. He squared his shoulders. "Tell me how I can make this process easier for you."

Luisa swallowed and sudden tears leaked from her eyes. "Damn it, Cam. Why do you have to be so decent?"

Cam found a laugh for that one. "Me? I'm a pain in this world's ass. Ask my brother."

"Mm-hmm."

The low roar of Jorge's beast of a car rounded the building. They both listened as a heavy door slammed and slow footsteps approached the door. Slight panic crossed Luisa's face.

"He'll be okay," Cam said. "Just tell it to him straight."

Jorge took the news silently and stoically. Afterward, outside with a thin sheaf of delivery slips gripped in one hand, Cam positioned himself in front of Jorge and said, "If the new owners decide to plow over these fields and build little houses, we'll find something else to do. You and me."

Jorge met this proclamation with a quiet nod and held out a hand for the slips. Cam passed them over and Jorge sorted them into order with Cam watching over his shoulder. No deliveries to Raymondskill Road.

Shortly after three that afternoon, Cam pulled his car into Melanie's driveway. She popped out of the front door before he'd exited the car, and crossed the front lawn to meet him.

"You must be a mind reader." She held up her phone. "I was literally about to text you."

"Yeah?"

"The mower. I jammed it again. Backyard, this time. I know, I know. I should have used the weed whacker first, but I thought the grass looked thinner."

"You're not mowing the top, though. You're mowing from the bottom."

A light snapped on in Melanie's eyes. "Huh. Four years of college and I don't know how to cut grass."

Laughing, Cam gestured toward the backyard. "Let's go fix your mower."

Melanie fell into step beside him. "What brings you out this way?"

"I was heading home from work and thought I'd stop in to see how it was going."

When he'd last been here, they'd put together an extensive to-do list for fixing up the house as well as the yard. Mostly exterior projects. Melanie hadn't invited him inside, and he hadn't asked. He was a relative stranger, after all.

"Good! I got a couple of quotes for the windows, and they're much more expensive than I thought they'd be."

Cam nodded. "It's worth getting good windows, though. They're going to help with your heating and cooling bills. And professional installation is probably the best way to go. I'd offer to help with a small window, but that big one at the front? You need a professional for that. It's got to seal right, all around."

Nodding and smiling, Melanie pulled out her phone and tapped at a note screen. Then they were at the mower, which was stuck at the end of one chewed-up stripe of not appreciably shorter grass. Chuckling, Cam patted the upright handle. "You poor thing."

Melanie laughed.

Once again, he took her through the steps for safely untangling the grass from the rotor. They had to take the blade off to get at all of it. He let Melanie reattach it and watched as she worked the wrench to tighten the nut afterward.

When she stopped, he twirled one finger. "Give it another turn, if you can."

She did that and handed him the wrench. "Want to check it?"

"Nope, you've got this."

The mower started at first pull, and Cam smiled in satisfaction at the healthy purr of the engine. He'd done a good job servicing it last week. "And you're off!"

Melanie killed the ignition. "After I trim."

"That too. Want a hand? I can trim and you can mow behind me. We'll get it done twice as fast."

"I don't know where you came from, but I'm glad you're here." *Damn.*

"If only to save you from blowing up the mower and ruining this lawn."

An hour later, Cam left Melanie to finish cutting the grass. He had another stop to make before he went home. He had spread Victor's mulch but hadn't planted the trees. He checked his watch. Nearly five. His stomach rumbled.

He'd dig one hole and call it a day.

Victor wasn't home. Cam stared at the empty spot in the garage and chewed on his lower lip a moment as he contemplated the bubble of disappointment trapped somewhere between his throat and his lungs. He hadn't seen Victor yesterday, but the sense he was there, somewhere in the house, had been enough. To say it had felt like companionship would be stretching the imagination, but it had. Cam hadn't been alone.

He turned to survey the tools hanging along the wall. Victor had a lot of tools—most of them geared toward various gardening purposes. He also had a space devoted to woodworking projects.

A small circular saw on a workbench that had obviously been built here in this garage. A jigsaw and electric drill sat behind a station of battery chargers, and a short row of handsaws. Drawers filled with screwdrivers and wrenches. A few hammers and mallets. The usual collections of odd screws and nails. Stacks of leftover wood. The most curious item in the garage, though, was the children's tool bench. Cam discovered it when he twitched a flowered drop cloth aside.

"Interesting."

He wanted to continue snooping, but he'd probably be halfway up the ladder to the garage attic when Victor pulled back into the driveway. It'd been a long day. He was too tired to think of a reasonable excuse for why he continued to poke into Victor's life.

Cam tugged a pair of gloves out of his back pocket, picked the shovel he wanted off the wall, and went to dig a hole. The day had cooled, and the darkening clouds promised overnight rain. Still, he was lathered with sweat by the time he was done. Cam checked the time. Nearly six. He checked the sky. The clouds had developed a bruised underbelly that promised a little thunder and lightning with the coming rain.

He should hit the road now.

The garage was still empty when Cam hung the cleaned shovel back on the wall peg, and he didn't run into Victor on his way out of the driveway. His mood settled somewhere between quiet and melancholy as he turned back onto Milford Road in the direction of home.

His phone rang and Cam glanced at the screen. He smiled when he saw his niece's name and answered the call. "Hey, you!"

"Hey, yourself!" Emma said.

Rain spattered the windshield, and Cam stuck the phone into the cradle on the dash so he could flip on the wipers. "What's up?"

"Are you driving?"

"On my way home."

"How's my car?"

"She's doing fine." A total lie. He hadn't fixed the electrical problem yet. He planned to, though. "How are you doing?"

"I'm doing great. Brooklyn is a lot of fun. Noisy, but fun. So, listen, I've got a long weekend coming up. Reiner doesn't need me for the California job—boo—and said I could take a couple of days. I figured I might come home, at least overnight. Hang with you and Uncle Nick."

A light tan shape flashed in the periphery of Cam's vision, and he immediately slowed, expecting a deer to burst from the trees and cross the road. The tan wobbled in place and collapsed, and Cam slammed on the brakes. He jumped out of the car and heard Emma call out from the dash.

"Uncle Cam?"

He ducked back inside to grab the phone. "Sorry, Em. I nearly hit a deer. I think someone else actually did. Hit it, I mean." He rounded the front of the car and stopped. "It's— Oh, shit, it's a dog!"

"What?"

"I'll call you back."

"Okay, make sure you do!"

He hung up, tucked the phone into his jeans pocket, and knelt beside the downed creature, heedless of the rain raising small puffs of dust from the side of the road. The scent of baked tarmac and hot dirt assailed him, combining with the warm peat rolling out of the forest. Thunder rumbled softly in the distance.

Cam focused on the dog. He didn't know much about breeds or whatnot, but it looked a bit like a beagle, only mostly tan with a splash of white across the chest and at the tips of each paw. It lay on its side, panting softly, and didn't seem to be injured. No obvious blood. But as Cam leaned forward, it whined and struggled, as though it wanted to get up. One of its front legs wasn't moving properly.

"Shh." He reached out slowly, letting the dog sniff his hand before cupping one ear in a soft caress. The dog whined again. Cam glanced over his shoulder in the vain hope another car had come along and stopped. Wouldn't it be nice if a vet happened to be driving home along the same road? Or someone who liked dogs.

No one. Just a deepening blackness across the tarmac as the storm rolled ever closer.

"Okay, then." Cam turned back to the dog. "I'm going to pick you up, and it's going to suck. I'll be as gentle as I can. Then I'm going to take you to someone who can fix that leg of yours." It could be fixed, couldn't it? No bones were jutting out.

Gritting his teeth, Cam shook away gristly memories and got to his feet. He trotted around the side of Emma's car and opened the back door. Then he returned to the dog and set about picking it up as carefully as he could, taking care not to disturb that one leg any more than he had to. The dog yipped a few times and let out a pained whine as Cam settled it across the back seat. He debated strapping a belt over it for about thirty seconds before deciding to drive slowly.

Then he hopped back behind the wheel, the seat squelching beneath him. Rain dripped from his hair into his eyes. He pulled his phone out of his jeans and checked for the location of the nearest vet. There was one a little north of town, wasn't there? Yes. He tapped the number to call them and tucked the phone back into the cradle as he started the car.

They were closed, but the recording listed an emergency number. Cam punched that into his phone. It rang twice.

"Dr. Sheehan, how can I help you?"

"I just picked up a dog from the side of the road. I think someone might have hit them. Doesn't want to move their front leg and cries when I get too close to it."

"Is the dog wearing a collar?"

"No collar and they're a bit rough-looking, as though they've been on their own for a while."

"All right. Bring them up to the hospital and we'll do what we can. You know where we are?"

"Yeah. I'll be about fifteen minutes."

"See you there."

Cam ended the call. He was about to turn to the dog, maybe offer some words of encouragement, or whatever you said to a dog who was suffering, when lights flashed in the rearview mirror. Another car.

As he put his car into gear and pulled away from the shoulder, a curious feeling spread through him.

The sense of purpose, he recognized. He always liked having something to do—even before he'd joined the army. That need was more intense now, and it wasn't always healthy. But for tonight, he had a task. A real one. And despite the disappointment of knowing he'd soon be out of work, he felt curiously upbeat.

When he examined that closer, a wave of almost sickness rolled through his torso. An injured dog was not a cause for celebration or cheer. What the fuck was wrong with him?

Chapter Ten

What was movement. Really?

Victor stepped back from the canvas and studied the slashes of paint with a critical eye. The dark red background he'd chosen was too red. The green, too green. The vertical, too vertical. The . . .

"It's crap. It's all crap."

Many of his paintings began as a combination of insecurity and determination. He'd have an idea in his mind—not so much a mental image, but a notion of what it could be. Sketches came next, a loose scrawl lacking in detail. He always understood what should be there, though. What he was supposed to see.

He saw it when he consulted his sketchbook, and with this being the sixth painting in the series, it should have been obvious—even without the fifth leaning against the wall of his studio, waiting to be framed.

Movement was not a new concept. He should not be feeling insecure. This painting should be a simple matter of connecting the dots.

His phone buzzed across one of the tables at the rear of the studio. After rinsing his brush, Victor laid it out to dry and went to check his texts. He smiled at the name at the top of the notification and swiped down to read Sage's message. A knock sounded at the front door.

"Coming!" he called.

The text, of course, had been Sage letting him know he was in the driveway. Sage never called in advance. He just showed up. Then he texted to let Victor know he'd be knocking in a minute or so.

If Victor didn't hear the knock, he'd text to say he was walking around to the kitchen door—which was rarely locked. The next message would be about how Victor should remember to lock the kitchen door, because anyone could come in.

Why Sage never used the key hidden under a rock by the front door, Victor would never know. Or simply keep a key to the house he'd grown up in.

He was an odd child. Really, both of his children were odd in their own, wonderful ways.

Victor opened the door and grinned at the sight of his son and his grandson. "Hello, hello!"

He put his arms out and Sage handed off his squirming bundle of joy. "Billy wanted to visit."

"Mm-hmm." Victor pressed a noisy kiss to the side of Billy's warm head. He smelled like cheesy crackers. Shifting Billy to his hip, he held out his other arm and gave his son a quick hug. "Lovely to see you." He frowned. "What day is it?"

"Saturday."

"Of course, it is." He'd been working on painting number six for four days and all he had was too much red and green, and too many vertical lines. Wonderful. Also, most of his trees were still in the driveway. Where was his deliciously defined landscape artist?

"Has Tholo been in touch?" Sage was eyeing him with concern.

"What? No. I've been painting." Victor carried Billy into the family room and set him down near the box of toys he'd pulled out of the garage a few months ago. He smiled fondly at the naked doll resting on top of the mixture of plastic food, numbered blocks—brightly colored and mostly indestructible plastic. He had always enjoyed watching his children play and derived the same satisfaction out of trying to guess which toy Billy would go after first and what game he would make out of it.

"The movement series?" Sage flopped onto the couch with a soft sigh. "This week, one of our artists submitted a cover concept that made me think of you. Let me see if I have it on my phone." He lifted a hip and dug into the pocket of his dark jeans.

"What's Ashni up to today?" Victor asked.

"Girls' day out. They have tickets to a matinee in the city and might do dinner afterward."

"Oh? What show?" It had been ages since Victor had ventured into Manhattan. He'd continued to haunt Brooklyn for a while after he and Tez had returned home to the Poconos to raise children together. For a few years, they'd carted their babies over to Park Slope and squashed onto the couches in the tiny apartments of well-intentioned friends before deciding they'd rather be the weekend getaway spot. For the next fifteen-or-so years, they'd hosted a different group every other week.

It had been nice. Nowadays, Victor much preferred the quiet of having the house to himself, but he still often felt a pull toward New York. Maybe Tez would be up for catching a show—though he really must stop relying on Tez for company. Did his missing landscaper ever visit the city? Was he into theater? Art?

"Dad?"

"Hmm?"

"Where'd you go? I was telling you about the show Ashni went to see and you were, like, a million miles away."

"Oh, sorry. Got lost somewhere down memory lane."

Concern returned to haunt Sage's gray eyes. "Are you sure everything's all right?"

Victor flapped a hand. "Work isn't going well, so I'm feeling a bit drifty. That's all."

Sage showed him the cover art commission, and Victor could see why his son had thought he might like it. The style was hauntingly similar to Victor's, with large abstractions and tiny details. But the energy of the piece felt different, as well as the color choices. The subject, another matter entirely. Victor didn't paint people. Not anymore. He captured nature. Landscapes, mostly, in bold lines and blocks of color.

The picture on Sage's phone featured the outline of two people with heads bent together. It resembled the view through an infrared camera, with the centers of the figures a blazing red and concentric rings of cooler color radiating outward. The detail was at the heart of each figure, where the artist had inscribed sketchy mechanicals.

"This is stunning work," Victor said. "Thanks for showing it to me."

"Sure." Sage glanced at the screen, his eyes lighting with a measure of pride before he shut off the phone and stuffed it back into his pocket. "It's for a book I found. A manuscript. From the slush pile. Two weeks after I started with Hot House."

Ah. "Congratulations on seeing a project to completion."

Sage blushed. "I had very little input. I don't even know if they used the notes I submitted." He shrugged. "But the fact I found it definitely upped my cred."

"I'm sure it did."

Billy smacked the naked doll onto the carpet three times and said, "Boom!"

Victor side-eyed his son. "Have you been playing *Warhammer* in front of your impressionable child again?"

The color in Sage's cheeks intensified, giving his skin a distinctly rosy hue. "So, when are you going to plant all those trees in the driveway?"

As an attempt to divert Victor's attention, it was a good one.

"Funny you should mention the trees." Victor took the bright green block Billy held out to him and mimed juggling. Billy quickly retrieved another two blocks. "I had someone all set up to put them in the ground for me, but he's MIA. Or is it AWOL?"

"I guess it depends on whether you had a contract for the work."

Victor began flipping his three blocks, one after the other. Billy instantly clapped and cooed. Victor cooed back before smiling in Sage's direction. "He's so much like you at this age."

Sage grinned at his son. "I get the impression he's quieter and nicer than I was."

"Maybe a little. Give him time. I mean, with a name like Billy, he's bound to have some rough edges."

"Are you ever going to give up on your campaign to rename my son Basil?"

"Never. And if you clone yourself again, I'm going to insist you reconsider herbal alternatives to whatever conformist drivel you and Ashni come up with."

Chuckling, Sage said, "If we do end up with a girl, Ashni is all for Marjoram. She didn't like Basil. Said it would make him sound old before his time, and I agree."

"Cardamom, then. You could have called him Card!"

"Wasn't your other suggestion Dill? So cruel."

"Are you insulting all the Dillards on this planet?"

"Apparently so."

"You should have just gone with Bergamot and been done with it."

Still chuckling, Sage pushed up off the couch. "Got any soda? Can I get you anything?"

"There's still some in the fridge from the party. Grab me a can?"

One by one, Victor caught the blocks he'd been juggling and handed them to Billy, who made an adorable attempt to toss them in the air. His coordination was about three years off, but he'd get there. Then, apparently bored with toys, Billy pulled himself up using the nearest chair and began what would likely be the first of multiple circuits of the living room. He'd been cruising for a couple of months and had recently graduated to actual steps between furniture. Victor found the whole process as amusing as he had with his kids.

Sage returned with two cans of soda, a box of apple juice, and a bag of chips. "Have you checked the hole out back for your garden guy?"

"Hole?"

"There's a great big hole at the end of the patio."

Unfolding his legs, Victor got to his feet. "Ugh, remind me not to sit cross-legged. I am not as young as I used to be."

"No kidding."

"Rude!" Victor tottered out of the family room on stiff legs.

He had managed to walk normally by the time he reached the kitchen. As usual, the patio door was unlocked. He opened it and stepped out. And, there, at the end of the patio, was the hole.

It was in the right spot. Victor definitely wanted a tree there. But why was the hole so large? It could accommodate two trees, easily. Also, why wasn't there a tree in the hole? Or even close to it?

What he really wanted to know, of course, was where his gardener was.

Victor pulled out his phone and looked for Cam's number. The only one he had was for Shepard's Tree Farm. Well, it was Saturday. They'd be open, wouldn't they? Then he remembered that Cam had accepted the landscaping work independently.

He put his phone away.

Sage stepped out onto the patio, leading Billy by the hand. Billy tugged free and tottered toward the first piece of furniture.

"Best not let him get too near the hole," Victor said. "We might lose him forever."

"Are you putting in a hedge?"

"No, a tree. But Cam generally seems to know what he's doing. There will be a reason why the hole is so big."

"Cam?"

"The landscape guy."

Victor could feel Sage's attention like an itch on the side of his face. He turned to his son. "He delivered the mulch and trees and then offered to spread and dig."

A hint of a smile twitched across Sage's mouth. "Uh-huh."

"It's not like that. Besides, I'm still getting over Tholo."

"I think you were over Tholo a while ago."

"Then why did I spend a week crying into every bottle of wine in the house, hm?" Victor had tried to inject a tone of *you think you're so smart* into his retort but succeeded only in sounding petulant.

"Because you live for excuses to swan around in silk and faint onto nearby couches, a bottle of whatever clutched in your hand."

"That's . . ." Victor spluttered for about ten seconds before giving into laughter. "Entirely true. For the record"—he sought a contrite expression—"I'd been sober for at least twenty-four hours before Billy's party. I was sleeping it all off when your mother found me."

"She told me."

Victor's phone burbled with a familiar ringtone. Anticipation warred with lightly buttered dread as he retrieved it from his pocket and woke the screen. "Jazmine! How lovely to hear from you." Victor arched his eyebrows at his son.

Sage returned a smirk. He knew Jazmine. She'd been Victor's agent since about the time Sage had started kindergarten.

"Hallo, Victor." Jazmine had a smooth voice that always reminded Victor of Lindor chocolate ads. "Is this a good time?"

No small talk? A prickle of unease touched the back of his neck. "It's always a good time. You know that. What's up?"

"Natali Wirth is bumping your show."

Victor parsed each word twice and still didn't quite understand what Jazmine had said. "What do you mean?"

"The official word is that they've been presented with a one-time opportunity to showcase an emerging talent and the only dates they can accommodate her are September fifteenth through the thirtieth."

"But that's when they're supposed to be accommodating me." He'd been exhibiting with Natali Wirth ever since they opened in New York. "I'm a cornerstone. They can't bump me."

"Actually, they can."

"But . . . how?"

"The numbers for your last show dipped below contractual obligations."

"They *what*?" At Victor's screech, a bird startled out of the garden. Billy squealed, clapped, and tottered toward the edge of the patio. "Why didn't anyone tell me?"

"I told them it was a blip."

"A blip."

"A momentary—"

"I know what a fucking blip is. What I'm asking is why no one told me about this fucking blip."

Sage put a finger to his lips and jerked his head in Billy's direction.

With a frustrated wave, Victor strode to the opposite side of the patio. He'd need to burn off some energy soon. He'd start by circling the house a few times. Perhaps if he walked fast enough, he'd be too tired to see if there was any wine left in the dining room.

"Is this the first time my numbers have trended downward?" He hadn't sold a lot during his last showing, but he rarely sold out an exhibition anymore. "How many of those paintings are still listed?"

"Everything that remained afterward."

The prickle at the back of his neck became a pinch of cold fingers. "And when were you going to tell me this?"

"I wasn't concerned, Victor. You're on a low swing of the pendulum. Your next series will see your worth rise again."

His next series. The one he was having trouble finishing. Trouble conceptualizing. The series that now had no show. "Who is going to see these damn paintings if Natali Wirth won't show them?"

"We can wait to see when they'll have an opening or look for a new gallery."

"Wait to see . . . What, you mean, they don't have a new date for me?" He was screeching once more. Victor glanced at the front door as he strode past, and the echo of his show there, nearly two weeks ago, felt bitter. He continued on around to the south side of the house.

Jazmine sighed. "Vic, can I be honest with you?"

"Oh, please do."

"You're so talented."

"I thought we were being honest," he said, pushing some of the bitterness he felt into his voice.

"We are. And I am. I love your style. But it's not as unique as it was. Heck, nothing is. The market is cluttered and becoming more crowded every day. You don't stand out the way you once did, even as a mainstay."

"Don't call me a mainstay! I refuse to be compared to a product line at Walmart."

"If you don't want your prints to become the new backing paper for their buy-one-get-twenty-free frame deal, you need to come up with something new."

Victor stopped outside his studio and panted into the phone. "I . . ."

"Look. I know you explore a different direction with every series. That you're constantly testing the boundaries of your style to see where it will go. I admire that. A lot of people admire that. It's why you're still popular. But you're not exactly painting anything new, Victor. You're not breaking those boundaries or reaching outside of yourself."

Staggered, Victor contemplated dropping to the ground. The grass beneath his feet was longer than it should be and inviting in all its lush greenness. Could he hide there until his son left, then perhaps crawl to the kitchen in search of solace?

No more drinking.

He started walking again and stopped by the hole at the edge of the patio garden. Leaned forward to study the deep brown depths.

Jazmine kept her silence, which he appreciated—though the sound of her voice, or rather, the content of her small speech, continued to haunt him regardless. *"You're not exactly painting anything new, Victor. You're not breaking those boundaries or reaching outside of yourself."*

She was right. And had they had this conversation last year or the year before, she'd also have been right. He thought about the canvas in the studio, the painting that hadn't progressed beyond too red, too green, and too vertical. He'd been clinging to a formula. Had conceived this series based on a fucking formula. Why hadn't he recognized that?

Then there were his teaching plans for the Hearts & Crafts program—recycled so often, they were no longer new objects. How did he still have students?

"Vic?" Jazmine, her voice quiet but not consoling.

"I'm staring at a deep hole and wondering whether I should crawl into it."

Sage, who was still on the patio with Billy, looked up sharply.

"Maybe for a little while? But don't let yourself be buried. Think for a while but don't roll over. And if you want to talk about it, I'm here. If you want to toss around any . . ." She hesitated.

"New ideas?" Victor filled in.

"I'm here. You know that. Always."

"Don't we have a contract with certain obligations?"

"You'll never be just a contract to me. You could sell nothing and I'd still represent you."

Could relief and self-pity coexist? Yes. Yes, they could.

"I'm going to go," Victor mumbled.

"Want me to call in a few days to check on you?"

"No. I'll be fine. Assume no news is good news."

"Okay. I'll talk to you soon."

With a sigh, Victor ended the call. Then he blinked away the tears lurking behind his eyes and drew in a deep breath. The sorrow on Sage's face nearly undid any attempt to pull himself together. Victor shook his head at his son. His full-of-feelings-and-not-afraid-to-show-it boy whom he loved with a ferocity he would never be able to adequately describe. "I'm okay. I'll will continue to be okay. I'm not dying. Just my career is."

Sage opened his mouth.

Victor waved him off. "Please don't say anything. I love you, dear son, and I know you mean well, but I need to sit with this for a while."

Gaze darting toward the kitchen, Sage failed to hide a wince.

"I promise I won't drink myself into another coma." A promise he might have to break. Perhaps he could smoke himself into oblivion, instead.

"Can I say one thing?" Sage asked.

"One thing. And it cannot be about my art or me as an artist."

Sage would have heard enough of Victor's side of the call to have put together a fair approximation of what had happened.

"One of the reasons I stopped by today was to check on you. I was worried last week when Mom told me what you'd been doing." Sage's brow creased. "It's been a while since you drank." He held up one hand. "This isn't an intervention. I don't think you have a problem with alcohol. Not much of one, anyway."

Victor sometimes wondered if he did, though.

"I think it's more you . . ." Sage shifted from foot to foot.

Victor sighed.

Sage got on with it. "I know you prefer not to talk about depression. No one from your generation does. But I'm here and I'll always be here. I'll listen or sit with you if you feel you just need to be. I'll never tell you to smile and bear up. And if you, ah, want"—his fidgets increased—"to talk to someone, I'll help you find the right person. If you want me to."

Victor's first urge was to ask his son to leave. His second was to grab hold of him and use him as a life preserver. The need to be the adult and *male* warred with the desire to find his robe and a fainting couch. The correct reaction, of course, was to hug his son. To accept his gift.

Victor knew his eyes were shining as he stepped forward and tugged his son into a rough embrace. Oh, his boy. His precious young man. How had he ended up with such perfect children?

Sage hugged him tight, and Victor coughed back a surge of emotion.

"Thank you," he rasped into Sage's shoulder. "I actually have a therapist, whom I should probably call for a check-in." Should but probably wouldn't.

Sage's lack of reaction suggested he already knew about the therapist. Then why . . .? Victor pulled back and frowned.

"I wasn't sure if I was supposed to know about that."

A chuckle worked its way through all the knotted emotion inside Victor's torso. "Her name is Sahar. Your mother connected me to her when . . ." The brief amusement faded. His son might accept that he saw a therapist for his regular bouts of depression, but did he need to know where it all came from? Sage possessed an equanimity of character that tended to indicate he'd never need such help. Hopefully. "When I needed to clarify my thoughts."

While Sahar was always willing to talk, however, she thought he needed more. A psychiatrist and a prescription. Victor suppressed a frown. He'd managed this long without pills, he could last—

"I'm glad you have someone," Sage said, interrupting his mental wandering.

Victor initiated another gentle hug. "And I'm glad I have you."

Chapter Eleven

From the bottom of the stairs, Cam kept his face turned toward the front door. If he didn't peek into the living room, the dog wouldn't—

A soft whine emanated from the pile of blankets in front of the couch.

Damn it.

He'd never had a pet before. Was he a sucker for needing to rush to the dog's side every time it made a noise?

"I already took you out this morning," he said as he sat on the edge of the coffee table. "Now I gotta go to work. It's been a week, buddy. You can do a day by yourself."

She—his temporary companion turned out to be female—hadn't necessarily needed a babysitter for that long, but every time Cam left the house, he worried she'd try to climb over the furniture and break another leg. The vet had assured him this was unlikely. Apparently, she was an older dog and seemed to have quite a sensible disposition, which made it stranger that she'd been out on the side of the road during a storm.

Still, Cam had spent three days entirely at home, caring for the dog's whims. On Friday, he'd taken her to the tree farm with him and let her spend the day nested in Luisa's office. He'd worked Saturday too, leaving the college students who ran the front office to fuss over her. Sunday, he'd killed a six-pack of beer while watching back-to-back Pirates of the Caribbean movies.

Today, Cam wanted to leave the house alone. The dog needed to learn to do its own thing for at least a few hours every day, or

Cam might never get laid again. He hadn't been *out* out for over two months.

"Which isn't totally your fault," he explained to a pair of warm brown eyes. "I haven't felt like it lately. Maybe I'm getting too old for sex."

She opened her mouth and let her tongue loll out in a soft pant, almost like a chuckle.

Cam snorted. "I know. Stupid idea."

More likely, it was that when he was preoccupied—when his dreams got bad, or when the need to occupy himself 24-7 needled and prickled—he preferred to be alone. Safer that way. Fewer *Are you all right?* questions.

"Well." Cam put his hands to his knees and made to rise from the coffee table. "Good talk. Now I gotta—"

There went the whine.

"Fine, fine, you can spend the day with Luisa, but after work, you're going to have to hang out in the back seat of the car, because I have holes to dig and trees to plant." Though, Cam half feared Victor would have finished the job himself. That would suck on levels he'd rather not examine right now.

After a week of practice, he'd figured a way to lift the dog and one blanket without disturbing the cast around her leg too much. The cast she'd have for about seven weeks, maybe, depending on how well she healed. Thankfully, the leg had been the only dire injury. She'd been in shock from pain and exposure, and hadn't eaten in two days by the vet's estimate, but was otherwise sound and healthy.

And his, for the time being.

Cam had tried to leave her at the animal hospital, but they hadn't had the space for stray animals. He'd considered a shelter for all of thirty seconds before nixing that idea. So, here she was, lying in his arms and gazing up at him with those ridiculously large and soulful eyes.

"Quit it."

A warm tongue lapped the side of his face.

"I said stop."

With another whine, this one along the lines of *I know you love it*, she wagged her tail and nestled.

A traitorous grin pulled at Cam's lips. *Damn dog.*

He strapped her carefully into the back seat of Emma's car—now fully functional thanks to his three days at home—and drove to work.

Luisa met him at the door, arms out, and wearing a bigger smile than he'd seen in a while. "I hoped you'd bring her today." She gently hugged the dog to her chest before bending to kiss one ear. "Did you name her yet?"

"I'm still trying to decide between Kibble and Shark Bait." His lips twitched before he got on top of the whole keeping-a-straight-face thing.

Luisa shook her head.

"Heh. Does she need a temporary name?"

"Might not be temporary," she said. "No one has called, have they?"

Word had been spread, calls made, and posters pinned. A grumble circled low in Cam's throat. "No."

Luisa hugged the dog again before transporting her to the pile of blankets in front of the office couch.

"Spoiled. That's what we should call her," Cam said.

"She's precious, though. I can't help spoiling her."

Jorge arrived, delivery slips were printed, and the dog received all due attention, including a smile and pat from Jorge, who knelt beside her blankets and cupped her jaw for a second, before everyone left.

"You want a dog if no one turns up to claim her?" Cam asked as he and Jorge walked toward the yard.

"No." A hint of a smile played about his lips. Then, as if he and the smile had reached an agreement, Jorge grinned in Cam's direction before jerking his chin toward the backhoe. He held up the slips in the order they'd agreed upon, and that was that.

The first delivery was to an older gentleman down past Bushkill. Cam had no sooner dumped the gravel at the end of the driveway, when the guy asked, "I forgot to ask on the phone. Can you spread the gravel?"

"We usually only deliver, sir." Cam scanned the yard. "Where did you want it? Along that path?" If *threadbare* could be used to describe a gravel walkway, it would apply here. The stones were mostly embedded in the dirt and clumped with weeds.

"To the front door, yes," the elderly man said.

Cam checked the docket. His name was Fincher. "Well, Mr. Fincher. I could quote you a rate for it." He only had three other deliveries. If no more came in, he could spread the gravel before he stopped by Victor's to dig the rest of those holes. Wasn't too hot a day.

"Oh, if you could, please."

Half an hour later, Cam left the old man with an estimate scrawled on the back of his delivery slip. Once on the road back to the farm, he dialed Luisa's number.

"What's up?" she answered.

"Hey, so if customers want me to spread the gravel or give them quotes for other jobs, do you want me to . . ." He wasn't sure what he was asking. "Would that fit under what you pay me? I mean, I'm not working all the hours you pay me for now, but—"

"We don't offer those services."

"Yeah, I know, but people keep asking me if we do, and I have the time. I was thinking it could be extra revenue for you, you know?" Also, it felt wrong not to pull Luisa into the loop.

"If you want to spread someone's gravel and I don't need you here, you go ahead and do it."

"How much do you think I should charge?"

"Whatever you think is a fair rate for your labor. It's your time, Cameron."

"But it's your time too."

"And I barely have enough work for you as it is. Do you like spreading gravel?"

"It's a job." He'd rather spread gravel than look for odd jobs around the tree farm, like counting the trees or restacking pots. Sitting by a phone that rarely rang.

"How about the extra money?"

"I do have some vet bills to cover."

"There you go, then." Luisa's voice lilted as though she were smiling.

"You sure you don't mind?"

"I do not mind. I would pay you more. You and Jorge both, but—"

"Now, now, let's not start on that. I accepted the job you offered, remember?" Thirty-one hours a week delivering trees and mulch; one hour under the limit where Luisa would have to pay extra taxes and offer him benefits. Back before the big box store had opened, he'd worked overtime for cash. Over winter, he'd found work driving a plow and helped out with his friends' various small businesses. Holding market stalls and cleaning kitchens. Moving shit.

His expenses were few, so Cam didn't mind not making a lot of money. As long as he could afford to eat and put a little away for a car he didn't need at the moment, he was good.

He'd worried about Luisa, though. She and her husband had built this business from two acres of Christmas trees. Shepard's was an institution. Seemed like people cared more about low prices on imported shrubbery than supporting a local endeavor, though, which was why, in general, people sucked. People Cam wasn't friends with, anyway.

Also, this was why, despite the everlasting sting of embarrassment, Cam held a thread, buried deeply, of gratitude for the woman who had duped and dumped him. He wasn't cut out to run his own business. Not when it came to dealing with the sorts of decisions Luisa had faced.

Much better to dig holes and spread gravel.

After making the last delivery, Cam drove the truck back down to Mr. Fincher's and spent an hour and a half shoveling gravel into a wheelbarrow and spreading it along the front path. Fincher paid him in cash, which sat nicely in Cam's back pocket as he drove away. Maybe he'd head out this weekend.

He ran a hand over his messy hair. It was probably time for a haircut. Then he could put on a shirt with buttons, dig out his clean jeans, and polish up his boots. Find someone to overlook the dangerous glint he'd been told lurked in his eyes. Or someone who wanted to go there. Have some fun.

He was whistling when he pulled into Victor's driveway, the dog once again strapped carefully into the back seat of Emma's car. She seemed to enjoy the sound. Her head had stayed cocked and alert for most of the drive.

As he stepped out of the car, Victor's front door banged open. Cam glanced up with a start.

"There you are." Victor strode toward him.

"Here I am," Cam murmured.

Victor wore acid-wash jeans that he'd presumably hidden in his closet at the end of the eighties or had liberated from a thrift shop, and a loud purple V-neck T-shirt. Oddly, the brightness of his shirt didn't wash out his skin. In fact, Victor looked as though he'd gotten a little color over the weekend. He'd lost the pallor and thumbprints beneath his eyes. The pale gray-blue of his irises remained the same, though. And his eyes flashed with a danger all their own.

"I thought you might have died or something." Victor planted himself in the driveway, a hand to either hip.

"Died? Why?"

"You disappeared. For over a week. And I have a hole beside my patio. A huge hole!"

"Sorry. I, er . . ." Cam gestured limply toward the back seat of his car. "I've been taking care of the dog."

"You brought your dog!" Shrillness edged Victor's words. "It better not shit on my lawn. Or eat my cats."

"She's pretty well-trained. Will poop when I tell her to and she won't be chasing anything. She has a broken leg."

As though Cam had hit a button or maybe pulled a plug, Victor's expression immediately softened. "Oh no! The poor dear." He rushed forward to peer into the back seat. "Oh, and she's so pretty."

He glanced over his shoulder, the lightning storm now missing from his eyes. "What's her name?"

"Spoiled, because everyone wants to give her everything." A half grin tugged at Cam's mouth. "She's a stray. I found her on Milford Road last week. The night it rained?"

"That's every night, lately. What is with all this rain?"

Cam stared at Victor, amazed by the sudden change in his attitude. "Right."

"So, this hole. Why is it so big?"

"For the bodies I've got stashed in the trunk."

Victor gaped. Cam laughed.

Shaking his head, Victor continued on as though Cam hadn't made a bad joke. "I only want one tree on that side of the patio."

"I always dig a large, wide hole if I can. You want a lot of room for the roots to spread out."

"Huh. Okay, that makes sense. Those trees down there?" Victor pointed out an uneven row of Bradford Pears on the lawn side of the driveway. "They didn't do much the first couple of years after I put them in. Would that be because the roots couldn't push through the clay or whatever?"

"Roots are pretty hardy and tricky. They can push through just about anything, though the soil here can be kind of shit."

Victor's eyes widened slightly, and Cam made a mental note not to use the word *shit* in front of a customer. Because that's what Vic was. A tree farm customer but also a . . . fledgling landscape-business customer.

Where had that thought come from?

Regardless, he should attempt to clean up his act. Limited cursing and no jokes about dead bodies.

"The soil isn't good," he said in his most professional tone. "Did you feed the trees?"

"I did not. I meant to, but time gets away from me." Victor waved toward the glass-fronted studio. "I can go into the studio in March and not come out until May sometimes."

"Seriously?" Did he sleep on the floor? Shit—crap—take a dump in buckets?

"Metaphorically."

"Oh. Well, ah, sorry for not showing up for so long. I had to take care of the dog. But I plan to finish digging the holes today. Or try to."

"With both of us working, we should get them done."

Cam frowned. "You're paying me to dig the holes. Technically, that means you get to open up a bottle of wine and watch from the patio."

Eyes widening again, Victor opened his mouth and closed it. "I could do that." One corner of his mouth lifted in a half smile. "I could definitely do that."

Uh-oh. They were flirting. How were they flirting?

When he turned it on, Cam could flirt the paper off a wall, but standing there in scuffed and grimy jeans and a shirt stiff with sweat, he wasn't exactly feeling it. Or was he?

He licked his lips.

Victor's eyes followed the movement of his tongue before flicking up to meet Cam's gaze.

Turned on and now completely off-center, Cam disengaged. He busied himself opening the car's back door. "Mind if I set her up on the patio? She won't go far, and I've got a stash of plastic bags for, ah, poop. She shouldn't need to go, though. Luisa took her out a while ago."

"Luisa?" came the voice at his back.

"My boss, at the tree farm." Cam got his arms under the dog and eased her off the seat. He turned around. "She's allowed to hobble a little. Meant to be good for keeping her muscles conditioned. But no running, climbing, jumping. She seems to know the score."

Victor was gazing adoringly at the dog. "I can't believe she doesn't have a name. There was no collar? No one seems to be missing her?"

"Nope."

Reaching out a hand, Victor let the dog catch his scent before gently ruffling her ears. "I'd call you Honey for the color of your coat."

She let out a soft yip and nuzzled Victor's hand. He looked up with a beatific smile, and the sense they could flirt again, as inappropriately as last time, passed over Cam in a cool rush.

After settling the dog on the patio, they quickly discussed the location of the three remaining holes. Victor retrieved two shovels from the garage and they set to digging. Cam moved out to the edges of the lawn, and Victor tackled the last hole, closest to the house. No more was said about wine and watching. Cam decided he wasn't disappointed. He didn't know what he was feeling, really, so he concentrated on putting the edge of the shovel to the dirt and biting down. Lifting with a swing and doing it all again.

After finishing the second hole, Cam leaned on his shovel and wiped sweat from his face with his sleeve. His shirt was so wet, he could probably wring it out. Spying a faucet near the short tower at the back of the house, he went for it. He set the shovel against the wall and stripped off his shirt before turning the water on and thrusting the wadded-up bundle of material beneath the cool stream. Dirty water gushed down the first time he wrung the shirt out. Cleaner water the second time. Cam splashed water over his face and arms and used the shirt to mop the excess away.

When he looked up, Victor was watching him. He hadn't set out wine and crackers or whatever. He'd grabbed a couple of bottles of water and a large bowl of sliced fruit.

"I thought you might enjoy some refreshment," he said.

Cam eyed the fruit. "You just cut this up?"

"Yes."

"For me."

"Yes?" Victor seemed confused.

Cam swiped a bottle of water and twisted off the top. He chugged half of it before putting it down. "Hope you don't mind I rinsed off under the faucet over there."

When Victor's gaze latched on to his bare chest, Cam wondered why he'd spoken. Why he'd invited the look. Victor was so far from his type, they could be a comedy act. The Odd Couple or some shit. But his interest was plain, and though slender, age-appropriate, well-dressed, refined and obviously educated men weren't his usual purview—too much conversation required—Cam was interested too.

But why?

Victor intrigued him. With his quicksilver moods but also because he was, in some way, unreadable. He had secrets. Stories he probably wouldn't or couldn't share over a quick beer while any thought not engaged with making polite conversation was already moving toward the bedroom.

A man like Victor would require more work, Cam guessed. Though, the way their eyes kept catching, maybe not?

But before Cam could shift the gears in his head toward whether he'd sleep with a client—of Luisa's business or his—Victor asked the question guaranteed to redirect his thoughts.

"How did you get those scars?"

Chapter Twelve

C am's grin didn't have the same ease he'd shown earlier. But neither did he appear pained. Either way, Victor refused to feel censured or embarrassed. Questions formed the shortest path to answers, and the more direct the enquiry, the better the results.

Besides, if Cam preferred not to discuss his scars, he wouldn't have taken his shirt off. Twice.

Right?

After swallowing the rest of the water in his bottle, the plastic crackling under the squeeze of his fingers, Cam wiped his forearm across his mouth and said, "Alligator wrestling in Louisiana."

Victor eyed him suspiciously. "That's a thing?" He studied the scars again, looking for bite marks or . . . bite marks. When he glanced up, Cam's eyes glinted with dark humor.

Hands on hips, Victor shot him a disapproving look. "Where are the bite marks?"

"Oh! You mean *this* scar?" Cam dropped his chin so they were both studying his chest. "I was hitchhiking through New Mexico and got picked up by aliens. Sliced me from hip to right here"—he touched the top of the longest scar—"and left me in a bathtub full of ice."

Honey whined. With a quiet chuckle, Cam rubbed between her ears. "This is why you don't hitchhike," he said with mock seriousness.

The dog whuffed softly and pressed her nose against his arm.

Victor snorted. The likelihood of Cam wrestling alligators or aliens felt equally remote. Also, if he wasn't mistaken, the two lumps near his shoulder were bullet wounds. Still, he could play along.

Victor pointed one out. "Let me guess. This one is the result of a ray gun?"

Cam inspected the rounded lump closest to his clavicle and sobered. "M16."

And . . . game over.

Victor swallowed the embarrassment he hadn't felt earlier. If he'd spared a moment for thought, it would have been obvious. The speed with which Cam had arrived at his side the day they'd met, and the genuine concern regarding any possible injuries. His calmness and efficiency. His occasional gruffness. Yes, Victor could be describing any number of people, but the facts also fit one particular profile. Cam was a veteran. Of course he was.

"Where did you serve?" Victor asked.

"Afghanistan."

And obviously during the worst of it. Then again, much of it had been "the worst of it," Victor imagined. "Does it make you uncomfortable when people say thank you?"

"Why, are you thinking about it?" Cam's lips crooked into a grin that was difficult to read. Not exactly cheeky or mischievous but definitely teasing.

"I was generally curious," Victor said. "I've observed several reactions."

"Probably because some days it's like, sure, and others it's . . ." His smile faltered.

Victor watched him for a few seconds. When Cam turned away, it seemed clear he wasn't going to continue. Victor wouldn't press. Also, the tattoo behind his left shoulder was now on full display and quite interesting up close. A ribbon, rippling back and forth, each pass imprinted with a date. The artistry and ink differed slightly between the lines, as though each had been added at a different time. The most recent was about five years ago, with the earliest being from 1992.

What Victor had taken as a patch of moles across his right shoulder blade was a second tattoo. Were those . . . fireflies? And stars, each with a yellow-orange corona.

How curious.

"I think you could be one of the most fascinating people I have ever met," Victor murmured.

"I think we should finish putting those trees in the ground." Cameron put his empty bottle on the table and jerked a nod toward the garage.

Victor prepared to follow him around the side of the house, only to nearly collide with his back as Cam stopped to pet the dog again. To give the impression that had also been his plan, Victor gave Honey a soft stroke as he passed.

He could feel Sinister watching him from the kitchen. Turning toward the window, he made a shooing motion. "Off the table."

The cat, of course, did not comply. A moment later, Dexter joined him, the pair resembling outsized and fluffy salt and pepper shakers. When Victor moved, they continued peering through the window at the dog.

"She'll be going home soon," he assured them as he trotted toward the garage.

Cam had the larger of Victor's two wheelbarrows in the driveway: a four-wheeled cart that would comfortably hold two of the trees.

"Will you be all right pulling that back up to the patio?" Victor asked as he helped load the second tree. "There's a slight slope, and the wheels sometimes sink into the gravel."

"I'll yell if I get stuck."

With a nod, Victor went to pick up the third tree. He squatted by the pot, wrapped his arms around it, and begged his thigh muscles to perform the impressive task of lifting him upright without failing. Thankfully, his decision to work out rather than descend back into Wineland after Saturday's call with Jazmine proved sound. His thighs did their job, and he hefted the tree with reasonable (rather than unreasonable) effort.

Cam also managed to drag the cart up the path, muscles straining nicely as he tugged at the handle, and together they arrived on the patio huffing and puffing.

Victor dropped his tree near the first hole. "This one here."

"Any preference on these two?" Cam asked.

"Nope." He'd ordered two varieties of dogwood and had split them into mixed groups for the patio and lawn. "Whatever you think works."

Grunting, Cam continued pulling the cart off the other side of the patio and onto the lawn. Victor busied himself planting his tree, first patting his pockets for the knife he knew he didn't have before trotting back to the garage for a spare. After liberating the tree from the pot, he slid it into the hole and admired the amount of room he'd given the roots to grow. Cam did have a good point there.

He spent ten minutes shoveling the dirt back in and grabbed the hose to water it down. Then he got the second tree situated and watered.

His trees taken care of, Victor circled the house to the south lawn. Cam had his first tree settled and was working on the second.

"Did you water this one yet?" Victor asked.

Cam shook his head. By the time Victor had given the first a drink, the second was ready for his attention. While he watered, Cam gathered up the tools and laid them in the cart. Victor caught up with him in the garage, where Cam was hanging away the cleaned shovels. He'd noted last time that Cam cleaned tools before putting them away and had decided he liked that about him. Disorder and disarray could be comforting, but tools should always be well-maintained.

"Can I get you another bottle of water or perhaps a beer?" Victor asked when Cam turned to him.

They were close enough for him to smell the honest sweat of Cam's skin and feel the heat of his exertion—his presence—and despite not having a particular preference for masculine partners, Cam's robustness very much appealed. He was just so there. So capable. So vital and engaged. But also unknowable, which meant Victor needed to know. To try to, anyway.

For his part, Cam appeared more relaxed. Or perhaps Victor simply couldn't see the scowl lines. It was a little shadowy in the garage. His eyes, as he met Victor's gaze, held amusement.

But when Victor sought a reciprocal interest, Cam let him down.

"This isn't going to work out how you think it is."

"What isn't going to work?" Victor tried, putting on his most nonchalant expression.

"Whatever it is you want from me."

Heat flushed Victor's cheeks. Hopefully, the dim light of the garage would also hide his discomfort. "What I want is to thank you for your—" He'd been about to say *service* but had meant *work*. When had this become awkward? "—work."

"I assume you're still planning to pay me?"

"Of course."

"Then I'll consider myself thanked."

"Why are you being so prickly?"

Cam stepped back, shaking his head. When he looked up, he wore a rueful smile. "I'm not, usually. I dunno, maybe I am. Ask my brother and he'd tell you I'm his number one annoyance." His smile faltered. "Or I used to be."

Victor's thoughts flashed to the dates behind Cam's left shoulder. "Oh, no. I'm sorry."

"What? No, he's not dead. He's thinking of getting married, which I can't quite wrap my head around. Not that I didn't ever imagine him partnering up. Actually, no, I didn't imagine it. I mean, why would I? Anyway, he moved in with his boyfriend last year. So, ah . . ." Cam spread his hands. "What were we talking about?"

Victor couldn't quite remember because his mind had latched on to the word *boyfriend*. Cam had not seemed fazed by Victor's obvious attention to his body. His casual flirtation. But he did seem bothered by the fact his brother lived with a man.

"Do you not see your brother much now?" Victor asked.

"I see him often enough." The lighter smile returned. "I invite myself down there now and again to mess with him. And I work for Oliver, sometimes. That's his boyfriend. Partner? Significant other? What do you call it when two adults are in a relationship?"

"Lovers?" Victor let one of his eyebrows arch.

Cam snorted.

"So." Victor tried not to succumb to an up-and-down look, but Cam wasn't wearing a shirt and his dirt-streaked and tightly muscled skin was on full display. He still smelled enticing. Victor cleared his throat. "We could be having this conversation on the patio. With refreshments."

"What conversation are we having?"

"Honestly? I've lost track. But I do enjoy talking with you."

Sucking his lower lip into his mouth, Cam considered him for a few second before nodding. "I could use a beer. I suppose."

"Don't put yourself out or anything," Victor returned with a playful smirk.

"Wouldn't dream of it." Cam put his hands out again. "Mind if I clean up a little? I could use the faucet out back again, but some soap would be nice."

"Come on into the house. There's a bathroom behind the kitchen."

While Cam used the bathroom, Victor washed his hands in the kitchen and mopped his face with a damp paper towel. He then glanced down at his T-shirt. It looked as though he'd hugged a tree and then gotten down into the hole with it. Should he change?

Cam emerged from the bathroom, still shirtless.

Victor quickly pulled open the fridge and grabbed two bottles of beer. He handed one to Cam, who inspected the label with an approving nod before twisting off the cap. "Trash?"

Victor held out a hand. Cam dropped the cap there and lifted his bottle in a toast. "Thanks."

"You are very welcome."

After disposing of both bottle caps, Victor snagged a box of crackers from the pantry and put together a quick tray of nibbles to go with the fruit. By the time he arrived on the patio, Cam had put his shirt back on (boo) and was seated in the chair closest to the dog. He had a hand on her head and appeared both comfortable and at home.

Victor slid the tray onto the table. "Help yourself."

"Thanks." Ignoring the food, Cam waved around the patio. "You do all of this?"

"The garden or the patio?"

"Both?"

"The garden is a work in progress, mostly finished." Victor turned in his chair. "When we first bought this house, it was the converted barn, which is the family room, a small library or den, and bedrooms upstairs. What you see from the front. We added this kitchen because the original one was awful and not at all useful. Plus, we had plenty of room to expand."

"It's a pretty spot."

"It is. We planned for the patio back then, and I've been planting around it ever since. The same as the rest of the garden. I'll plant a few things, see how they grow in, and then fill any gaps the following year." He pointed out the south lawn. "There were more trees there, but when I put the studio on that side of the house, I cleared a few so I'd have enough light."

"Makes sense. What about the tower?" Cam pointed out the blocky, two-story addition between the kitchen and the studio.

Victor laughed. "It's so funny you should call it that. Sage, my son, used to call it the tower too. Still does. That's the main staircase. There used to be one near the front door, but it took up half of the living space and made a mess of the upstairs floorplan, so we moved it back here."

Cam wore a frown. "You have a son?"

"I do. And a daughter."

"Were you married?"

"No. Not that I'm against marriage. A friend and I simply decided to have children together. We both wanted them." Victor smiled to himself at the memory of his and Tez's "pact" as they'd called it. "You know those movies where best friends declare that if they're not partnered up by a certain age, they'll do the deed? It was like that, only we didn't set an age and we decided we'd rather not get married. We didn't want to raise our children with that sort of pressure, if that makes sense."

Cam's lips were parted, as though he was searching for words. He shook his head. "Ah, no, that makes no sense whatsoever. What pressure?"

"That you need to be married to have children, or straight, for that matter. We did live together until the kids were in high school. Then Tez fell in love and moved out. We tried to foster the idea of family but not as a legal unit. As people who chose to live together." Victor allowed a rueful smile. "It sounds a lot more complicated than it was. Really. Most of it was living with a person I adored and raising two wonderful children with her."

"So, did you and . . . Tez, you said?"

"Tereza, Tez."

"Did you date other people?"

"On occasion. Each of us had a lover move in at some point."

"And that wasn't disruptive?"

"Oh, no. We always had friends staying. Sometimes for months. I enjoyed having a lot of people around. I think the kids did too." Victor gazed at his house, the place that had been a true home to so many, and tried to ignore the wave of sadness rolling through him. He enjoyed living by himself, didn't he?

Perhaps it *was* time to consider becoming an official foster parent.

"What about the guy you tossed out a couple of weeks ago?" Cam asked.

Victor turned his attention back to Cam. "Tholo?" He waved dismissively and then reached for his beer. "He lived here for a while, when we began our relationship. But he travels a lot for work. He was a model with his sights set on Hollywood when I met him. Now he's acting full-time. I'm happy for him, of course, but . . ." He shrugged. "Truthfully, I was over Tholo a while ago."

"Didn't look like it."

"Who doesn't love a little drama?"

Cam laughed quietly. "Me." He finished his beer and put the bottle down.

"Another?"

"No." He glanced over his shoulder at the setting sun. "I should head home. Honey will want to eat."

Victor grinned. "Aha! See, it is a good name."

"It'll do for now. Until her people come for her."

The look Honey gave Cam showed Victor she considered her people to be right here. But Victor knew if he'd lost such a lovely dog, he wouldn't stop searching until he'd drawn his last breath.

He stood and patted his wallet pocket. Not there. "I'll be back in a minute."

"Sure."

But when he returned to the patio, Cam and Honey were missing.

Then Cam appeared at the top of the path from the driveway. "I carried her to the car."

"She's very well-behaved. She sat and watched me while I dug my hole and planted the tree."

"Yeah. She's not at all excitable. I could probably leave her at the house? But I think she likes having company."

"She certainly seems to."

They were talking about the dog, but standing there, face to face, perhaps a foot and a half between them, all Victor could think about was Cam and how the words suited him. *Not at all excitable. Did well on his own, but seemed to enjoy having company.*

Heh. They suited Victor too.

In the low light of the setting sun, Victor made a quick study of Cam's face. Still not classically handsome, but not unattractive. More familiar than last week or the week before. He'd seen Cam happy now. And sad. Concentrating. Telling a joke—or spinning wild stories. He was getting to know this face, and the more he got to know—

"Still not a good idea," Cam said softly.

Vic lifted his gaze from Cam's mouth. "What's that?"

"You want conversation and commitment. That's not who I am."

I think you could be. "Maybe I'm only looking to—" *Do* not *say "blow out the cobwebs." Dear lord.*

Cam held out a hand, palm up.

Vic stared at it, confused, then remembered the soft weight in *his* hand. His wallet. He flipped it open and sorted through the bills there. "Would you be interested in another job?"

"What's that?"

Vic counted out five twenties, then added an extra. He handed them over and watched as Cam tucked them into his jeans pocket.

"I would like to draw you. Sketches, for a painting, perhaps." A feeble tremor touched Victor's torso as complicated emotions knotted and unknotted behind his breastbone. At one time, he'd loved capturing portraits, especially of people he felt connected to. Perhaps it was time to try again. Time to move past the block, past the moment that had changed the course of his career and his life.

Try for that new direction Jazmine thought he should explore.

Waiting for Cam's answer, Victor held his breath.

Cam's eyebrows scrunched together. "Draw me?"

Victor exhaled softly. "Use you as a model. Have you pose while I draw."

"Me?"

Victor couldn't help his grin. "If you're comfortable with it. I'm looking for inspiration for a new series."

Cam's expression could only be called dubious. Then he shrugged. "Sure."

"Really?"

"As long as I can bring my dog."

"Yes! I mean, well, yes. So, ah, I'll call you?"

One last smile, this one sly. "I'll call *you.*"

Chapter Thirteen

Cam's thoughts had wandered toward the sense of abandonment Honey might be experiencing at being left home, alone, when a blur of motion to his left pulled him back to the present. He was at his brother's place for game night. And, stupidly, missing the dog he was trying not to bond with.

Nick plucked a card out of Grayson's hand and shuffled it to the bottom of the deck. "You can't choose your specialty before the smoke quest."

Had anyone but Nick pointed this out (and snatched said card), they would have done so with more exasperation or weariness. But not Cam's brother. When discussing rules—or enforcing them—Nick always spoke with cool collection.

Gray—Oliver's oldest friend—shared one of his easy grins with the group gathered around the coffee table before drawing in a breath for the explanation he gave every time he and Nick butted heads over this same point. "But my orc already knows what it wants to be when it grows up."

"Smoke. Quest."

"Ambitions," Gray shot back.

Gray's boyfriend, Aaron, patted the air in a peacekeeping gesture and looked to Oliver for help. Oliver passed responsibility to Cam with a relaxed shrug of the shoulders.

With a long-suffering sigh, Cam touched his brother's arm. "How about if we all choose our specialties before the quest? To try a different spin."

"But the rules state—" Nick inhaled, chewed on his bottom lip, and then nodded.

Surprise rippled around the table.

"Seriously?" Gray was already reaching for the deck.

"Sure. Fine. The balance will be ruined, but let's try it."

Nick was probably right. When it came to numbers and statistics, he was always right. But gaming with friends wasn't always about who won. It was about what happened along the way. And Orcs & Swords was supposed to be a cooperative effort—until it wasn't.

On his turn, Cam selected a specialty card and shuffled it into his hand, readying it for deployment after his smoke quest, assuming he had enough points. Nick did have something there. They'd all have to reconsider their strategy—whether to go big now or save it for later.

Sorting his cards into a vague plan, Cam asked after Gray and Aaron's new collaborative project. Gray had suffered a (thankfully) mild heart attack last year and had ended up selling his café so he could bake full-time and design board games with his boyfriend.

It felt like a weird career choice. Cam couldn't imagine being in such a conceptual field. He much preferred to work with his hands. But he did enjoy playtesting the games.

"Okay," Aaron started, his pale, freckled skin already flushing with excitement. "Our new idea is kinda weird. We're thinking subterranean spy thriller. We'll build the board or play area similarly to the last game, with players picking up and setting down terrain tiles. But instead of vying for and using resources to build a society, they'll be gathering clues, information, and influence. Something to do with politics in this, like, underground setting."

"Weird," Cam said.

Gray laughed. "Yeah, it is, but we've got a lot of cool story notes for it. I think we can make it work."

"It sounds fascinating," Nick said. "And using the tile system again gives you a brand."

"Just what I was thinking," Oliver put in. He turned to Aaron. "Are you going to illustrate the faction cards again?"

"Some? Maybe not all. I dunno. It took me years to do the last set. I'm not sure we want to sit on this for that long. We might see if we can outsource the bulk of the art."

"What sort of terrain are you thinking?" Cam asked, thoughts zipping to the one and only artist he knew.

"Think *Journey to the Center of the Earth* and *The Lost World*," Gray answered before taking his turn.

Play resumed for a round, with each of them revealing their strategy for the rest of the game. Predictably, Gray had put down his specialty card. Interestingly, so had Nick.

"I'd love to see what another artist might do with the concept," Aaron said. "That's also a part of why I don't want to do all the art myself."

"I might know someone." Cam had, at this point, investigated Victor Ness using his brother's favorite collaborator: Google.

Victor's style of art hadn't at all surprised him. His paintings were bright, colorful, and tantalizingly abstract. Mostly landscapes but from varying distances. The closer in he painted, the more detail he included, but not in a way that necessarily made sense. Cam had spent nearly ten minutes scrutinizing an enlarged corner of a small painting, trying to determine how Victor had known where to place each streak of color and every fine line.

Some of the larger paintings had the appearance of being behind water-beaded glass. Others had a verticality of movement Cam still hadn't worked out. He also hadn't decided whether he exactly liked the paintings. He thought he did.

"Who's that?" Aaron asked.

Cam pulled his phone out of his pocket. "Victor Ness? He's a, ah, landscaping client."

"Landscaping?" Oliver asked at the same time as Nick said, "I know Victor."

Cam blinked at his brother. "You do?"

"He teaches painting and drawing at the LGBTQ Center in Milford. Where I used to teach. His program is called Hearts & Crafts."

Like on the T-shirt Victor had been wearing the day Cam had thought he was dead. "Yeah, that's him."

"Do you have his details?" Aaron asked.

Cam passed his phone over. "Here's his stuff. Check it out and if you think he might work, I can ask him if he's interested and then put you in touch?"

Aaron took the phone and showed it to Gray. The pair leaned together, their faces almost touching, and Cam hid his smile. He'd never have pictured Gray and Aaron as a couple. They were so different, and not only because of the color of their skin. Aaron was devoted to fitness and Gray hadn't met a carb he didn't love.

Aaron swiped the screen, and they murmured over several of the pieces before looking up with scarily similar smiles.

"Definitely ask him," Aaron said. "His style is wild. Like, totally different to what I had in mind, but I'd love to chat with him about the project."

"Sure."

Oliver leaned forward, resting his elbows on his knees. "What's this about a landscaping business? Is Shepard's branching out?"

"No. It's just me at the moment." *What do you mean "at the moment"?* Cam frowned lightly at his internal voice before shoving it aside. "I mean, it's not really a thing? I've been doing some work for a few people. Spreading the mulch they order. Planting their trees. And I have two mowing clients." Melanie was commuting to New Jersey now and had hired him to maintain the yard so she could concentrate on the house over the weekends. She'd also recommended him to one of her neighbors. "And a couple of inquiries about larger projects. Digging out a bed and advising on the planting."

Laying it all out, it did sort of sound like a business. Cam cupped the back of his neck, which felt unaccountably warm, and shrugged. "It's just a little extra work. The, ah . . ." He glanced around the coffee table to gauge the interest of his friends. They were all waiting for him to continue. "The farm's been losing business ever since that huge hardware store opened on the other side of Dingmans Ferry. It's been slow all summer and—" his gut tightened "—Luisa is thinking of retiring. Actually, she seems pretty set on it."

Nick looked properly horrified. "But Shepard's has been there for forty-three years."

Cam nodded. "From Christmas tree farm to full-service landscaping supplies."

A pall fell across the table, and Cam immediately regretted sharing the news.

"That sucks," Aaron murmured before adding the positive spin Cam had come to expect from him. "It's good you're putting together a backup plan, though."

"But if the tree farm closes, where will his clients order their landscaping supplies?" Nick asked.

Cam shot a wry smile at his brother. "Thanks for the reminder."

"You could approach another supplier," Oliver suggested. "Set up an arrangement."

"Something to consider."

"We'll spread the word. Anyone needing garden work should call Cameron Zimmermann," Gray said.

"Thanks, man."

"I'll chat with Dev and Leilani about who maintains the property around our gyms. We might be able to offer you some work," Aaron said. He was a fitness instructor and personal trainer. He, his sister, and sister-in-law owned and operated three gyms around the Stroudsburg area.

"Only if you're not satisfied with whoever you're using now," Cam said. "Times are tight for a lot of people."

Aaron nodded. "I hear you."

The game continued, with Gray and Nick battling toward chieftain, which was how a night of Orcs & Swords usually turned out. Gray ended up winning by a margin of two points and the pair shook hands over the board.

"Do we want to play another game?" Aaron asked as he packed up the cards and tokens.

Preparing to stand, Cam put his hands to his knees. "I've got a full day tomorrow." And a dog to get home to.

Oliver glanced over at Gray. "Are you doing a market?"

Gray shook his head. "I haven't done a market all summer. I'm too busy filling bread orders and listening to Aaron drone on about subterranean caverns."

With a grin, Aaron nudged his partner's shoulder.

Oliver turned a quietly stricken look on Cam. "Are you holding a stall for someone else?"

Cam laughed. "No. I've got one of those yards to do and a plan to lay out for that larger job, and, ah . . . another job for, um, Victor." He'd decided to give the modeling a try for reasons that would not be shared here because that would involve mentioning that he'd accepted a job where he might be taking his clothes off. For money.

He didn't actually know whether Victor wanted to draw him naked. Shirtless had been mentioned, though. Victor seemed inordinately fascinated with his torso, and Cam figured it wasn't all about the scars.

"Awesome! So, you can mention the game?" Aaron pulled out his phone. "I'll text you a couple of concepts. A sketch or two."

In his pocket, Cam's phone started dinging.

"Thanks." He shared a wry smile with Gray before getting to his feet. He lifted his empty soda can. "Anyone want anything from the kitchen while I'm in there?"

A chorus of "No, thanks" followed him out of the room.

Because Nick lived in the apartment, a corner of the kitchen had been turned into a recycling center. Oliver had provided a sliding closet door and Nick the six labeled bins. Cam was studying the labels to determine where he should put his can when he felt his brother's presence behind him.

He knew it was his Nick. No one else ever managed to stand with the same feeling of potential, as though gathering every thought that could be shared during an allotted time.

Cam aimed his can at the paper bin and grinned as Nick huffed. Correcting his throw, he tossed it in with the other cans and turned. "How's the proposal planning coming along?"

Nick's eyes widened. He threw a glance over his shoulder before grabbing Cam's elbow and steering him deeper into the kitchen. "I have questions. About pillows. I'll call you on Sunday morning."

"Pillows?" What the—

"Shh! Sunday."

"Ohh-kay. But not too early." After having spent an evening with coupled-up friends, Cam decided he had plans for Saturday night. Him, a reactivated app on his phone, and whoever was in driving distance.

"Is Luisa planning to sell the tree farm?" Nick asked.

Cam rocked back a little, surprised. "Um, yeah, I guess so."

"You should consider buying it."

Laughter bubbled up from Cam's midsection. "With what? The two coins rubbing a hole in my wallet?"

"What about a loan?"

"My credit is pretty much that hole in my wallet."

"Why?"

Ah, his brother. Always with the questions. "Because I'm not you, Nicky." At Nick's glare, Cam corrected himself. "Fine, *Nick*. I'm sorry. I don't have your memory, either."

"There is nothing exceptional about my memory."

"Uh-huh."

"What happened to your credit score?"

Cam wrapped a hand around his nape. "That's a whole story you probably don't want to hear."

"I asked, didn't I?"

"Yeah, well, suffice to say, when I arrived on your doorstep two years ago, I didn't even have those two coins in my wallet because of some, ah, bad business decisions. I got . . . I'm not . . ." He didn't want to say he wasn't smart, because that would be untrue. Cam had never doubted his own intelligence, though his superiors in the army had seemed to make a habit of questioning it. Cam knew he didn't possess street smarts or business savvy, though. The quick-wit that enabled some people to rise to the top of the cappuccino like foam.

That wasn't a particularly apt analogy, was it?

Suffice to say, he'd have been *smarter* to hand his checkbook to someone who made their home under a bridge. At least then his money would have done some good.

"Cam?"

Cam mustered the driest tone he could manage. "I don't have the money or the credit to qualify for a loan."

"We'll figure something out, then."

"We?"

To the uninitiated, Nick's facial expressions could sometimes appear awkward. Cam easily read the concentrated concern wrinkling his brother's forehead, though. Nick was the kind of guy who always put family first, even when his family—especially his brother—annoyed him. He was the most loyal and deeply caring person Cam had ever known.

After a short hesitation, Nick gripped Cam's shoulder. "You like working at Shepard's, helping people choose trees and plants. You don't mind making the deliveries. You love being outside, digging and planting, and planning. The job suits you. So, let's find a way to make it work."

Swallowing over a sudden lump, Cam offered a quick nod in reply.

Nick returned one of his lopsided smiles. Then, with a cheeky glint in his eyes that Cam was still getting used to, he said, "Tell me how you know Victor."

Now would be an excellent time to share the fact he had someone to get home to, even if that someone had floppy ears and a tail.

Chapter Fourteen

At the sound of voices in the driveway, Victor hopped off the couch—where he absolutely had not been waiting with his hands in his lap like a debutante—and crept to the front door. He could peek through a window, but curtain switching wasn't his thing. Neither was feeling as though he and Cam were about to embark on their first date, but there he was, leaning against the door with his heart pinwheeling inside his chest.

He clapped a hand there, left of center. "We are done with men, remember?"

In Victor's mind, his heart said: *No, we're just done with love. For the moment.*

Outside, the voices continued.

Victor cracked open the front door, expecting to find Cam talking to his dog. Instead, he found Cam talking to a human who more resembled a mountain than a man. Tall, with the broadest shoulders Victor had seen since his barhopping days, dark shaggy hair, and a weathered complexion. Warm and engaging eyes. And listening to Cam as though he had all the time in the world.

Between them, stood Honey. Spying Victor, she yipped and hobble-trotted toward him. Cam turned and winced lightly. "Victor, hey. Sorry I'm so late. My car broke down. Thankfully, Jorge was with me, so here I am." He gestured at his filthy jeans and T-shirt. "But I didn't have time to go home. I guess I could have but—" He shook his head before turning back to Jorge. "So, yeah, um, can you pick me up around eight?"

Victor glanced at his watch. It was six now. That didn't give them a lot of time. "I can drop you home."

"Huh?" Cam's brow wrinkled.

"Later this evening."

"Oh, yeah, that'd be great. I think we have one Uber driver between here and Milford and her car smells like week-old Chinese food."

Lovely. "Isn't there a local taxi service?"

"He seems to quit at five."

Behind Cam, Jorge's granite visage softened toward a smile.

Cam offered his friend a casual salute. "I'll see you at eight."

But wasn't Victor driving him home?

Jorge responded with a nod and climbed into a vintage Mercury Cougar. Cam stepped back to let the car swing past and waved him out of the driveway.

"I'm confused," Victor admitted.

"What about?"

"I thought I was driving you home."

"Oh, you are. Jorge is picking me up tomorrow. We've got six acres to clear."

"That's a lot of grass."

"And all of it bumpy and rocky. There's about one acre of it flat. I kinda wish we had a third person. Heck, four would be ideal. Two to clear and two clean up."

"Is that what you do when you're not bullying your clients into planting their trees?"

Cam chuckled, then shrugged. "Maybe? I just sort of started this thing. Had hours in the day to fill, you know?"

Oh, Victor knew. After Sage left for college, he'd become an expert at dealing with extra hours. He hadn't always turned to his friends Chardonnay and Sauvignon. Once upon a time, he'd developed hobbies. He just couldn't seem to remember what they were.

Well, there'd been one named Tholo, but better not to think about his trashy ex right now. He had a filthy gardener shedding dirt onto his driveway.

As though he'd read Victor's thoughts, Cam was once again examining his clothing. "I meant to shower and change before I came over, but the job Jorge and I were on ran long. Not six acres long, but a lot of digging. Then my car wouldn't start." He indicated a row of darker streaks up one arm. "When we couldn't figure that out, we hatched the plan to have him drop me off."

"You could have called."

Cam's head whipped up. "Huh. Yeah, sorry 'bout that. I kept thinking . . . We never established, ah, this modeling. Did you want me to take my clothes off?"

Victor swallowed, and the sound seemed to echo around the gravel circle of the drive, which should have been impossible. "I did not expect you to disrobe completely, no. I planned to start with clothed and perhaps without a shirt, if you were comfortable with that."

Truthfully, Victor had no plan. He was operating on a feeling and the remembered joy of sketching faces and torsos. He used to love drawing faces. Adored the complexity of expression. Why had he let such a passion go?

A face, one rendered in loving detail, flittered past his consciousness. Oh, Sunshine. Would the pain of losing his father ever fade completely away? Thankfully, a sense of excitement for sketching Cam fairly burned along his shoulders and down to his fingertips, banishing his ghosts for the time being. This evening, he'd capture something new; maybe even the outline of what might become a plan.

"Sure." Cam plucked at his shirt and winced. "Would it be weird if I asked if I could take a shower first?"

Victor smiled. "Not at all. Come on in. I can lend you some sweats and a T-shirt while we run your clothes through the laundry. And I took the liberty of preparing a light dinner. I wasn't sure how long we would have for this session, and I didn't want you to starve." *Stop rambling.* They were, by now, at the door, Honey hobble-trotting in front of them. Victor bent to ruffle her ears. "How is she doing?"

"Getting stronger every day. I have to encourage her not to walk more often than not." Cam squatted next to her and slung an arm around her neck. "But you're a good girl, aren't you?" He smiled up at Vic with obvious pride. "Always sits when I ask and curls herself into the neatest donut on her blankets when

I suggest she rests awhile." He nuzzled the side of the dog's head. "That's what you're going to do this evening, little lady. Rest a while. Then we'll take a walk."

Gentleness, itself. Victor might melt all over his own doorstep. "Would she rather be in the studio with us, you think?"

"For sure."

"I have a cat bed in there that Dexter and Sinister never use. Let's introduce her to it and then I'll get you a towel and some clothes."

Cam blinked at him. "You named your cats left and right?"

"It was either that or salt and pepper."

A slow grin captured Cam's mouth (and Victor's imagination). "You're all right, Vic."

Vic?

Victor braced for the shudder he might have to suppress, but it failed to arrive. Apparently, his aversion to having anyone but Tez play with his name had dissipated.

Thirty minutes later, Cam was showered, dressed in snug-fitting sweats and a plain white undershirt, fed, and pacing around the corner of the studio Victor had cleared for him. Outside, long shadows streaked the lawn. The sun wouldn't disappear fully until after eight, but the studio only benefitted from morning and early-afternoon light. Still, the soft glow through the windows would highlight the planes of Cam's face in interesting ways, while deepening shadows and hollows.

Ideas began to multiply as Victor sat on a stool with a large drawing pad on his lap.

Finally, Cam stood in the center of the space and put his hands on his hips. "What do I do?"

"That works for now."

Cam nodded toward the sketch pad. "You don't use one of those tablet thingies?"

"Not often. I haven't developed the hand-eye coordination for it. Cori, my daughter, is quite adept. She's offered to teach me a few tricks, but you know what they say about old dogs." Victor marked a few spots on the page that would guide this first, quick sketch. Eyes, nose, ears. When he found himself trying to focus on the exact distance between each, he shook off the need for precision and drew. A curving line for Cam's chin with just the right tilt. Neck, shoulders . . . back up for his ears—were they too far apart?—brow line, hair line. Huh, Cam had a high forehead.

"It's like a big, clunky sketch pad," Cam was saying. What was he talking about? "Nick got one last year. By the way, my brother says he knows you."

Victor focused on Cam the person instead of Cam the model. "Oh?"

"Nicholas Zimmermann. He knew about your program at the center up in Milford."

The pencil nearly escaped Victor's fingers. "You're Nicholas Zimmermann's brother? Wait, oh my God! I can't believe I didn't recognize you. You look like him." Older, more lived in, and not nearly as reserved as Nicholas, but definitely from the same family. Flattening the pencil against the pad for a moment, Victor scrutinized Cam for other differences. Cam wore his hair shorter and stood straighter. "You know what? I remember him mentioning you, years ago. I'd asked, because I vaguely remembered going to school with a Zimmermann, but he was much too young. What is he? Forty?"

"Forty-one this year." Cam narrowed his eyes. "Wait. Oh, wow. Victor Ness. I thought your name was familiar. You were two years ahead."

"You remember me?"

"Duh, you were the only kid at Delaware Valley with purple hair. And your whole group was weird. We *all* knew you."

Victor laughed. "Good. My past self is pleased. My ego was much more delicate back then." He considered Cam through the lens of thirty-or-so years. "You played football, didn't you?"

"Heh. Yeah. Not well."

"And didn't you win some award? For science?"

"Physics. My popsicle-stick bridge. Yeah. Largest single span. Built that whole thing without a lick of glue, if you can believe it."

"Wow." Victor shook his head. "All this time, we sort of knew each other."

"Milford isn't big."

"No, it's not. Your brother is extremely talented by the way. You know, he used to teach classes at the center, but then he stopped. About five years ago." Victor dredged his memory. "His sister passed, I think. Oh . . ."

"Rebecca. Yeah. Nick took her death pretty hard. They were really close. After our parents died, she practically raised him."

Their parents too? "That, I did not know. Cam, I'm so sorry."

A flash of old pain pinched Cam's brow, briefly, and Victor found himself wishing he could freeze the moment. Sketch it. Then he berated himself. So not his style or his business.

Then he recalled the dates of Cam's tattoo. 1992. And the most recent from five years before.

A slim skewer slid into his sternum as he mentally placed the dates in between. Afghanistan.

Cam had lost his pose and was now standing loosely, shoulders down, hands dangling at his sides. Victor flipped his page and started a new sketch. He left off placing elements and went straight for long, flowing lines, the angle of Cam's shoulders, the tilt of his chin. The length of his arms and legs. The slight dejection of his stance but also the strength of it. A man down but not out. Not yet.

Apparently noticing he'd resumed drawing, Cam lifted his chin and watched.

"I . . ." Victor paused. "I wanted to capture you that way. I'm sorry if . . ." Embarrassment warmed his skin.

"It's cool." Cam showed him a weak smile. "You said you were in New York for a while?"

"Brooklyn." Having outlined this pose to his satisfaction, Victor flipped the page. "If you're ready, would you mind putting your hands back on your hips?"

Cam complied, and as Victor had hoped, the movement lifted and squared his shoulders. His chest popped out a little, his tight physique visible beneath the stretch of white cotton. Victor again sketched the longer lines of a full-length pose, noting the trimness of Cam's waist and how the borrowed sweatpants hugged the muscles of his legs. The bulge front and center? Victor tried not to linger there but found it difficult.

He did find cocks interesting, after all. Personally and professionally.

What were they talking about? Brooklyn. "After college, a bunch of us set up there. Four of us tried the loft thing in the Village, but we decided we'd rather eat than look good, so we moved across the river and lucked into a converted warehouse. Space for us to live, love, and paint, draw, sculpt, whatever. It was marvelous while it lasted." Glancing up from his drawing pad, Victor shared a world-weary smile with Cam. "I distinctly remember feeling as though I was living my dream. Quite literally—I would wake up and pinch myself. And then the beautiful man next to me. My career was taking off with regular shows at reputable galleries, private commissions, and a little commercial art. What I enjoyed the most, though, was working with the community art programs."

"Like with kids?"

"That, but also collaborating with others to raise awareness of the arts. To keep art in schools and fund extracurricular activities. To foster a culture of creativity." He twirled a finger through the air. "Can you turn three-quarters? A little more. There. Thanks." Victor flipped to a new page.

"How did you end up back here?"

That face. That sad, but kind, familiar face. Victor mentally shook Sunshine away for the second time that evening. Cam didn't want to hear about his loss, as devastating as it had been. Cam had been to war.

"I . . . One day I woke up and . . ." He could still remember the sound of the phone ringing. The call that had changed the direction of his life. "There came a day when I looked around and realized I was done with the city. The noise and the bustle. My primary work has always focused on nature, and while there are lovely parks in New York, the green isn't the same as it is out here. You can't hear the wind in the trees and there are no hills. The birds sound different."

"What do birds have to do with paintings?"

Victor chuckled. "It's hard to explain, but when I paint a scene, I try to capture the essence of that location. I want anyone looking at that painting to be able to smell the sunshine and hear the birdcalls. To feel as though they're outside."

"Huh."

"So, I told Tez I was done with the city and she admitted she was too. We moved back here, bought a house together, and decided to have kids."

"Simple as that, eh?"

"Pretty much. But aside from having a family, do you know what the best part about moving home has been?"

Cam shrugged. "The birds?"

"Hah! No. Though I do enjoy them. But the programs I was trying to create in Brooklyn? They're needed there. And all over New York. For kids who don't have access to art or creativity. But they're also needed *here*. At home. Maybe more so. Funding for public education is . . ." A sigh gusted out of him. "A conversation we can have over something stronger than beer one night. What I have loved, living here, has been working with the schools *my* kids attended, and starting programs for after school and summer vacation. Finding other artists interested in donating their time. Raising the money for it all. Mostly, it's about sharing art with kids, though. Seeing the wonder in their eyes when they get it and knowing they'll never look at the world quite the same way again."

Cameron was nodding as if he understood.

"What about you?" Victor asked. "Do you draw or perhaps paint?"

Laughter tossed Cam's head back. The sound was rich and warm and maybe a touch self-depreciating, which suited the Cam that Victor was getting to know. "Nah," he said. "I stick with what I'm good at. Digging holes and fixing cars. Though, the latter hasn't been going all that well for me lately."

Victor considered his model a moment, then flipped to a new page of his sketch pad. He held out his pencil. "Want to try?"

Chapter Fifteen

C am was used to being the subject of focused attention. His brother could become quite fixated when trying to figure stuff out. *Stuff* having been Cam for nearly a year after he'd returned to Pennsylvania.

Victor's attention wasn't like that—or hadn't been until he'd started drawing. Cam had supposed he'd feel a bit like a vase or a bowl of fruit or whatever it was artists drew when they weren't asking near strangers to drop their pants. He'd expected Victor to look through him, or around him, or . . .

His expectations had totally missed the mark.

Victor's attention carried weight. Not all of it was substantial—his eyes flicked up and down, over and around. His gaze sometimes alighted quickly and other times fell heavily. Cam's skin prickled with each and every pass. He didn't exactly feel turned on, but he could be. If he thought about it.

He was definitely trying not to think about it.

Victor's expression now, however, and the way he was offering his pencil and drawing pad? Victor was seeing something Cam couldn't guess at. Seeing something in *him*.

First instincts were usually correct. Cam immediately obeyed his. He could not draw. Lifting a hand, he offered a quick, dismissive wave. "I'm good."

"You could be, but you'll never know if you don't try," Victor said.

What the . . .

"No, I meant I'm happy not to try."

"Why?"

"Because I'm not an artist. That's Nick's job. And Becca's. She designed all the gardens around our—ah, the house." Though, to be honest, Cam still thought of the place where he resided as *our house*, meaning his, Nick's, and Rebecca's, though Nick was only holding the deed until Emma turned twenty-one.

One more year.

Given that Emma still had two years of college remaining, Cam reckoned he had a bed and a roof until then. Still . . .

"Everyone has the capacity for art." Victor had lowered the pencil and pulled the pad back onto his lap but hadn't resumed sketching.

"But is it good art?" Cam asked.

"What do you think is good art?"

"Nick's houses are amazing." Cam gestured toward the easels around the studio, the paintings stacked against tables and slotted into wide shelves, and the sketches tacked to the walls. "Your paintings are incredible. But I don't need to tell you that. I assume you're making enough money to live comfortably. You know you're successful."

Victor shrugged lightly.

Cam frowned. "Is it a trick question, then? Like, whether art is good or not is irrelevant?"

Chuckling, Victor rose from the stool and slid his sketch pad onto a nearby table. "Well, sure. We all have our own sense of taste, some more developed than others. And 'good' is a relative term. It's also kind of loaded. I mean, if it's not good, is it bad?"

Cam grinned. "Evil art. Art bent on world domination."

Laughing, now, Victor nodded. "Pretty much an established concept."

"Heh. I'm sure whatever I tried to draw would fail the evil test. It'd be plain bad."

Victor tapped the sketch pad. "But you haven't tried."

"Because you're paying me to stand here for your—" *Do not say pleasure.*

Given Victor's expression, Cam might as well have said it. He reached for a different word and found, "Convenience."

"Mm-hmm." Victor looked him up and down, his light blue eyes glinting with interest.

"Stop that," Cam said.

"Stop what? Measuring you for my next sketch?"

Cam jerked his chin toward the closed sketch pad. "The one you're drawing in your mind?"

"I'm conceptualizing."

"More like objectifying." Cam lifted his brows but kept his expression light and humorous.

"You don't strike me as the sort of person who minds being looked at. You're fit, attractive, outgoing, able, and not averse to a little objectification yourself."

Cam huffed as he stalked toward the table. "When have I looked at you the way you just looked at me?" Of course, he wanted to *now*, and the fact he'd only be reminding himself of assets he'd already catalogued did not pass him lightly. "Okay, maybe I have. I'm . . . You're . . ." How had Victor put it? "Fit, attractive, outgoing, able, and not averse to a little objectification."

Shaking his head, Victor smiled widely. "Not. At. All."

They were standing too close. As close as they'd been in the garage. Cam leaned forward and Victor drew in a short, sharp breath. Smirking, Cam snatched the pencil off the top of the sketch pad and rocked back on his heels.

He spun the pencil through his fingers. "Fine. What do you want me to draw?"

Victor exhaled. Smiled. He flipped the sketch pad open to a blank page. "Whatever comes to mind."

Cam frowned at the stark white rectangle of paper. *Whatever comes to mind?* Right now, that would be how Victor might taste. How firm or soft his kisses might be. How he liked to fuck. The sounds he might make. Would he scream or yell?

Squeezing his eyes shut, Cam breathed quietly and deeply as he sought alternate inspiration. Then again, he could draw a cock and balls and be done with it. Except, he didn't want to end up in bed with Victor, up against a wall, or with one of them bent over a table. He did not want to sleep with this man.

When he opened his eyes, Victor hadn't moved. He stood as still as Cameron, as though shifting would break a spell. His eyes, though. God damn, the way Victor looked at him.

Cam pulled his attention away from Victor and stared through the paper on the table. Then he gripped the pencil and put the point down. Sketched.

He'd doodled before. But he'd never tried to draw much more than stick figures or perhaps a crude map. He'd diagramed an engine repair, once, with instructions.

Sensing Victor would prefer something less dry, Cam drew a doughnut; a fat toroid with a wavy line around the outer edge. Then he put ears on it, floppy ones like Honey's. A face beneath, the snout outlined against the doughnut's edge. Paws, four of them, little nubs in pairs. A tail curving up and out . . . No. He turned the pencil over and used the eraser to correct the angle of the tail, sketched it curling close to the head.

It was the worst drawing he'd ever seen. Silly too.

Cam put the pencil down and grinned at Victor. "There."

Victor's smile already lit his whole face. He laughed and shook his head. "Very good."

It was Cam's turn to laugh. "Good? It's terrible. Worst drawing in the history of drawing."

"Not so terrible I can't tell what it is."

"I'll try harder next time."

Victor smiled softly at the dog curled onto the cat bed in the corner. Thankfully, Honey was small and the cat bed on the large side, because she only just fit. She looked cozy and content, as though she'd always lived in this house, and when Victor knelt to stroke her head, she barely cracked an eye.

"Good little doughnut," Victor crooned.

"Maybe I should change her name."

Victor stood. "But Honey is such a perfect name."

Cam opened his mouth. Closed it. Fought the prickle of heat moving across his cheeks. Spinning on one heel, he prepared to stalk back to his modeling corner. The sooner they finished this session of whatever, the sooner he could go home and figure out the rest of his Saturday-night plan. Because this wasn't it. He'd wanted to hook up—with someone other than Victor.

Why had he agreed to this modeling thing?

He flicked his fingers in Victor's direction. "C'mon. Clock's ticking. What's next, Leonardo?"

Victor glanced down at the dog. "I thought we might take a break. In case *Honey* needed to go out."

Cam pressed his lips together against the laugh fighting up his throat. Then he let it go because why not?

Victor laughed with him while he picked up his sketch pad. "I suppose I should get my money's worth before you get totally pissed off and leave. Would you be comfortable removing your shirt?"

Cam put his hands to the hem of his T-shirt and stopped. Eyed Victor. "Ah, fuck it." He pulled the shirt over his head and tossed it onto the easel closest to him. "How do you want me to stand."

"That's great."

Cam glanced down at his pose. He had his legs slightly apart, hips square to Victor, one hand tucked against his hip, the other dangling. Huh. Weird.

"Chin up?" Victor made an upward motion with his free hand.

Cam lifted his chin.

"Look at me."

"Not a good idea."

Victor's grin was sly. "I know."

The push-pull of attraction between them only intensified as Cam met Victor's gaze. Breathing became a conscious effort, and Cam could feel every heartbeat. Then not as he once again imagined the feel of Victor's mouth.

Victor's gaze flipped away, to his sketch. Up, then back down.

Cam thought about what he'd taste like—beer or wine or the salad stuff he'd put together for their dinner. Peppers, tomatoes . . . Did they have a flavor that lingered? Beets. Who the hell put beets in salad? They'd been good, though. White beans, pecans, lettuce, shredded purple cabbage, and spinach. It'd been the healthiest damn meal Cam had eaten in a month.

No wonder Victor seemed effortlessly lithe. Not skinny, not exercised to a scrawny leanness. But slender. Toned. When not taking a week's vacation inside a wine bottle, Victor obviously looked after himself.

With an odd flash of something, Cam decided he admired that.

"Turn your head to the left?"

Cam turned. When his shoulders moved to follow him around, he asked, "Like this?"

"I want to see the movement on your right side. Over your ribs. Can you lift your arm forward a little? Perfect, thank you."

Victor had him adjust his stance a few more times before he folded the top of the sketch pad back over and set it down. "Okay, I'm done. For now."

Cam relaxed. Rolled his shoulders. "For now?"

"I'd like to do this again."

"Uh-huh." Once more, Cam fought his attraction to this man. Why did he want to flirt so badly? They weren't . . . they couldn't . . .

They shouldn't. Enough said.

"But we could," Victor said quietly.

Cam shook his head. "Don't do that. It's creepy."

"Tell me you haven't been thinking about pushing me up against a wall since you got in here and I'll say I haven't been imagining it either. Or what you taste like. The sounds you might make."

"Fuck."

"Are you not . . ." Compassion creased Victor's brow. "Does your sexuality make you uncomfortable?"

"What? No. I know who I am and what I want."

"I thought that maybe having served in the military, you might be less inclined to—"

"That's not it."

Somehow, they'd drifted across the studio toward one another again and were standing by the table where Victor had put his pad. Cam on one side of a corner, Victor on the other. In the quiet lulls between their conversation, the house had creaked and Honey had snored. This pause felt loud. As though the words they didn't voice crowded unseen edges.

"I told you. I'm not about conversation and commitment." Cam kept his voice low.

Just as quietly, Victor said, "Maybe that's not what I'm looking for."

Scoffing, Cam managed a backward step. "Yeah, right."

Victor stepped toward his side of the corner. "What are you so afraid of?"

Breath caught in Cam's throat. Sirens seemed to ring in his ears. "Nothing. I am afraid of exactly nothing." He felt his shoulders draw up. "If you'd seen what I've seen, man. You'd know."

Victor immediately dropped back. "Cam, I'm sorry."

"No, don't." Cam shook his head. "*I'm* sorry. I shouldn't have brought that here. Used it."

"I pushed too hard. It's my fault."

"I led you into it. I shouldn't have."

Sighing, Victor glanced over his shoulder and retreated toward his stool. He sat heavily.

Cam grabbed his T-shirt from the easel. He had it halfway over his head before he remembered it wasn't his. As he pulled it back off, he caught the scent of Victor's soap and cologne. The detergent he used. Longing hit him square in the chest. His body almost vibrated with the need not just to fuck but to be with. To spend a night wrapped in a scent and to wake up with it. To smell it on his own skin.

Melancholy got him next. A deeper yearning. He knew, without thinking about it, that Victor could give him what he wanted. What he'd always wanted.

But for how long? When would fate take it all away?

It was better to be the one that left.

Better to always be leaving.

"I should go." Cam held out the shirt like an offering.

Victor eased off the stool. "Your clothes are probably dry." They'd moved them from the washer after eating.

While Cam dressed, Victor took Honey out onto the lawn "Just in case."

Then they helped her into the back seat of Victor's small SUV and took their places up front.

"Where to?" Victor asked.

Cam supplied his address, and the drive passed in relative quiet except for the annoying whine every time Victor turned the wheels past thirty degrees.

"You need to check the power steering fluid. You might have a leak," Cam said when they pulled up in front of his house.

Victor glanced over at him, mouth slightly open.

"The whine," Cam said. "When you turn?"

"How did you know that?"

"It's what I did in the army. I was a mechanic."

"Why don't you do that now?"

"I prefer digging holes." He still liked fixing cars, but the smell of engine oil and grease often took him to places he didn't want to go. To the couple of years before the end, working happily and quietly side by side with the soldier who'd been a brother to him. And then to that day, that awful day when he'd lost another person he had loved.

"Cameron."

Cam glanced over at Victor's shadowy silhouette. "Yeah?"

Victor had apparently watched as Cam strolled along memory lane. His expression was now guarded but not unfriendly. All traces of flirtation had been packed away. "Thank you for this evening. It may not have felt like it, but I accomplished a lot. Drawing-wise."

"Okay."

"I'd love you to model for me again, but I'll understand if you don't want to. The offer is there, nonetheless. I'd also like your help with a gardening project. If you'd be interested."

"You don't—"

"I've long wanted to cut a path through the trees at the front of my property. Down to the road, following the driveway. With steps." Victor gestured toward the three short steps Cam had dug into the slope from the front lawn to the mailbox. Cam had framed them out with wood before filling them in and planting around them, giving the impression that the steps had occurred naturally or had always been there.

"Getting down to my mailbox in winter can be treacherous," Victor continued. "A path would be easier to navigate. More protected from the snow as well."

Cam turned back to Victor. "There are other people. Real landscapers who—"

Victor touched his hand. Cam controlled the urge to flinch. The following urge to cover Victor's hand with his.

"I'd enjoy planning the project with you. You're easy to work with. I'd like . . . for us to be friends," Victor said.

Cam exhaled into the warming atmosphere of the car. With the engine off, the A/C had stopped humming. Friends wasn't a good idea, but . . . "Sure. We can do that."

Victor smiled.

Cam nearly leaned in to kiss it from his lips. Instead, he moved in the other direction and opened the door. Slowly, he withdrew his hand from beneath Victor's. Then, not quite understanding what he was doing, he made a soft fist and nudged Victor's upper arm.

Victor's wan smile said he understood.

"Call me with the details," Cam said as he got out of the car.

"I still don't have your number. Only the tree farm."

Cam reached into the back seat to encourage Honey onto the sidewalk. He offered Victor a playful smile. "Guess I'll be the one calling you, then."

Chapter Sixteen

Victor finally found a parking spot off 8th Street, and after reassessing the moody sky, he reached back into the car for his umbrella. The four-block walk to the restaurant where he and Tez met for their regular lunch date passed in a blur of familiarity and memory. He hadn't grown up in Stroudsburg, but the town had become a second home when Tez had moved down here.

He stepped inside the tiny Italian bistro right as the wind picked up, and closed the door as rain began to patter against the pavement outside. The aroma of garlic and tomatoes quickly squashed the dusty wet scent of the turning weather, but Victor had already tucked it away. He loved that smell and had been trying for years to capture it in a painting.

Tez waved from a table along the wall of the narrow restaurant, and Victor wended his way down the center aisle to join her, stooping to kiss her cheek before claiming his seat.

After greetings were exchanged and drink orders taken, Tez leaned across the table. "How are you, really?"

Victor narrowed his eyes at his best friend. "Just fine. Really." He waved at the server's retreating back. "I ordered the lemonade." Elderflower rose lemonade, to be precise. He ordered it every time he and Tez visited this restaurant.

"You're not still bulldozing your way through the wine cellar, then?"

"When did we get a wine cellar?" Victor asked.

"You didn't put one in after I moved out? I naturally assumed that's what you would do with my bedroom."

"Your bedroom is not subterranean. And I don't drink enough wine to warrant a cellar." Not usually. "Also, as you well know, I have maintained your room as a shrine to the mother of my children."

"Our children."

"Yes, dear."

They shared a laugh. Then, leaning back in her chair, Tez folded her arms. "How's work, then?"

"Ugh, can we talk about you?"

"We can most definitely talk about me." Tez pulled a purse the size of a suitcase onto the table and rummaged through it until she found her phone, which she produced with an "Aha!" A moment later, she thrust the screen at him, and Victor was confronted with a shoulders-up photo of a lovely woman with creamy skin, auburn curls, and a cheeky smile. The lines about her eyes and mouth indicated her age, which would be in their neighborhood. She obviously took better care of herself than he did, though.

Victor glanced up at Tez and feigned being blinded by her glow. With a hand in front of his eyes, he said, "Have you been on a date, yet?"

"No." Tez was now mooning over the photo. "We're still chatting. But we're chatting well, if you know what I mean."

"I don't."

"We're already getting deep and meaningful."

Victor squashed the urge to be anything but excited for her. They'd both had such poor luck in love. Maybe this time it would work out for the woman he loved not-like-a-sister-because-that-would-be-weird. But loved all the same. He gripped the hand she had resting on the table. "Thinking good thoughts for you."

The server returned with their drinks and they ordered lunch. An appetizer to share, though they'd both complain about how much they'd eaten later, stuffed ravioli for Tez and a hearty eggplant parmigiana for Victor, half of which he planned to take home for dinner. Whether that happened would depend on how distracted they got. He had a terrible habit of overeating with Tez.

"Thank you." Tez handed their menus to the server and turned to Victor. "Now, what about you? Are you back out there yet?"

"Dear lord, no. It's only been, what, three weeks?"

"But you were over Tholo months ago."

"In my mind, yes. But perhaps not my heart. Or maybe it was the other way around." Victor probed his feelings—in particular whether or not he wanted to start dating again—and discovered only weariness *and* a desire to invite a certain person over for several rounds of rejuvenating sex. Huh. Not that his desire to sleep with Cam was a surprise. That he could consider doing so without planning the rest of their relationship was, however.

Perhaps Cam had been wrong.

But when Victor slotted Cam into the role of a rebound remedy, his newfound aversion to attachment fell apart. Sex would only be the beginning, and Victor most definitely was not ready to start anything.

"Earth to Victor." Tez tapped the back of his hand.

"Sorry, I apparently had a little thinking to do."

"About whom?"

"How do you know it wasn't a what?"

"Because you look like Dexter does when you let him drink the milk out of your cereal bowl. If you'd started licking your lips, I was going to have to smack you."

Victor chuckled. "No, I was thinking about . . ." He bit his lip. Should he tell Tez about Cam? If he did, he'd have to update her on the full story as it unfolded.

"Who is he and where did you meet him?" Tez asked.

Letting out a sigh, Victor pulled out his phone. "He's . . . Don't laugh, okay? Not a single wicked chuckle."

Tez used her hands to squash her cheeks inward.

"Stop that."

She grinned.

Victor scrolled to one of the detailed sketches he'd started, using the studies from Cam's session and the few photos he'd snapped before they finished. Although terribly out of practice when it came to faces—to people, to detail—he liked the way this piece was shaping up. Of course, he had absolutely no idea what he'd do with it. Whether he'd attempt to paint Cam or confine his interest to a series of drawings.

He showed the picture to Tez and watched as her smile narrowed and disappeared.

Was that good or bad?

"Vic," she breathed.

"I think I've made him more attractive than he is." He angled the phone back in his direction. "I haven't quite captured his nose. It should be crooked. And his eyes aren't even. His face is almost too angular, you know? Which makes it hard to draw—"

"No, yes, sure, all of that. But the drawing is stunning! I didn't know you were drawing people again." She shot him a carefully questioning look.

Victor drew in a shallow breath. "I'm not, not really."

"Remember all those portraits you did in Brooklyn?"

With a slow wave, Victor cast a deliberate haze over the years they'd spent in the city. "I remember painting some rather terrible portraits. They were in the style of my landscapes. Too abstract for recognition. I always thought I needed to make them smaller, for the detail, but I wanted to paint big. Either way, they were terrible."

With the exception of the piece upon which the pendulum of his future had unknowingly swung. Objectively, Victor knew the painting had had nothing to do with his father's death, but the timing had been uncanny. And he'd put so much of himself into every single stroke. Every thread of color had been a connection between him and the most sincere and gentle man he'd known.

"The sketches you did for them were always spot on, though," Tez was saying. "Just gorgeous. I was sorry you stopped drawing that way." She gripped his hand. "I know portraiture is tied to the loss of someone so dear to you, but I always felt that was why you should explore it. Because it makes you feel."

"I think I already feel entirely too much." Victor checked the screen of his phone again. Tapped it when it started to dim. It *was* a more than competent drawing. Despite the defects, he knew who it was, and Cam would probably recognize himself. But when he looked deeper, he saw what Tez saw. The lines and the shading, the way he'd successfully molded Cam out of paper, drawing him from the blankness that was white pulp to give him life. The eyes, though not properly spaced, danced with merriment and secrets. The slight uptilt of lips hinted at a joke waiting to be told. Even the angle of Cam's jaw and chin were there.

It was a *good* drawing. It almost lived and breathed.

Licking his lips, Victor met Tez's gaze. "I didn't consciously stop drawing. I still sketch out my landscapes. Several times, as you know. But you're right. This is different." He frowned. "The same in a way, in that I'm trying to capture his living face. Him as an alive being. Not a moment in time, but who he is." Which was what he liked to do when he painted. Not just capture scenery but life. The feeling of being there; the brush of wind against skin, the scent of newly green leaves. Or the sharp tannin of fall foliage. The brackishness of a creek along with the lap and trickle of the water running over round boulders and skipping down a waterfall. Life.

"Who is he?" Tez asked.

"Cameron Zimmermann."

Her forehead wrinkled. "Any relation to Nicholas?"

"Yes! His brother."

"I didn't know Nick had a brother."

"I did, though I hadn't remembered. He was two years below us in school."

Tez snatched the phone. "No." She woke the screen using his password, stared at the picture, and shook her head. "Nope. I don't recognize him. Except to say he does look a little like Nick? I don't spend a lot of time checking out men, though." She handed the phone back. "How did you meet?"

"He's working for Shepard's. He delivered the mulch and trees I ordered to spruce up the patio for Billy's birthday."

"The mulch that's still in your driveway?"

"Oh, no, it's spread now. And the trees are planted. Cam did it for me. Well, I helped with the trees."

Eyes narrowing, Tez put her elbows on the table and cupped her chin with her palms. "I'm sensing a story."

"There's a lot of story. Too much for one lunch." He waved her back.

Tez might have refused, but their appetizer had arrived. They ate for a moment, scooping chopped tomato, onion, and herbs onto perfectly toasted rounds of bread.

After demolishing his share, Victor dabbed his mouth with a corner of the napkin and reached for his drink. "You know, every time we eat here, I swear I'm going to plant some tomatoes. They're so good in season."

"Where would you put them?"

"I'm half tempted to say everywhere. In between flowers in the beds. I already have herbs all over the place, which I both love and hate. They keep the deer away from the flowers, but I always liked the idea of having a dedicated herb garden. Where would I put a dedicated vegetable garden, do you think?"

In the middle of the discussion about the best location for a patch of vegetables, Victor's phone rang. He glanced at the screen and smiled. Shepard's Tree Farm.

"Do you want to answer that?" Tez said.

"Would you mind? I'll be quick."

She nodded and he took the call.

"Hey," Cam said. "Is this a good time?"

"I'm actually at lunch. I'd ask if I could call you back, but I still don't have your number."

"It's cool. I wanted to see if you'd be home on Friday afternoon. Later. Say, six or six thirty? I'm booked to mow in your neighborhood and can stop by afterward to look at this path project."

"Works for me. Bring your appetite. I'll cook."

"You don't have to—"

"I don't mind."

"Okay. I'll bring beer."

"Perfect. See you then." After ending the call, Victor noted Tez's *Aww* expression. "Stop that."

"You like him."

"Yes, I do. But he's not interested. And his reasons are sound." He put the phone aside. "I'm incapable of just sleeping with someone. I always want to make a relationship out of the most unremarkable meetings."

"I love that about you, though. You make your lovers feel special."

"And look where it's gotten me. Fifty-two and still single."

"Be fair to yourself, Victory. We both spent a good decade being little other than parents, and our situation can be weird for some people."

Thinking on Tez's own string of failed relationships, Victor reached for her hand. "Do you regret it?"

"Not for a minute," she answered quickly and decisively.

He squeezed her fingers. "Me neither. Our children are beautiful people."

"They are."

Their meals arrived and they returned to the topic of Victor's vegetable garden while they ate. As predicted, Victor finished his plate and barely had the strength to stop himself from ordering more bread to mop up the sauce. He reclined in his seat and patted his rounded gut. "I don't think I'll need dinner."

"I never do when we have lunch here. I sort of count on it, actually. Not having to cook or bother about eating again. I can go home, put my feet up, and digest."

Victor laughed. "Sounds very middle-aged and kind of perfect."

She grinned. "Tell me about the sketches. Cam agreed to model for you?"

"He did."

"Are you thinking of doing something other than landscapes next? After your show."

All of Victor's good cheer swirled into a muddy puddle. "I'm not doing the show."

"Whyever not?"

"They bumped me." Now he wished he'd ordered wine. A drink would feel good right about now. "For an emerging artist."

"They what? But you've been at that gallery for years. Surely they can't do that."

"My agent says they can. My last couple of shows haven't met the contracted terms, which they were apparently content to let slide until they found someone to take my place."

"Victor—"

Holding up a hand, he shook his head. "I'm still working through it and trying not to turn your room into a wine cellar in the process. Can we talk about something else?"

"How are your summer classes coming along?"

He breathed out a sigh. "I've been wondering whether the kids are simply there out of habit. I need to change my lesson plans. Explore new territory. I have a student who is currently homeless, by the way. They have somewhere to stay for now, but as you know that could change quickly. Keep an ear out for a couple of good spots? One year left of high school. If we can get them past that, they'll have a wider array of opportunities."

"Of course. You're not thinking of housing them, are you?"

"I'm keeping a room put aside, in case."

"I'm not sure that'd be a good idea. You've got so much going on. Are you sure you're okay? I worry about you. You're drawing portraits, again, of a man you want. You're still angry over Tholo, *and* reevaluating your career. It's a lot, Vic. Do you think you should call your therapist?"

"Sage already asked. I'm fine. I spent a week feeling sorry for myself after I chose to throw Tholo out on his ass, but after hearing about the show, I didn't fall back into the bottle. I've been doing my best to remain constructive." He tapped his phone. "Hence all these sketches."

"Just try not to get fixated."

Only Tez could say that and not flinch. And not fear his reaction.

Victor sighed and then produced a smile that felt weak. "I asked Cam if we could be friends, and I honestly think that's for the best. He's right, you're right. Everyone is right. I promise I'll take it easy. Not leap before I look and all that."

Tez had his hand again, and for a moment, he missed her. The life they'd built together for all those years. No, they hadn't shared a bed. Not for sex, anyway. But they had slept to either side of their children on many occasions, and they'd often curled up together to talk. He missed having a constant. A companion for his soul.

No regrets. None.

She squeezed his fingers. "Keep sketching, then. What you showed me is amazing, Victor. Really strong work. Fresh and vibrant. So like you, but new too. Maybe that's what Cam is here for. To inspire you artistically."

Finding a better smile for her, Victor lifted Tez's hand and kissed her knuckles. "Maybe."

Chapter Seventeen

C am was wrestling with the laptop Emma had gifted her penniless uncle when she'd started her second year of college. She'd bought herself a new and improved model, slightly larger, but oddly lighter. And the keyboard lit up like a rainbow. Pretty, but even glowing keys wouldn't help him with the message currently blocking the screen of her cast-off piece of junk.

Input what software key? It'd been working last week. Why did he suddenly need a key?

Maybe the new and improved, rainbow-keyed laptop didn't need keys.

"Fine."

From under the table, Honey huffed. Probably a yawn, but Cam reached down to ruffle her ears. "I know. Stupid computer."

Honey gave another huff and flopped her chin back over his socked feet. She had taken to following him from room to room so she could lie with some part of her extended over some part of him. At first Cam had found this odd. He was so used to being alone. Now he welcomed her company.

He canceled out of the program and searched for another. He just wanted to make a list. One he could rearrange and assign dates to. Maybe add a scheduling sort of affair. He and Jorge were taking on more garden maintenance and landscaping jobs each week, and Cam woke up every morning panicking that he'd forgotten something.

Maybe he could use the calendar? Plug all the details in there? Sync the contacts from his phone?

Hmm . . .

The chime of his cell phone interrupted his musing. Absently, Cam scooped it off the table. "Hello."

"Mr. Zimmermann?"

Uh-oh. Calls that began with *Mr. Zimmermann* rarely brought good news. "Speaking." Cam pulled the phone from his ear to see if Verizon had matched the number to a contact yet. It had not.

"Hi, I'm calling from Milford Animal Hospital. We've had an inquiry about your dog. The dog you found. Someone who believes she might be their dog."

A pit didn't actually open up in Cam's middle, but he felt hollow all the same. As though someone had scooped a big old hand through his midsection and taken out everything that had mattered.

"Are you there?" the now faraway voice asked.

Cam looked down at Honey, who was gazing up at him. Her eyes reflected the confusing sorrow he felt. "Yeah," he said into the phone. "I'm here."

"Would you be available to bring her by the office?"

"Now?"

"If you have time."

Cam checked the microwave display. Five thirty. His only plan for the evening had been to figure out a scheduling mechanism, eat the rotisserie chicken he'd bought on the way home, and queue up a movie or two. Or three. Why not take a trip into Milford to give away his only happiness?

Maybe we should schedule some time to brood over why you're not happy.

Shut up.

"Yeah, sure. I can come now. I'll be there in a few."

After coaxing Honey into the back seat of the car (repaired once again, but wheezing oddly every time he approached the top of a hill), Cam ran back into the house for her favorite blanket and the two toys he'd picked up for her. She seemed to like the fuzzy banana with the dangling rope legs best. She carried it upstairs every night to bed. Well, he carried it. And her. With her cast, it took her nearly ten minutes to hobble up the stairs—a fact he'd discovered one night after hearing a sound by the front door. When he'd gone to investigate, he'd found Honey halfway to the top, the banana clamped in her jaws.

Back at the car, Cam sat behind the wheel and stared through the open garage door. If he drove all night, he could make Indianapolis by dawn. He and Honey could simply disappear. Tour the open road. Not that Emma's car would make it to the other side of Pennsylvania.

"Damn it." He started the car and sped out of the driveway. Best to do this quickly. Rip off the bandage before he felt the pain. Except he was already feeling it. "Damn. It."

At the animal hospital, Cam carried Honey, her blanket, and her banana inside. He spotted them right away, the couple who'd lost her. Amiable-looking folks. He turned toward them and watched hope brighten their faces like a sunrise. Any minute now, Honey would try to leap from his arms. He tightened his grip a little. Wouldn't do for her to break another leg.

When he reached the couple, Cam squatted down to let Honey loose. She hopped to the floor and looked up at him, and he handed her the banana, which she dutifully took in her mouth. Cam stood and mustered a smile. It felt like one of his brother's. Lopsided and awkward.

The receptionist had rounded the desk to crouch by Honey and was enthusiastically stroking her ears. "You're such a good girl," she crooned. "So sweet."

She sure was.

The vet who'd fixed up her leg arrived, all smiles.

Sick of the stretched elastic feel of his own mouth, Cam prepared to make his exit. He glanced at the couple.

They weren't smiling.

This time, the mysterious hand that scooped out the insides of sad people seemed to sweep the room. Everyone lost their happiness all at once. Even Honey, who'd been enjoying the sudden attention.

"It's not her?" the vet asked.

They shook their heads.

Cam's knees trembled. Two weeks. He'd had this dog for two freaking weeks. What was he going to do if another two weeks passed before her owners turned up? He looked to the couple in quiet appeal. The woman met his gaze and shook her head, but gently, as though she understood exactly what he was feeling. Then she crouched to get in on all the petting.

"She's a sweetheart. What do you call her?"

"Ho-ney." Cam's voice caught halfway through.

"Perfect."

Conversation continued, with Cam only half-aware. The vet took a few minutes to examine Honey's cast. "While she's here." He checked the muscles above, her shoulder joints, and her other legs and pronounced her fit and healing nicely. "Let her walk a little more if you can. Not too far."

Then Cam was back behind the wheel, Honey in the back seat, both of them sitting there, contemplating the drive to Indianapolis.

"I don't know why that'd be our first stop, except I've never been there."

Honey huffed.

Cam drove home.

Nick's truck was parked in the driveway, and there was a shadow behind the wheel. Bizarrely, only an hour had passed since Cam had left. The afternoon seemed barely to have aged, the midsummer sunlight only now starting to dull toward evening. But the phone call might have been a year ago. Man, he was tired. Maybe he'd be able to sleep tonight without the sound of the TV.

Nick hopped out of his truck as Cam was carrying Honey back out of the garage. He broke into a smile at the sight of her. "When did you get a dog? What happened to her leg?"

"I found her on the side of the road one night. She'd been clipped by a car. I just got back from meeting with some folks who might have been her people, but they weren't."

"Oh." Nick's face shifted into processing mode. "You're taking care of her for now, then?"

"Yeah."

"It'll suck when her people turn up."

"Yeah." Cam nodded toward the house. "You could have gone in. You didn't have to wait out here."

"I just got here. I was about to call you."

"Okay." Cam led the way to the door. Rather than put Honey down, he handed Nick his keys. "She can walk, but stairs are hard for her."

"Okay." Nick let them into the house and immediately looked around. "Oh, wow, you repainted in here. It's so much brighter!"

Last year, Cam and Nick had made a lot of improvements to the house they'd grown up in. It had been a bittersweet journey, replacing windows, tearing out bathrooms, hanging new curtains, refinishing the kitchen. At times, Cam had felt as though they were ripping up pieces of their childhood. But after the death of their sister, Nick had let the house—already old—begin to fall apart around him. The work had needed to be done.

Cam had never liked the color they chose for the hallway that formed the connective tissue of the entire house, though. They'd picked blue for Emma. But it had always felt temporary, as though the walls were simply testing the color out. So, he'd painted again. Downstairs and upstairs.

He smiled at the dove gray walls. "It's the original color if you can believe it. But three and a half decades fresher. I also repainted the stair rails using a softer white. Less glare and less prone to show wear." With the dark wood of the stair risers, the combination was homey.

"I like it."

"Come check out the kitchen." Cam deposited Honey onto the floor and tossed her blanket over the chair closest to the family room door before hurrying his brother toward the back of the house. "I finally replaced the fridge."

Proudly, he opened the shiny stainless door to display his sweating roasted chicken, tub of mashed potatoes, and six-pack of beer. There wasn't a lot else to dull the bright white of the new interior, easily seen through the clean glass shelves.

"Nice," Nick agreed before running his finger over the countertops and cabinets they'd refinished together. He cocked his head at the wall beside the fridge. "You painted in here too."

"Yeah. The white felt too clinical. I think the green looks good against the windows. Especially now, with the garden in bloom."

Nick checked the windows overlooking the backyard. Cam waited for the flinch. His brother had a complicated relationship with the backyard. He'd been unable to venture out there for three years after Rebecca had died. But now, he turned and showed Cam one of his more relaxed smiles. "It all looks great."

"Thanks." Cam gestured toward the fridge again. "Want a drink while you're here? Water, beer? I can put on some coffee."

"I just came to drop off the truck." Nick dug keys out of his pocket and put them on the kitchen table, next to the laptop.

Distractedly, Cam noticed the screen was blank and wondered whether he'd turned it off before taking Honey over to the vet. If not, he'd have to dig out the cord and charge the damn thing back up again. He checked back in with Nick, who was watching him with an expectant expression.

"Why are you dropping off the truck?" Cam asked.

"Because you need it more than I do right now."

"I do?"

"For your landscaping and garden maintenance business."

Cam felt his jaw unhinge. "You can't give me your truck."

"Yes, I can."

"But, Nick. You need it to deliver your houses. Plus, it's *your* truck."

"I can use Oliver's van."

"But—"

"How else are you going to transport the equipment you'll need?"

Thankfully, most the clients he'd picked up thus far had their own mowers and trimmers, and he and Jorge had managed the six-acre job with the equipment they already owned. The guy who'd wanted the land cleared had seemed a little surprised when Cam had shown up with a weed whacker and a wheelbarrow wedged into the trunk of Emma's car. Jorge's beast of a vehicle had room for a mower and another trimmer, but it had been a less-than-professional look.

Regardless, they got the job done. But if he and Jorge planned to grow the business, they would need better vehicles and equipment. Thing was, if they made that sort of commitment, then, well, they'd be making that sort of commitment. And, to Cam, *commitment* was a dirty word. No, a scary one.

He and Jorge should have a conversation. One where both of them talked.

Studying the keys, Cam chewed thoughtfully on his lip. Then he searched his brother's face for what he'd never find. Nick didn't have an ulterior motive. A hidden agenda. He simply wanted to help.

And, hell, if the whole business failed—it was bound to, wasn't it?—Cam could give the truck back.

Stepping in, Cam lifted his hands in a gentle warning and then pulled his brother into a hug. Kissed the side of his head. "Love you, little bro."

Nick folded his arms around Cam's back. "I love you too."

Cam let him go. "Give me a minute to let Honey water the lawn and I'll drive you home."

Nick nodded toward the fridge. "Maybe we *could* have that beer together first?"

The hollow inside, the chasm that had opened up at a single phone call and developed into some sort of permanent canyon during the drive to and from the vet's office, began to fill. The sides closed in and the pit lost its depth. The night didn't feel as endless, and Indiana was now farther away than Cam wanted to drive in a single stint.

"Want to sit outside?" Cam asked. "You need to catch me up on your proposal plans."

Nick cocked his head. "Do people like public proposals? Like at stadiums and theaters? Or does that only happen in movies?"

Trying not to wince, Cam waved his brother toward the patio. "You'd better tell me what you have planned."

Chapter Eighteen

Victor hummed as he released the lid on the slow cooker. Steam curled up from the dark, rich chili, carrying the aroma of black beans and the sweet and spicy sauce. Stomach rumbling, he stirred in the chopped chipotle pepper and replaced the lid. The best part of Crock-Pot cooking was also the worst: smelling dinner all day.

A knock sounded at the front door. Victor tugged at his apron, pulling it off and using it to wipe his hands at the same time, then tossed it over the back of one of the chairs on his way to the door.

Cam wore his usual smile: happy with an almost sardonic twist, as though he saw the lighter side of life but didn't always feel welcome there. Honey was hobbling up the couple of steps behind him, and in the driveway sat a shiny silver pickup.

"New truck?"

"It's my brother's."

"Ah." Victor bent to greet Honey. "Hello, there. How's the leg today?"

"Vet said she can get some extra exercise."

"Good for you," Victor told the dog. Then he straightened and returned Cam's smile. "Hi."

Inexplicably, Cam's cheeks pinked. Just a little. "What smells good?"

"Oh, that's dinner. If you want to stay."

"Maybe." Cam squinted skyward. "Looking like it might rain again. We should check out the path, or where you want to put it."

"Do you— Ah, yes, of course." When had he become this awkward?

"Honey, stay," Cam directed.

The dog flopped down on the stoop, legs splayed inelegantly beneath her, and dropped her chin onto her cast.

Victor pulled the front door closed and followed Cam across the circle at the top of the driveway.

"Isn't all this gravel a pain in the winter? For plowing?" Cam asked.

"It is, but the driveway is so long. It would cost a fortune to have it paved." Victor's art allowed him to live comfortably by any standard, but every winter, he compared the twenty grand estimate for paving with the five-hundred-dollar snow removal service and chose the cheaper way out. He didn't have to drive the plow, after all. He just had to rake gravel out of the beds and off the lawn come spring.

"I can see that. So, where do you want this path?"

Gesturing, Victor broke into the wooded acre between the front of the house and the road. "Anywhere in here. I thought it might be nice to have it wander a little. Back and forth with wide, shallow steps."

"Like a switchback down a mountain."

"Yes, but maybe not as tight as that? I haven't decided yet whether I'll plant around it or encourage the ferns back in."

They'd reached the top of the slope, before the land tipped sharply down toward Raymondskill Road. Cam paused there, hands on hips, and surveyed the forest. He looked up, through the tops of the trees and Victor followed his gaze. Even in the middle of the day, it would be darker here, quieter when the road lay quiet. With rain clouds building castles over their heads, evening had come early.

The wind kicked up, pushing from the northwest, and Victor watched as the trees rustled and undulated in a wave across his property, swayed by the freshening breeze but almost seeming to follow it at the same time. That was what he'd wanted to capture in paint. The way air could ripple through a scene as though it were a living entity.

"I love the way the wind does that, or the trees," Cam said. Victor glanced over at him, surprised. Cam smiled. "I watch it from the patio behind my house. The wind. It flows along the creek like it's following the water."

"Nature is . . ." Victor wanted to mark the occasion with profound words, but the moment—both of them standing at the top of a short hill, surrounded by tall trees and whispering leaves—felt deep enough. Special, in a way. And if he didn't shake it off, he might do something stupid. Clearing his throat, he wrestled his thoughts back to . . . where? The path. "Do you think a short terrace would work here?" He looked toward the house, barely visible through the trees. "We could clear a little to this point. That dead tree has to go anyway, and maybe the one next to it. A spot of light, a small garden. Lilies along the path, a rhododendron where that tree was . . ."

Victor continued to point out the markers of his imagination, and Cam nodded along, adding a comment here and there as they tackled the slope, both of them sidestepping down the steepest part. Together, they mapped a tentative path to the road, one that curved back toward the mailbox after the last bend.

"A couple of steps down to the road?" Cam suggested. He had his phone out. He'd snapped a couple of pictures, mostly where they'd decided the path should turn. He showed Victor the screen. "How's this?"

Victor's lips parted. There, on the phone, was a map. A jagged red line crisscrossed the top half and Raymondskill Road scored a line across the bottom. "How did you do that?"

"GPS. I tracked our walk. We wandered a bit near a couple of turns, but this should do for a start. Help us figure out how much gravel we'll need. Wood for the frame. I was thinking old railway sleepers. We could get them for next to nothing, and they're solid enough to last generations. What?"

Victor had not managed to close his mouth. In fact, his lips only moved farther apart as Cam talked. "You're a natural at this."

The pink returned to Cam's cheeks. He ducked his head and shrugged. "It's just logic."

"No, it's not. I'd *never* have thought to map it out like that. You're a genius."

Cam laughed. "Sure."

"I love the idea of using railway sleepers, by the way. Railways are such a storied part of local history."

"They are that."

Victor gazed back up the slope, intending to muse over how the path would look when it was done, but he could barely see between the trees. He checked the sky again, the corridor of cloud over the road, and did not like what he saw.

"We should start heading back up."

Cam followed his gaze. "Yeah."

Thunder boomed in the distance, and Victor indicated with a hand-wave they should hop down to the trench that served as a gutter on this side of the road. "And we should take the driveway this time."

"Definitely."

The wind gusted sharply, icy fingers pushing at their backs, and thunder rolled closer. Then the rain happened, as though a trapdoor had swung open to release all the water in the sky at once. Lightning arced overhead, disappearing somewhere behind the next curve of the driveway. Likely miles behind the house, but out here, with the wind threatening to drive them through the rain, it seemed closer.

Victor shook off a shiver and ran. Cam's rapid footfalls crunched beside him, the sound nearly obscured by the sudden storm. Victor led the chase into the next turn and veered too close to the side of the drive. When his foot slid into a rut, he tilted sideways, and a firm hand caught his elbow, yanking him upright.

"Thanks," he panted.

He could have shaken Cam off at that point. Cam could have let go. But they ran on that way, with Cam holding his arm, until they rounded the final curve and spilled out into the circle at the top of the driveway. Honey stood in the doorway, yipping softly. Cam let go of Victor's arm and broke across the gravel with an extra burst of speed. He stopped long enough to scoop up his dog and then pushed through the front door.

Victor followed, and the wind sucked the door out of his hand, slamming it closed.

Shit, that meant the kitchen windows were open.

From somewhere inside the house, Dexter wailed. Honey yelped back.

"I have to close the windows in the kitchen." Victor took off in that direction, his feet squelching, his clothes—chosen so carefully for this . . . this . . . whatever this was—flapping wetly around him. Cam appeared no better off, his green Shepard's polo plastered to his skin, his jeans a darker shade of indigo. Muddy puddles spread from his boots. "I've got some towels in the laundry," Victor added.

He ran into the kitchen and spied a wet black cat engaged in a furious bath by the door. "Get caught outside, Sin?"

Sinister didn't deign to respond.

Cam chuckled at the sight, and Honey padded over to the scraggly cat. Sinister paid no attention to the dog, either, as if acknowledging Honey would make her real. Apparently stumped, Honey sat in the middle of the kitchen floor and thumped her little tail.

Victor started on one side of the kitchen, pulling the windows closed. Cam began on the other side. They met in the middle, both of them standing in puddles of rain that had blown inside. "Good thing you have a tile floor," Cam murmured, looking down at their feet.

"Yep." Victor chose to look down also—away from Cam's shoulders, broad chest, his Adam's apple, a chin darkened by stubble. His mouth. Taking a step backward, Victor pointed toward the laundry. "In here. I can grab those sweats again if you want to change out of your wet clothes."

Cam's gaze traveled the length of Victor's body, leaving a heated flush, and then a chill. A half smile crooked one side of his mouth. "Sure."

Rather than trail water all the way upstairs, Victor followed Cam into the laundry. He'd grab a towel first. The room was long and narrow, the washer and dryer side by side, with a shelf above.

Folding closet doors covered the opposite wall, ending in an alcove for the fuse box and generator connections.

"The dryer is . . ." Victor gestured toward the second unit.

Cam flattened himself against the wall so Victor could pass. But when Victor was in front of him, their chests an inch apart, their thighs almost touching, Cam put a hand to his shoulder. Victor looked up, his eyes once again level with Cam's chin. His lips.

"What smells so good?" Cam asked.

"You stopped me here, right here, to ask what smells so good?" Victor said to Cam's chin, his mouth. He glanced up.

Cam's eyes glinted in the sketchy light. "No. I . . . Yes. Jesus, Vic."

He grabbed Vic's other shoulder and held him in place—the space between them now not enough to slide a piece of paper through. The laundry was not a party room. But with Cam in front of him, his body heat evident through their wet clothes, Victor's libido was already sliding into disco mode.

When Cam dipped his chin, Victor lifted his.

He expected Cam's kiss to be rough and urgent. For his mouth to crash down and claim. For there to be a loss of control, however slight. Any kiss would definitely signal a loosening of both their wills. Instead, Cam's lips brushed his. Once, then again. He exhaled, his breath hot. He dripped, water from his hair dappling the side of Victor's face.

Victor was the one who pulled them closer.

With a groan, he tucked one hand behind Cam's head and drew him down so their lips meshed together properly. So the kiss could deepen, broaden, grow to encompass the entirety of Victor's world. The firmness of Cam's lips, the taste of rain, the scent of his soap and deodorant, the musk of sweat beneath. The prickle of his stubble—and then the gentle insistence of his tongue.

It was only when Victor let his hips rock forward, another groan tearing free, that he remembered this wasn't supposed to happen. But Cam felt so good against him. Hard and warm. Giving and forgiving.

Cam had *wanted* to kiss him. What were their reasons for not doing this?

Why weren't they pulling off these wet clothes and getting down to business?

Oh, right. Victor was done with love.

And Cam apparently didn't do . . .

Cam's tongue slid along his, and Victor lost all thought. Their hips bumped together, and Cam's groan traveled through their lips and down Victor's torso.

Fuck. Me.

Mustering every ounce of his will, Victor broke the kiss. He wedged his arms between them and flattened his palms over Cam's warm, broad, hard, *wet* chest. The beat beneath his fingers had to be Cam's heart knocking out a siren tattoo.

Dear lord.

"We shouldn't," Victor more gasped than said.

"We really shouldn't," Cam replied.

"I'm so not . . ."

"Not what?"

Thunder shook the house. The lights flickered. Dexter howled.

Cam's hand found the side of Victor's face, then his lips were close again. His breath washing across Victor's skin.

Don't lift your chin.

He shouldn't, but he did.

Chapter Nineteen

Victor tasted of summer, like kisses stolen out of time. Creek water and sunshine, sudden storms, wind and rain. He trembled against Cam, as though holding his body back just enough to resist the crush, the collide that would end this delicate moment. Rocket them from kissing to touching to grinding to release.

Experience taught it wouldn't be long. They couldn't stop the oncoming crash. They could control it, though. Cam didn't want to do this standing up in a laundry. He was too old to frot in front of a washing machine.

He ended the kiss, caught another whiff of cologne and sunshine, and traced his lips along Victor's jaw. He'd shaved that afternoon.

For me.

Lips pressed to Victor's ear, he murmured, "Bedroom."

Victor jerked backward. Reflexively, Cam tightened his grip on Victor's shoulders. Then made his fingers let go, one by one. If Vic didn't want this—

"Are you sure?" Victor asked.

His eyes were searching, his lips reddened and slightly parted. The muscles beneath Cam's fingertips still quaking softly. When was the last time he'd been with someone this responsive? This sensitive? If they didn't put some space between them— fast—Cam was going to come in his jeans. Already, he was so hard, he ached.

"Yes, I'm sure."

Victor started to edge out of the laundry. Before their bodies lost contact, he ducked back in. "We need towels. The floors . . . Slippery when wet." He grinned.

Cam laughed.

Victor bent to yank open the dryer door, and Cam eyeballed the curve of his ass. Would they fuck or would Victor make him wait? He had a sense Victor might like to tease. There he was, bent over the dryer. Knowing Cam had to be checking out his ass.

Cam tucked two fingers inside the denim at Victor's hip.

Victor gasped and Cam closed in on him, pressing his restrained cock to that reciprocal curve.

"*Oh.*" Victor shuddered and straightened. He pushed a warm towel into Cam's hands. "Leave your boots and jeans here."

And so began the comedy routine of two viciously aroused men attempting to peel wet denim down their thighs in the confined space of Victor's laundry.

"If I bang my elbow on the washer one more time, I'm going to break something," Victor growled.

"I'm wondering why that damn shelf sticks out so far." Cam rubbed his temple. "You have, what, five acres here? And a corridor for a laundry."

"We could be in the garage. That's where I had the machines when we first moved up here. Before we built this extension."

Finally succeeding in tugging his jeans all the way off, Cam let them drop into a wet puddle and reached for Victor. He pulled him into another kiss, reveling in the feel of their thighs finally brushing together, the tickle of hair and the firmness of the musculature beneath. Two straining cocks. Cam smoothed a hand over Victor's hip and down his leg. When he wrapped his fingers around the back of Victor's thigh, Vic lifted that leg to curl it around Cam's calf, then knee.

Oh, yes. This was going to be amazing.

Then the lights went out. Bizarrely, the thunder shook the house after the loss of power, as though mocking them.

"Oh, the fun of living in the Poconos," Victor said.

"Is it my imagination or are the storms worse this year?"

"Definitely worse, but it was so dry this winter. We need the rain. Have you seen the river?"

Cam dotted a kiss to the closest skin and grinned as he landed it on Victor's nose. "I have."

"Well, we won't be washing or drying your clothes tonight." A hand found his and, somehow, they extracted themselves from the laundry room without dislocating any joints. The kitchen was a jumble of shadows, occasionally lit by a flare of lightning. Cam followed Victor to the counter, where he plucked a flashlight from a wall socket and flicked it on. "This way."

Victor directed the beam back toward the large living room that seemed to take up most of the floor, past the new staircase, and to a room that poked out of the opposite side of the house: the northwest corner.

"Two steps up," Victor said.

From somewhere in the house, a cat yowled. Nails clicked in an uneven rhythm against tile, then hardwood. Honey, following.

In the wavering beam of the flashlight, Cam caught the edge of the mentioned steps and lifted his foot. Then they were in a large bedroom, lightning flickering through the windows combining with the flashlight to reveal wooden beams framing cream-colored walls, a tall stone fireplace, polished plank floors, and what would be, in the right light, explosions of color. Rugs, paintings, cushions, curtains. A large bed spread with multiple quilts and pillows. A white pile of fur.

Victor tugged a quilt from the end of the bed and folded it into a corner beside the fireplace.

"For Honey."

Cam beckoned her over and settled her with a gentle pat. She sat and licked his hand. He grinned at her. "You're a trouper, you know that?" The storm seemed to be bothering him and the screaming white cat more than her. Cocking her tawny head, she panted at him. He cupped her ears and kissed between them. "Stay."

"Off the bed, Dex. Go squawk in the closet. Sinister! Come sit with your brother!" Victor called out. Then, "Oh, Dexie, it's all right, you dope. Just another storm."

A laugh edged up and out. One minute Cam was about to come in the laundry, the next they were soothing pets in Victor's carnival of a bedroom. But with the power out and no other plans pending, they could be outside time. It didn't matter how long it took to get Victor into that bed of his. To lay him out, pull his shirt over his head, his underpants down. Explore all of his lean musculature. His nooks. The valley between his ribs, the other one at his spine. To see whether he had dimples over his ass. To taste, to smell . . .

Yeah, okay, Cam was hard again.

Swallowing a growl, Cam stepped behind Victor and circled his slim waist. He liked that Victor wasn't tall. That he was well-built but slightly smaller. Leaner. That he could easily be wrapped in Cam's arms. Held and protected.

Thunder rumbled quietly in the distance. Cam bent to kiss the junction of neck and shoulder. Victor shuddered and moaned. Then he climbed away from Cam, onto the bed, and Cam followed.

Victor lay on his back and held up his arms, and Cam covered that lithe body with his, touching down, finally, a deep moan pulling from his feet as the hardness of his cock pushed into the heat of Victor's groin and a corresponding hardness prodded his hip. Vic reached down and adjusted their angle so nothing broke, and Cam resumed the kissing.

He'd always enjoyed kissing. Vic seemed into it too. Nipping, tasting, blending. The need to press into someone else rolled up from the soles of Cam's feet, curving his body into an undulating wave. He ground down and arched back. Twice. Three times. Kissed Vic's reddened lips with bruising force. Buried his face in a sweet-smelling neck. Found Vic's ear again and nipped the lobe.

"Want to fuck you," Cam said.

"God, yes." Vic fastened his hands over Cam's hips and pulled him down. Pushed up. Pressed them together so hard Cam saw stars. Then he leaned away. "Let me grab some stuff."

"Yeah, cool."

Kneeling, Cam stripped off his shirt and tossed it over the side. After Vic dropped a condom and bottle of lube onto the side of the bed, Cam reached for Vic's shirt and eased it up and over, not looking where he tossed it as he bent to kiss Vic's chest. His clavicle, the top of one pec. Small springs of hair surrounded his nipples. Cam bit one tiny nub and kissed across to the other. He slid a hand down to his new favorite handle—Victor's hip—and pushed at his underwear.

Vic wriggled out of the damp cotton, and Cam kissed his way down, playing his tongue over ribs, into the narrow valley of belly button and lower, the scent of Vic's arousal testing his control all over again.

He licked and sucked, pulling gasps and cries from his new lover. Explored. Nipped at Vic's inner thighs. Spread his legs, slid fingers behind his balls. Found his hole and circled. Stroked. Probed. Prepared.

By the time he was sheathed and pressing himself inside, Cam had forgotten the storm. The shake and rattle of the windows and rolling growl of thunder were him. His body crying out for release. The tremble in his thighs as he held himself in check, the yell building inside him as he slid into the tight glove that was Victor's ass.

Then he was *in* and the sudden quiet could have been a stroke or the inside of a tornado for all he cared. *Take the damn house to Kansas.* Braced over Victor, Cam stared down at the tousled, silvery-blond hair, sleepy gray eyes, and red lips. The flush of arousal across Vic's cheeks and neck, the darker shade of Cam's passage, where he'd kissed and marked.

"You're gorgeous," he said.

Victor smiled. Then he clenched. Pulling a groan out of the earth, Cam began to move. Stroking in and out, matching breath for breath. Covering Vic's hand with his, tugging together on Vic's cock, feeling the same joy in their symphony of movement.

Vic climaxed first, arching, shuddering, his knees banging into Cam's ribs. Come pushing between their fingers. Dipping his head and steadying his arms, Cam thrust harder and deeper. Wanting to follow. Needing to. Vic grabbed his ass, his fingers sticky and warm, and Cam moved faster.

"That's it, oh God," Vic ground out, eyes fluttering closed. "I think I'm going to— I could . . ."

Cam's orgasm tore free and he let it fly loose. Victor shuddered again, his dick jerking. Cam could feel his voice inside his throat, knew he was making sound. Wordless and joyful. A release that had been too long in coming. His body spasmed. His soul unhooked.

Then that damn cat yowled and a bubble of laughter rolled up from his belly.

Beneath him, Victor broke into a wide grin and chuckled. "Dex knows when a good thing is going."

"We're storming it up too much for him." Cam was still rocking his hips. Gently now, forward and back. "Did you actually come twice?" He bent to kiss Vic's chin. Moved up to his mouth.

"No. Just sensational aftershocks. It's been a while since I last bottomed. I'd almost forgotten what it felt like to come and then feel someone else come."

"Yeah?"

"Mm-hmm." Vic cocked one light eyebrow. "Never tried it?"

"Not often." Took way more trust than Cam could usually muster for a partner he intended to spend less than twelve hours with. Securing the condom, Cam withdrew, hissing in chorus with Vic, and flopped onto his back. He rolled his head toward the middle of the bed and met Vic's sleepy but curious gaze. "Haven't had a lot of male partners. Not sure why. I like men and always have. I usually feel more comfortable with women in bed, though."

"You felt comfortable inside me."

Chuckling, Cam could only agree. "Very." His smile narrowed. "I think I wanted to do that from the minute I saw you. Don't ask me why. I never know why I'm attracted to someone. Sure as heck wasn't the shrieking you were doing that day. Or that robe." His lips curved upward again. "Though, putting that much skin on display might have done the trick."

"Really? I've never considered myself particularly attractive in that manner."

"What? Naked? You're fit and toned. You have the kind of legs I like. Long but strong."

A crease appeared in the middle of Victor's forehead. "You're not like anyone I've been with before."

"I'm going to take that as a compliment."

"You should. Because you are *not* my type."

"You're not mine."

"From what you've said, I'm not sure you have a type. Except someone with legs."

Cam smoothed a palm down Victor's finely muscled and sticky thigh. "Legs like these." He let go to deal with the condom. "We should clean up."

"We should."

"Does your water run without a generator?"

"It does not. The well pump is all electric."

"Oh, the joy of the Poconos in a storm."

"Wind, rain, snow, flood. All it takes is one tree over a powerline and we're thrust back into the dark ages."

The outline of a jagged tree floated in his mind's eye. The sound of a knock at the door haunted his ears. And a swell of melancholy rolled through the calm of Cam's postorgasmic high. He'd lost his parents on a night like this. He didn't think of them every storm, but the small mention of a powerline had been enough to thrust him back in time.

Could he not enjoy one amazing moment without myriad sadness poking holes in his bliss?

Pulling his shoulder away from Vic's, he rolled off the side of the bed. "Where will I find a towel? In the bathroom?" He could wave it outside a window for a second, get it wet enough to at least wipe them down. Then they could see about firing up the generator.

Vic sat up. "Is everything okay?"

They'd left the flashlight on the mantel over the fireplace, the beam pointed toward the ceiling. Cam's eyes had fully adjusted to the dim light and the concern on Vic's face was clear. So he forced a smile. "Yeah, fine. Back in a sec."

Chapter Twenty

F*ine* hardly ever meant *fine*. Victor had tossed the same word out so often, he could barely remember the true meaning. The one he liked best, though, pertained to lines and edges. To him, *fine* meant *I'm balancing*.

Watching Cam tiptoe out of the bedroom, Vic pondered his fineness. He'd already reassessed his original opinion of Cam's attractiveness. In that sense, Cam was *fine*. He had the sort of face that might not mean a lot at first glance. Features that lined up well enough but sat there without flare. He had a nice face. The regular brown of his eyes and hair and squareness of his jaw, straight brows, and crooked nose, all said: *I'm here to do what needs to be done. You can probably trust me.*

But the more he got to know Cam and his face, the more Victor saw. His eyes weren't simply brown. They were the loam beneath the trees, the fertile earth hidden by the mulch of fallen leaves. Touch the color with sunlight, though, and they shone like lake water. Brown and green and the tiniest flecks of blue. A glint of yellow. If Victor were to paint Cam's portrait, he'd need at least four tubes of color to replicate the varying moods of his eyes.

Physically, Cam was beyond *fine*. He wore his years well, his body shaped by activity and determination. Victor suspected Cam rarely sat to do nothing. He was a man who moved. Lying there, thoroughly fucked in a way unachieved for longer than he liked to admit, Victor could attest to the absolute fineness of Cam's fitness.

Footsteps padded back toward the bedroom. Victor thought about picking himself up, maybe sitting or gathering some pillows so he could try to lie attractively. But Cam's fineness had pretty much done him in. He did manage to look up with a smile, though, a smile that felt stiff as he noted the distracted expression on Cam's more-than-fine face.

We need another word, hon.

Kneeling on the side of the bed, Cam offered a damp towel. Victor accepted the gift and set about cleaning the—*don't say it . . . ah, fuck it*—*fineness* from his hands and stomach.

"What's the grin for?" Cam folded his knee so that he sat. Naked, still, and obviously comfortable in his skin.

"I have been pondering the various meanings of the word 'fine.'"

Cam's eyebrows quirked upward. "Okay."

Finished with the towel, Victor tossed it toward the floor. "It's such a reflexive word."

"How do you mean?"

"It's what we say when we're not fine. I mean—what is fine? As far as mood or mental state? If you think about it, like, really think about it, what we're saying is that I am in neutral. Neither good nor bad. Just fine. But what we're also saying is that I'm standing on the edge of something. I'm clinging. I'm fine now, but I could easily not be fine."

Cam blinked at him.

Victor continued. "But what we're mostly saying is, 'I'm experiencing an emotion or pattern of thought I'm not ready to talk about. Or would prefer not to share with you. So I'm going to say I'm fine and you're going to nod and we will move on.'"

Lips twitching, Cam offered a gentle nod. "I see."

The rain had hastened the end of the day, the light outside now obscured by heavy clouds. Victor could still see Cam's face, though, one half illuminated by the up-thrust beam of the flashlight on the mantel, the other by memory. He wore a thoughtful expression.

Then, leaning back on his hands, Cam nodded again, his chin bobbing up and down. His lips twisted. His brow pinched. When he turned to Victor, his mien had changed. Now he seemed sad.

"What is it?" Victor asked.

"Conversation leads to complication."

"Complication doesn't necessarily mean commitment, and we've talked before."

"We have."

Victor touched Cam's hand, brushing his fingers over the knuckles folded into the quilt. "If you prefer to remain *fine*, I won't press."

Cam gazed at him for a long, long time. If Victor had a clock that ticked, the quiet beat would have sounded over and over in a steady rhythm beneath the thrum of rain and the creak of old timber and they'd be starring in their own gothic horror movie.

But, no, they were sitting on rumpled sheets, sated by good sex—and he had, inexplicably, decided to destroy the mood. Victor patted the knuckles he'd been stroking. "Let's get dinner, hmm?"

Cam scrubbed his face with his other hand. "My parents died on a night like this. A storm caused flooding on a road outside Milford and the edge broke away. Their car slid off the side, bounced off a power pole, and rolled. The power was already out when the cops showed up to tell us what had happened. We thought it was the lightning. It had hit our damn yard, striking a tree outside our front door. The cops had to walk around half a smoking tree to tell us our parents were dead."

Victor curled his fingers over Cam's hand. "I'm so sorry."

"It was a long time ago, Vic. A very long time ago. But when I think back, when I'm looking for reasons, that's where it all starts."

Where what starts?

He might as well have posed the question aloud, because Cam answered: "Four weeks later, I enlisted in the army." Easing his hand out from under Victor's fingers, Cam scooted back toward the side of the bed. "So, now that I've shit all over our parade, I should go."

"No." Victor scrambled off the bed and caught Cam's wrist. "You can leave if you want, but you don't have to go. I asked, Cam. I opened this door, even though you have hinted, many times, that I should not." Victor slid his fingers back over the knobby bone of Cam's wrist and tugged on his hand. "But I didn't ask for the sake of connection. Well, I did. But only because that's who I am. I've never been fond of anonymous sex. But I can do friend sex. That's what I'm doing here. We both wanted this, and we're both old enough to see it for what it is. Just because we talk doesn't mean it's more. Okay?"

Cam considered him for another long, quiet moment. The invisible clock ticked, but outside, the wind had eased. The thunder was gone. Dexter had stopped howling a while ago, and the house no longer groaned under the pressure of a storm.

Then Cam nodded—once—and squeezed Victor's hand in return. "Okay." A familiar grin tugged at the side of his mouth, poking a previously unseen dimple into his cheek. "But only because whatever you made for dinner smells so good."

Victor laughed. "Thank goodness I planned ahead, hm? Or we'd be having peanut butter and jelly sandwiches."

"Food of champions and never say it isn't."

"Oh, I wouldn't dare."

And just like that, the atmosphere lightened, as though the storm had moved on from inside the house as well.

After dressing in sweats and tees, Cam once again pleasingly attired in Victor's too-small clothing, Victor ventured out to the garage to fire up the generator. Cam took care of the interior connection, flipping the fuses on the auxiliary board to power the well pump, the kitchen, and a few other scattered lights. Then Victor served them each a hearty bowl of chili, and they sat around a corner of the kitchen table, Honey flopped over Cam's feet, Sinister on his own chair, his triangular black head poking up over the top of the table, and Dexter probably burrowed into a warm nook of the abandoned bed.

"Gang's mostly here," Cam observed. He appeared to take in the five empty seats. "Must have been nice growing up here. For your kids."

"I like to think it was."

"You still see them much?"

"I do. They stop by unannounced at times, which I love. That they're comfortable enough to think, 'Hey, I'll visit Dad,' and just show up. I feel like it means I did something right."

Nodding, Cam dipped his spoon into his bowl and brought up a steaming mound of black beans. He blew across the top and then tasted it. "This is good."

"Thank you. It's one of Tez's recipes. Her parents are from Texas, and this is, apparently, a completely authentic recipe. Except for the beans. It should be made with cubes of chuck steak, but beans are heart healthy, and apparently I should be watching my cholesterol."

"Heh, me too." Cam patted his belly. "Every now and then I'll get all healthy and cook, you know? Spend a day making stuff to pack the fridge and freezer. But in between, I exist on bacon sandwiches and beer. Or chicken and whiskey. Those are my main two diet plans."

"I'm more of a wine and cheese man, myself."

"You don't say."

They shared a laugh and ate in silence for a while. Vic assumed it was a comfortable silence until Cam said, "Seeing as we're doing the friend thing, can I ask a question?"

"Sure."

"How come you're not married. To a man, I mean." His eyebrows dipped downward. "You are gay?"

"A hundred percent and thank you for not asking whether I slept with Tez in order to make our babies."

"Oh, that was next." Cam grinned, but the angle of his eyebrows suggested he was lying. The question didn't seem to have occurred to him.

"As to why I am not married . . ." Victor shrugged. "It's funny you should ask. Or not funny, but coincidental. Tez and I touched on that subject this week. We were having lunch and wondering, again—this is something we think about a bit, I suppose—whether our decision to have kids has somehow mucked up our romantic aspirations. We wanted so badly to raise our children together and that was almost twenty years of our lives. Sometimes I ask myself if I could have found someone else to do it with. A man. But the men I was enjoying back then weren't interested in having families, and the men I met out here were so often already married with children and I was their secret on the side."

Cam winced.

"What about you?" Victor asked.

Cam put his spoon down and wiped his mouth with a napkin. "If I ever got married, I'd want a partnership like my mom and dad had."

Victor's heart squeezed. Of all the answers he might have expected, this was not on the list. Especially as he'd supposed Cam might never talk about his parents again.

"They were best friends. Like you and Tez. Good people too. Not perfect, but even at twenty, I loved what they had and aspired to achieve the same one day. I had a girlfriend before I went away, a friend from high school. Do you remember Cindy Marks? She was a year ahead of me."

"You were dating the captain of the cheerleading squad?"

"Go big or go home, man."

Victor laughed.

"She still lives locally. Married a guy she met in college and they moved out here to be close to her parents. We met up shortly after I returned from Afghanistan. A couple of years after." He waved a hand. "I had work to do when I first got back. Rehab and stuff. But then I came home for a bit, and we caught up and it was great. We could still be friends, you know?"

"Did you break up with her to go away?"

"I did." Cam's smile was sad but not tragic. "That's when my love story died."

"And you haven't met anyone worthy since then?"

Cam shrugged. "There was someone else a while ago, but she wasn't as into it as I was."

"Another *she*."

"I've never had a serious relationship with a guy."

Victor smirked. "I see. We're just for fun, then."

"Hey, it's all just for fun." Cam picked up his spoon and seemed to concentrate on finishing his chili.

Victor did the same.

"What about your parents? They still live around here?" Cam asked after a minute.

Victor felt his good humor begin to fade and quickly bolstered it. "They moved to Oregon of all places. As if we don't get enough rain here."

"They get a lot of rain out that way too? I thought that was Seattle."

"I think the whole northwest is relatively wet."

"Were they good parents?" Cam's question was quiet. Wary.

With a gentle smile, Victor nodded. "They were. All three of them."

Cam blinked.

"Sunshine, Moonbeam, and Rainstorm."

After a beat, Cam said, "You're not kidding, are you?"

"Nope. I was raised by three loving people. They were living with many, many friends, a commune, I suppose, past Mount Airy, when my mom got pregnant with me. When I was four, the three of them moved to Milford to start their own little four-person collective." Victor grinned.

Cam put a hand to his mouth. "I'm trying so hard not to laugh."

"It's cool."

"How did you end up with a name like Victor? Is your real name Victory or something?"

At Victor's blank stare, Cam covered his mouth again. "Oh, man. No."

"And we will speak of it no more." Only Tez was allowed to call him by his birth name and only once a month or thereabouts.

Pinching his thumb and forefinger in front of his lips, Cam made the universal sign for locking a secret away. "What about your last name?"

Victor smiled. "It's my mom's. The name on her birth certificate was Mary Ness and she had white-blonde hair and pale blue eyes, so figuring out whether Sun or Rain was my father would take a paternity test. I always suspected it was Sunshine, though. Our personalities are similar. Our moods."

"He's bright and colorful and totally in love with drama?"

Victor chose to laugh. Softly. "You could say that."

Cam looked around the house again, as though Victor deciding to live with the mother of his children while occasionally hosting their other lovers now made sense. "That's kinda cool."

"Yeah."

"You see them often?"

Despite his efforts, the sadness crept back in. "Sunshine, whose legal name was Stan, he . . . died when I was twenty-seven."

If Cam picked up on Victor's hesitation, he ignored it. "I'm sorry."

"Thanks. I don't know if a three-person relationship makes the death of a loved one harder or easier. I was glad Mom and Rain had each other, but watching them grieve together was awful." His own grief . . .

It was time to lighten the conversation. "Mom and Rain live in one of those retirement villages now. Say it's almost like a commune. They still grow vegetables and have drum circles and braid each other's hair. And then play golf and go to book club and all the regular old people things. Tez, the kids, and I fly out there every year to say hello."

Cam wore a thoughtful expression. "We both had great parents. Do you know how unusual that is for people like us?"

"What do you mean?"

"Men who like other men."

"Your parents knew?" After the mention of a high-school sweetheart, Victor had assumed Cam's parents thought he was straight.

"Oh, yeah. They caught me kissing my best friend when I was about thirteen."

"What did they say?"

"'We love you, but be careful.'"

"Huh."

Honey whined softly and twitched in her sleep. Cam bent and scratched her behind the ear. "Having a dream there?" He looked up. "How about you?"

"I think it was almost expected that I wouldn't be straight. I mean, I had two dads who adored each other and a mom who loved them both. Honestly, the biggest surprise in our family has been my son, Sage. When he told us he was into girls and only girls, we were all, like, 'No. How is this possible?'"

Cam chuckled, Victor smiled in return, and they sat there smiling at each other until Victor felt a bubble of laughter working its way up from his diaphragm.

"What?" Cam asked.

"Look at us. Connecting."

Scowling, Cam said, "Don't."

Victor forced himself to sober up. "It's all good. And as you know, I recently got out of a relationship. You and me, we're still getting to know each other. So this—" he gestured between them "—what we're doing right now? This is all I want at the moment. I'm not ready for more."

Cam nodded. "Cool."

"Of course, me also being me, I want to know what you're so afraid of, but I've asked enough pressing questions for one night."

"You have. But I've got another one for you."

"Oh, yeah?"

Reaching between them, Cam rested his hand on Victor's thigh. "How many times can you get it up in a night, old man?"

"Old man!" Victor spluttered. "I'll have you know I am in my prime."

Cam leaned in. "Oh, yeah? Ready to back up that claim?"

Victor met him in the middle and whispered against his mouth. "More than ready."

Cam's lips tasted of black beans and BBQ sauce. Victor wanted to devour him. He also wanted Cam to be the one splayed out on the bed this time, his body laid out like a buffet.

Ending the kiss, Victor drew back. "I need to feed the cats. See if Honey wants to run outside for a minute? Then we'll rustle up something for her too. *Then*, we can play."

"Need time to muster up some strength and fortitude? I get it."

Laughing, Victor shoved at Cam's chest. "Speak for yourself."

Cam pulled him in for another kiss and Victor groaned. Then he hopped astride Cam's lap and said, "Damn you."

Chapter Twenty-One

Luisa glanced up with a smile when Cam walked into the office—a smile that faded when she noted the absence of Honey. Before she could ask the question that had haunted Cam all weekend, he shook his head.

"She's at home today. My neighbor is going to let her out for a bit after lunch."

"I wouldn't have minded her company," Luisa said.

"I know. But Jorge and I have a long job this afternoon. If that fits in with what you have for us, of course."

"It's Monday, Cam. I have exactly one delivery for you."

One? Damn.

Cam stopped by the coffee maker. Luisa's mug was missing, so he filled his and carried it to the couch. "How was the weekend?"

Holding his breath, he searched her face as he waited for a reply.

"Not bad," she said. "I had to come in for a while on Saturday afternoon because the kids were overwhelmed."

"Your weekend manager couldn't handle it?"

Luisa's lips compressed.

"What?"

"I had to let her go, Cam."

"I'm sorry."

She shrugged.

"Any movement on your plans to sell?"

"Some. A developer is interested in the land, but I'd like to sell the farm as a business." Luisa lifted her chin. "How about you and Jorge? How's the landscaping and such coming along?"

Cam swallowed the vague sense of panic that arrived with every mention of the fledgling business. "Suspiciously well."

She laughed. "I've thought about it before, providing extra services. Landscaping, lawn care, snow removal. It would mean working year 'round, though. And I do enjoy winter in California."

"I get that." Cam dug his phone out. "Hey, while we're here, I've taken a job to cut a path into a hillside. Down to a client's mailbox." On Saturday morning, he'd measured the route he'd traced. On Sunday, he'd transcribed his map onto paper as a scaled drawing. "I still need to price out the materials, including fill and gravel. But I want to use railway ties for the steps. Any idea where I can get my hands on some? I figured they'd be cheap but strong."

Luisa chuckled softly.

"What?"

"Have you ever been out behind the last shed? The one behind the greenhouse."

"Maybe? I don't know."

"You can have whatever you find there, and don't forget to charge yourself the contractor's rate for the rest of your supplies."

Cam glanced up from his phone. "I'm sure he's expecting to pay full price."

Victor didn't seem the type to expect unreasonable discounts because they'd slept together. Cam's skin warmed at the memory of Friday night and Saturday morning. When he returned his attention to Luisa, she was eyeing him curiously.

"What?"

"The difference is yours, Cam. You pay the contractor price. He pays the consumer price."

"Oh, right." He knew that. Had even made a mental note to ask Luisa about it—before he'd started thinking with his little head. Thank fuck he had no plans to see Victor for the next few days. He needed time to get him out of his system.

Jorge arrived and helped himself to coffee. Silent greetings were exchanged. Then he pulled out his phone, scrolled around for a bit, and showed the screen to Cam: a local marketplace ad for a reconditioned, heavy-duty ride-on mower.

"Six acres, man," was all Jorge said.

Continuing to do the job with push mowers wouldn't kill them, but with a ride-on, one of them could mow while the other cleared. They'd finish faster and potentially accomplish more. What they needed was an extra team. And another truck.

The sense of panic rose again, and Cam had a harder time beating it down. With a racing pulse, he handed the phone back. "Did you hear from your cousin?"

"If we can match what he's making at the hardware store, he's in."

That would be a proper salary—for a proper employee. Fuck, fuck, fuck.

"He also has a plow attachment for his truck and a couple customers leftover from last year." Jorge's face did an odd thing, then. After a second, Cam realized he was smiling. Had he ever seen Jorge smile before?

The tension across his shoulders eased by a small degree. "You thinking of putting one on the Cougar?"

Jorge's shoulders jumped a little. A chuckle. "Nah, man." He flipped to another screen on his phone and handed it back. A plow.

Would Nick mind if Cam used the truck over winter too? He'd have to ask. Or maybe offer to buy it from him. And try not to get overwhelmed by the idea of it all. He did have that cash put away, after all.

"A sound plan." Cam blew out a breath and levered up off the couch. "Let's take a walk out behind the nursery. I've got another job I want to talk to you about."

Later that afternoon, Cam dropped into Luisa's chair and started pricing out the materials he needed for Victor's job. The thought of charging himself one price and Victor another didn't sit quite right, but that was the way contracting worked. If his discount was high enough, he could cut Victor in on it and still make a little extra. Especially as the wood would cost them next to nothing.

The stacked railway ties behind the nursery had been meant for beds Luisa had planned to extend across the lot between the nursery and the orchard—until she'd figured out she made better money spreading hay and pumpkins across it in the fall.

He was counting out the number of ties he'd need for the steps when the office phone rang. Glancing up at the wall clock, he debated answering it. The farm was closed, but the call could be for a delivery. Luisa needed the income. He answered on the next ring.

"Shepard's Tree Farm. Cameron speaking."

"There you are."

Conflicting emotions battled for dominance as Cam recognized Victor's voice. A bright lift of joy and a sharp pang of—not regret. Something like fear, but not. Victor had called him. Why was Victor calling him?

Before he could finish examining the darker feeling creeping up through his chest, Victor said, "Cam?"

"Sorry. Ah, sorry." *Wow.*

After a beat of silence, Victor said, "You're surprised to hear from me."

No. Yes? Why was he so surprised? "I wasn't expecting you to call here."

"If I had the number for your cell, I wouldn't have to."

About that. By some miracle, Cam stopped himself from suggesting Victor shouldn't need to call him. Because obviously they did need to be in touch. For the job. The shop number would suffice for that, though, wouldn't it?

After muttering quietly, Victor spoke again. "Okay, well, I'm sorry to have bothered you at work. I was planning to leave a message. You left Honey's banana here on Saturday. I thought you might want it. I can call back tomorrow to discuss the front path, if you prefer. During business hours."

All of the air Cam hoped to either pull into his lungs or push back out stuck fast in the middle.

On the other end of the line, Victor sighed, muttered, and hung up.

That was spectacular.

Pushing away from the desk, Cam sprang to his feet and paced around the small office, shaking out his arms and hands. What the actual fuck? What had just happened? Why had he been such an ass? A phone call didn't equal commitment. It was . . . a phone call.

Maybe he was on edge because of the whole new-business thing. His conversations with Luisa and Jorge about all the equipment he needed to purchase. The realness of actually seeming to start a business.

The office door opened, and Cam jumped out of his skin. Whirling, he nearly dropped into a crouch . . . and stopped as Jorge's large frame filled the doorway. "Fuck, man."

Jorge lifted his chin, which was his way of asking if Cam was all right.

"I'm fine." Cam pressed a hand over his ribs. "Freaking out is all." He frowned. "What are you doing here?"

Jorge looked between Cam, the couch, and back again. He had a damned pillow and a folded blanket tucked under one arm.

"You're *sleeping* here? Does Luisa know?"

He shook his head.

"Where do you go before she gets here?"

Breakfast, obviously. And somewhere he could shower or wash.

"Jesus fucking Christ, Jorge. Why didn't you say something?" Cam held up a hand to forestall any reply, not that Jorge appeared ready to start talking. He'd probably used up all his words that morning.

Cam pointed toward the door. "Grab whatever you need. You're coming home with me."

There was no point in asking why Jorge had to sleep on Luisa's couch. Not only had he likely used up his verbal allowance for the day, he might prefer not to share the story. Cam got it. He'd been there—a few times, now.

Jorge insisted on bringing his car, and they parked side-by-side in Cam's driveway. They'd gone from one lonely vehicle to three in a short space of time.

Cam led the way to the front door. "So, this is the place. It's in trust for my niece. I'm looking after it until then." He didn't know all the specifics of how the ownership would transfer, he just figured someone would tell him when it was time to move out.

Inside, they greeted Honey, giving her ear rubs and belly pats. Cam put her on the long leash he'd attached outside the back door and let her out for a bit while he toured Jorge through the rest of the house.

"Help yourself to whatever is in the fridge. There's not much. We can shop tomorrow if you want." Having someone else around would mean they could plan meals and such. "TV's in there." He pointed out the family room. "Bedrooms and bathrooms upstairs. You can have my brother's old room." Cam opened the door and leaned in. A smile spread across his face. "I grew up in this house. In this room." He turned his smile on Jorge. Clapped him on the shoulder. "It's yours for as long as I'm here."

Jorge studied him for a long, silent moment, and Cam expected nothing more than a nod at the end, and for Jorge to disappear into the neat and somewhat impersonal bedroom Nick had left behind.

Quietly, Jorge said, "Thank you."

"Sure. I just wish I'd known you needed somewhere to stay sooner. Why didn't you say so?"

Jorge didn't answer.

"Want something to eat?"

Jorge followed him back to the kitchen and sat at Cam's bidding. Cam pulled out the leftover burgers he'd grilled up the night before and set them on the table with fixings: buns, cheese, lettuce, tomatoes, mayo.

"Mustard, ketchup, or both?"

Honey scratched at the door, and Jorge let her in. Then, together, they fed her and themselves. While he sat there chewing, watching Jorge chew, listening to Honey chew the scraps that kept miraculously falling in the vicinity of Jorge's feet, Cam contemplated their situation.

He put his burger down. "Some, they come home and pick up right where they left off."

Jorge nodded.

"Why didn't we?"

After swallowing his mouthful, Jorge sipped his beer, set the bottle back on the table, folded his hands, and looked Cam square in the eye. "If I had an answer for that, I'd still be married and you wouldn't be living in your niece's house."

Cam's dinner turned into a black hole intent on devouring his stomach from the inside. "You have any friends?" he asked. "I don't mean why aren't you staying with them. I mean people you can sit with and not talk about Afghanistan but know they're hearing every word anyway."

A smirk twisted Jorge's mouth. "You."

"You can talk out loud to me. If you need to."

Jorge lifted his chin. "Same."

Cam gnawed on his lower lip, bit a little too hard, and soothed the sting against the lip of his beer bottle. Then he put the bottle down. It hadn't occurred to him until he'd made the offer, but Cam wanted to talk. Jorge probably wasn't the right person to listen. Not to what he had to say at this moment.

Maybe Nick?

Cam tugged his phone out of a pocket and turned the warm rectangle over in his hand. He did need to talk, but not about war. Not right now.

You know who you need to call.

"Help yourself to another burger if you want. I'm gonna—" Cam nodded toward the backyard. "I need to make a call."

He ducked outside and crossed the patio. Wove around the fruit trees he'd planted eighteen months ago. Their leaves were green with summer, and three of them had little apples going. Cam smiled at the fruit. Behind the fenced veggie patches, the lawn sloped down to a line of trees that ran along the creek. Cam stopped there and woke his phone. He'd had Victor's number

stored in his contacts for a while, but had yet to use it because . . .
Because.

He hit Dial.

"Hello?"

"You having my number means you can call me, and I don't know why that feels like such a big deal, but it does."

Quiet. Then, "I understand."

"Do you? Or are you just saying that?"

"Cam . . . I like you, okay? Not because we had a great time on Friday night, but because you're a decent person. The day we met, you jumped out of your truck to help me, even though we were strangers. Then you kept coming back because that's who you are."

And because with his lithe body, blue-gray eyes, and colorful clothing, Victor was, inexplicably, stuck fast in Cam's mind.

"I'm not going to apologize for wanting to stay in touch with a decent human being," Victor continued. "Plus, there was Friday night."

And Saturday morning.

"Can I stop by tomorrow to pick up Honey's toy?"

"I'll be home all day."

"I could . . . You want me to bring food?"

"Are you inviting yourself over for dinner and *dessert*?"

A grin edged across Cam's mouth. "That's what friends do, isn't it? Eat. Share something afterward."

"I don't sleep with all my friends. Just so you're aware. Could get rather messy."

Cam laughed. "Good to know." The creek burbled in front of him and the scent of the water wafted up on the evening breeze. "I don't sleep with all my friends, either."

He had no idea why he'd said that, or why it seemed important. What he even meant.

On the other end of the phone, Vic exhaled quietly. "Good to know."

Chapter Twenty-Two

"You win. Dear God . . . Stop, I can't. You win!"

Victor flopped onto his back, pulling his over-sensitized-but-still-hard dick away from Cam's hand and covered his groin protectively. Cam grinned evilly at Vic's cage of fingers before rolling backward. Victor panted and sought unsexy thoughts.

Beside him, Cam sighed in satisfaction. "When do I get to claim my prize?"

"Do you really want your backrub now?" High stakes wagers, all the way.

"Fuck no. It's like a hundred degrees in here."

Dexter, who'd been cleaning himself at the end of the bed, took the opportunity to slide up between them, his soft fur unwelcome.

"Seriously, Dex," Victor warned. "Come any closer and I will use you as a come rag."

"Hollow threat. You didn't come."

Victor clutched his slowly deflating penis. "Not for lack of trying. Apparently twice is my limit, for one afternoon, anyway."

Cam thrust two fists into the air. "Aha!"

"Gloat away. You'll be dry for the rest of the week."

Smile narrowing, Cam turned his head in Victor's direction. "You think?"

"Honestly, I don't know? I've never had a come-off with anyone before. What the actual heck, Zimmermann?"

Cam's shoulders shook with laughter. "You suggested it."

"I must have temporarily taken leave of my senses."

Cam leaned in and kissed him, the touch of his lips swift but firm, and in that instant, that seemingly inconsequential moment, Victor felt his grip on sense loosen by another thread. *Oh no.*

Propped up on one elbow, Cam continued to smile over him, the tired lines of his face somehow making him look younger. He was relaxed, Victor realized. In one place and relatively still. Not that Cam exhibited hyperactivity, but he did seem to loathe doing nothing for the sake of doing nothing.

And his damn face kept growing increasingly attractive. Victor could no longer remember a time when he didn't think Cam good-looking. He especially enjoyed the cheekier smiles and the light that sparked in his eyes when he made plans.

He very much liked the way Cam touched him.

Stop.

Before Cam could touch him again, Victor sat and swung his legs toward the side of the bed. "Let's eat. I'm starved."

"Good plan." Cam lifted his chin toward the ceiling. "What's above this room?"

"Just sky. It's one of the extensions. Why?"

"It's on the hottest side of the house in summer."

"And in the path of storms in winter." Victor nodded toward the fireplace. "Hence my solid wall of heat."

"I wonder if a sky light, or those higher windows—clerestory?—might improve the ventilation in summer."

Victor studied the ceiling, picturing a windowed bump in the middle. It would have been cheaper to have included it when he'd planned and built the extension. But he could see Cam's point. "When it gets hot, I sometimes sleep in the studio."

"On your yoga mat?"

"Heaven forbid. No, I toss couch cushions in there and drag my quilt over them."

Cam turned a fond smile on him, and the stitches sealing Victor's heart shut loosened by another thread.

"Ever swim in the creek to cool off?"

"Not since the kids were little."

Cam seemed to check himself, then. Clouds edged toward the sunshine of his face, the lines about his mouth and eyes—across his forehead—deepening slightly to leave him looking less weary and more straight-out tired. "It's one of the things I always remembered fondly about living up here. How there were so many creeks. Or cricks, as we say. Nick and I used to swim in the one behind our house. When it got deep enough, we could swim. Otherwise, we'd float there with the water running around us. I remember playing this game to see who could lift up off the bottom the best, make themselves stiff enough to catch the current. Nick always won. He was skinny. And younger."

"I've done the same."

"It's a good place to grow up."

"Want to cool off with a swim before we eat? Or take a snack with us? It'll still be light for another hour."

August had arrived with a lengthening of late afternoon shadows and a sunset closer to eight than nine.

Cam pushed off his side of the bed. "Yeah."

While he pulled on a pair of shorts suitable for swimming, Victor toyed with the idea of putting a halt to their trek through the woods. It felt dangerous. Not to him; he craved this kind of connection. The sharing he and Cam were doing had started to fill the empty spaces inside of him. But a part of him—a substantial part—suspected Cam would wake up tomorrow with regrets. That this deepening of their friendship, sex aside, might be too much for him. Or maybe, just maybe, Victor was worried about himself. He already cared too damn much.

In the kitchen, he grabbed a bag of cheddar popcorn and a couple of bottles of water. Slung them into a tote he pulled out of the laundry and added two towels from the dryer.

Cam watched the preparations with a slightly sardonic grin. "We've upgraded."

"I am well beyond the age where I would run through the woods barefoot and think I could air-dry on the way home. We are also taking bug spray."

"This is no longer feeling spur of the moment."

Victor laughed.

Summer had thickened the woods into a jungle with barberry bushes establishing fortresses between the trees. But the air was cooler, a light breeze stirring the treetops, and the simple joy of being outside drew him on. They heard the creek before they saw it, and a moment later, they pushed through the last of the trees.

Despite the rain, the creek would not be deep enough for swimming in the traditional sense, but they could get wet.

Cam had already shucked his boots. He dropped his jeans beside them and waded into the shallow stream wearing only his underpants. Victor left his shoes with Cam's but kept his shorts. A life-long fear of leeches, however ridiculous, remained strong.

The water was cold. Goose bumps raced up Victor's legs and arms. He clutched his torso and shivered. "Bracing!"

"Feels amazing." Cam found a steady space where the water lapped across his knees and sat. He leaned back, planting his hands behind him in the water, and tipped his head toward the strip of sky overhead. "I could die happy in this moment."

The comment sent another chill up and down Victor's spine. Shaking it off, he stalked through the cold water until he found a good spot and plopped down next to Cam. He hissed at the shock to his genitals. "Hope we're done with sex this evening. All of my externals have run for cover."

Cam chuckled. "Mine too."

Quiet blossomed around them, the only sounds the water, evening birds, and the wind. Victor absorbed the soft burbles and chirps, the peace of them, and let his thoughts roam. They didn't wander far. Cam sat less than six inches away.

Victor realized, then, that Cam was the first man he'd slept with who'd grown up here. Not just in Pennsylvania but in Milford. He wasn't counting the boys he'd played with before going away to college, because that hadn't been this. Two men of a certain age sitting in a creek and thinking thoughts. Sated because they'd played a silly game, but also content to simply sit.

It was so damned restful.

Cam turned to him, then, his beautiful face serene in the soft evening light. "What'cha thinking about?"

"Not a lot. How peaceful it is." *How happy I am to be here with you.*

"Same."

"How's your business coming along?" Because if they sat here talking about thoughts and feelings for much longer, Victor might share things Cam would definitely rather he did not.

Cam let a beat of silence pass before answering. "I'm at the point where I need to start thinking about it that way. As a business. Like, doing legal stuff." He shook his head as if bewildered by the thought. "I mean, the cash is nice, but if we want to do this properly, then we need to do it right. I'm starting to think Jorge needs it as much as I do."

"Oh?"

"He's been sleeping on the couch at the tree farm. I had no idea. I took him home. He's going to live with me."

Victor's heart swelled because of course it did.

Cam moved on, his brow wrinkling. "We've got his cousin Estefan in with us now, and he wants to know if we plan to do benefits, because his wife wants to change jobs. I'm all like fuck if I know. That makes it real." Panic edged his voice. "And if I want to bring on additional workers, I'll need to decide that. And whether this is worthwhile."

"Do you enjoy it?" Probably a silly question. That relaxed and replete expression Cam had worn earlier? He always looked like that with a shovel in his hand. He obviously loved working outdoors and with tools. Victor had only seen the garden at the front of the house Cam lived in, but he'd noted how lush and well planted it was. Tidy too.

"I do. But . . ." The frown returned. "I don't know if I'm a business person. If I can be . . . that person."

"I think you are. Look how quickly you've put it together so far."

"There is that."

Connections sparked in Victor's brain. "I might know someone who's looking for part time hours. A young person. Thrown out by their parents because they're transitioning. They've been in my summer program for three years and they love the outdoors. Always seemed like a conscientious worker too."

Cam nodded quickly, almost distractedly. "Send them my way. Do they need somewhere to live? Only room I have left is Emma's. I can ask if she'd mind."

"No, they're living with a friend for now, and last I heard, planning to switch to cyber school for their senior year so they can keep working part time hours and get a place of their own."

"Cool."

Cam adjusted his hands, drawing them out of the water and wrapping them around his knees. "I could stay here all night."

Taking the change of subject for what it was, Victor replied, "I am numb from the waist down."

Cue a mischievous grin.

"No," Victor warned.

Cam coiled inward like a snake preparing to strike.

Even before he moved, Victor was pushing away, but Cam caught him and pushed him back into the water. Water rolled over his face, and Victor closed his eyes. His fingers leaped toward his nose, pinching it shut, and his legs kicked upward. A joyful laugh burst from his lungs. A laugh that gurgled once before he broke the surface, spitting out water and chuckles.

"Numb all the way yet?" Cam asked.

"No. Yes!"

Victor was plunged a second time, and it was only when his back failed to touch the rounded pebbles beneath the surface that he realized that Cam had tucked an arm around him first.

The care. Always the damn care. Did Cam even know he showed it?

Bracing himself, Victor pushed up faster than Cam's rescue and rolled Cam backward for his turn. He failed totally in getting an arm around Cam's shoulders in the same way but did succeed in dunking himself again. Face-first, this time.

Once he flailed back to the surface, he had to work hard at prioritizing breathing over laughing. Thankfully, Cam was fighting the same battle.

When he caught his breath, Victor said, "I think I am sufficiently refreshed."

Cam chuckled and leaned back on his hands, whipping his head about like a dog's at the same time.

"I just realized you don't have Honey with you."

"Jorge is babysitting."

Victor wanted to know Jorge's story, then. He'd only seen the man once, in the driveway when he'd dropped Cam off. He'd been large and stoic. But with the same cautious gentleness Cam exhibited so often.

Before he could ask, though, Cam turned the conversation back on him. "How's your work?"

Victor shook his head. Shrugged. Shot Cam a rueful smile. "Let's just say I'm glad I can make a reasonably comfortable living off the sale of prints." His body of work was large enough that residuals continued to trickle in. The absence of a mortgage also helped.

Am I sliding into retirement before I make a plan? Felt that way sometimes.

"You're not painting? I've been waiting for the abstract Cameron."

"The abstract Cameron is a work in progress." And only mentally.

Victor made a study of the water, the fading light making it hard to see below the surface ripples. They'd have to start back to the house soon.

Cam swirled his hands through the stream, cupping water and letting it trickle through his fingers. When he touched Victor's upright knee, his fingers were both warm and cold.

Victor looked up.

Brow pinched, eyes darker now, the light not sufficient to show the depth of color, Cam seemed to move words around in his mouth a moment. Then he shared his thoughts. "I don't know what we're doing, Vic. I know we're trying to be friends, but . . ." He shook his head. "I started in the wrong place. What I'm trying to say . . ."

He dropped his hand. Played in the water.

Victor waited, not sure what he could offer in response.

Finally, Cam tried again. "Is there anything I can do? To help you paint?"

Another thread pulled free. But instead of the thrill of connection, Victor felt sadness. And fear. Despite his best efforts, he'd started to fall and losing Cam was going to hurt. But he couldn't see how else this might end.

Why, oh why did he have to start thinking about the end?

Cam was a beautiful man, and Victor already cared too deeply. But he was also a broken man. And he wasn't the only one. Victor's heart harbored deep wounds that hadn't been left there by departed lovers.

Maybe that's why he understood Cam so well. They shared another sort of loss, one that had apparently shaped them over all the years that had followed.

The fading light started to feel inconsequential and, measured against the blackness rolling in toward Victor's soul, it failed. Because, while night always ended with the dawn, a tide of sadness might last for days.

Not now. I will not do this now.

With a sigh, Victor found Cam's hand in the water and tangled their cool fingers together. He forced a smile. "Just be you, hm? That's all I'll ever ask."

Cam's smile was gentle.

Victor softened his and started planning for the oncoming storm.

Chapter Twenty-Three

When he got no answer to his knock, Cam dug out his cell phone and texted Nick. *At the back door.*

A minute later, the left-side door at the rear of Nick and Ollie's shop creaked open and his brother's smiling face peeked out. He had one earbud in. The other bud rested in his fingers and a slim note of music fluted up from his hand. "Hey."

"Hey, yourself."

Nick pulled the door wide. "Are you coming in?"

"Please."

Nick shut off his music and pocketed both of his earbuds. "Let's go upstairs. I think there's still coffee."

"Where's Ollie?" Cam had expected them both to be here on a weekday.

"In the city visiting Dani and Adam."

Oliver's daughter and her boyfriend had an apartment in Manhattan. Very low on the East Side. The actual area had a name, but Cam could never keep all those city neighborhoods straight.

Upstairs, Nick retrieved the carafe from beneath the coffee maker and poured out two cups. Cam sat at the breakfast bar and Nick slid a cup toward him.

"Cheers." Cam took a swallow and hummed in satisfaction. Even half a day old, the coffee tasted better than whatever he usually managed to put together. "How is it you make such good coffee?"

"Precise measurement." Nick grinned.

"That can't be all it is. I measure!"

With a shrug, Nick sipped his own coffee. Cam thought he detected a note of mischievousness in his brother's eyes, and it warmed him. That his brother could still play. Nick had often been a serious kid. Had always seemed such a serious adult. He'd been a complete mess when Cam arrived home two years ago, though.

"What's up?" Nick asked.

"Yeah. Okay." Cam spread his hands across the counter and breathed for a second. *It's not a big deal. Just breathe.* "I need to start a business. Or register one. Or whatever it is you do to make yourself legit. I have actual employees now, and one of them needs to show income so they can rent themselves an apartment."

Showing no surprise whatsoever, Nick nodded. "Do you have a list?"

"A list?"

"Of what you need to do?"

"Oh, yeah." Cam retrieved his phone again and opened his notes app. "So, um, get a business name and bank account. That's all I've got so far. I googled business names and found this website. It's from the PA government, and there are checklists. Like, six dozen of them." That was when his heart had begun to flail. Cam looked up. "I need help, bro. You're good at this kind of thing. Organization and whatever." He shoved the phone across the counter. "Tell me what to do."

Nick did not pick up the phone. "Do you have a name?"

"For the business?"

"Yes."

"Um, no."

He'd tossed a few ideas around with Jorge last night while they sat side by side on loungers on the back patio, peeling the labels from their beer bottles. As usual, Cam had done most of the talking with Jorge interjecting a grunt now and again. Cam had yet to figure out whether Jorge's "comments" had been in the affirmative or negative, however.

"Let's start there."

"With a name?"

"You'll need it for all the paperwork."

"Shit."

"You don't have to put whatever you register on the side of your truck. You can use a trading name. But you need something for the business paperwork."

"Your truck," Cam muttered.

"What?"

"It's your truck."

"I gave it to you."

"I'm borrowing it, okay? But if I offered to buy it, how much would you want? I'm going to need some assets for this business, aren't I? Fuck." A familiar roiling moved through his gut. Flat air seemed to push at his ears. Cam edged off the stool. "You know what, let's just forget it. I'll—"

Nick grabbed his elbow, and the movement was so unexpected—his brother never reached out unprompted—Cam stood still.

"What's happening?" Nick asked.

"What do you mean?"

"In your head. Why is this so hard?"

Resisting the urge to shake off Nick's hand, Cam sighed and sat. Then he touched Nick's fingers, sort of squeezing them and peeling them off his arm at the same time.

Nick sat on the stool beside him and pulled Cam's phone across the counter. He opened a fresh note and put his thumbs to the tiny keyboard. "Milford, Zimmermann, landscape, lawn, care, terrain, beautiful, garden, aspect, prospect, grounds—"

"What are you doing?" Cam leaned over to watch the progression of words on Nick's list.

"Listing keywords. We can bump two together as a business name."

Could it be that easy?

Cam started joining words. "Milford Lawn, Milford Beautiful, Milford Grounds." It was harder to marry his name to the ideas on Nick's growing list, but he tried a few. "Zimmermann Landscape, Zimmermann Garden, Zimmermann Prospect. How about Zimmermann Projects? That sounds good."

"Either that or Cam Do."

"Cam what? No, oh, no. That's terrible."

Nick grinned. "We'll start with Zimmermann Projects. It's versatile. You can fit a few business models underneath it. Now we need to figure out whether or not the name is already registered."

The roiling returned. What if someone already had the name? He'd be stuck. And how long would he have to wait to find out how stuck he was?

Nick flipped back to the website Cam had found and brought up a search tool. He handed over the phone. "Type it in."

Cam put the phone on the counter and drew in a deep and not refreshing breath. He picked up the phone with a trembling hand and put it down. Fuck. He tried again and nearly dropped the phone. The kitchen started to spin, and it was as though he hadn't been breathing at all. A roaring started up somewhere inside his head, and he had to fight the urge to cover his ears. His back hurt and every one of his scars ached.

Shit. *Not now.*

It'd been more than two years since he'd fought dread so strong, he nearly blacked out. But with as hard as he'd been avoiding thinking, he almost wasn't surprised to feel it now—strong fingers of doubt pressing at the base of his skull and the noise. Why was panic always so loud?

Pushing off the stool, Cam stood still for long enough to ensure his feet were on the ground and then took off. Or tried to. Nick grabbed his arm again. He might have been talking, his mouth was moving, but the crashing waves inside Cam's skull drowned him out.

Shaking his head, Cam jerked his arm out of Nick's grasp and made for the door.

Nick beat him there and spread his arms from side to side, forming a barrier.

"Don't." Cam pushed ineffectually at his chest. He didn't want to hurt his brother. Not Nicky.

When Nick didn't move, Cam pushed a little harder.

The roar inside his head was now so loud, it hurt. And he still didn't seem to be getting any air. Black spots crowded in around the edges of his vision, and the sense of being exposed crept across his shoulders. The need to duck and cover swamped him. Turning, Cam scouted the room and chose the couch in the living area facing the kitchen.

Somehow managing not to knock over anything in his path, he lurched toward his destination, bundled himself into the farthest corner of the couch, hunched forward, and curled his arms over his head.

Breathe.

If he didn't, he'd pass out, which might be a mercy.

Air ripped down his throat and his lungs convulsed. He managed another breath, and the roar started to fade. The hum beneath remained steady, though. No, the hum was new, the hum was . . .

Tears pricked his eyes.

The hum was his brother, sitting next to him on the couch. His skinny little brother who had followed him everywhere, day and night. Through the house, out into the yard. To the creek where they'd float side by side until Nicky was old enough to play games. Up and down the street where Cam taught him to ride a bike. In the basement, batting a ping-pong ball back and forth.

Cam remembered waking up with the sun on Saturday mornings to find Nick sitting at the end of his bunk—he'd had the upper one—stacking cars or blocks or books or whatever the fuck he'd carried up there. He'd look up when Cam woke and show him that awkward, lopsided smile.

It hadn't always been them playing, though. Nick had had such a hard time connecting with others. He'd come home from school bewildered and in tears and sometimes he'd yell and scream and rock into walls.

Cam remembered rocking with him. They used to try to stop him until they figured out that he needed the rhythm of movement—and that he could be left to do it on his own as long as he wasn't in danger of hurting himself. Cam had never liked leaving him alone, though.

Until he had.

Now, he read the concern in Nick's eyes. Saw what few others would see. The love beneath. Nick's emotions on full display.

"I'm sorry," Cam whispered.

"It's okay."

"No, you—" It was too hard to explain.

Nick allowed a beat of quiet to pass between them before speaking again. "Is this because you want to start a business?"

"Yes."

"Why?"

Cam didn't have to think about it. "The responsibility."

A wrinkle appeared between Nick's eyebrows. "Why?"

"Because I'm a fuck-up, little bro. Everything I've ever tried has crashed and burned. This is gonna be no different."

"What else have you tried?"

Always with the questions.

"It's better if no one else is relying on me. That way, if I don't show up, I'm the only one who gets hurt."

"Why wouldn't you show up?"

Cam jerked his head up. "Did you not see what just happened? I freaked out over a business name."

Nick appeared to digest this. "I think you freaked out over starting something new."

"Same deal."

"Will you tell me about when you came home?"

What was he talking about? "Huh? When?"

"Two years ago."

The desire to leave itched along Cam's legs, but his body felt too heavy to lift off the couch. Despite years having passed since his last full-on panic attack, he remembered the exhaustion that followed. He flopped his head back and sighed. Tried not to ruminate on all the ways in which he had failed and why he'd finally decided to come home. "I ran out of money."

The couch creaked quietly as Nick moved. Cam closed his eyes and breathed.

Nick moved again, then started talking. "This therapist I'm seeing? One of the things we do is go over the events I'd prefer not to think about. I can verbalize the memory, or write it down. I . . . It's hard. But it helps. Do you remember when you told me talking helps? You were right. So, talk to me."

Nick had come so far. Cam had never doubted he'd grow up to be a good and kind man. Sensitive, but in a good way. He was glad Nick had turned out okay.

Cam took a deep breath. "I invested every cent I had into a business venture with a friend. With a woman who I thought was my friend. It was for a franchise. I'd been working dead end jobs ever since I got back. I didn't mind so much. Go in, lift, carry, pack, whatever for twelve hours, go home. But I had some savings, money I was putting away for Emma, you know?"

Nick offered a nod.

"I saw the opportunity to make my money do more. A way to get somewhere. Be someone. Own a business." The swirl in his gut turned sour. Cam swallowed. "She took it all and ran."

Face showing little emotion, Nick said, "This was the woman you wanted to marry."

Cam winced.

"I'm sorry," Nick said and he looked as though he meant it. As though he hadn't plucked the phrase from a list of acceptable reactions.

Concentrating on that rather than the fact he didn't need such words from his brother, Cam shrugged. "If I was a fully functioning adult, I'd have seen it coming."

"Probably not."

"What makes you say that?" Also, points to Nick for not arguing the adult part. Or the functional part.

Nick studied him for another long moment, as though consulting his list of acceptable responses or maybe just searching for the appropriate words. Cam waited with the patience he'd learned growing up with his uniquely thoughtful little brother.

"You are the most caring person I know," Nick finally began. "You always want to help people, no matter who they are or who they are to you. It makes you susceptible. But wouldn't you rather get hurt trying to help people than never connect at all?"

"I'd rather have my thirty grand."

"Did you go to the police?"

Cam sighed. "I don't have a good record with the police, man. A couple drunk and disorderlies. One DUI. They weren't going to take me seriously."

"You don't know that."

"Trust me. In that town? I did know that. Like I said, I'm a fuck-up."

Pain flitted across Nick's face. "I wish you wouldn't say that."

"Why?"

"Because—" His lips flattened into a hard line. "You served. You went away to war. A horrible war. You got hurt."

Surprise lifted Cam's eyebrows. "How did you know I got hurt? Oh. My scars."

"And the dates."

His tattoos? Did Nick think they were—

"Your tours didn't line up exactly. You came back early."

He had. "They sometimes don't, but yeah, I got hurt. I'm fine now." Mostly.

That thought plucked a smile out of nowhere and fixed it to one side of his mouth. Melanie reckoned he was *mostly* harmless. Mostly sane. Mostly trustworthy.

But not great with money. Mostly gullible.

Nick got up from the couch, grabbed their coffees and Cam's phone, and brought them back over. He handed Cam the phone. "C'mon. Let's see if the name you want is taken."

Recognizing that the moment had passed, Cam took the phone and stared at the screen until it went to sleep. He breathed in and woke the screen again. Typed: *Zimmermann Projects.*

Less than a second later, he had his answer: *No results found.*

Stomach cramping, he looked up to meet his little brother's lopsided smile. Felt a reciprocal curve pluck at one corner of his mouth. "I guess I have a name."

Nick grinned. "I guess you do."

Chapter Twenty-Four

"**B**rush, meet canvas. I know it's been a while, but you two used to be the best of friends." Victor prodded the tip of his brush closer to the washed canvas in front of him until the bristles touched. "Now talk, damn it."

The brush remained still in his hand.

He'd start at the top, with hair. No, that was a terrible idea. He needed a face first. Victor glanced at the sketch pad propped on the easel next to him. An ear? He could outline the face from the right ear down, around the jaw and up to . . .

This was why he didn't paint people. Trees didn't have ears or noses. They didn't need to be distinct.

Dropping the brush back onto the palette, Victor slumped onto the stool behind him. He put his head in his hands and groaned.

Maybe he should go back to landscapes. Tez had been wrong. Portraiture didn't come naturally to him. Not anymore. He *had* enjoyed sketching Cam and the other studies he'd done over the past few weeks—of Cam at work on the path, his friend Jorge, the young Beck, Estefan, and the new, fifth member of Cam's ragtag landscaping team, Estefan's wife, Renata. But he hadn't had any success transferring his ideas to a canvas. He still wasn't painting, which was not aiding his efforts to keep the darkness at bay. But he was determined not to succumb to the feeling that all, if not already lost, soon would be.

Victor pulled the sketch pad from the easel and flipped through studies he'd done of kids at the center. Cassidy painting. Nayana cutting paper for a collage. Lionel hunched over a computer. Victor smiled at the steep curve of the young man's back. Did he have elastic for a spine?

He had sketches of his son and grandson. His number two daughter (Sage's girlfriend) and a drawing of his number one daughter, though he hadn't seen her in weeks. He'd used a photo as a reference. He had a whole series of Tez, who had patiently made faces for him for an hour or so on his last visit to Stroudsburg.

And he had pages and pages of Cam.

Perhaps he needed to start with a subject he was less afraid of.

Humming softly to himself, Victor compared his sketch pad to the wash of paint he'd used for a background on his current canvas. A combination of oak and gold in preparation for Cam's brown on brown coloring. Should he have used blue instead? Added ochre highlights to Cam's hair?

He put the sketch pad aside and stood to sort through the tubes in the paint-splattered cart he'd parked close by. Burnt umber, camel, wheat? No, too light. Sienna, black bean, burgundy. He dotted a fresh palette with color and began mixing. Then, with a conscious lack of thought, he introduced the brush to his canvas again, moving it in short, downward curls. Dark layers first, moving outward. Lighter, a shadow beneath there, lighter still. Another shadow. He mixed and painted, mixed some more, chose a lighter shade, and finally started applying highlights to the cap of varied brown. Ochre and a touch of orange. Using a much finer brush for the slimmest threads.

The golden background was wrong, but he could fix that. Also, no one was going to buy a painting of someone's hair, so whatever. He was painting and that was all that mattered.

After dotting a final touch here and there, Victor dropped his brush into the jar of water, where it collided with the three other brushes he'd used. The water had that murky puddle color he always tried so hard to replicate on canvas, and the studio smelled of paint—a curiously flat odor—and sweat.

A chewing sound caught his attention, and he checked the corner where Cam had encouraged Honey to curl up and nap. He'd dropped her off a couple of hours ago, asking Victor to keep an eye on her while he and the team continued work on the path project. He was worried about her being too close to the road. Given Honey had made her debut on a roadside, Cam's concern was relevant.

The end of the cast closest to her paw had a rather frayed appearance. Victor smiled. If he had fur, he'd probably want the damn thing off too.

He ambled over, crouched at her side, and ran a hand along her short coat. Had her belly been this round when Cam found her? Probably not. She licked his hand.

The front door opened and closed, and a voice called out, "Hello!"

Smiling, Victor stood. "In here."

After a scuffle that likely involved Cam pulling his dirty boots off, a shadow appeared at the other end of the family room. Victor only felt silly after he waved, but left his hand suspended in the air. Cam's smile as he approached made the gesture worthwhile. He looked tired but restful as he joined his hand to Victor's, threading their fingers before folding his over in a squeeze, and then leaned in to kiss him.

He tasted sweet and salty, like caramel soda and hard work.

Pulling back, Victor murmured, "All done for the day?"

"Yeah. We got the first three terraces finished. Want to come see?"

"Seeing as I'm not allowed to work on this project with you, maybe I should wait until it's completed."

Cam squeezed his hand. "What's the point of paying me to do some work if you're going to do it with me?"

"I could stand the exercise."

"Start clearing for the vegetable patch you want to put in. Or the herb garden behind the patio. Chop some wood. Winter is always coming."

Victor chuckled, and his mood rose up from the anxious knot in his gut to spread across his shoulders like a warm blanket. Cam always had this effect on him. Victor could be spiraling downward and one glimpse of Cam's smiling face would halt the cycle.

Cam peered over his shoulder with a light frown. "Is that a dead bush?"

Victor glanced back into the studio and laughed. His painting did resemble a brown bush. Or a pile of turds. *Take your pick.*

"Something like that." He'd rather not tell Cam it was hair. *His* hair. Who painted just hair, for goodness's sake?

Maybe that could be his new direction. Victor Ness—hair artist.

"Hey."

Victor snapped his eyes forward and met Cam's curious gaze. "Hmm?"

"Everything okay with you?"

"I'm . . ." He pressed his lips together. Cam knew his thoughts on *fine.* "It's been a long day."

"Don't I know it. Come see the path."

"Where's everyone else?"

"Gone. On their way home."

"Is Jorge expecting you this evening?"

Cam chuckled. "No and I think he might be having a friend over." He frowned again. "He made a point of asking if I was coming home tonight, so . . ."

"Maybe he wants to fart in peace. Or watch something other than Star Trek."

"Hey, now. That's quality television."

Victor hooked his arm through Cam's. "Show me what you've done with the path."

Together, they crossed the driveway, circling the lichen-covered fountain at the center. The gap in the trees on the other side still surprised a little. Victor was so used to seeing skeleton limbs from the dead tree poking above the canopy. Clearing that and the tree next door had left a good-sized space for the top of the path, and he looked forward to planting a few perennials there later in the fall. The rhododendron he'd imagined, which would provide a nice splash of color in the spring and early summer. And some bulbs, maybe, though chipmunks would probably eat most of them before they had a chance to sprout.

From the clearing, the path angled away from the driveway into the first gentle turn. The second turn was a little sharper. The path continued to switch back and forth down the slope until it spilled out by the mailbox. Victor could see all of it from the top of the hill, including the frame for the first three turns, and something new.

"What's this?" he asked, jumping onto the shallow steps connecting the first and second loops.

Cam climbed down to stand beside him. "In winter, you'll want to follow the path. Or when it's snowy or slippery. But right now? If you were in a hurry, you could use these steps and cut out the curves. I'll put another set between each switchback on this side." He smiled. "I mean, the driveway would get you there faster, but I had the extra wood. And I figured someone always wants to cut corners anyway."

"It's brilliant. I love it." Victor punctuated his statements with kisses, grateful for the lighter moment. Cam was all too adorable when he got excited about his work.

From below the top, Victor surveyed the path again, the sweeping curves of the main project and the steps in between, and nodded with satisfaction. Even before they filled the frame with dirt and gravel, he could picture the end result. Could already imagine the forest growing back in to surround it and the small joy he'd feel taking this way down to the street. It would be his road less traveled. His outdoor break.

He'd think of Cam every trip.

Stop that.

Cam was looking at him.

"What?" Victor asked.

"You want to go out?"

Victor frowned. "What do you mean?"

"Like, to eat. Or for a drink. Out, out."

"A date?"

Complicated feelings flitted through Cam's eyes but he nodded.

"I thought we weren't doing that. We're friends who fuck."

Cam winced. Licked his lips. "I figured it might be fun. To go out. Together. As friends."

Victor looked away, his own emotions beginning to feel complicated.

Beside him, Cam shuffled, his unlaced boots scuffing against the dirt. Then, with a puff of breath, he climbed the steps and started back toward the driveway, leaving Victor standing alone in the woods.

Victor scrambled up the hill after him. "Cam."

"Just gonna grab Honey." Cam crossed the driveway, kicked his boots off outside the front door, and disappeared inside.

A part of Victor wanted to let him go. It would be easier to let this moment ebb rather than have it break the relationship they were building. A greater part wanted to fix the misunderstanding. If he let Cam go now, it would affect their friendship. He had no doubt Cam would finish the job on the front path and that he'd do spectacular work. But Victor's joy would fizzle and pop. He would hate the path.

You're going after him to save a damn pathway?

Cam reappeared in the doorway, Honey in his arms. He wore a stoic expression but managed a sort-of smile. "I'm doing a market for Ollie and Gray tomorrow. Sunday, my niece is coming for dinner, so, ah, I'll be back Monday—no, probably Tuesday to finish out the framing. I forgot we've got two lawn jobs on Monday afternoon."

"Cam."

"I'll call you if my plans change." Cam had shoved his feet back into his now-loose boots and was clumping toward his truck.

Victor followed. "Cam, please?"

Cam settled Honey on the front passenger seat and turned. "What?"

Throat tight, chest heavy, Victor sorted through the minute differences between what he wanted to say and what he needed to say. Cam had half-turned away again when Victor finally managed to get a word out. "Stay."

"I don't think that's a good idea."

"None of this has been a good idea, but here we are."

Still turned away, Cam shook his head. "I told you this wasn't going to work out the way you thought it would."

"You did. But you had no idea what I wanted."

Cam faced him again. "No?"

"I wanted to sleep with you. Touch you. Discover you. I didn't want . . ."

"This." Cam sighed. "Neither did I."

"And, yet, here we are."

"Maybe this is where it should end."

Victor glanced over at the front door—still ajar—as though he could pinpoint the spot of gravel where he'd entertained a similar thought. Or had he been standing on the steps? No matter. He turned back to Cam, thought about putting a hand to his chest, decided that was too dramatic, then did it anyway. "Is that what you really want?"

In the time Cam took to think about his answer, Victor's heart soared and dipped. It hurt. How had they managed to come so far in so short a period of time? It'd been, what, a month?

"What do you want?" Cam asked, fixing him with an intent look.

Tell him to go.

Ask him to stay.

It was going to hurt either way.

"I want you. I want whatever this is to continue. Our friendship and everything that makes this more than what we want. I'm not ready for it and I know you didn't want it, but we're here now, and I feel as though calling it quits would mean losing not only what we have, but all of it."

"We should have known we couldn't just have sex." Cam wore a wry smile.

"We did know. The both of us."

"Yeah." He rubbed his forehead. "I guess we did." Cam dropped his hand. "So, listen, the reason I, um, wanted to, ah, go out tonight . . . Christ, why is this so hard?"

Victor badly wanted to take his hand. Thread their fingers together again. Draw Cam into a kiss. The moment their bodies touched, they'd forget all about the concept of words and the diagrams that defined their relationship. They'd pull off their clothes, tumble into bed, and—

"You wanted to do something that wasn't sex," Victor said, suddenly certain he'd gotten it right.

Cam nodded. "Because I wanted to invite you to meet my niece on Sunday. My brother will be there too."

"Oh! Yes. I mean . . . Okay. How do you want to do this? Sunday, that is. Are we friends or more?"

"Honestly?" Cam snorted lightly and shook his head. "I don't fucking know. We're . . . You're . . ."

"Is this the most awkward relationship conversation you've ever had?"

"God, yes."

Victor laughed. "Nice to know we still have it."

"Not sure what *it* is, and speak for yourself, old man."

"You're not even three years younger. Two and a half."

Grinning, now, Cam reduced the space between them or tried to. His unlaced boot chose that moment to flop off his foot and he stumbled. Victor caught his arm, and they swayed together, torsos brushing, and then their hands and mouths were fused, Cam's all-day stubble scraping over Victor's jaw, their noses butting together, hands already plucking at shirts, hips grinding.

"You always taste so good," Cam said into his mouth.

"You always feel so good." Hard and soft, but mostly hard. Especially now. Victor palmed the erection pushing at Cam's zipper. "Want you."

Cam kissed the words away, his hands at Victor's shoulders now and turning him, backing him up to the truck. He started working the button of Victor's jeans, then slid down Victor's body with them, dropping to his knees as he pushed the denim down, lips seeking the exposed skin of Victor's hips.

Before Cam could take him into his mouth, Victor pushed at his shoulders. Gently. "Is this what you want?" It was a stupid question to ask with his cock caressing Cam's cheek. Victor knew what he wanted. But Cam had started the conversation in a different place. One they were about to forget.

Cam smiled up at him, apparently comfortable on his knees in the gravel, outdoors, under a late-afternoon sky. Thank Christ the driveway curved up a hill.

He kissed Victor's bobbing dick. Licked the side. Then drew away, leaving Victor to hiss and whine.

"This is what I want right *now*," Cam said, his breath warm against Victor's thighs. "Then I'm taking you out to eat. I've got a change of clothes in the back of the truck."

Victor's knees almost gave way. Cam had had a plan. He'd packed clothes.

This man.

Caressing Cam's cheek, Victor smiled and curled his fingers under that stubbly chin and nudged his mouth a little to the left. "Then we'd better get started."

Chapter Twenty-Five

C am stopped in the middle of the kitchen with a tray of sweet potato wedges held out in front of him. "Shit."

He'd been on autopilot most of the afternoon. Cleaning and tidying the house, sweeping the patio, and plucking stray weeds from the beds. He'd been about to chop wood for the firepit when Jorge had pointed out that he had enough wood stacked behind the garage to see him through forty years of winter.

When Cam had (not) wailed that he needed to mow the lawn, Jorge had pushed him inside with one word: "Chill."

Now Jorge was mowing and Cam was putting together what food he could before his guests arrived. And he'd just realized that he and Victor had forgotten to define their relationship. How was he supposed to introduce him to everyone else?

As Victor Ness, dummy.

Huh.

Cam slid the tray into the oven. A grin edged across his mouth as he set the timer. Nick would be proud. He'd scheduled the oven to switch on at five, meaning the potatoes should be ready by six. Or so. Now he had to remember to slide the mac and cheese casserole back in there at some point. Or should he microwave that?

Cam leaned out of the back door and waved Jorge down. The mower stopped. "How should I reheat the mac and cheese?" It was Jorge's baby, after all. He'd made it last night.

"Twenty minutes at three-seventy-five."

He'd set the oven for four-twenty-five for his potatoes. So, what, ten minutes?

Ten minutes.

The front doorbell rang, and Cam waved Jorge back to work before going to answer it. Emma stood there, looking so damn adult, Cam could cry. He pulled her into his arms. "What is it with this family and ringing the goddamned doorbell? This is your house."

"Yeah, but you live here," Emma said into his neck.

He released her from his embrace but continued to hold her upper arms. "Let me look at you." He eyed her up and down. "You had your hair cut." Now it was shoulder-length and framing her face instead of tied into a long braid. "And you might be taller."

She kicked out one foot. "Heels."

As always, she was dressed as though she had somewhere to go, in slacks and a blouse. He didn't think he'd ever seen his niece in jeans. The blue and green flowers on her blouse were pretty, though, and suited her. She still looked like Emma.

"Come on in," he said.

"Anyone else here yet?"

"Only Jorge." He'd told Emma all about his houseguest during one of their phone calls.

"I can't wait to meet him! When's Uncle Nick getting here?"

Cam glanced over her shoulder. "He didn't bring you? I thought he was picking you up from the bus?"

"I called an Uber."

"Not the car that smells like Chinese food?"

"The very one."

"Damn, girl. You should have called."

She shrugged and then turned at the sound of another car rolling down their street. It was Victor's SUV. Cam's stomach pinched. *Shit, shit, shit. Be cool. Stop sweating.* Jesus, fuck, were his hands shaking?

While Emma and Cam watched, Victor got out of the car and retrieved a bag and a box from the back seat. He looked good. Long, lean legs encased in the light denim he preferred, and a loose, billowy shirt in shades of purple and blue. Sorta like his robe.

Cam's stomach had nearly turned itself inside out by the time Victor reached the front door.

Victor shot him a sympathetic smile and held up the box. "Pie."

Cam took the box and Victor greeted Emma. "You must be Cameron's niece. It's so nice to meet you. I'm Victor."

"Hi, Victor." Emma shook his hand before arching one slim eyebrow in Cam's direction.

"Victor's my . . ."

An awkward pause bounced between the three of them.

Victor licked his lips. Cam waited for his body—which now felt brittle—to explode into a million pieces.

Smiling, Emma touched Cam's hand under the pie box. Then she turned her smile on Victor and said, "Now I'm *really* glad you're here."

Victor laughed and Cam wanted to die.

Somehow, they got inside the house, where Cam dithered around with the pie, trying to decide where to put it. Now that his and Victor's relationship status had been relegated to a silence that spoke volumes, he was free to ponder the next quandary: Why the fuck had he invited so many people over?

Jorge put the mower away and then ducked upstairs for a shower.

Soon after, Nick and Ollie arrived with Gray in tow.

"Aaron went hiking with his folks," Gray explained while shaking Cam's hand. "I was invited, but hiking with the Ashers is like a forced march up Mount Everest."

Cam laughed. "There's a heart-healthy turkey burger in the fridge with your name on it."

Gray looked crestfallen. "And here I was hoping you'd be my excuse to eat something fun."

Renata, Estefan, and Beck showed up next. Renata was married to Jorge's cousin Estefan. She was about his age and built like a bird. But, man, she could work and she had a wicked sense of humor.

Beck also worked hard and had an earnestness that reminded Cam of Nick and Emma when they were younger. They'd been pretty shy at first, and Cam understood that he and Jorge, Jorge in particular, could be intimidating. They were tall men. But by the end of the first week, Jorge's peaceful demeanor had won Beck over. Now they smiled along with everyone else at Renata's jokes.

As he'd expected, Emma immediately took Beck under her wing, leading them aside to chat quietly. Cam pushed everyone else outside—he hadn't swept the damn patio for his own amusement—and went to get the charcoal from the garage. He should have started the grill half an hour ago. Now he'd have to adjust the timer on the oven.

Nick caught up with him on the way there. "Why is Victor here?"

Ah, his brother. So direct.

"He's my . . . friend."

Nick's eyes widened. "You and Victor?"

Cam stopped walking. "What do you mean, me and Victor?"

"You hesitated and your face got all complicated. You're together, aren't you?"

A sigh gusted out of him, and it felt pretty good. He'd lost the brittleness of earlier, and his stomach had stopped cramping. "Yep."

Nick's smile was sudden and brilliant. "I like Victor a lot. I don't know him well, but he's very committed to the programs at the center. To working with kids. He's a good person."

Cam could only nod. "He is."

"I'm happy for you."

"Thanks."

"I'm going to go talk to Victor now."

"You do that." Cam watched him go, bemused.

Back at the patio, his guests had further broken into groups he might not have predicted. Then again, as he watched Gray feed words to Jorge, who nodded back every now and then . . . Yeah, he could have guessed at that one. Gray could be sunshine itself, but he also enjoyed a good brood.

Oliver had engaged Renata on the subject of food. Probably trying to sell her on the meatless, cheese-less life. *Good luck, buddy.*

Of course, in deference to his vegan little bro, Cam had planned for the joyless eaters. He had black bean and rice burgers chilling in the fridge, a dairy-free pasta salad, and plenty of green shit.

Nick sat next to Victor. Both of them held glasses of wine, though Nick didn't seem interested in his. He'd likely taken it to be polite, and Cam would find it abandoned later. After lighting the grill, Cam drifted in their direction.

Nick turned to him. "You didn't ask Victor about the cards."

"The cards?"

"For Gray and Aaron's game."

"Oh! Man, I totally forgot." Cam pointed a finger between them. "Did Nick tell you all about it? Sorry, I was supposed to mention it about a month ago."

"I gave him an outline of the game," Nick explained.

Over his head, Victor gave a serious nod. His eyes twinkled with mild amusement. Cam's stomach did weird things again.

"If you're interested, you should chat with Gray some," Cam said. "He's Aaron's partner. He'll have pictures of what Aaron has done so far on his phone. And from the other game they did."

"It sounds fascinating."

"What's that?" Emma asked, joining the conversation. Beck smiled shyly at her elbow.

"I was telling Victor about Aaron and Gray's new game," Nick said.

"Oh, I want to hear about that!" Emma looped her arm through Nick's. "And I want to catch up on everything you've been doing as well."

Nick's smiles were often awkward. Higher on one side than the other, as though he doubted the appropriateness of his response. When he was with Emma, all such filters disappeared. He'd been caring for her since she was a baby, after all. Might as well be her father.

Cam loved seeing them together. At first, he'd been envious of their relationship. Now he was simply glad for it.

They started chatting, and Cam turned his attention to Beck. "How are ya? Sore from yesterday? Jorge said you all shoveled dirt and mulch for four hours."

Beck rubbed their left shoulder. "Yep. It was hot too. We went swimming after. So, hey, is it cool if I switch with Estefan on Monday afternoon? I checked with him. Mr. Ness only has three summer classes left."

"Sure thing."

Victor poked Beck on the shoulder. "See you then."

They smiled, ducked their head in a shy nod, and then went to join Jorge and Gray.

Cam turned to Victor. "So, the sweet potato fries are probably burning and I forgot to put the mac and cheese back in the oven. Also, the damn grill isn't lit yet. I hope everyone's good with eating around midnight."

Victor laughed.

"I'm sorry I couldn't find an elegant way to introduce you to Emma. Or anyone else."

"I stood there mentally flailing along with you."

"We were supposed to talk about it on Friday night."

"As I remember, you had your mouth full, then I had my mouth full, and then we went out to eat."

Cam never blushed. Except, apparently, for right now. Moving closer to Victor, he traced a hand down his arm. "Yeah." Their fingers tangled together naturally, as though activated by proximity sensors.

"You should be lighting the grill, not looking at me intently enough to make me hard."

"Damn."

"I'm not sure we have to explain ourselves. Just stand together and it's obvious we'd rather be in bed."

Nick and Emma glanced over, and Cam's never-before-and-would-never-happen-again blush intensified.

Cam tugged Victor up off the chair he'd been lounging in. "C'mon. Let's light a fire."

"Here or upstairs?" Victor's light blue eyes sparkled merrily.

"*Here.*"

Somehow, he got the charcoal lit, then he led Victor back into the kitchen under the guise of "I need someone to help me get all of this shit timed right."

He hustled Victor into the nook beside the fridge and kissed him senseless. Was thinking about dragging him upstairs, when the oven timer dinged.

"Not that I need an alarm to tell you I'm ready, but . . ." Victor broke off with a laugh.

Cam grinned. "Okay, need to stop thinking about sex and start thinking about the fact I have invited people over to eat and that I would prefer to serve something other than burned crumbs."

"I'll help." Victor pushed up his sleeves. "What do we have?"

Cam took him on a quick tour of the menu, and they fell into step, prepping dishes, deciding what needed to be heated and how, and getting the variety of burgers ready for the grill.

"So much easier with you here," Cam said, leaning over to press a fast kiss to Victor's mouth.

Victor's eyes softened. "And here you thought I was all about complication."

"Oh, you are. But I'm starting to think I like it."

"Me too."

Chapter Twenty-Six

"Jazmine, dear, how are you?" Victor observed his lips moving in the mirror over his dresser and wondered whether he sounded as manic as he looked.

If so, his agent didn't seem to notice. "Victor! Great minds. You were on my list of calls today."

"Oh?" His reflection frowned, and Victor turned away. He wasn't in the mood to watch his face age five years for every beat of news his agent had to deliver. He hadn't been on her list of calls for over a month.

"I have a line on an opportunity you might be interested in."

Dear lord, save him from agent double-talk. "Mm-hmm."

"A new gallery in Brooklyn is putting together a show of former residents. Artists who got their start in the borough. It's their way of—"

"Trading in on the known to make themselves less unknown. I'm familiar with the concept."

"I see it more as paying tribute."

"Oh God. I've gone from homewares to hall-of-fame invitations?" Having not escaped his bedroom, Victor sat in the chair by the fireplace and eyed his bed—the sheets and quilt still rumpled from his overnight guest. A smile edged across his lips. Cameron wasn't quite a silver lining to his current cloud of career woes—thankfully, he occupied a completely different part of the atmosphere. But being with him *now* certainly made all of the skies over Victor's head brighter.

"Victor?"

"Hmm?"

"I said, I don't understand. What homewares?"

Victor forced his thoughts away from the night before and early morning with Cam, about when he might see his lover again, and focused on the present. He frowned. "Housewares?"

"Never mind. I'm going to assume you were being allegorical. Can I tell you about the show?"

"Did they reach out or did you?"

"They did."

His shoulders dipped in relief. "Book it."

"Are you sure?"

"No, but I don't have much else going on career-wise right now, and though I generally loathe the idea of being grouped with a random collection of artists, I would like to sell some art. New art, that is. Anything other than a damned mouse pad with some weird corner of a painting I can't remember working on."

"Your online store does good business, Victor. It could be the reason you were invited to participate in this show."

"Good to know I'm still relevant."

Jazmine was silent for a moment, and Victor listened to the birds outside. They were quieter now, as the morning waned toward noon. He used to paint in the mornings. Around the middle of the day, he'd work in the garden or on a project around the house. In the afternoons, he'd paint some more or teach classes, either at the center or at one of two after-school programs. In the evenings, he'd try not to drink, which hadn't been all that difficult during a series. He'd be so focused on capturing his theme and drawing it from one canvas to the next that his evenings had often seemed to swallow themselves. He'd sit outside and watch the stars breathe in the night sky. Sit inside and watch sparks dance over the logs in the fireplace. Let his mind rest. Then start over the next day.

Now, Jazmine's silence reminded him of his evenings before Cam. When he'd sit at the kitchen table and stare at the bottles of wine in the rack beside the fridge and try not to imagine what each one tasted like.

Finally, Jazmine spoke. "Do you want to submit the series you were working on for the September show, or something else?"

"I don't have anything else."

"Do you want to talk about that?"

Thank Christ he couldn't see his reflection. He could feel his eyebrows pulling down and his eyes squinting. Victor rested his elbows on his knees. The phone, warm and slippery now, slid over his ear. Clutching it, he pressed it close to the side of his head. "Not really. I'm . . . I've been experimenting with a few ideas." He sucked in deep breath and straightened. "You know what, let's declare this the end of an era. All in on this show. I'm going to participate as enthusiastically as possible, and then disappear for a while. Until I have a new direction. No more pre-bookings or contractual obligations. Let's cast ourselves adrift in a sea of possibility and wait to see where we land."

When she responded, Victor could hear the smile in Jazmine's voice. "That sounds like the Victor I know and love."

"Okay, then."

"Have we covered everything? You were the one who called me, remember?"

"Only to see what you had for me. And here you had a show. How fortuitous."

Another beat of silence, then, "Art never dies, Vic. You'll always be relevant. The beauty you have captured will always be there. So make sure you take the time to drift properly before swimming for the closest shore."

Possibly not the best advice for a man who struggled with depression and a slight reliance on alcohol, but Victor understood what she meant. Art couldn't be hurried and, sometimes, neither could the artist.

After ending the call, Victor wandered into his studio, pulled a stool out from one of the tables, and sat with his art. He closed his eyes and inhaled the familiar odors. The soap he used to clean his brushes and the flat, woody smell of his paints. The scent of color and the way it all worked in his head. The way he felt green and brown and blue. How different shades of each moved and breathed. The concept of movement, and how hard he'd tried to capture it in the series that would prove his last for a while.

Should he think about retiring? He'd never planned for an actual date. Had assumed he'd paint until he could no longer hold a brush but with the expectation he'd produce less over time. And, in his heart of hearts, he'd hoped his value would increase as his paintings became more considered and rare.

He had not imagined this, this slow roll down the other side of a mountain he called success.

In a blur of black fur and yellow eyes, Sinister leaped into Victor's lap, his long tail thwacking him across the cheek. Chuckling, Victor smoothed his hand down Sinister's back, settling him down, and then he sat with his cat, the rumbling purr warm across his thighs.

He might have stumbled, but he hadn't broken anything. He was still *able*.

And if he was brave, he had many places to go.

Reflexive fear gripped tight.

Victor turned to one of the smaller paintings adorning the studio's wall. A sunflower in the brightest shades of yellow, orange, and gold. He hadn't been able to keep the portrait he'd made of his father, but this painting had always felt true to Sunshine's spirit.

"I don't know if I can do it," he said to the flower.

In his imagination, Sunshine spoke quietly back. *You'll never know if you don't try.*

Victor was delighted to find Beck gathered with the other kids in his summer art group.

"I'm glad you could make it today," he said.

"Me too!"

With a smile and a nod, Victor moved to the front of the classroom and took a moment to check in with all the faces, meet the eyes of every student. It was a small group. But they'd been meeting in this classroom over summer for three years now. Two had graduated last year, taking their number from nine to seven.

Next summer, three more would disappear and he'd see a new crop of faces.

It was time to give these kids more than just a space to hang out. For him to find joy in teaching again.

Resting the back of his hips on the edge of the desk, he reached behind for the folder of printouts he'd prepared and flipped it open. "I realize we're close to the end of the session, but I have a new project I want to share with you."

The faces in front of him angled upward, flowers seeking sunlight.

"A friend of a friend—a couple of friends, actually—are making a game."

Beck's mouth opened, and he offered a slight nod in their direction. Emma had introduced Beck to Gray and Gray, of course, had mentioned his and Aaron's games.

"They asked if I would contribute some art for the cards, and I told them I'd think about it." He leafed through the concepts Aaron had emailed over, and the printed images of already completed cards. Aaron had a great style. Completely different to Victor's: delicate and precise.

Stepping away from the desk, Victor started distributing the sheets. "These are some of the cards from the previous game. As you can see, they're all in one style. It took the artist, Aaron Asher, five years to draw them all."

A few more mouths opened.

"For this new game, he wants a different look. He'd like the cards to still feel representative of his brand, which he'll mostly accomplish with layout and typography. But the images themselves? Wherever your imagination takes you."

He handed out another few sheets. "Here's what he wants. The characters, the creatures, the terrain, the objects." Victor glanced around at his student's faces, all of them now wrinkled into serious expressions as they absorbed the information in front of them. "This is for fun. Pick a subject you feel a connection to and try a few sketches. If you're not feeling it, work on a project that means more to you. Either from this summer, or this year, or a project you've been working on in your spare time. For some of us, this might be our last summer together. Our last few classes. I want to make them memorable."

One of his quieter students raised his hand.

"Yes, Omar."

"So, our own style of art?"

"Absolutely. I don't know if Aaron and Gray will use whatever we give them. So don't feel any pressure to produce the perfect piece. Have fun with this. Experiment. Plan. Whatever feels good."

Advice he should be taking to heart, which was another reason why he loved this class. And teaching. Being with the kids. Whenever they asked a question he could answer well, he felt renewed.

If this upcoming show flopped, he'd put all of his energy into teaching, he decided. Start another program. Fund it himself if he had to. Because this was where it was at. Right here with these young flowers.

After answering a few more questions, Victor sat behind his desk, drew his copy of the games notes close, and opened a sketchbook. He began to draw. Not movement. Not leaves rippling in waves across the tops of trees. Not his students or his family or the face he'd woken up next to that morning.

He drew nothing at first, just lines from his imagination.

Then he sketched possibility and watched as the marks on his page pulled together into an image of a place he'd never been before.

Not the shore he'd told Jazmine they were aiming for, or the one she'd urged him to cruise alongside for a while before landing.

Somewhere new.

Somewhere completely undiscovered.

Chapter Twenty-Seven

C am's butt hit the couch before he knew he would be sitting. From behind her desk, Luisa rolled out a sympathetic expression. "I'm so sorry, Cam."

"No, no. It's your business, Luisa. Your decision. I'm just . . ." He studied the floor in front of his shoes. "A little winded, I guess." Even though he'd known this was coming and had made a contingency plan—sort of.

Zimmerman Projects was starting to feel less and less like an offshoot, though. Or what he did in his spare time. He had *employees*. He did *paperwork*.

His head snapped up. "What about the trees?"

Luisa smiled sadly. "We'll sell what we can. Discounts start today." She wandered over to the printer to pick up the day's delivery slips. "Mention it to your customers. All trees fifty percent off. Including the pine and fir."

"Are we staying open through November and December for the cut-your-own sale? What about fall? Are we doing pumpkins?"

"Yes and yes. The harvest sale is too lucrative to skip, and it will remind people that we have Christmas trees. But December twenty-fourth, we're done."

Cam glanced over at Jorge, who stood still and silent, gaze focused on the coffee in his mug. Could they find enough business from December twenty-fifth onward to keep themselves in beer and burgers until spring? And what about his employees? Beck would be back in school, so only part-time.

Where would he source all the materials they'd been using for the landscape jobs? The dirt and mulch? The trees?

Luisa was talking. "Whatever's left is yours, Cam. At whatever you can afford to pay."

"What do you mean?"

"Materials, the plant nursery, trees. I'd love to give you the land too, but the developer's offer will mean I can retire out west with my kids and not have to worry about income."

Cam didn't have to force a smile. "That's a damn good thing. You've worked hard, Luisa. You deserve all the breaks." He pushed up off the couch. "So, this is it."

"Yep. I'm not going to order any new landscaping supplies. We'll fill the orders we can during the fall and that's it." Luisa leaned over her desk and tapped a few keys on her computer. "This is my list of suppliers." The printer started whirring. "I don't know if you've set yourself up with an inventory system yet. You can probably have this computer when we're all said and done. But this list will get you started if you need additional supplies for your business." She glanced up. "And you're going to need a place to store it. Some land of your own. You could maybe talk to the developer about acquiring a lot?"

Cam's head hurt. He nodded. "Okay, yeah. Thanks." He eyed the printout but left it on top of the printer. "I'll grab that later. Thanks, Luisa."

"Sure."

Shell shock was a feeling Cam knew intimately. Carrying the numbness and ringing with him, the sense of unreality, he grabbed the delivery printouts and exited the office. Jorge followed. Together, they crunched across the gravel toward the lot where the landscape supplies rested in huge, framed piles. To the shed that housed the backhoe and front-end loader. Cam supposed he'd need to ask about them too.

"I can't afford all of this." He waved the printouts in an arc that encompassed the back corner of the fir lot, the nursery, the tractor shed, and the front corner of the materials lot. "What the fuck was I thinking? I don't have the money for a lot or a stock of materials or a backhoe."

"I do."

Cam spun around. "What?"

"I have the money."

"Dude, you were sleeping on the office couch. How do you have any money?"

Jorge shrugged and Cam thought that was all he was going to get. Then, "Never touched my settlement. Soon after I got back, my aunt passed. Left me her house. Sold that. And I've been living cheap." His brow furrowed. "You want me to pay rent?"

"What? No, I don't want you to pay rent. You're a friend. Besides, I don't pay rent. I tried, but Emma wouldn't let me. I've been saving it for her to use after college instead." Cam sighed toward his shoes, which were getting undue attention today. "Not that she'll probably need it. My sister left her pretty well set up." He glanced sideways. "Then why were you sleeping on Luisa's couch?"

Jorge held out a hand, and Cam passed over the printouts. After sorting them into an order he seemed to like, Jorge said, "I was taking a break." He met Cam's curious gaze. "When did you get back?"

"From Afghanistan? 2008. You?"

"Five years ago."

They shared a moment of silence pregnant with meaning that only they would ever fully understand.

"I like trees," Jorge finally said. "I like working with you. Wouldn't mind if we kept on."

Swallowing a sudden lump, Cam squeezed the big man's arm. "Then we'll keep on."

As though they'd agreed on nothing more important than where to get lunch, Jorge nodded and handed the slips back. "We'll load this one first."

"Right on."

The sense of being dazed followed Cam all through the morning deliveries and the two afternoon mowing jobs. ZP, as he was starting to think of Zimmermann Projects, had enough business to split between two teams. Estefan, Renata, and Beck worked mornings. He and Jorge worked the afternoons. They met up sometimes for larger jobs.

It worked because Cam and Jorge were still being paid by the tree farm. With his own place in the new venture subsidized, Cam could afford to push work toward Estefan's team. Realistically, while he and Jorge lived rent free, he could continue doing so. But that would be half-assing the situation.

Every time he thought about what it meant to have a business, his gut curdled and he thought he might shit himself. But he still wanted to do it *right*.

That evening, after showering and changing his clothes, he found Jorge and Honey in front of the TV. "Wait, are you watching—"

"Shh." Jorge shooed him away and put his hand back over Honey's shoulders. "It's the episode where Tuvok and Neelix get fused together by the transporters."

Cam grinned.

"You can take that grin to your boyfriend's house. He'll appreciate it more than I do."

With a salute, Cam left.

Victor had dinner ready for them, and Cam settled into what had become his customary seat at Victor's long kitchen table. "Guess who's watching Star Trek right now? All on his own."

"As if the poor man doesn't have enough scars," Victor said drily.

"Jorge's a survivor. He'll be fine." Cam dug into the baked pasta Victor had prepared. The fat raviolis were soft and the sauce rich and flavorful. "This is good."

"Another of my slow cooker standbys."

"You cooked this in a Crock-Pot?"

"Mm-hmm. You use frozen ravioli. Dump in the sauce, sprinkle cheese over the top, and let it sit all afternoon."

"I gotta get myself one of those."

Stopping short of licking his plate, Cam put his fork down and leaned back in his chair with a sigh. "Just as well you planned a big meal, because I wanted to talk. If you're cool with that."

Their evenings more often consisted of food then sex, or sometimes sex then food. Food and talking happened occasionally. Usually when they ate something heavy.

Victor put his fork aside and picked up his wineglass. "Should I be worried?"

"Only about my sanity."

Snorting, Victor drained the last mouthful from his glass. "'Oh, you can't help that, said the cat. We're all mad here.'"

Cam chuckled. "What's that?"

"*Alice in Wonderland.*"

"Oh, man, and you think Star Trek could leave scars?"

"Aren't they always at the mercy of evil aliens?"

"No! Star Trek is supposed to represent an enlightened future where diplomacy trumps aggression."

Victor shot him a blank stare.

Cam chuckled and spread his hands. "They try."

Smiling, Victor put his glass aside. "What is it you want to talk about?"

Cam outlined the events of the morning. Luisa's decision regarding the tree farm, her offer to sell the leftover supplies to him and Jorge when the business closed, and how he'd need to find somewhere to put it all. Jorge's offer. Jorge, himself.

"He said he was taking a break. I've done my share of couch surfing since I got back, and I can tell you, it never felt like being on a break. It's being between, you know? It's fucking purgatory or limbo. It's nowhere."

Gently, Victor said, "Maybe that's where Jorge needed to be for a while."

Cam closed his eyes and nodded. Yeah, that made sense. Warm fingers found his and squeezed. Opening his eyes, Cam smiled across the table at his lover. At the improbable man who'd changed his mind about relationships. Then he stopped thinking about Victor in those terms because the fear was real. He swallowed.

"Want to talk about it?" Victor asked.

"When I got back, I knew there'd be this period of adjustment. They prepare you for it. Well, they tell you to be prepared for it.

But . . . At first it was the quiet. I didn't realize how . . . It's not noise, it's like a static in your head. This constant alertness to sound. And the need to be ready for the sounds to change." Was he making any sense? And why were they talking about this?

Victor's fingers were warm against his, though, and the ravioli was nesting in his belly.

"Voices, wind, the vehicles; it's constant noise. The hospital was too quiet."

Eyebrows dipping, Victor offered a short, encouraging nod.

"All I wanted to do when I got out was go home. But when I got there, it wasn't noisy either. My sister, brother, niece. They didn't make enough noise. Am I making any sense?"

"Yes."

"So, I don't get the couch thing. But maybe Jorge's dysfunction is different. Maybe he needs the quiet. Or the aloneness. I . . . don't. I was going crazy in that house by myself. I like having him there." A grin pushed at his mouth. "He likes being there. Fuck. Five years for him, a lot more for me, and we're both still clawing our way out. Sorry. I don't know why I decided to tell you all of this."

Victor squeezed his fingers. "Don't ever apologize. I've seen your scars, Cam. Your legs, your ribs and shoulder. The ones inside. You don't ever need to be sorry."

Cam pressed his free hand to his chest. "Have you lost a person you didn't quite know the value of until they were gone?"

Again, Victor nodded and his eyes held a knowing glint.

"I . . ." Cam swallowed. "I lost someone over there. That was why I came back. I couldn't do another tour after that. I think Jorge must have lost more, though. For all I'm messed up. Fuck, I don't know. Maybe he's got the right of it. Solitude and silence. He's probably mentally healthier than all of us."

"Could be." Victor let go of his fingers.

They sat in the sort of silence Cam used to hate for a few moments before Victor asked if he wanted coffee.

"Have you got any of that peppermint tea?"

"Sure."

Cam followed Victor into the kitchen, where they moved around each other in easy domesticity.

After putting the kettle on, Victor turned and leaned against the counter. "Are you going to take Jorge up on his offer?"

Cam settled his hips against the opposite counter and folded his arms. Checked in with his shoes and remembered he was only wearing socks. He'd left his shoes by the front door, lining them up with Victor's and the castoffs from Victor's family and friends.

When he looked up, Victor was studying him with a calm and patient smile.

Cam breathed. In and out. Then shrugged. "I think so. I mean, yeah. I kind of have to if I want to make a go of this. I don't have enough cash to do it on my own. I know Nick could help me out. Emma, even. But it'd be nice to build something without them. Hell, if I could do it without Jorge's help, I would."

"I imagine Jorge has been sitting on his money while he waits for the right opportunity. Now he's found it. He believes in you. Trusts you."

"And that shit is scary as fuck."

Victor grinned. "Isn't it, though?" He nudged one of his feet forward so their toes touched. "But I think his trust is well-placed."

"I'm not a businessman."

"You've come this far on instinct alone. You're going to be fine."

Cam groaned. "Aren't you supposed to be talking me out of this? Offering words of caution?"

"Is that what you need me to do?"

Screwing his face into an I-have-absolutely-no-clue expression, Cam took Victor's words on board and sat with them for a while. Sat metaphorically, seeing as he was actually standing in Vic's kitchen, the toes of one foot pushing against his.

Breathe in. Breathe out.

Cam looked up. "I think I just needed you to listen. I could have said all of this to a wall, or to Honey, but neither of them would have asked me that question. So, yeah."

Victor's shoulders shook with quiet laughter. "I'm so flattered."

Cam nudged his toe. "You should be." Unfolding his arms, he closed the distance between them and took Victor's face in his hands. Bent to kiss him. Hummed softly at the warmth and lingering taste of ravioli. The slight tang of wine.

Victor kissed him back, gently, then with urgency. Hands slipped beneath shirts, Cam skimming his palms up Victor's back, Victor's fingers splaying over Cam's heart.

The kettle burbled and switched itself off. Cam rested his cheek beside Victor's, his lips close to an ear. *I'm so tired of being scared*, he imagined whispering. *About all of it. You, Jorge, the future. You.*

Being with Victor was dangerous. Cam's need to connect was picking scabs away from wounds that hadn't fully healed. His need to succeed at *something* had him reaching for a dream that hadn't fully coalesced. It all came down to balance, with Cam portioning out how much of himself to give, how much to hold back.

Victor's arms closed around him, and as the quiet deepened, Cam couldn't help wondering whether Victor was thinking the same thing.

Chapter Twenty-Eight

Without looking over, Victor tapped his fingers along the edge of the table for his 4B pencil. He wanted a soft black line here. One he could smudge, draw out, or deepen with the tip of a finer black.

"When you think it's dark enough, go darker."

The Wisdom of Victory Ness. If he ever wrote a book, he'd devote an entire chapter to that one.

His fingers brushed up against fur. Smiling, Victor curled his fingers into Dexter's thick white coat and gave the cat a good pat.

"Are you sitting on my pencils, Dex?"

He'd been so absorbed by his work he hadn't heard the burbling chirp Dexter always uttered as he jumped up from the floor. Had there been a tinkle of pencils spilling from the table? Quickly, Victor glanced at the floor. No pencils. "Just as well. The replacements would come out of your allowance."

Graphite didn't shatter quite the way lead used to, but it could still break inside a dropped pencil, causing the tip to wobble after a certain point. Then would begin the endless sharpening, frustration building as the broken piece fell out, only to be replaced by another one.

Victor tucked a couple of fingers under Dexter's belly and laughed as Dex licked the back of his hand. "Stop, you old fool." He located the pencil, all warm and snug, and pulled it out. Returned to the sketch pad propped on the table easel in front of him. He'd chosen a larger pad for this piece in the hope that giving himself room to expand his lines would release the feeling of restraint he'd experienced in his smaller studies.

Working on the cards for Aaron's game had been illuminating. After playing with some nonsense landscapes, Victor had chosen character cards rather than terrain. He'd enjoyed putting together the landscapes, but they weren't far enough away from the old Victor Ness. The lines had been too familiar and subject matter not compelling enough.

The character list proved far more stimulating. So far, he'd completed preliminary sketches for a ravager, a scavenger (both dwarves), and a troll. The subterranean setting included many underground species, and he planned to tackle a kobold next.

They weren't exactly portraits, but close, and as each creature came to life, he could feel himself pulling closer to a line he hadn't been able to cross.

This morning, he'd decided to try. Plunking down the sketchbook with the most studies of Cam, he'd told himself it would be just another character portrait.

He added the soft black line. Found the need for another. Traced a shadow that could stand to go a little deeper and touched the pencil down another two times. Squinting at the paper, he surveyed the ratio of light to dark, the gradient of his shadows, and gauged the completeness of his sketch. No—this was more than a sketch. Something other than a simple study. This was a piece he'd pushed to completion. Not quite a painting, but close.

Drawing in a careful breath, Victor scooted off the stool and stood. He grabbed the pad and propped it up on the closest upright easel and stepped back for a proper look.

"Oh, dear lord."

He'd done it. The face on his sketch pad had the same half tilt to the lips, the same careworn eyes. But the angle of his chin, that slight upward lift, said he wasn't out of the fight. The direct gaze? Cameron Zimmermann wasn't done caring yet, no matter how tired he was.

Though the portrait was rendered in black, white, and various shades of gray, Victor could feel the entire canvas of brown. The warm palette of Cam's eyes, the tanned skin, more weathered across his forehead, softer and paler behind his ears. His nose, that crooked yet strong line. There, right there. The way his hair almost curled.

A face that was at once not handsome but utterly beautiful.

Victor massaged his chest and let go of a long, slow breath. A feeling he'd almost forgotten—or hadn't wanted to entertain— crept beneath his hand, gripping his insides tight. It hurt, and he knew if he gave into it, the sensation would overwhelm him.

He *loved* this face. Loved the person who wore it. Had fallen head over heels, which was perhaps the most apt metaphor for love he'd ever heard, and would never be a chapter of his book because he had spent most of his life avoiding it. Had perfected the art, choosing lovers who were too pretty or selfish or self-absorbed (two rather distinct qualities). He'd entertained men who rambled endlessly about subjects Victor found tedious, who dressed better than he did (so annoying), who exercised properly and proudly, who believed in deities Victor had never heard of, adhered to ridiculous diets, didn't read for fuck's sake, and who didn't understand art. Or who thought they did and continuously challenged Victor's talent. Or falsely bolstered his ego because they loved the feel of his mouth on their cock.

He'd collected men and pretended despair when he discarded them.

Tholo had hurt. It always *hurt*. But separating himself from Tholo hadn't been about preserving his heart. No, that had been all about his pride. About that damn magazine and the picture of Victor in that stupid little cutout. The terrible lighting and the fact he resembled a hundred-and fifty-year-old harpy.

That and the cheating. Victor could not abide infidelity. He'd have been willing to share Tholo had he been asked. Wouldn't have minded entertaining one of Tholo's other lovers. But to be kept on the side, or rather in the middle, while Tholo cruised the perimeter fence? No. Just no.

Victor turned away from the sketch to speak to Dexter, who had rearranged himself so that his back paws stuck out at right angles and was currently engaged in the all-important task of butt cleaning.

"It's a simple life, but a good one," he told the cat, his throat tight.

Dexter continued licking. His inattention to Victor's spiraling emotions served a purpose, however. Victor stopped circling the drain. Mentally, he cast Tholo aside—*Good riddance, you trite little fuck*—and turned his thoughts back to the disaster at hand.

He'd fallen in love with Cameron, and this was so not good. Not good at all. The stupid part? He'd known it was going to happen. Had guessed it the minute he'd started seeking beauty in Cam's features. Not because he needed to be with an attractive partner, but because the more one got to know another person, the lovelier they became.

Feeling panicky now, he pulled out his cell phone and called Tez.

"Hey, you," she answered. "What's up?"

"I'm in trouble and I need your help."

He could almost hear Tez coming to alert. "What happened?"

Breath caught in his throat, and his heart seemed determined to continue beating faster, his pulse increasing until it launched from his chest and took off to orbit. Victor clamped a hand over his breastbone. "It's Cameron. I . . . I drew him again, properly this time. All the shades, my full set of pencils, and . . . Fuck, Tez. We've been seeing each other, and it was too soon after Tholo, and now I've gone and fallen for him and it's going to end in disaster and I'm not ready. I'm not ready!"

"Victor! Take a breath."

He sipped at the air.

"Take another one. Deeper. Count with me. In-two-three-four, out-two-three-four." Tez repeated the pattern a few times, and Victor counted the breaths off in his head. His pulse slowed and the rocket launcher under his heart petered out.

"Okay." He studied the drawing again. The art he'd been working on all morning, outlining, shaping, molding, and shading, until he'd brought a face out of the paper and kissed life into it.

His pulse sped up.

"Not working," he stuttered.

"Being in love is not the worst thing in the world!" Tez sounded exasperated.

"Oh, but it is, Tez. It absolutely is. It's going to hurt when he gets tired of me. It already hurts."

"What if he doesn't get tired?"

"Have you met me? I'm exhausting."

"I'm still here."

Was he imagining her grudging tone? "But we're not in love." As soon as the words left his lips, he regretted them because of course they were in love. Weren't they? *He* adored his best friend and would be beyond devastated if he never saw her again. His world would end. "Oh, dear god. You're not allowed to depart this earth. Ever. You hear me?"

"*And* we're on schedule for your five-year freak out where you assume everyone you love will die and leave you alone and in pain for the rest of your life." A definite note of weariness had crept into Tez's voice.

Victor slumped onto the stool in front of the table. "You make it all sound so dramatic."

"It *is*."

"I'm not . . ." A different hurt circled his heart. "I'm an emotional being. I always have been. You know this about me."

"And I love this about you. I do. You are and always will be my best friend. My soulmate." They'd long ago agreed that the concept of matched souls was always meant to uphold a platonic ideal because while each of them hoped one day to meet the person they were destined to have sex with until they grew old and, well, *dry*, they would always have each other.

Over the years, they'd adjusted their beliefs to accommodate various lovers who might have been The One. And still, they'd always had each other.

Tears beaded Victor's lashes. "I don't want to be in love with him, Tez. Not only because he'll hurt me, but because it's too much emotional investment. For both of us. I'm not . . . I've had a difficult year. You saw how I moped after Tholo left, and I didn't love him half as much as I do my cats. And the whole time I've been falling for Cam, warning klaxons have been sounding off in my head, all the way down a long tunnel. I can feel the end coming. I can feel a pit of despair opening up ahead and the ground sloping toward it. Sometimes I think I'm already sliding, and I'm not sure how long I can hang on."

"Oh, Victor. Why didn't you say something?"

"I'm saying it *now*."

Tez was well acquainted with the currents of his moods. The highs and the lows, and the fact that every so often, to a timetable that could not be predicted—her quip about his five-year freak-out cycle not withstanding—a deeper swell would sweep through, bobbing him a little higher but with an awful consequence. Once the wave withdrew, he'd touch bottom. He'd be down there with all the grit and detritus of life, and so damn heavy, he'd lack the buoyancy to bob to the surface again.

A beat of quiet passed between them. Dexter had finally moved from his ass to his legs and was currently chewing one of the toes on a back paw. Tez breathed quietly into the phone.

When she finally spoke, her tone held caution. "Do you think you should call Sahar?"

Victor chewed on his lips. Thought about how Sahar might react when he told her he'd fallen in love and how terrible it was. About what she'd recommend. He'd made it this far without medication—well, not really, if one counted wine and weed as medication, but they only dulled his sense for a short amount of time, for when he needed to feel dull.

Oh, but he was tired of battling the pendulum. So very tired.

A shadow appeared in the open doorway, Sinister slinking in from the family room. He rounded the corner of the table and dumped a small, gray mouse at Victor's feet. The poor critter had probably died of heart failure because there wasn't a mark on it.

"Sinister brought me a gift."

"Oh, dear."

"I'm trying very hard not to take it as an omen."

"Vic."

He straightened the curve of his spine. "You know what? I'm actually feeling a bit better." Not so much a lie as a false representation of the truth. He no longer felt as though he might fall off the top of a roller coaster and crash toward the ground, breaking every limb along the way. Instead, a numbness had started to spread through him. A sense of disconnection. Not exactly a good sign as Victor recognized it as his body and mind retreating from a decision. But he could operate like this. He could rest here for a while.

"Are you sure?"

"I'm going to pull out some of my old journals. Read over Sahar's previous pearls of wisdom and see if that helps. If not, I'll call her."

"You promise?"

"Don't make me promise. I'll call her if I think I need her."

"Call me too. If you need me. I'm always here."

Victor exhaled sharply and felt the breath leave his chest. "I'm here too. If you ever need me. I know I'm the more dramatic member of this duo, but I'd crawl up from the center of the Earth to be there for you."

"I know." He could hear her smiling now and could picture her face. The softness middle age had brought to her cheeks and the always warm and comforting brown of her eyes.

It was little wonder he'd fallen for a man with similar coloring.

"I love you, Tereza."

"Love you too, Victory."

Chapter
Twenty-Nine

"What do you think?" Cam asked as he surveyed the two acres spread in front of him and Jorge. Honey sat between them, a third observer.

They'd have to excavate and level, which meant renting the appropriate equipment. A road would have to be brought down from Dingmans Turnpike. More equipment. More work. Permits too. The business of starting a business seemed only to get *more* complicated.

Cam pressed Pause on that thought spiral and indicated the flattest corner of the hilly, bumpy lot. "Should we build an office or buy a trailer and park it there?"

"Hmm." Jorge turned a slow circle, and Cam followed him around. "When we clear this lot, we'll have two fewer acres to keep up with," Jorge said.

Cam laughed. "True that."

As they had suspected, buying a parcel of land from the developer who'd made an offer on the tree farm had proven beyond their means. It had been Jorge who'd suggested they approach the owner of the six-acre lot they'd cleared and continued to maintain. The guy had a deal in place for the front four, and they had their choice of the back two parcels, or both of them if they wanted.

Cam wasn't sure they needed two acres. Normally, he'd be all about the go-big-or-go-home idea, but in this instance, *big* equaled *expensive* and he was heartily tired of thinking about money. But it would be easier to acquire the land now than have to move later. The price scared him spitless, though. He'd done the research; it was fair. But the last time he'd gambled tens of thousands of dollars, he'd lost. This time? He didn't have even have half the money he needed.

Breathe. In and out.

Jorge turned back to him.

Cam squinted against the light of the lowering sun before shading his eyes. "What do you think?"

"I'm down with it."

"Okay." *Shit, shit, shit.* "Okay." Cam dropped his hand and sought solace in the rocky soil at his feet. The tufts of grass and weed he'd driven their ride-on over about ten days ago. "I need to talk to my brother."

Jorge didn't comment, but Cam could feel the weight of his gaze. Hear what he was holding back. Jorge could buy the property outright on his own and didn't mind being the money guy. Cam needed it to be an even split, though. No loans between them. Just a straight partnership. They'd already started the paperwork, which cost money. Because of course it did.

"We can start with a trailer," Jorge said, answering his earlier question. "Estefan knows a guy. It's a piece of shit, but it'd cost us nothing. We could park it at the top, here."

Jorge walked to the spot and Cam followed, Honey trotting behind. She was due to get her cast off in a week and probably wouldn't miss it, but she walked so well with it now, she'd have to readjust her gait. Cam bent to ruffle her ears, and she pushed her head into his hand before veering off to nose her way through a dense clump of bracken.

"Behind this hill." Jorge pointed back toward the road. "We should leave the slope at the front here. It'll give us a natural barrier between us and whatever they build up front."

"Good idea." Cam narrowed his eyes at the hill and recalled an architecture documentary series he'd watched years ago. "We could eventually build into the side. Like one of those eco houses. Grow some grass over the roof." Letting his imagination go made a nice change from stressing about money. "Extend a greenhouse out that way and put the plant nursery on the other side."

Jorge took over. "Gravel lot in front for parking and getting the vehicles in and out. Shed for the equipment. Steel?"

Cam nodded.

Jorge continued. "With doors at each end, so we can drive through. Then the materials."

"We can plant any trees we get from Luisa at the back."

"A few up here, too, around the office building. It has to all look good. 'Specially the green house. We can sell a structure like that."

"With all this mowing and building and landscaping, we won't have time to deliver supplies."

"We could keep that service for clients."

"Then there's the plowing and leaf service."

"We're going to be busy." Jorge looked as though he might be smiling.

They were already busy. Cam felt as though he hadn't sat down in a week. It'd been a couple of days since he'd last seen Victor, and nearly a week since he and Jorge had last managed an episode of Star Trek. Life was . . . not what Cam had been expecting. Not now. Not here, at nearly fifty.

Busy did have one blissful side effect, however. He'd never slept so well—when he wasn't fretting over money and responsibility.

Honey bounded back over, her one leg flying out sideways as she ran, and skidded to a halt in front of Jorge's boots. The large man scooped her up and hugged her to his chest, kissing her between the ears. She licked his face.

Jorge handed her over, and Cam got his cuddle in, holding the wiggling body of the excited dog with an ease unconsciously mastered. She got a kiss from him too. He got a thorough licking in reply.

Grinning, he put her back on the ground. "I have a feeling she'll be coming to work with us every day."

"She already does."

Smiling, Cam turned another slow circle, but he didn't need to. He could see it all as he and Jorge had described. Their business—or the center of the operation. The heart. There'd be a point where his fear became true excitement, wouldn't there? He lifted his chin in Jorge's direction. "We should change the name.

Zimmermann-Castellano. Do up a ZC symbol for the trucks and stuff."

"You sure?" Jorge's eyebrows crunched together. "You know Luisa never wanted her name on the business because—"

"Fuck that shit. We're partners. Both names. We can put yours first if you want." Cam suspected Jorge would decline the offer.

Sure enough, he shook his head.

"Just your name?"

Another shake.

"ZC it is." Cam extended a hand and they shook on it. Cam was about to express the wish that he'd known Jorge over there, that they'd been able to serve together. He thought he saw a similar idea flicker through Jorge's eyes. But then the handshake was done and the moment passed.

Just as well. Because when he thought about it again, Cam was glad they hadn't met until afterward.

"You want to call the guy? I'll drive, drop you and Honey home, then I'm off to see Nick."

Jorge bent and tapped a broad hand against his shin. Honey put her paws up on his legs, and he lifted her into his arms and carried her to the truck. By the time Cam dropped them back at the house, Jorge had finished talking to the owner of the land and they had a deal.

Cam parked behind his brother's shop and sat there with his fingers folded over the steering wheel of his brother's truck and wondered how he was going to ask his brother for money.

He sat there for thirty minutes, undisturbed, with his thoughts tumbling between whether the sickness in his gut was hunger or nerves before finally settling on nerves. The only other conclusion he'd come to was that Victor's texts over the past couple of days had definitely been too short. He needed to make time to stop by and see what was up.

All of that decided and with no idea how he was going to accomplish his current mission (impossible), Cam climbed out of the truck.

Seven o'clock had come and gone, and the early-September sun wouldn't be up much longer. Deep shadows had already swallowed most of the lane behind the shop, and the last of the day's light glinted only from the highest windows.

He knocked on the double doors and waited.

Oliver pulled open the left, dressed in one of his aprons (he seemed to own many, each of them a different color and design) and raised a floury fist for a bump.

Cam knocked their knuckles together. "What's cooking?" He sniffed, brow wrinkling. "Is that *bacon*?"

"Does it smell like bacon?" Oliver leaned forward, his expression all gleeful anticipation.

"It does."

"Want to try it?"

"Depends on what it's made of."

"Fungus."

A man should not be so proud of a word like *fungus*, or the fact he was trying to pass it off as bacon. But that was Oliver for you.

"Yeah, I'll pass. Nick around?"

"Upstairs. I'll pack up a few of these quiches for you to take home. I'm sure Jorge will enjoy them."

"Yeah, you do that."

Cam aimed for the stairs, as though distance could save him. He found his brother in the living area of the apartment, reclined on the couch with his socked feet propped up on a pillow. He had an elastic bandage wrapped around one ankle.

"What happened?" Cam asked.

Nick glanced toward the door to the stairs, then back at Cam. "Where is Oliver?"

"Cooking fungus." Cam shuddered.

The trademark awkward grin flashed across Nick's face. He tucked his hair behind one ear and nodded toward his propped ankle. "Dancing lessons."

"Dancing lessons."

"I wanted to learn how to do the tango."

"Should I ask why?"

"The proposal. I thought—"

Cam held up a forestalling hand. "Just ask him, Nick. Make a nice meal, sit him down, and push a ring box across the table."

"But—"

"It's one moment. It's the ever after that counts."

"People reminisce about the proposal, though."

"So make the meal *really* nice."

Nick frowned at his ankle.

No doubt they'd be having this conversation again. Hopefully not with Nick in a body cast because he'd decided to take up skywriting.

"Do you need to talk through it some more?" he asked before flopping into the chair next to the couch.

"No. I'll text you when I have a menu plan."

Cam chuckled. "You do that."

"Why are you here?"

And they were down to business. "Jorge and I found some land."

Nick's eyebrows jumped upward. "Where?"

"Right off the turnpike. Less than a mile from the tree farm. It's a part of the six acres we cleared for that guy." He didn't know how much detail Nick had retained from their brief conversations about his new business but supposed a detail like the number six would stick in his mind.

Nick nodded. "How much does he want for it?"

"Twenty thousand."

"That's a good price."

"I know."

"Do you have twenty thousand dollars?"

Cam pressed his lips together. Nick bumped one hip upward as though reaching for his wallet. He pulled out his phone, instead.

Holding up one hand, Cam called a halt to whatever it was he was doing. "Jorge has the money, but I want to partner equally with him and I don't want that partnership to start out with me owing him anything."

"I understand."

The sickness returned, bringing along breathlessness. Cam wanted to clutch his gut and his chest at the same time, and he was almost sorry Nick had the couch, because the corner he'd curled into for his panic attack was calling his name.

Breathe in, breathe out.

"Thing is, little bro, is that I can't guarantee I'm going to pay you back. This whole business idea might not work out. I'm not going to say it's because I have no idea what I'm doing. I've worked with Luisa for long enough to have a handle on the materials side of it, and adding in the lawn service and landscaping work has been pretty seamless. Estefan already has customers lined up with plowing contracts over the winter, and Jorge's started selling a leaf service. It feels like all we have to do is good work. Turn up on time, get the jobs done, and leave while everyone is still happy."

Cam had laced his fingers together. Now he pulled them apart and peeked at the couch.

Nick caught his eye and held it for what seemed like a long time before looking away. He flipped his phone over in his hand and turned back. "Do you want me to chart all of that out for you? Like a projection?"

Cam huffed. "Way ahead of you. We did that."

"Does it work?"

"It works."

"Then why are you worried?"

"Because I'm me? Because I nearly lost my marbles trying to register a business name. Which I need to change because if Jorge is going in on this with me, his name is going on the side of the truck. Also, I want to buy the truck."

"You can have the truck."

"I'm buying the damn truck. I checked the blue book price, and I'm going to make you a crappy offer, but you're going to accept it."

Frowning, Nick put his phone on his thigh. "Okay."

"Here's the deal. I have eight and a half thousand put away. It's yours, for the truck."

"It's worth eleven-point-five."

"Nine and a half, tops. The head gasket is about done."

"Oh."

Cam rested his elbows on his knees. The new position put pressure on his gut, which helped with the nausea. The change of subject did too. "Yeah, it's a rough idle and has started leaking oil."

"I'm sorry."

"Hey, it's a twelve-year-old vehicle. There should be more wrong. You took good care of it."

Nick scooted backward on the couch a little. "Do you want me to lend you your half of the twenty for the land, then?"

"Yes." Like ripping off a bandage, except the sting lingered, and Cam didn't have a wound to press his hand to. And he needed more than his half of the twenty. "Plus some for set up. We need to put a road down the side of the lot. Build a shed. Pay Luisa for the leftover supplies and vehicles."

Cam pulled his own phone out, then, assuming Nick would want to see the numbers. To his surprise, Nick waved him off.

Instead, he asked, "Are you going to resent me for lending you this money?"

"What?"

"I made it hard for you when you came back. I wasn't kind. And I'm your little brother."

"Nicky—Nick. No." Cam abandoned his phone and pushed his hands through his hair. "Have I ever told you how proud I am of you?"

Real emotion rippled across his younger brother's face.

"And not only of who you've become. *Always*. How fierce you were as a kid, how you stuck by Rebecca, how you did your best by Emma. You're one of the most amazing people I know. It's hard for me to ask you for this money, and my pride is taking some scrapes, because I always wanted to be the one who looked out for you. But knowing you're someone I can come to? Knowing you're here? That means everything."

Nick sat up and swung his legs over the edge of the couch. Cam tried to push him back, but Nick leaned forward so their knees were touching. "If this business doesn't work, I'd lend you the money to start another one. And another, and another."

Why?

Answering the unvoiced question, Nick said, "Because you were always there, even when you weren't. I missed you so damn much when you went away, but I was proud of what you were doing. I kept you in my head. When I had a hard time, I imagined you were telling me to keep trying. Now I have you back and *that* is everything."

Chapter Thirty

The journals were a terrible idea. An awareness of his mental state pricked at Victor's consciousness the moment he picked up the first of the neatly labeled notebooks he kept in a low cupboard in the studio.

That the books were all the same, somber gray had soothed him in the past, as though he was taking his mental health seriously. Now, as he stared at the regular spines, the undulating wave of sober color—or lack thereof—told him something else: he despised these books and what they represented. If he loved them, he'd have bought a different color for every year. If he enjoyed them, he'd have deliberated over the covers, the style of binding. He'd have bought beautiful journals he couldn't bear to write in.

"Which would have been so not the point," he said to the book clutched in his hand.

He shelved the journal and closed the cupboard door. Winced as he straightened and decided his creaky back had a better idea. He'd do some yoga, then he'd go for a walk. Exercise might keep the oncoming swell of depression at bay—build a bulwark, a levee.

Victor unrolled his yoga mat, collected his earbuds from the charger, and queued up a favorite yoga instructor on the app he kept on his phone. Ten minutes later, hands pressed together in front of his heart, Victor lifted one foot, tracing his toes over the bone in his opposite ankle and up the curve of his calf to below his knee. He wedged the foot there and looked for a point of focus. His gaze landed on the portrait of Cam.

Those eyes. Even in varying shades of gray, they were warm and inviting. He'd marveled over Cam's eyes before. They could be his best feature. Often sparking with merriment, with verve, snapping with intelligence, and always a balm.

"I love his eyes."

In Victor's ears, the instructor replied, "Breathe out and raise your hands past your face, straightening your arms, lifting them over your head."

Victor complied, lifting his arms ceiling-ward. His posture wavered a little, and he concentrated on his focus. Cam smiled back at him. Victor's heart squeezed and thumped.

"I'm going to hurt him."

Cam had the ability to hurt Victor, an undeniable fact. But Victor knew Cam wouldn't do it carelessly. If—when—the end came, Cam would let him down as easily as possible. He'd care about the mess he'd made and try to clean it up. He wouldn't just disappear. Oh, dear god, he'd be one of those people who'd believe they could remain friends.

So Victor would have to be the one who did the letting down.

His pose collapsed, and he planted both feet on the ground, bent forward, and clasped his knees. There, he hung panting softly.

Why was he imagining the end? They weren't even close, were they? What was wrong with him he couldn't simply fall? Drown in love rather than despair?

His gaze cut sideways to the low cupboard housing his journals. Eleven volumes of thoughts that were supposed to help him clarify the process. The triggers that sent him toward a downward slide, the hooks that might hold him suspended and safe.

The navigation markers along a road designed to keep him on the most level route possible.

Ripping the buds from his ears, Victor stood up and breathed. In for four, hold for seven, out for eight. He flattened a palm across his belly and breathed deep. His heart pecked away at the underside of his breastbone, the feeling almost a pinch, and his thoughts rabbited around inside his head until he wanted to tug his hair and yell.

"Time for a walk." Raising his voice, he called his intent to the two furry inhabitants of the house. "I'm going out for a while, kids. Lock up the valuables while I'm gone, hm?"

Come to think of it, why didn't he have a lockable cupboard for the wine?

Because he'd have to replace hinges every time he took a screwdriver to it.

Two days passed in a glory of effort and sweat. He did not read his journals, but neither did he drink. He walked five miles a day, every roll of his sole against the uneven pavement alongside Raymondskill Road a shovel full of dirt in the levee he built against the storm.

The sense of his depression, the oncoming wave of it, roiled off to one side, a brooding hurricane he intended to thwart by sheer will alone. Tez thought he could do this. His therapist had told him he could. But by the end of the second day, he couldn't remember who all the effort was for. Him or Cam? For both of them?

Fate chose that moment to connect them, his phone buzzing in his pocket. Victor pulled it out and almost grimaced at the notification pane. Cam had texted him, and why was it so, so hard to text back? Cam was his lover, his friend, a beautiful and kind man. He loved Cam.

But did Cam love him back? And what would happen next?

"Stop, just stop."

Wonderful, terrific, he was clutching his head and talking to himself on a public road. Spying a path into the woods, Victor stepped into the privacy of the trees and sank to the ground. His phone lay heavy and insensible against his palm.

Victor woke the screen and accessed Cam's text.

Super busy today. Deliveries and two mowing jobs. I could come over and collapse next to you, but I'll probably smell like gas fumes and sweat. I will most definitely snore. Loudly. And you need your beauty sleep. Going equipment shopping with Jorge tomorrow. Miss you. Catch up this weekend?

Victor found a smile for the check-in. It was so Cam. Newsy, but still personable. And he couldn't be happier that Cam's new business had taken off so spectacularly.

As quickly as the positive thoughts arrived, however, they fizzled. Fading from his mind until only afterimages remained, and darker thoughts soon rolled in to replace them. And they made no sense. Life should have purpose, and Cam was so, so lucky to have found his. And if Victor were to confess his dark thoughts, his insecurities, Cam would take those on board too. He'd make room in his schedule.

There was nothing to fear in all of this.

"Answer the text."

Victor tapped out: *Miss you too.* He hit Send and pocketed the phone. He'd send more later. Tell Cam how he felt. Wish him all the best. Say something worthwhile.

He found a blank journal at the end of the row, one so new the spine still creaked when he opened it. Spreading it across the kitchen table, Victor shifted his buttocks against the chair, picked up a pen, and contemplated that first, awful page.

Then he touched the pen to the paper and wrote: *I don't know why I feel so sad, why my control is slipping or even if it's a matter of control. All I know is that the wave is there, right off the shore and the longer I ignore it, the bigger it gets. I wish I knew why it was there. Why acknowledging the fact that I love Cameron brought it in from the ocean. Why I'm so fucked up.*

Long experience moved the pen from those first few sentences where he did little more than ask questions and look for meaning, into pages of similar statements. Eventually, he'd connect all the parts together and he'd see a way through.

I'll hurt him.

Why?

Because I can't help being sad sometimes and when I am, I can't talk about happy things. I can only lie there and feel the heavy weight of it all, breathing shallowly beneath it, gripped by the fear that one day, I'll stop breathing, that I'll want to stop breathing, and let it all crush me.

With a wordless cry, Victor dropped the pen. Then he did what he'd promised he wouldn't do. Not reach for the closest bottle; he wouldn't give in and start drinking. He went back to the cupboard and pulled out the sketchbook hidden behind those bland, gray books. The sketchbook that had broken his heart. Torn it up in a way he wasn't sure would ever mend.

And there, slumped on the floor of his studio, legs splayed out in front of him, back curved against the open cupboard door, he revisited his father. The man who'd chosen the ironic name of Sunshine.

He had been so often sunny, though. When Sunshine had been up, he'd been very up. But when he'd been down, he'd been very down. In between hadn't happened often. There'd be a day, an odd day or two, where he'd be like everyone else. And it would be weird. As though someone had forgotten to load his program and switch him on. Then Sunshine would return with cloudless skies and endless optimism and they'd believe that this time, he'd stay.

Swallowing a lump in his throat, Victor traced the lines of a beloved face. "Sometimes I wish you weren't my father. That I hadn't inherited whatever this is." He knew what it was. Thankfully, he didn't suffer as badly as Sunshine had. That didn't mean he didn't struggle, though. "But then I wonder what it would be like not to feel so deeply. Not to believe in love so fiercely that I fear it. Not to see the joy in every small glint of light."

The hole Sunshine had left in his life would always be felt. But for a while, as Victor sat there with his saddest sketchbook open across his lap, he almost made it to the top of the levee. Calm started to spread through his middle as though the act of connecting with his father and telling him his troubles might be what he'd needed.

Then, as inevitably as the weather, his mood turned as he remembered he had two parents left, two perfectly lovely people who had lost and grieved both with their son and by themselves. And the selfishness, wanting only what he couldn't have, washed in, the first splash of cold dread over the top of the dirt mountain he'd been trying to build.

Muddy emotion spilled across his shoulders, and then the weight behind his back collapsed, and he was falling, forever falling, too sad to pick himself up when it was so much easier to close his eyes and lie on the floor and go away for a while.

Chapter Thirty-One

C am was pretty tired by the time he turned his truck toward Milford. He and Jorge had bought a second mower, two trimmers, and sundry other equipment from a friend of a friend of a friend of someone's who planned to retire. He should be anxious about having spent most of the money his brother had lent him. Instead, quiet purpose thrummed through his veins.

He could do this. With Jorge at his side and Nick at his back, he could make it work. Plus, he had Estefan, Renata, and Beck, part-time. Melanie already had another name for them, for when they needed more workers. Luisa was giving them all of her clients.

And then there was his relationship with Victor.

Cam didn't *need* a romantic partner. After Donna cut him loose and fled with his last dream (and cash), he'd decided to keep things to just sex. The first time he'd kissed Victor, that notion had taken wing and flown out the nearest window. But still, he'd tried to keep it friendly. Until he hadn't.

It was Nick's fault, he decided. And Emma's. If he hadn't had to introduce Victor to his family as *someone*, he could have kept up the charade of friends who fucked forever.

Awkward as it had been, though, he'd liked having Victor with him for Emma's visit. He liked having Victor in his life. Victor added so much light and brightness to everything he touched. Cam smiled into the night closing around the truck. For a man so pale, Victor always traveled with so much color.

He flipped on his turn signal and guided his truck onto Raymondskill Road. Lifted his hand in a half wave as he passed

Melanie's house unnoticed, and pulled into Victor's driveway. His text that he'd be stopping by had gone unanswered, and it was only when he reached the circle at the top that Cam acknowledged the slight anxiety he was carrying below the weariness.

Vic didn't strike him as the type to keep multiple partners (unless agreed upon), but they hadn't had an exclusivity conversation. Coupled with the lack of real communication over the past week, Cam had started to wonder if the shine might have worn off. He'd tried to console himself by remembering how Victor had looked the last morning they spent together: spread across a jumble of colorful quilts, his pale skin aglow, sweat beading his brow. Victor had not worn the expression of a man who needed more or someone else.

Still, the thought that things had shifted niggled.

The house appeared quiet. A quick check of the garage showed Victor's car in residence. Cam knocked at the front door. When he got no response, he tried the handle. Locked. He crunched across the driveway and took the path around to the back patio.

The kitchen lay in darkness, the laundry light slicing a wedge across one corner of the long table and the front of the breakfast bar. Putting his hands to the glass, Cam peered inside, looking as best he could through the doorway into the family room. He couldn't see any other lights.

He tried the kitchen door and found it open as always. The black cat, Sinister, appeared out of nowhere and pushed past Cam's feet to get inside. "Don't you have your own door?" Cam asked as he caught his balance against the doorframe.

The cat disappeared as quickly as it had arrived.

Cam called into the dark. "Vic? You here?"

Rustling came from the direction of Victor's studio.

Cam picked his way across the dark kitchen, loathe for some reason to turn on any lights. At the family room, he switched on a lamp. He'd break his neck, otherwise.

Then he saw Victor, not in the studio, but sprawled on the couch, eyes closed, dressed in underpants and robe.

Déjà vu skipped across the back of Cam's neck. Nope, no. But also, why? What the fuck had happened to plunge Victor back into despair? Cam cautiously sniffed and couldn't detect the telltale odor of old wine and sweat. Maybe Victor was napping.

The sandwiches said otherwise. There were four of them, each on its own plate, each missing only one bite, and now that Cam could see them, he could smell that at least one had gone bad. And there, under the couch, a bottle of wine. Empty. No glass anywhere.

While Cam stood there thinking about his next move—wake him or leave him—Victor opened his eyes. He blinked a couple of times, then focused on Cam. "Oh, it's you."

Yeah, it's me.

At Victor's careless tone, Cam almost turned to leave. He was pretty sure he didn't want to be a part of whatever conversation happened next. He licked his lips, pushed the plates aside, and sat on the coffee table.

"So, um, what's up?"

Victor stared at him.

Cam checked in with his gut, his emotions, and came up confused. He'd wanted to share his optimism with this man. The hope he carried inside, and his plans for the future. He'd assumed Vic would care. That he'd smile that sweet smile of his, the one that crinkled his gray-blue eyes with more amusement than should be possible. That he'd be happy because Cam was cautiously happy.

Now, sitting in a darkened room next to moldy sandwiches, he felt sympathy for the man on the couch. Obviously, Victor was dealing with something. Cam could be the adult, here. He could put aside his cotton candy and pull out the medicine if need be.

"You should probably go," Victor said.

"I don't have to. I can clean up a bit. Get you a bath. Stay the night."

Victor shook his head. "No. You don't understand. I don't need you, Cam. I never needed you and I'm sorry if I sounded like I did."

Yeah, okay, so maybe still a bit drunk.

"Want me to come back tomorrow? We can have this conversation then."

"No." Victor pushed himself up on the couch. "No. What I mean is, I can't do this. I can't love you."

Oh-kay. But inside, a large boulder had appeared out of fucking nowhere and had decided to roll down Cam's midsection, stretching, crushing, and destroying. Taking him down with it.

"I didn't ask you to love me, Vic. We were having fun."

"I'm not capable of fun."

"You know what, we're not going to do this now. I'll come back tomorrow. Day after?" Cam shook his head. "But I'm going to call tomorrow. Or text. Because if you're not showered and dressed sometime soon, I'm going to have to call your son, or Tez, or someone who knows what to do when you pull out the robe and underpants."

Victor was shaking his head. "This will happen again and again, don't you understand? I can't maintain the line. I can't stay happy. I can't be with you and make you happy."

Cam reached out. He meant to take Victor by the shoulders and if not shake some sense into him, then at least connect. But Victor fell away before he could touch him.

"Don't."

"Vic—"

"Please go. And . . . Just go. Please leave me to do my thing."

Cam stood and smoothed his hands down the front of his jeans. His suddenly sweaty hands. The boulder was lodged somewhere between his diaphragm and his lower intestines, causing pain and making breathing difficult.

His heart hurt.

But he'd been here before. So many times. Down and supposedly out. He knew the score.

"Fine, you win. I'm going to head home. But if you don't text me tomorrow to let me know you're alive, I'll be back." He couldn't switch off the care overnight. He'd never been able to. "Same deal with the next day. And if I don't like how you sound by Monday, I'm calling Tez."

"You don't have her number."

"I can get it." He knew people who knew people. How many ceramic artists could there be in Stroudsburg? If Nick didn't know her, Oliver likely would. Or Aaron or his sisters. The gay community in this corner of the world wasn't big.

Cam took a deep breath. "We can talk about us when you're feeling better, but right now? I'm your friend. Whatever happens, I'm your friend. I don't have so many of those that I can drop them like an old sweater, which I probably wouldn't drop because old sweaters are the most comfortable fucking kind."

Anger had started pushing through. Cam breathed. *In. Out.*

"Until then, be kind to yourself. Remember you have people who love you, whether you want to believe you're capable of returning it or not."

And with that, he left. He didn't want to. Fuck, no. More than anything, he wanted to drag Victor through a shower and into bed where they could hold each other all night. But he had to let Victor pull himself together. At least, he thought he did.

Also, he had to be kind to *himself.* And all Cam wanted right now was a shower. To warm up. Figure out a way to dislodge the damn stone buried in his gut.

Then maybe steal Honey away from Jorge and let her lick his face until it didn't hurt anymore.

Chapter Thirty-Two

The first text read: *Are you there?*

Victor had no idea how long ago it had arrived, but the absence of a follow up indicated perhaps not eons ago. As in ice ages hadn't come and gone between when he'd thought his phone might have chimed, wondered who had turned the sound on and plugged it in, and found it in the kitchen.

Without taking the time to check the time and date, Victor tapped out a simple reply: *Yes.*

The second text arrived that evening—time and date clearly discernible because it was dark outside and Victor was still curled into the corner of his couch: *What are you wearing?*

The lack of wink emoji had saddened him. But acknowledging they'd formed enough of a relationship to have had an in-joke—Cam had texted him twice before with the same question, usually around eleven on a night when they hadn't gotten together—only hurt more.

I am such a fool. Victor looked down at his bare torso and wrinkled his nose at the funk rising from his skin. *A stinky fool.*

His reply was short: *You don't want to know.*

The temptation to shove the phone across the coffee table and pull his robe up over his shoulder prodded, but not insistently. Victor sat there, in the moment, and marveled at the quiet after the storm. It wasn't over yet. He still had to climb out of the hole he'd dug for himself—a better metaphor likely to be found when he wasn't recovering from however many days of moping on his couch—but he was starting to feel again. Mostly relief that he hadn't drowned.

The third text concerned food. Victor didn't answer that one. His cats were eating and that was all that mattered for the time being. He'd showered by that point. Spent the night in his bed and had awoken feeling if not refreshed then at least rested.

The worst part of spending so long pinned in one position, or the same position in various places across the living room, was how exhausting it always was not to move.

But now that his brain had started to come back online, the remorse kicked in.

Why had he pushed such a good man away?

"Because you're ugly when you're down."

Except Cam had seen him that way twice now and he still apparently cared enough to text: *Have you washed that godawful robe yet?*

Dutifully, and because cleaning and tidying always felt good after a bout of depression, Victor tucked a laundry basket under one arm and went in search a full load.

Then he found his earbuds, pulled up his yoga app, and went to retrieve his mat from behind the table. It wasn't there—because he'd left it on the floor . . . when? A week ago?

Now he really didn't want to check the date on his phone. Dear lord, had he missed a class with the kids? He had, hadn't he? How long could he keep doing this? He glanced at the journal cupboard and thought, seriously, for the first time in a while, of calling his therapist.

Maybe it was time to try something new. Research medication. It couldn't be all bad, could it? Because, while he was back in the land of the living, he felt as though he'd left an essential part of himself at the bottom of the ocean. Not his heart, but maybe a reason to keep it beating?

He'd do his yoga, clear his head, and then call.

One step at a time.

Victor winced at the series of pops along his spine as he pushed his hips up and back into downward facing dog. There had been a time when he'd imagined his vertebrae exploding into dust and his body collapsing into a loose heap. He might have been high. Had most probably been high, and not pleasantly so. Why he'd been doing yoga instead of digging a hole in a beanbag chair so he could spend seven hours in contemplation of the webbing between his fingers and wonder whether he was descended from mermen was a mystery for the ages.

After counting off thirty seconds, Victor lowered to his hands and knees. The pressure that had been building in his skull eased, the pounding against his temples fading to a dull throb. Dear Lord, his head.

Dexter hopped up from the corner of the mat, where he'd been systematically poking holes in the rubber, and wound through Victor's arms. Victor pressed a kiss between the cat's silky ears and choked back a sob.

Maybe it was too early for yoga and repentance. He wanted more wine. More oblivion. More impenetrable darkness and the suffocating but somehow comforting weight of the entire world on his chest.

He wanted not to be moving.

He also wanted not to have Tez discover him clinging to the couch in his underwear.

Cam did not strike him as a man who issued idle threats.

His throat tightened, and the sharpness that appeared only when one was quite sad cut deep.

Your own damn fault.

Victor pushed his sore body up into another downward facing dog and counted silently to thirty. His head filled with regret and pain and his temples pounded fit to burst. His back screamed. His throat posted a sign reading "None Shall Pass." At thirty, he dropped to his knees, then his elbows, and then his side, and lay on the rubber mat, sunlight streaming cheerily through the studio windows, and listened to the sound of Dexter chewing the fur between his toes.

He curled his knees up and wrapped one arm around them, folded the other arm under his head and closed his eyes. Time drifted for a while, and the sunlight shaded into a comfortable orange, darker at the edges and traced through with spidery lines of dark brown. The warmth of the light felt like a blanket. Dexter's licking and chewing faded away. Victor clung to the edge of consciousness for a while before giving in to the drift, the slope, and the downward rush of sleep.

When he awoke, no time seemed to have passed. The sun still warmed him. Dexter hadn't moved. The arm tucked beneath him had not turned numb. Victor blinked and smacked his lips.

A soft vibration drew his attention to the floor. His phone had woken him. Someone was texting him. Uncurling his arm, Victor reached for the phone and pulled it into view. He registered no surprise whatsoever in seeing Cam's name at the top of the screen.

The text read: *Have you been outside today?* Followed by: *Not answering this text will result in a call to you know who.*

Sighing, Victor put the phone aside.

Let him call her. Let her come. Why did any of it matter? If Tez stopped by today, she'd find him already showered and dressed. He was doing *yoga* for the love of all things breakable. And it would take her at least forty minutes to get up here from Stroudsburg, giving him plenty of time to relax his fetal curl and push into an inspiring pose.

Minutes rolled by in an easy quiet, the house creaking companionably around him, the smell of old wood, dust, and paint comfortable and familiar. Outside, a bird squawked and another answered. The icemaker rattled from the kitchen.

The cat door thwacked open, and Sinister chirped his way into the studio, spied a ghost in the corner of the family room, and took off at a run.

Dexter resumed chewing his paws.

Victor drifted in one of his favorite places: the in-between. Where he felt neither happy nor sad. Nothing poked or prodded or begged. He just was.

Of course, it couldn't last. His phone vibrated again. Victor snatched it up, opened the text without reading it, and swiped his thumbs across the stupidly small keyboard. *I sent you away for fuck's sake. My health and well-being are no longer your concern.*

He tossed the phone aside and sat up. Waited for his blood to equalize and pushed to his feet. Maybe he'd beat everyone at their own game, including himself, and go outside after all. Cam's team had finished building the steps and had already packed them with dirt. The gravel for the top lay piled in the driveway, in front of the garage. Victor would fill a barrow and wheel it to the path. Spread it. Rinse, repeat. He'd finish the damn project and make the path entirely his.

He would not think of the beautiful man who'd taken his vision and run with it. The plants they'd chosen together. The extra steps. The afternoon they'd sat at the top to admire the completed framework. How rough Cam's lips had been after a day out in the sun with not enough water. The calluses on his fingertips.

His phone rang. Victor snatched it up. "What?"

"Hello to you too."

"Oh, Tez, sorry. I thought you were Cam."

"Ah." Then, "Do I need to come up there?"

"Has he already called you? Jesus. It was, what, ten minutes?"

"I have no idea what you're referring to, but your last text seemed to indicate you two are no longer together, which probably means you're lying on the couch in your underwear counting the row of wine bottles along the coffee table."

Victor pulled the phone away from his face and checked his text messages. He'd sent his last as a reply to Tez's casual *What's up.* Fan-bloody-tastic.

"I am dressed, in my studio, standing on my yoga mat, and thinking about going outside to shovel gravel," he informed her.

"Do you want to talk?"

"About me and my idiocy? Not really. How are you, my dearest?"

"Oh, you know. Same old, same old. I'm going on a date tonight and expecting I'll be home by eleven."

"What happened? I thought you liked this woman?"

"We texted better than we talked."

"Oh, well, if you're not excited by this date, why are you bothering?" Victor snagged a stool and sat down.

"Remember what my grandmother used to say?"

"That sitting on cold concrete would give you piles?"

Tez's laughter knocked a chink into the armor of sadness he'd built around himself over the past week or so.

Victor tried again. "No, wait, I have a better one. If you were making that face when the wind changed, you'd be stuck that way forever."

Another chuckle. "And absolutely everything was bound to put hair on my chest whether I wanted it or not."

A smile. A real, honest-to-goodness smile. Victor touched his cheek and massaged the sore muscles there. "What would be her advice regarding your date this evening?"

"They could be a friend you don't know yet."

"And we can always use another friend," Victor finished for her. Idly, he opened the top sketchbook and winced as he recognized it. The one he'd pulled out to torture himself with during this latest descent into depression. He flipped the cover closed. "Tez?"

"Mm?"

"Thank you for always being there. As my best friend and as the one who kicks me off the couch when I've wallowed hard enough."

"Thank you for always being my best friend, even when I thought bright blue hair worked with my complexion. For buying us a house and never asking me to kick in until I could. For laughing at all of my jokes, especially when they're awful. For letting me cry when my grandmother died. For holding me throughout those same months. For raising our kids so I could go back to school."

Victor's eyes welled with tears. "Thank you for sharing our children with me," he said, his voice strained.

"Are you all right?"

"I sent him away."

"Are you going to go get him back?"

"I don't know." Victor flipped open the sketchbook again and paged through until he found the sketch that always hurt him the most. The study for the painting that had broken his heart. He adored all three of his parents and had always counted himself lucky to have had two fathers. Rain had taught him to love the outdoors. The thrill of sinking his hands deep into soil. They'd caught worms together and carried them around in cupped hands. Frogs. Salamanders. Fireflies.

Victor's thoughts drifted forward and sideways to the tattoo on Cam's shoulder. The stars and fireflies. He'd never asked about it. He'd never asked about the dates, either. The lack of understanding left him feeling as though they had unfinished business.

He closed the sketchbook.

"There's a part of me that wants to go see him and apologize. He's so good for me, Tez. It's been a while since I felt so engaged with the world. But I don't want him to see the ugly parts of me, though I realize it's already too late. I mean, he met me on one of my worst days and he saw me this week."

"And he's still texting you? That's a man you want to hang on to."

"Unless . . ."

"Unless," Tez prompted.

"Does it make sense to say I'm scared of being too happy?"

"No. Did you call Sahar?"

"Not yet, but . . . I think this time I will. I've fallen over twice in a few months. Despite my love of drama, I think I need to talk to her. Also, I'm tired of being depressed."

"Let me know how it goes?"

"I will." The sound of a car in the driveway had his pulse quickening. "Someone is here. I have to go. Try to enjoy yourself tonight, hm? And if it doesn't work out, pop by tomorrow, and we'll sit outside and laugh about it together. Or hold hands and cry."

"Look after yourself."

"You too."

While he made his way to the door, Victor thought about his relationship with Tez. How he wouldn't have as firm a grasp on reality if not for her. She'd been the one to console him after Sunshine's death. The one to listen while he'd explained his theory that Sunshine was his biological father.

Sunshine, the dad who'd danced. The man who'd loved to dress up with Victor and put on small, two-person plays for the benefit of Moon and Rain. The father who'd read a book a day and related the stories to everyone at night. The dad who'd dreamed.

The man with moods. With heights of happiness that had lifted him clear of earthly worries. With depths so far below the plane of mere mortals, he might never have risen again. He had always managed to, though—except for the time he hadn't.

Victor opened the door.

"Oh." The sound was involuntary because the man he most wanted to see was not standing on his doorstep.

The delivery driver held out a paper sack that smelled of lasagna and garlic bread. "Victor Ness?"

"Yes," Victor whispered.

The bag was thrust toward him. "Here you go."

It could have been Tez, Victor thought as he carried his dinner back inside the house. But it hadn't been. There was only one person kind enough to have sent him food. To send him a meal he'd be tempted to eat.

Cameron Zimmermann.

Chapter Thirty-Three

C am put his phone on the breakfast table, face down, and sighed.

"Proof-of-life request?" Jorge mumbled from Nick's old seat—back to the windows. He dipped a spoon into his cereal bowl and filled his mouth with another mound of wet cardboard.

Cam winced at the imagined taste. "I swear, it's like living with Nick all over again. Bacon is the only fit breakfast."

"Heh. Turkey burgers aren't going to save you if you keep eating that way." Jorge nodded at Cam's plate, where only the crumbs of a bacon and egg breakfast bagel remained.

Shrugging one shoulder, Cam reached for his phone and then picked up his coffee cup instead. He sighed with resignation in the direction of the cell. "I don't know why I care."

Jorge's snort had almost hurricane force. "Whatever gets you through the day."

Hitching up his other shoulder, Cam sipped his coffee. Breakfast continued in silence, Jorge munching soggily, Cam ignoring his phone—easy enough as it did not buzz with a return text.

The morning passed with a similar blend of peace and agony. Cam stewed over Victor's lack of response *and* the way it made him feel. The blame fell squarely on his own shoulders. He'd told Vic things wouldn't turn out the way he'd wanted, no matter whose feelings Cam had been trying to save. He suspected he'd known it would be his. That he'd be the vulnerable one in the equation.

That they'd chosen to go on anyway was his fault too.

At the farm, Luisa had eight delivery slips for them to deal with—the result of her advertisement that Shepard's was going out of business. It had been the same all week: deliveries and small landscaping jobs vying for every available hour. On the one hand, Cam welcomed the packed schedule, returning to the mindset of the previous year—work, work, work. He didn't have to think when he was working.

On the other hand, he missed the spare hour he might have taken with Victor. The thrill of a quick interlude. Sex for sex's sake.

As they arrived at their last job of the day, Jorge glanced pointedly at Cam's phone and raised an eyebrow. Cam shook his head. Jorge directed the truck into a driveway, and Cam hopped out with the paperwork and met the client in front of the garage.

"Thank you so much for delivering and spreading the gravel on the same day!" she enthused.

A meeting with Luisa late last week meant Cam and Jorge now owned all of Shepard's landscaping materials, and all deliveries came with a quote to spread such materials at the client's pleasure. It had been Luisa's way of handing over her client list. They'd also bought her trucks. After December, the Shepard's phone number would point in their direction too.

Cam and Jorge were officially in business.

Sweaty business.

August might have been wet, but early September was hot and humid. They were both drenched and gritty by the time the path was done.

They were on their way back to the farm to swap trucks when Cam's phone rang. As he was driving, he handed it to Jorge. "Who is it?"

Jorge frowned at the screen. "The animal hospital."

Oh, no.

Jorge took the call since Cam couldn't make his hand reach for the phone. He couldn't even bear to look at Honey when they got back to the farm. She was waiting inside, curled up on the couch in Luisa's office. She hopped down when she saw him and trotted over with her endearingly awkward gait. Cam dropped to his knees and pulled her into a little hug, his eyes squeezed shut. "Hey, girl," he whispered over her head.

Man, it hurt. For a moment, Cam wasn't sure he'd be able to stand up again. To let go of the dog wriggling ever deeper into the loose circle of his arms. Above him, Jorge and Luisa were talking. He let their voices drift into meaningless word babble.

He thought to ask Jorge if he could take her to Milford. But one glimpse of Jorge's bleak expression killed that notion dead. Still, when Jorge offered to come for the ride, Cam tucked away all pretense and nodded a simple yes.

He couldn't meet Luisa's gaze before he left. Could only keep his head down, his face pressed into Honey's fur.

The sweat on his back was itching by the time they got to Milford, and the grit under his shirt chafed. Cam bore both with the stoicism of a martyr as he carried Honey into the reception area. When he spied no one in the arc of plastic chairs, his spirits rose. Maybe pictures had been exchanged and a decision that no, this wasn't the right dog, had been reached. Then an office door opened and an elderly couple shuffled out.

Honey turned her little brown head, her ears flapping over Cam's arms, and pushed off with her back legs.

"Whoa, girl." Cam knelt to let her down before she broke another leg and then stood and rocked with silent body blows as Honey bounded into the old woman's arms, yipping and licking in that way she did when she was happy. Her entire body seemed to wriggle, every leg independently, the casted one bouncing off the woman's ribs. Then she was passed—still wriggling—into the old man's arms.

The woman approached Cam, one hand extended. "I don't know how to thank you."

You could try not existing.

Cam swallowed over Mount Everest as he thought about simply turning around and leaving. Not saying a word. It'd be rude. But what did he care? He'd never see these people again.

Instead, he forced himself to take her hand, and then she was sobbing against his chest and somehow, he had his arms around her and was patting her back awkwardly, this stranger, this dog loser and retriever, this breaker of his heart.

Jorge received her attentions next. Cam met his eyes over the top of the little old lady's head and they shared a WTF look.

After handing Honey to the vet for what would presumably be a final checkup, the old man approached, one hand out.

I swear, if he hugs me and sobs, I'm done.

Thankfully, he confined himself to a businesslike handshake. "Thank you, son." *Not your son.* "We'd all but given up hope."

Cam unstuck his throat. "How long?"

"Nearly six months."

Damn. "Where?"

As though fluent in Cam-Speak, the old guy said, "We moved to New Paltz. New York."

"That's over an hour away."

"That it is. Name's Fred, by the way. And this is Ginny."

Cam blinked at the man in front of him. "Like Fred Astaire and Ginger Rogers."

Fred laughed. "You look far too young to have made that connection, but just so." He sobered a little as he nodded toward the open examination room where the vet had taken Honey. "That's Lucy."

At her name, Honey turned and panted, tongue lolling out in a doggy smile.

Cam resisted the urge to press his hand over the wound in his chest. *Never show them how much it hurts.* Stupid advice, but he'd follow it to the letter. He forced a smile. "We called her Honey."

Fred glanced between him and Jorge. "I can see she was in good hands."

Ginny arrived at Fred's side. "How much do we owe you for her care?"

"No-thing." Cam backed up a step. "So, ah . . ."

Fred and Ginny put on matching frowns. Ginny spoke. "Do you want to say goodbye? Maybe we could exchange numbers? If we're down this way, we could stop by and let you all visit. I'm sure Lucy will miss you both. You've obviously taken real good care of her."

Cam shook his head. "No need." His own frown was in an effort not to let the tears gathering behind his eyes spill out. "Take care of her, okay?"

Honey—Lucy—watched his retreat, and when he got to the door, she scrabbled as though trying to make a leap from the examination table. Cam's heart collapsed inside his chest as he turned away from her and pushed through the doors and out into the parking lot.

He made it to the truck but lacked the strength and coordination to open a door. Instead, he sort of molded himself to the side and hid his face in the dark space of an open window.

A heavy hand landed on his shoulder, and Jorge's solid, implacable presence rested beside him a moment. Every breath Cam managed sounded wrong, as though he'd run a mile in this stupid September heat. The humidity was the killer. He could have run ten miles over there, in that other heat. Without this pain in his chest. Could have—

"Want to go get a drink?" Jorge asked.

Cam nodded vigorously. *Fuck, yes.* "Let's take a bottle back to the house so we don't have to drive, because in about an hour, I plan to be insensible."

With a nod, Jorge held out his hand for the keys. Cam passed them over, climbed into the passenger side, and closed his eyes against the ever-present need to cry.

Chapter Thirty-Four

Victor sat at one end of the long kitchen table and turned his phone over in his palm like a bar of soap. After several rotations, he checked the notification pane, not expecting to find anything new but compelled to look anyway.

Cam hadn't checked in for three days.

After Wednesday had passed without a text, Victor spent his evening wavering between giddiness and a flatter, duller feeling of inevitability. Cam had given up on him. That he had expected but not the disquiet that came along with it. When had he come to rely on the fact Cam would be back? When had fantasy become his reality? Or had his reality diverged into unreality?

Stop.

If he let his thoughts continue along that line, he'd be on his knees in front of the wine rack. "I should get rid of all the wine in this house."

He wouldn't. He should, but he couldn't.

Sahar, when he'd called her, had been supremely unhelpful on that score. *"It's your choice, Victor."*

Choice could go get mired in fudge.

She had put him in touch with a psychiatrist, however, and they had tentatively planned a course of medication meant to help balance his moods. He'd been warned that alcohol and the prescription wouldn't mix. He'd decided to think about it over the weekend. While he journaled. Because Sahar still felt it was important for him to work though his feelings.

If only she knew.

She probably did.

His textless Thursday had been more difficult to bear. Thankfully, he'd had back-to-back afternoon classes, the extra session a poor substitute, really, for the class he'd missed while wallowing in self-imposed grief.

He still felt slowed, but that was perhaps all for the good. A slower climb to equilibrium usually signaled a longer period of evenness. But it was Friday now, and Cam's absence remained a bump in his otherwise smooth road.

Victor had no reason to call him, except to apologize for being an ass.

A pang of longing hit Victor hard in the chest. If he wanted this feeling to go away, he'd do better not to call. Not to stay in touch.

What he couldn't figure out was the why. For any of it. Why he'd decided he needed to give Cam up and why he wanted him back. The giving up made sense from a certain perspective. Victor always did away with what made him happy while on a downward slide. The need to take Cam back up was pricklier.

"We don't always get what we want."

In his hand, the phone rang. Startled, Victor nearly dropped it. After frowning at the unknown number, he answered. "This is Victor Ness."

"Vic, it's Jorge."

A rather large lump of coal wedged itself between Victor's larynx and esophagus. "Jorge," he squeaked.

"Cam's friend."

"I know who you are. I'm just, ah, surprised to hear from you."

"Heh. So, listen. Cam's not doing so great."

The kitchen dimmed. That the sun had slid behind a cloud only occurred to Victor after he'd checked that his heart was still functioning by trying and failing to feel the beat through his chest. "What do you mean?"

"Honey's owners showed up and took her home."

Oh, no. Oh, dear lord. It had happened on Wednesday, hadn't it?

The way Cam felt about that dog would have been evident to anyone living on the moon. "I'm so sorry to hear that. I'm sure it's a good outcome for Honey, but Cam must be devastated."

"He's doing his best impression of you."

"What do you mean?" Jorge barely knew him. What stories had Cam been spreading?

"He won't talk. Too still. Cam's never still."

No, he wasn't. "Did you call his brother?"

Silence rolled over the line.

"Jorge?"

"Cam's super protective of his brother. I don't think he'd want Nick to see him this way."

Oh, Cameron.

"I see."

"He needs someone and it's not me."

Jorge left that thought there, and Vic didn't press for details. He got it. It was his turn. No, it was his *last* turn. If he didn't act now, he'd lose a good man forever—whether they were destined to be friends or more. And *that* was not what Victor wanted.

His life would be less complicated without Cameron Zimmermann, but also simply less.

"I'm on my way."

Jorge had left by the time Victor arrived. They'd agreed it might be best if he went out for the evening. That Cam might be more receptive if he knew he and Victor were alone.

Receptive to what, was the question. Victor had spent the short drive going over what he might say and had come up blank. He hadn't even brought props. Just himself.

Bypassing the front door, Victor circled around to the back, admiring the immaculate landscaping along the way. He remembered the first time he'd seen this small, unassuming house, and how much sense Cam had made as a person in that moment. It was right there in the obvious care taken with every detail, from the cleanliness and repair of the siding and gutters, the new windows and freshly painted front door. The new paving stones along the front walk, the steps to the mailbox. The trim of every tree and shrub. The multitude of flowers.

The back garden showed the same attention. The grass was a little long but thick and darkly green. The vegetable beds flourished; late summer flowers still bloomed. His orchard trees were heavy with fruit.

And there was Cam, lying on a wooden lounger on the patio—one of a pair he might have made himself, the wood stained a rich oak and then covered with bright red cushions. The patio paving was a work of art—mismatched slabs of slate, mined no doubt from the yard, and spread in an interlocking pattern across light gray gravel.

In the two years Cam had lived in this house, he'd clearly cared for it. But the garden showed the most inspiration. The most love. To see him inert on a lounger rather than enjoying the reward of his labors hurt.

He didn't look up at Victor's approach. He barely seemed to be breathing. When Victor spied the half-empty whiskey bottle on the patio, Jorge's comment came into focus.

"He's doing his best impression of you."

Maybe it *was* time to reevaluate the need for a wine collection. Or wine in general.

Victor sat on the lounger next to Cam's, kicked off his shoes, and lay back. The view was rather lovely—the periwinkle blue of an early evening sky framed by leaves in silhouette. Victor could hear the creek at the far end of the yard. The warmth of the day rose from the patio stones, and when the air stirred, the scent of old charcoal drifted over from the grill and firepit.

Okay. He was here. What now? Cam hadn't moved, even to acknowledge his presence. Would it be terribly cowardly to get back up, collect his shoes, and go?

Victor studied Cam's profile. From this side, his nose made a crooked line, and Victor wondered when he'd broken it. Had it been in a fight? During the war? Sometime since? A simple accident, perhaps? He noted, also, that Cam hadn't shaved in several days, a fact not immediately apparent because of the color of his stubble: more silver than brown. He had deeper lines about his eyes. The corners of his mouth turned uncharacteristically downward.

A sudden movement startled Victor: Cam closing his fingers around the bottle of whiskey and lifting it to his mouth. He swallowed once, then held the bottle out toward Victor. Lacking for anything better to do, Victor took it. But he didn't raise it to his lips. He set the bottle on his stomach and traced a line around the outside of the label.

"You're not going to drink?" Cam's voice was quiet and unsodden. However long he'd been out here, he hadn't drunk all of this whiskey today.

"No." Victor set the bottle down on the slate paving.

"Then why are you here?"

Why, indeed?

Victor turned back to Cam and met a weary brown gaze. He seemed so tired, so defeated, so *done*. And that hurt. God, it hurt. To know Cam was suffering and he hadn't been here to help ease that burden. What sort of friend was he to let Cam down like this?

What sort of man?

Pressing his lips together, Victor cast about for the perfect way to express all of this. For words of apology and restitution. Had he already left it too long? Had what they'd had counted at all?

He grasped at a straw. "It occurred to me that I had neglected to ask about your tattoos."

Cam blinked. "You're here to ask about my tattoos?"

"The dates I figured out. I think I even know why they're on your left side. For your heart. They're the people you loved, and you keep them close. The ache of their loss felt sharply one final time, then forever with you."

Did the pain of each lessen as the tattoos healed? Victor doubted it.

Cam was staring at him, his expression mildly dangerous.

Victor quickly moved on. "The other one, the fireflies and stars. I wanted to ask about that."

Cam held a hand out toward the whiskey bottle. Victor passed it over. After another small swallow, Cam put it down close to his lounger and returned his gaze to the darkening sky. Rather than give in to the feeling of defeat souring his gut, Victor mirrored Cam's posture. He'd lie there and meditate. Wait for the stars to come out.

When Cam spoke again, his voice floated into the gathering night. "It's for Nick. One of his favorite things to do in the summer was chase fireflies. He never wanted to catch them; he wanted to run around stirring them up. Used to say he was running through the stars, and I always liked the image of him running through the sky."

"That's beautiful."

Cam snorted softly and took another swig at the whiskey bottle.

"I was sorry to hear about Honey," Victor said.

"Jorge called you."

"He was worried."

Another snort.

"I'm sorry about . . ." Victor trailed off long enough to pull up his big boy pants. "I'm sorry I was such an ass. It wasn't you."

"'S'cool. Would've happened sooner or later. Everyone leaves, Vic. Got a list of dates on my back to prove it."

Frowning, Victor sat up. "Your brother is still here."

"Nick has left the nest." Cam made a fluttering motion with his hand and then wrapped his fingers back around the bottle neck. "It's all good, though. He doesn't need me anymore. Honey just needed somewhere to stay for a while. Never should have got attached." Cam glanced over at him. "You too."

As regarded attachment or needing somewhere to stay awhile?

Victor swallowed.

Cam's expression darkened. "Becca needed me. I fucked up there. Donna? She only needed my money. Leland . . ." He turned sharply away.

"Who's Leland?" Victor asked.

Cam angled his left shoulder forward. He was wearing a shirt, but Victor let his gaze land on the ink resting beneath.

"August fourteenth, 2007. I couldn't walk so I held him while he bled out. I told him he was going to be okay even though I knew he wouldn't be."

Victor wanted to reach across the space between them and take Cam's hand but he refrained. "I don't know what words are appropriate in this situation, except: I'm sorry. That your friend died. That you were injured."

He pictured the scars on Cam's legs and torso and put together a brief story in his head. Cam hadn't been able to save his friend because he'd been too hurt. So he'd held him as he died. Bleeding and broken, he'd held another man's life in his arms and watched it ebb away.

Victor couldn't imagine such pain. Feeling small and sick and out of place, he pushed back up off the lounger and reached for his shoes.

What the fuck are you doing? Sit your ass down.

He was *not* going to run away from this. From a man who needed him. If he did, he might as well keep running. Besides, enough fucking people had left Cameron alone. Victor was not going to add his name to that list.

With a sigh, he wrestled the whiskey bottle away from Cam and raised it to his lips. He swallowed the sweet and rough rye without widening his eyes, determined not to wince. Then, as softly and with as much care as he could muster, he said, "I need more than somewhere to stay. I think you do too."

Across the space, on his own lounger, Cam let out a quiet sob.

Good job, Victor.

With a sigh, he put the bottle down and dropped his head into his hands.

Chapter Thirty-Five

Lying there, chest aching, Cam worked to suppress a second sob. One would do it, thank you very much. At least until Victor left. Then he might cry a little, but only for a minute. It was too beautiful a night to do otherwise. When he wasn't focusing on the endless procession of bus wheels rolling over his head and heart, he could appreciate that. The sky and the stars. Could think about his little bro, remember him cavorting across the lawn in weird, sideways cartwheels and froggy leaps. Uncoordinated as fuck but special because of it.

Their parents would be sitting about where he was now, on the old lawn chairs he'd found tucked away in the back of the garage, labeled because of course Nick had labeled them. They'd have been sitting side by side, talking quietly about nothing. Just chatting. They'd been good friends, his parents. Cam had always liked that about them because when they'd fought, which hadn't been often, they'd done so without too much drama.

Rebecca would have been sitting on the back step, stretching the long cord of the telephone to its limit. And Cam would have been sitting at the edge of the lawn, watching Nick play while wondering whether his father had counted the cans of beer in the fridge.

A typical summer evening.

"I need more than somewhere to stay."

That was it, in one of those proverbial little nutshells. Cam needed *more*. More than somewhere to stay. More than a job digging holes. Wasn't that why he'd continued caring for and updating Emma's house? Why he'd started a business with Jorge?

But his fear of collapse, of an end—either big and noisy, or a quiet slipping away—nipped constantly. The dogs of Hell baying at his heels.

He'd been waiting for weeks for the sky to fall in on him. And now that it had, how long would Jorge wait for him to emerge from the rubble? To stop cowering with his hands over his head—or sleeping on a patio lounger with a whiskey bottle clutched in one hand?

Maybe he should give up now. Leave before it all fell apart. A sodden breath escaped him, the sound suspiciously like another sob.

God fucking damn it.

Victor's fidgets stopped. "Cam—"

"Everything I touch falls apart, and here I am starting a business with a man who trusts me, who maybe even needs me, and I can't do it. I'm too fucking scared to try."

"But you're already there," Victor pointed out.

"Not right now I'm not, and it's only a matter of time before it all turns to shit."

"Why do you think that?"

"Because I left when my parents died. I fled the war when my friend died. I left Delaware when my girlfriend stole all of my money. I should leave Pennsylvania before this falls over. Just get it done."

"Or you could stay and let the people who love you help you."

Tired—beyond tired, but unable to express it succinctly, Cam plucked the whiskey bottle from between Victor's feet and took a swallow. "I sit out here sometimes, on a good day. Birds chatting to each other, squirrels playing chase across the lawn. The creek all happy. The grass is super green because I mowed it and I can smell it. It's warm and beautiful, you know? And I lie out here on my lounger, and I think about all the people dying of starvation and disease. The people murdered because of what they believe in or who they love. And it fucking hurts. That I'm here and whole."

Sensibly, Victor remained quiet. Or maybe he simply didn't have the right words.

Regardless, Cam rolled on, "Then I get this dog, a dog I do not want, and I help her and it felt pretty good to know she'd lived because I picked her up." A pressure bubble of emotion was swelling beneath his breastbone. "And now she's gone, and it's like . . . She's a dog, Vic. Why am I so cut up about a fucking dog?"

Tears rolled down Victor's cheeks. "Because you loved her, and because the person you'd come to rely on to be there for you wasn't there to hold on to while you let go."

Cam drew in a sharp and painful breath against the third sob building in his chest. It was getting difficult not to give in, and he wasn't sure why he was fighting so hard. Maybe because Victor was crying enough for the both of them, which sucked. Victor didn't need to be crying. He had enough sadness of his own to deal with.

"I'm sorry," Cam whispered.

Victor blubbered quietly and waved. "Why are you sorry? I'm the one who should be sorry."

"You didn't have to come."

"No, I did. I absolutely did. I have been so selfish."

"You're not selfish."

"Oh, I am. But let's not make this about me. I'm here for *you*. I'm here because I care, Cameron. I'm sorry you've lost so much, but the one thing you haven't lost? *You*. You're an incredible person. A man who knows how to *human* on a level the rest of us only aspire to. You give and give and give. When people happen to you, you give them your all. You're beautiful. So beautiful. And it hurts to see you so low, to think of you not believing in yourself enough to grow a business that means so much. To do what you're good at and have others support you."

The back of Cam's scalp prickled.

"Jorge knows who you are," Victor continued. "He's lucky to have you as a partner. I know this because I'm lucky to have you, and I sincerely regret my attempts to push you away. I was secretly glad that I appeared to be failing." Vic swiped at his tears. "So, if you want to know why I'm here, that's it. Not so much because you lost Honey or because Jorge asked me to come. But because I am not ready to let you go. I have been waiting for someone like you. And the only way I'll leave now is if you ask me to."

It would be easy to pull Victor into his arms and believe that all that needed to be said had been said. That Victor's little speech could seal the wounds of the past thirty years. But if the movies Cam had watched on the nights that he couldn't sleep had taught him anything, it was that crying and hugging didn't fix shit, no matter how good it felt.

He missed the feeling of being close to someone, though. Had missed falling asleep next to Victor and waking up beside him. The sex in between, yes, but also the small moments. Bumping for room in front of the bathroom mirror. That they could piss in front of each other without being embarrassed. That he knew what Victor liked to eat and the sound he made when something tasted good. And just talking. *Sharing.*

He'd never had a relationship with someone where he could hang out and talk—mostly because he hadn't encouraged it. Except with Donna. He'd tried there, he really had. Now he could see all he hadn't back then. She'd been the Cam in that relationship. There for a good time, not a long time. Oh, and the money.

All Victor had ever wanted was his company. How had they ended up here?

"Why did you push me away?" Cam asked.

Victor swallowed audibly and reached across the space. He wrapped his hand around Cam's and eased the whiskey bottle out of his fingers. Cam let it go. Victor studied the bottle for a few seconds, sighed, then put it down by his feet.

"I think we've had enough."

Agreed. Cam remained silent, though. He didn't want to distract Victor from the question.

Finally, Victor met his gaze. "I pushed you away because the last person I put on canvas or paper with so much of myself, with all I felt, with love for every little line, was my father."

A small frown pulled at Cam's forehead.

"I told you I didn't know who my biological father was," Victor continued, "but that I always suspected it was Sunshine. We were alike in so many ways, but most especially our moods. Though he had a much harder time than I have ever had. His highs were manic, his lows so far down, he seemed to sink under the ground."

Victor paused for breath and his eyes glistened again. "Sunshine took his own life when I was twenty-seven, and it changed me fundamentally. I promptly fell out of love with the man I was dating, moved home, and asked my best friend to have babies with me." He reached out a hand, and Cam took it. "I haven't really risked my heart since. Not so much because someone I loved died, or took himself away, but . . ." His voice lowered. "I think I feared I might do the same one day." He squeezed Cam's fingers. Exhaled. "The thing is, it's a baseless fear—or not entirely baseless. I've never wanted to die, not even when I'm so low all I can do is breathe. I simply want to not move for a while."

Victor eyed the whiskey bottle.

"You seemed pretty broken up over Tholo," Cam said.

"He embarrassed me. I was pissed off, tired, and my work wasn't going well. *And* I do like to put on a show now and again. Mostly, though, he was my excuse to wallow for a while. But I didn't stay down because you appeared. And when I tried to push you away, you didn't go." Victor squeezed his fingers again. "Anyone who truly knows you would know that would never work. You are not the man who leaves, Cameron. You are the man who stays, no matter what."

Tears beaded Cam's lashes. "I left after my parents died. I didn't stay to watch Rebecca die."

"You were looking after yourself, both times. When your parents died, you reacted by signing up to defend everyone else. And exactly how far away were you when your sister passed away?"

"I was down in Delaware. Why?"

"Not far, then, and you're not going to leave now. *No one* is leaving. You're going to stay here and continue building your business with Jorge. And you're going to let me help you."

Cam shook his head. "How?"

"By loving you. Let me love you, Cameron. Let yourself love me in return."

At this juncture, his late-night movie binges let him down. Declarations of love did not come with jagged, tearing pains. They shouldn't hurt like this. Cam heard himself gasping, and then Victor was beside him, one hand warm against his back and moving in slow circles.

"Just breathe. In and out."

Had Victor said that? Or had he whispered it to himself?

Either way, it was good advice. Cam breathed. In and then out. And he leaned against Victor's side, trusting the slimmer man to take his weight. Victor pulled him close, and they breathed together. In and out. Tears tracked down Cam's cheeks. Victor's breaths were wet.

"This is way too dramatic," Cam managed.

Victor chuckled. "It is, isn't it? One out of ten, would not recommend."

Laughter bubbled upward. Fighting against it hurt, so Cam let it out. "Great, so our relationship is starting off with a bad rating. Good going, Vic."

"What would you give it?"

Cam waited for his breath to calm, then considered. "Five out of ten, needs work."

"That I can agree with." Vic touched the side of his face. "At the risk of sounding altogether corny, do you want to work on it with me?"

Cam turned to face him, found he was too close, but couldn't bear the idea of moving away. He closed his eyes and rested their foreheads together. "Yes."

Panic threatened again. He pushed it back.

"I can feel our score rising already."

Choked amusement pushed past Cam's lips. "If that's a euphemism, I'm done."

Victor laughed. "No, but I'm going to remember that for another time."

Cam angled his chin forward so he could touch his lips to Victor's. "I don't know if I can say it and not spiral. Or laugh. Or start sobbing."

"We have plenty of time. Not going anywhere, remember?"

"Thank you for coming over."

"All Jorge's doing."

"Not really."

"We'll thank him later." Victor laced their fingers together. "Right now, I want to take you upstairs and push you through a shower. You smell like me after communion with the wine rack. Then I'm taking you to bed."

Feeling strangely pliant, Cam let himself be lifted away from the lounger. "Okay."

"Will you make love to me in the morning?"

"Yes."

Victor tugged on his hand, but Cam pulled him up short. "It's not going to be this easy. Not always."

"You thought this was easy?"

Cam shook his head. "You know what I mean. We're going to hurt each other again. We'll fight and we'll say stuff we don't mean. We'll get depressed, because that's who we are. There's too much pain in our pasts to forgive and forget."

"Perhaps we could put Jorge on a retainer."

The sharp bark of laughter hurt Cam's throat.

Victor smiled. "Back to business, as they say: Yours is going to be what you make of it, Cam. I can't promise you'll be wildly successful, but with Jorge and me at your side, you can make of it whatever you like. What do you want?"

You.

But also Jorge at his side. And a business they were proud of. Something they'd built and could pass on. "I want to stay. Will you stay with me?"

Vic nodded.

Cam pulled him close and kissed him, his intended sweet touch giving way quickly to hunger. Breathless, he leaned away but left their fingers joined.

"We'll be patient with each other," Vic said quietly. "We both have good examples to live by. Parents who loved unconditionally, both each other and their children. We'll remember that, and our friends. And that *we* are friends. Friends forgive each other. Friends are there for each other. And friends don't leave."

Finally, the words came, and Cam delivered them with a smile. "I love you, Victory."

Victor's beam was beautiful to behold. His smile, everything Cam loved. Bright, colorful, and transformative. Sunshine in human form. So stunning, he didn't need to hear the words Victor said in return.

"I love you too."

Epilogue

December

Breathing deeply of the bright but chill morning, Victor nodded with satisfaction. The sky was the sort of blue only December could produce, and the sunshine peeking across the treetops carried enough warmth for lighter sweaters and maybe even rolled-up sleeves. It was the perfect day for a party.

Victor surveyed the patio for leaves he might have missed and spied a clump behind the stacked furniture. He put the broom aside, pulled out the short tower of chairs, and then swept behind. The smell of crushed leaves rose from the misty gray flagstones, and the colors of fall danced through his head. A smile edged across his lips as he thought of the series of tiny paintings he'd completed only the week before, each an explosion of color one probably wouldn't find in a subterranean cavern. But the brief had called for autumn in the underworld, so Victor had delivered prehistoric trees with leaves the size of blankets, the scale made absurd by the dimensions of the game cards.

He'd almost forgotten what it was like to paint for fun, and when he'd shown them off, the audience he'd enjoyed the most was his after-school art club—kids from the summer program and the few faces who'd joined them. Together, he and the kids had signed a contract to provide all the art for Aaron and Grayson's upcoming game. Aaron had insisted they couldn't afford an artist of Victor's pedigree. Wanted to tap him for the few major pieces they had planned, such as the box and booklet art. Victor had insisted on doing some art for the cards as well, though, citing the size as a welcome challenge. They could pay him whatever they could afford; he simply wanted to paint without considering the value of each brushstroke. He'd forgotten what that was like too.

The door to the kitchen creaked open, and a black shadow slipped out and along the wall in the direction of the garage.

"He does have a cat door," Victor remarked.

Cam leaned in the doorway, arms folded, one of Victor's favorite smiles curving his lips. The slightly sardonic one. "I know, but there is something to be said for the feeling of being useful that letting him in and out gives."

Victor arched an eyebrow. "Did I not make you feel entirely useful this morning?"

Cam's grin widened. "And then some." He lifted his chin. "How long until everyone starts arriving for this party you insist I need?"

"Fifty only comes once and you have so much to celebrate! Your family, your friends, your business." Victor leaned the broom against the stack of chairs and crossed the patio. Cam's arms unfolded at his approach. Victor moved between them and reveled at the warmth closing about his back as Cam hauled him in for gentle hug. "You make fifty look good."

"Mm." Cam caressed his lips in a sweet kiss.

"So, now that you're a year older, any further thoughts on moving in permanently?" Victor asked.

Cam spent five or six nights a week at his house. Victor wanted all seven. To wake up next to this man every morning. He'd invited lovers to move in before but had never looked forward to sleeping next to someone as much as he did Cam. The sex was amazing but so was the talking and the cuddling. The whiff of engine oil and hard work Cam always seemed to carry with him, and the way Cam always asked after *his* work.

They bickered but were still new enough to enjoy making up afterward.

It wouldn't always be this simple. Nothing worth having ever was.

Cam bumped their noses together. "I think your mind is going, old man. It's only been six weeks since the last time you asked."

Victor chuckled. "Just taking an opportunity where I see it."

Hands closed about his waist. "Speaking of opportunity—"

Victor's phone buzzed in his pocket. Sighing regretfully, he pulled it out. "In answer to your earlier question about how long we have until people start arriving?"

"Sage is in the driveway?"

"Yep."

"If he didn't text, he'd catch us in bed nine out of ten visits."

Victor smirked. "True." He pocketed his phone and held out a hand. "Shall we?"

Sage wasn't alone in the driveway. He had Ashni and Billy with him, of course, but Cori's car was parked close behind, and she had Tez with her. No Raya today, apparently. As though half the party had coordinated a simultaneous arrival, Grayson's Mustang crested the hill of the drive and pulled into the circle behind Cori's car. His car carried two additional passengers, Aaron and Oliver.

"Where's Nick?" Cam asked.

"He was picking up your gift." Tugging his phone out, Victor checked the time. He grinned as he tucked the phone away again and his heart squeezed in a few extra beats. He and Nick had worked hard to find the perfect gift for Cameron, with Jorge and Oliver helping when they had time. Victor hoped it seemed as perfect today as it had last week when he and Nick had filed the paperwork.

Cam frowned. "He needed a whole extra car for it?"

"Mm-hmm."

Hugs and kisses were exchanged, with Billy passing from adult to adult as they all fussed over him. When Victor pulled Ashni in for a quick embrace, he blinked down at her midsection, which felt a little rounder than it had over the summer. "Are you . . .?"

She and Sage swapped a knowing smile. "Marjoram will be here in March."

Slapping his hands over his mouth, Victor worked furiously to prioritize his emotions. "I don't know if I'm more excited about another baby or that you've picked one of my names."

"Both." Ashni laughed. "You can be excited about both."

Tez squealed with delight, and Cam was all smiles. Victor had only introduced Cam to his kids at the end of September. Over the past couple of months, they'd bonded. Cori apparently had his cell phone number. She said they only talked about park dimensions and urban landscapes, but he'd heard Cam's end of their conversations. They'd become fast friends, and little delighted Victor more than seeing his loved ones together.

Gray was holding Billy upside down, much to the toddler's delight. Beside him, Oliver flapped his hands. "If he gurgles, pull him up slowly. No one wants to start the day by choking on vomit."

Aaron was shaking his head at the pair. "And my mom thinks Gray and I should adopt. I think Gray and Oliver should adopt and Nick and I can look on in horror." Aaron turned to Victor. "So, hey, I loved the fall series you did for the cards. Amazing, truly."

"Thanks. I liked them a lot, myself. Have you finished going over the latest submissions from the art club?"

"I have, and I wanted to talk to you about that."

Oh? "As in we should go somewhere private or chat here as we continue watching Gray and Oliver torture my grandson?"

Oliver had Billy by the waist and was attempting to fly him like an airplane.

Tez appeared at Victor's side. "Is the patio all set up or are we grilling in the driveway today?"

"Why don't you organize everyone while Aaron and I talk about the cards for a minute?"

"Will do."

Victor turned to Aaron. "What's up?"

"Gray and I love what you and the class have been giving us. We only have a few issues, and they're super minor. Could we maybe visit the class one afternoon to talk to the kids?"

"They'd love that. Let me know your schedule and we'll keep a day open for you."

"Awesome. How'd your show in Brooklyn go, by the way? Wasn't that last week?"

Victor nodded. "Week before and it went quite well. I sold all the pieces I contributed, including two from a new series." Unaccustomed warmth touched his cheeks. "Portraits, both."

Aaron slapped him on the shoulder. "Good for you."

Tez had said the same thing when he'd shared the news. Cam had been there when Victor had taken the call, and Sage had sent him a bottle of non-alcoholic cider with which to celebrate. But every time Victor shared the news, a glow kindled inside him. Excitement unfurled. New directions rolled out around him. Forty years of painting and he still had so much to explore.

They'd reached the patio where Cam had the fire pit going and Oliver had given up playing with Billy in favor of commanding the grill. Tez was carrying out platters of various burgers Cam had assembled last night, grumbling all the while that he shouldn't need to cook for his own party and then suggesting yet another low fat or vegetarian option for his friends to try.

Gray sat with Sage and Ashni.

Cori and Billy were playing with the cats.

Jorge, Estefan, Renata, Beck, Melanie, and Luisa arrived, and the patio fairly groaned beneath all the boots and shoes. Victor ran to the garage for additional chairs. He'd just set them up with Beck's help when his phone vibrated again. He pulled it out and nearly swallowed air. Nick was in the driveway. Pocketing the phone, Victor trotted around the side of the house and popped out into the circle of cars to find Nick holding the most adorable creature ever to possess floppy ears.

"Oh my God. She's even prettier this week."

Nick shot him an awkward smile and made to hand over the wriggling puppy. "And furrier."

"No." Victor held up his hands. "I think you should give her to him."

"You don't want to?"

"I want to watch his face as he takes her from you."

Nodding as though this made perfect sense, Nick set off up the path. Victor trotted close behind and overtook him before they reached the patio.

The burble of voices from the back garden filled him with happiness. His house was made for occasions such as these. For family and friends and celebration. Unable to help his grin, Victor started clearing a path to the grill. Cam stood there chatting with Oliver, pointing out the different burgers. He looked up at their approach, smiling, and then gaped.

"Nick's here," Victor said unnecessarily. "And he has someone we'd like you to meet."

Nick held out the wriggling puppy.

Cam closed his mouth, opened it again, and then his expression shifted through a series of emotions too complex to capture with paint: Joy, grief, surprise, fear, consternation. All of them. Everything a man could feel and not break apart. Tears tracked down his cheeks. His lips moved.

But he didn't hold out his arms.

The puppy wriggled and whined in the space between him and Nick, and Victor wondered, for a horrible half minute, if they'd made a mistake.

Then Nick pushed her forward, all out-sized paws and golden fur. "She needs someone like you."

Cam took the puppy and hugged her to his chest.

Pretty much everyone on the patio cried. Victor could barely see through his tears. Still, he leaned against Cam's side and whispered, "Do you need help picking out a name?"

Cam shook his head. "She'll tell us who she is." He kissed between her ears. "Won't you, sweetheart?"

"Us?"

"I can't raise her on my own. She'll need me to live here, won't she?"

Victor let out a great sigh and circled an arm around Cam's waist. "That she will."

Cam shifted to make room as Nick dusted invisible dirt off the retaining wall and sat next to him. He'd been watching Aaron and Gray play with the puppy and had been caught in a weird bubble of *where am I and what am I doing*. Some days, the noise of war and the pain of loss felt recent enough to heat his skin and dig at his heart. Other days, everything that should rest in the past remained there as distant scrapes. Significant dings in the breakfast table of life but only noticed when he looked, rather than every time he set a cup of coffee down.

Today, he felt balanced between past and present. A birthday like fifty couldn't help but have a man thinking backward. He'd been content in his memories, though, caught up mostly in the good moments. His little bro starred in a lot of those.

"How are you doing?" Cam asked.

"Fine. Do you like your gift?"

"I love my gift." Cam curled an arm around his brother's shoulders and pulled him into a sideways hug. "Not sure if I said thank you, but yeah. She's perfect."

"Good. Victor was worried you might not want another dog."

"I wouldn't have thought of it myself." A lie. He'd thought about it, especially in the weeks following Honey's return to New York. But he hadn't got much past imagining all the ways he might lose another companion. No such thoughts intruded now, however. He was simply happy.

"She's a golden retriever mix. I think Australian shepherd or border collie." Lifting one hip, Nick dug a card out of his back pocket. "This is a trainer recommended by the shelter. Apparently, dogs are happier when they're well trained. Less confused about good and bad behavior. What the rules are."

Taking the card, Cam studied Nick's expression. He seemed slightly wistful. "Thinking about a puppy for yourself?"

Nick shook his head. "No. I was thinking about the training. It would be useful for humans, don't you think?"

Cam chuckled. "Definitely." He held up the card before tucking it away. "Thanks. So, how are the proposal plans coming?" After choosing and rejecting sixteen elaborate dinner menus,

Nick had moved on to researching weekend getaways. He'd been investigating scuba diving in Hawaii (because he and Oliver had watched a documentary and Oliver had said it looked pretty out there under the water) when Cam had suggested Nick research activities they already enjoyed sharing rather than a holiday that might end up in catastrophe.

Recently, Nick had returned to the dinner plan, and the menus had started arriving in epic texts once again.

"I'm thinking eggplant scallopini," Nick said now. "I know Oliver likes eggplant. The hard part is choosing a dish I can cook without his help, though. He's much more comfortable in the kitchen than I am."

"Here's an idea: Why don't you invite Oliver to cook with you?"

"But he always cooks."

"It's an activity you like to do together, though."

Nick's forehead wrinkled. Leaning forward, he tucked a lock of hair behind one ear, and then nodded, dislodging it again. "I could invite him to cook a special meal with me and then propose after dinner. If everything goes well."

"That sounds nice."

"It's not boring?"

Cam glanced over at Victor, who was seated between his adult children, one arm around each of their shoulders. All three were laughing. Tez was looking on fondly. He pointed out the scene to Nick. "Remember when we all used to sit out on the back patio? When we were kids?"

"Yes."

"Those are some of my favorite memories. Us, all together. Not doing anything special. Just enjoying a nice night."

Nick turned back to him. "It's a single moment. It's the rest of it that matters."

Cam clapped him on the shoulder. "Now you're getting it."

Nick smiled and it was brilliant.

Cam watched as the last taillight winked down the driveway about an hour later, leaving him, Victor, and the unnamed puppy standing outside the front door. The day might have been seasonable, but it was still December and the night promised to be chilly. Vic was already shivering.

Cam pulled him close. "C'mon. Let's go get you warmed up. We can finish clearing the patio in the morning."

"Why do I have the feeling we won't get back out there until January?"

"We've got a puppy to train. We'll be out there every day."

"There is that." Vic smiled. "Thought of any names, yet?"

"Why don't you tell me your list?"

Victor would have one. He'd have started adding names to it the moment he set eyes on the pup.

Grinning excitedly, he started reeling them off. "Goldie, of course. Chrissie for reasons I cannot articulate. It just came to me. Then there's Daffodil."

"Daffodil is cute."

"I have many more."

Leading Victor back into the house, Cam gestured for him to continue.

"In the flower theme, I also have Begonia, Lily, and Pansy, though I'm not overly fond of that last one for obvious reasons."

"Mm-hmm. Go on."

Victor paused in the front hall. "Then there are the epicurean names. Mango, though she's more yellow than orange. Couscous and Pumpkin."

Perhaps sensing they were talking about her, the puppy cocked her head.

Looking down, Cam said, "Don't worry. I'm not calling you Pumpkin. Or Couscous."

"What about Bumblebee?"

Cam laughed.

"The Latin for *yellow* is *Flavus* if we want to link her thematically to Sin and Dex. Flavia, maybe?"

Cam considered the color of her fur. "What about Aura? She's more golden than yellow."

"Aura! I love it. Can we call her Rori for short?"

"Because Aura is so long."

The puppy yipped.

Cam stooped to pick her up. "What do you think? Do you like Rori?" She wriggled and licked his face. "I think we have a winner."

"We should see if she likes the bed my cats have disdained. We can buy her a bigger one as she grows."

It was horribly domestic, this dragging of the cat bed into Victor's bedroom and choosing the perfect spot for it. Cam delighted in the wasting of minutes, though. Neither of them had any place better to be or anything else to do. And it was this simple togetherness that made his relationship with Victor more real than any he'd previously enjoyed—that sometimes they just did things. Cooked, lay on opposite ends of the couch with their feet tangled, watched TV, tossed furry mouse toys to the cats, shared mugs of hot cocoa, and talked about places they might visit together when they both had some time off.

Cam had never imagined he'd enjoy such quietude. Then again, when he thought back to his childhood, he couldn't imagine how he'd never had this before.

From the bathroom attached to Victor's bedroom came the telltale rattle of a pill canister. Cam went to lean against the doorframe as Victor swallowed his nightly dose and reached for a toothbrush.

"How's the new prescription feel so far?" Cam asked.

Victor shrugged one shoulder. "Better than the last, I think."

It'd be a while before they knew whether the pills would help balance his moods. In the meantime, it was a matter of managing side effects.

This, too, the daily conversations about whether a pill made his lover feel more or less like sex—or more or less like himself— wasn't something Cam could have imagined. But it was perhaps his favorite aspect of it all. That he was inside someone's skin, living their life with them in the present moment.

"How about you?" Victor asked. "Feeling sleepy or should we choose a movie?"

And having that same person live inside him.

Because, finally, after thirty long years, he felt as though he'd come home. That he'd found a place where he could *stay*.

Cam slipped into the bathroom and wrapped Victor up in a loose hug. Kissed his cheek, the corner of his mouth, then his lips. "I love you."

"God, do I know it. I don't know if I've ever had someone love me so well."

Tears beaded Cam's lashes. He didn't know if crying more easily or frequently was a good thing, but so long as it was with Victor, he didn't mind so much. "I think I was waiting for the right person."

"Me too, my sweet Cameron, me too."

Explore more of the *Hearts & Crafts* series:
riptidepublishing.com/collections/series-hearts-crafts

Dear Reader,

Thank you for reading Kelly Jensen's *The Leaving Kind*!

We know your time is precious and you have many, many entertainment options, so it means a lot that you've chosen to spend your time reading. We really hope you enjoyed it.

We'd be honored if you'd consider posting a review—good or bad—on sites like **Amazon, Barnes & Noble, Kobo, Goodreads, Twitter, Facebook, Tumblr,** and your blog or website. We'd also be honored if you told your friends and family about this book. Word of mouth is a book's lifeblood!

For more information on upcoming releases, author interviews, blog tours, contests, giveaways, and more, please sign up for our weekly, spam-free newsletter and visit us around the web:

Newsletter: riptidepublishing.com/newsletter
Twitter: twitter.com/RiptideBooks
Facebook: facebook.com/RiptidePublishing
Goodreads: tinyurl.com/RiptideOnGoodreads
Tumblr: riptidepublishing.tumblr.com

Thank you so much for Reading the Rainbow!

RiptidePublishing.com

ACKNOWLEDGMENTS

I always put bits and pieces of myself into my characters. It's how I make them feel real—to me, anyway. I put everything I had into this book, and Cam, Victor, and just about every other character took those pieces and developed them far past what I could have imagined. They became actual people—people I have lived and worked with for almost two years. I'm going to miss them. I already do.

The story told here isn't a typical romance. I seem to have forgotten how to write those. But it *is* a love story. It's a redemption story. It's a collection of stories I have long wanted to tell. Characters and themes I have been waiting to explore. And, here, finally, I have. I love this book. If *The Leaving Kind* is the last novel I write—for a while or forever—I am content.

As always, I have a lot of people, here in the real world, to thank. They all know who they are. They all know how much I appreciate their kindness, love, and support. That without them, I wouldn't be here and neither would this book. But again, thank you. Always, thank you.

And to you, dear readers, I hope you found the joy in these pages. The beauty I wanted to share. That this book changed you, just a little bit, as it did me. And that you will remember it fondly. Thank you for taking this journey with me.

ALSO BY KELLY JENSEN

ABOUT the AUTHOR

If aliens ever do land on Earth, Kelly will not be prepared, despite having read over a hundred stories of the apocalypse. Still, she will pack her precious books into a box and carry them with her as she strives to survive. It's what bibliophiles do.

Kelly is the author of fifteen novels—including the Chaos Station series, co-written with Jenn Burke—and over a dozen novellas and short stories. Some of what she writes is speculative in nature, but mostly it's just about a guy losing his socks and/or burning dinner. Because life isn't all conquering aliens and mountain peaks. Sometimes finding a happy ever after is all the adventure we need.

Connect with Kelly online:
Website: kellyjensenwrites.com
Facebook: www.facebook.com/kellyjensenwrites
Twitter: twitter.com/kmkjensen
Instagram: www.instagram.com/kellyjensenwrites

Enjoy more stories like
The Leaving Kind
at RiptidePublishing.com!